BLOOD IN THE WATER

BLOOD IN THE
WATER

RICK OUTZEN

Waterside Productions
Cardiff-by-the-Sea, CA

Blood in the Water is a work of fiction. Names, characters, places, incidents, and events described are either the product of the author's imagination or used fictitiously. Any resemblance to actual incidents or actual persons, living or dead, is purely coincidental.

Printed in the United States of America

First Printing, 2020

ISBN-13: 978-1-941768-50-1 print edition
ISBN-13: 978-1-941768-51-8 ebook edition

Waterside Productions
2055 Oxford Ave
Cardiff-by-the-Sea, CA 92007
www.waterside.com

In memory of Big Boy, who would have thought this tale was about him…and he would be right.

1

"**What the hell are you doing?**"

I looked up from the bar and saw Dare Evans staring down at me. "I'm talking with someone."

The someone, a drugstore-box dyed blonde with wild hair that looked like it had been combed with a handheld mixer, interrupted. "I'm Catelyn, with a 'C'," she said as she reached out to shake Dare's hand.

"Of course you are," replied Dare, without extending hers or smiling.

Not wanting either of them to mess up the rhythm of my drinking, I gave a side-eye to Dare and explained, "Catelyn and I were discussing the relationship between the national debt and butterfly tattoos."

"Walker, we need to talk."

Leaning into me, Catelyn asked, "Is she your wife?"

The fruity fragrance of her Tommy Girl perfume overpowered me and made my eyes water. I shook my head, "She's my wicked step-mother."

Dare came at me again, repeating my first name to let me know she was serious. "Walker, you've got to get your shit together."

Catelyn straightened up, swept back her bushy hair, pushed her horned-rim black glasses back up to the proper place on the bridge of her nose, then grabbed her tiny gold purse and whiskey sour. "I think I best go back to my friends."

She walked to the other side of the mahogany bar that hadn't been polished since the Carter administration and joined a cadre of legal secretaries that was surrounded by white males dressed in fashionably wrinkled linen blazers, tight slacks, loafers and no socks. Honestly, I was relieved to not have even two more minutes of conversation with Catelyn.

Concentrating hard on my words so I didn't slur any, I asked Dare, "Who invited you to this party?"

As she sat on the bar stool next to me, she answered, "Rochelle. She's worried about you."

The tall red-haired bartender moved away from our side of the End O' the Alley Bar and tended to the legal secretaries and what I called the "legacy boys," those twenty-somethings who worked for their daddies and would eventually settle down to marry the right kind of girls, most likely the daughters of their mommas' friends. But for now, during happy hour, they were bold and adventurous with the wrong kind of girls who had dollar signs in their eyes, ones who hoped to land a ticket out of their studio apartments they still shared with former boyfriends because those dudes rarely made them pay rent. I predicted none of their nights would be memorable.

"I hope this isn't an intervention," I said, focusing back on Dare. "You know I'm not much for—."

She slapped my face hard.

The bar went quiet for a few seconds, people watched to see if anything interesting might happen as a result, and seeing that it wasn't, went back to their conversations. They'd already seen plenty of women slap me.

"Screw you!" she punctuated.

"I was working up to that," I mumbled as I took a long sip of my Jack and Coke. The boys and girls club giggled but stopped when Dare looked in their direction. When she held her chin up and locked her eyes on you, she was almost as intimidating as I was when I was sober.

Pointing to my left forearm that was wrapped in white gauze, she asked, "What happened to you?"

"He said last night he cut it breaking a window," Rochelle answered for me as she handed Dare her Chardonnay. "Ten minutes ago, he told the girl with the wild ass hair and the knock-off Chloe handbag that he was hurt in a knife fight."

"To avoid the knife, I jumped through a window." I quipped shoving my empty glass towards Rochelle, pretty pleased with my one-liner. "Another, please."

Dressed in a black Giorgio Armani pants suit with a white silk blouse and pearls, Dare didn't find me funny and instead disapprovingly shook her head, then as instinctively as a bird preens its feathers, swept her natural blond hair away from her brilliant sky-blue eyes. "I'm worried about you."

"The doctor's gonna take the stitches out in a few weeks." I quickly grabbed my drink a second after Rochelle had set it on the bar. "It's okay, I don't use my left arm much."

Dare squeezed my right hand. "Please stop and listen."

Yes, I was being an ass, an ass to my dearest friend. Maybe I should have told her what was eating me inside. Instead I went with, "What's there to worry about? I can walk back to the loft. It's only a block away."

"Stop, dammit. I'm your friend."

"No, Rochelle was my friend until she ratted me out," emphasizing "friend" loud enough for the bartender to hear me. "I don't like snitches."

Dare wouldn't let up. "Let's go sit in the courtyard."

Pointing to the skinny, gray-haired musician in a faded DeLuna Fest t-shirt playing on the small stage outside of the End O' the Alley Bar, I answered, "Not if we have to listen to that guy play 'Brown-eyed Girl' again."

Dare whispered something to Rochelle, gave her a twenty—a minute later the musician's microphone went dead. We moved to the brick courtyard where Catelyn and her gang had relocated to a corner table under a palm tree where the girls smoked cigarettes, still hoping to land a big fish, while the boys puffed cigars, still hoping for an easy lay.

I, Walker Holmes, owner and publisher of the alt-weekly *Pensacola Insider*, didn't have a drinking problem, but my demons needed to be soothed.

Dare Evans had been my friend since we were freshmen at Ole Miss in the early nineties, but that didn't give her the go-ahead to lecture me. However, she didn't care what I thought I needed. Once we sat down at a low, wrought-iron table near the waterless fountain, she started up again. I should have said continued because it was the same conversation we had several times before.

"You can't drink your way through life. This town depends on you. I depend on you."

The town was Pensacola, Florida. Before St. Augustine, Jamestown and Plymouth, Don Tristan de Luna sailed into Pensacola Bay to establish what the Viceroy intended to be the first of a series of settlements along the Gulf of Mexico. Within weeks of celebrating the first Mass in America, a hurricane wiped out the place, and thus, fame and historical significance slipped from Pensacola's grasp, as it repeatedly would over the next four hundred fifty-plus years.

"What's the point?" I sneered as I waved to Rochelle to bring me another drink, even though my glass was more than half full. She ignored me. Definitely, Rochelle was no longer my friend.

Big Boy, my spoiled seven-year-old chocolate Labrador mix, wandered in and stretched out under our table.

Dare asked, "How did he get in here?"

"He's my service dog."

"Big Boy isn't a service dog."

"Hush now, you'll hurt his feelings."

A smile appeared on her face for half a second. Big Boy edged closer to Dare. The dog lately had preferred other people's company over mine. *Join the club,* I said to myself.

We heard clapping from Apple Annie's. In August 1967, retired naval aviator and trumpeter Bob Snow bought the abandoned Pensacola Cigar & Tobacco warehouse and opened Rosie O'Grady's, where his Dixieland band played nightly. Gradually he expanded into the surrounding warehouses, creating Seville Quarter with several themed rooms. End O' the Alley was for us hardcore drinkers. The restaurant Apple Annie's shared the long, narrow courtyard with the bar.

"What's going on in Annie's?" I asked.

Dare studied the crowd. "Pretty sure I heard about Commissioner Monte Tatum and one of your investors, Reuben Crutcher, hosting a campaign fundraiser there for Sheriff Frost."

"The personal trifecta of Walker Holmes' haters," I mused.

"I'd recommend you slip out through the courtyard's side gate when you leave."

"Agreed. Frost wasn't happy with my coverage of Rachel Townsend's murder."

"She's the runaway?"

"Rachel wasn't a goddamn runaway," I insisted, then downed the remnants of my drink and started on the second bourbon and Coke that a waiter had just delivered to the table.

My voice had an edge to it, more than I intended. Dare lowered hers and spoke softly in an effort to calm me and avoid a scene. "Why the anger?"

Looking in my glass and avoiding her eyes, I tried to explain, "Every investigative article takes a piece of me. I keep thinking about how I could've covered it differently. I tried to protect her, but maybe I should've done more."

"Her death reminded you of Mari, didn't it?"

Mari Gaudet was our classmate at Ole Miss. She was kidnapped and murdered during our senior year, weeks before she and I were to be married. I didn't want the conversation to go in that direction so I gave Dare the coldest stare I could muster after a half dozen drinks—but it didn't work.

She rolled her eyes. "Okay, we don't want to talk about the runaway or Mari."

The waiter brought another glass of wine for Dare and a bowl of water for Big Boy just as the musician walked towards the stage. Dare slipped the waiter a ten, and a minute later the musician sauntered back to the bar.

"Is Bree coming this weekend?" she asked, trying to find a safer subject. Dare knew my girlfriend had often driven over from New Orleans and spent the weekend with me, but she didn't know Bree was now my ex-girlfriend.

I shrugged and lied, "I don't know. Called, texted and she hasn't responded." I took a sip and savored the bourbon. "I probably did something wrong, again."

Dare wasn't going to let me play the victim. "What happened the last time you two talked?"

I ignored her question as I watched the secretaries and legacy boys try to pair off. The heights, weights, and intellects didn't match, and the combinations had little hope of working unless they started doing Tequila shots.

"What happened?" she persisted, and I relented, "It's Tatum. Bree can't stand to be in Pensacola with him having any political power."

Bree Kress, a local graphic artist who relocated to New Orleans two years ago, and Tatum had a history, not a good one, from his days as owner of The Green Olive. Until Tatum's appointment to the county commission, Bree and I had seen each other every other weekend, but the visits had fallen off to once a month, then every six weeks, and finally stopped all together. Though I had fought for weeks to block Tatum's rise to power, Bree couldn't get over it. She pinned it on me, and when I didn't do so well with her ultimatums, the relationship died. The only loose ends were some of her things were still in my apartment, and she was stopping by later that night on her way to Destin to tie up those ends.

Getting drunk before seeing Bree wasn't my brightest idea, but bright ideas had not been my strong suit since Rachel's murder. I dreaded seeing Bree and facing another failed relationship.

I looked at my watch. Bree would be at the loft at seven, which gave me forty-five minutes to both tidy the place and sober up. But I only really needed thirty minutes so I had the waiter bring me a double.

The couplings of the millennial hipsters began to fall apart. They each congregated back into their original tribes, girls under the palm in the courtyard, boys inside at the bar. As predicted, no one was getting laid. Maybe I should hire myself out as a hookup prognosticator.

Dare interrupted my thoughts, "The word on the street is you're days from shutting down."

"That's what the *News Herald* wants my advertisers to believe. I'm a little behind on my bills but no more than sixty days. Payroll checks aren't bouncing." Owned by the largest newspaper chain in North

America, Barnett Press, the *Pensacola News Herald* was the town's daily newspaper.

She reached across the table and grabbed both my wrists almost causing me to spill my drink. "Stop this. People look to you to uncover the truth, but you have to be sober to do it."

"Sobriety is overrated," I countered. "Ernest Hemingway used to say, 'Write drunk, edit sober,' and I've been focusing more on my writing."

Dare let go of my wrists. "Damn you."

"Agreed."

Frustrated, she struggled to compose herself, fighting back tears because she cared for me. *Why was I such a jackass?*

Dare threw out a lifeline, "You can't keep taking on these lost causes and think someone'll rescue you."

"I don't need to be rescued."

"Look at you. You haven't shaved in days. You smell of stale beer. For chrissakes, what are you wearing?"

Smoothing down the wrinkles of my Hawaiian shirt and checking to be sure I had zipped the fly of my paint-splattered khaki shorts, I answered, "My happy hour attire. We got another issue to the printer today. Big Boy and I are celebrating."

"No, your staff finished it up after you abandoned them to get drunk," she corrected me. "I passed them as they were heading to a concert at Vinyl Music Hall."

"Well, drinking was Big Boy's idea."

Dare shook her head. I wasn't sure if it was out of pity or disgust. No, it was pity.

"I'm worried about you. This town turns to you to tell us how to look at things. You've been the one constant in this crazy place for the past ten years."

I let out a heavy sigh. "You know what, I'm tired of fighting everyone's battles."

"Finally, you say something that's real."

"My mistake." I wanted to tell her that taking on the world had cost me everything and everyone I had ever cared about. I wanted to talk to her about Bree and ask her for her advice on how to get her back. I wanted to beg for Dare's forgiveness for treating her so horribly. But instead, in one smooth motion I swigged down the last of my drink and stood up.

Dare hugged me, and whispered in my ear, "I need you, Pensacola needs you. You can't let the good ol' boys win."

I clumsily saluted, "Yes, ma'am."

As we were walking out, I heard the musician start the first chords of "Brown-eyed Girl."

The April sun was setting as Big Boy and I tried to get through the courtyard behind Apple Annie's without detection. Through the huge glass doors that had been salvaged from the Ursuline Convent in New Orleans, I saw the back of Sheriff Frost as he spoke from a small stage with all eyes focused on him. It looked like we would clear the courtyard unnoticed.

"Holmes, I hope you're not driving," Chief Deputy Peter Krager drawled as he stepped from behind the second large fountain in the courtyard, the one that actually worked.

"Shit, Peck!" I jumped back. "No, I'm walking the dog back to our loft."

"Shame."

"Peck" Krager stood five foot six inches and weighed 165 pounds. Since being promoted to chief deputy, he had become a fitness nut, running, working out at a gym five days a week; all lean and mean now. The rumor was he used steroids, and he displayed all of the signs—muscles that stretched the buttons on his shirt nearly to their breaking point, thinning, greasy red hair, high school acne, and breath that smelled like a dumpster.

I tried to walk past him, but he blocked our path pinning us between the fountain and a couple of tables outside the doors to Apple Annie's. Big Boy growled, forcing me to tug on his leash to keep him close to me. I didn't want to give Krager an excuse to hurt my dog, or me.

"Get your mutt under control," he snarled and rolled a toothpick to the corner of his mouth. "The dog shouldn't be in here."

"I've got him. Peck, step aside and we'll be on our way."

"You're not staying?" he asked taking a step towards me. Pre-steroid Krager was all bark and little bite. This version was nothing but bite. I pulled Big Boy's leash tighter and silently willed him to be still.

Krager jabbed my chest, "You should be covering this for your piece-of-shit newspaper. We've raised forty grand tonight. Tyndall doesn't have a chance."

"Maybe you should cut back on the 'roids." I tried again to push past him. Alphonse Tyndall was my friend, an African American attorney, and it so happened, running against Frost.

"Bad move, Holmes." Krager punched me in the gut. I doubled over but had the presence of mind to jerk the leash tightly and fall on top of Big Boy before he could leap at the bastard.

While I fought to catch my breath, Krager pressed his boot hard on my bandaged forearm, bent down and spit the moist toothpick in my face. He whispered in my ear, "Don't fuck with me or my boss." Then he cackled and walked through the glass doors back into Apple Annie's.

Big Boy squirmed out from underneath me.

"I'm okay, boy. Give me a second." I fought off the urge to vomit while thinking, *a sober Walker Holmes still would've gotten his ass beaten, but I'd have made a better showing.*

After getting to my feet and then walking across Jefferson Street, I heard the loud creak of a rusty car door and a woman shout, "Mr. Holmes?"

Rachel Townsend's mother, dressed in a long, frumpy black dress, climbed out of a pale blue Honda Civic with a smashed right taillight covered with masking tape and a bumper held in place by a frayed rope. A head band held back the short, squat woman's long mousy brown hair streaked with gray and exposed a weathered, grieving face that no amount of makeup could help soften.

"Mr. Holmes, I was hoping I'd catch you." Her voice was as worn out as she looked.

"Ms. Townsend, I planned to call you tomorrow," I lied. "There was no need to come downtown on a Tuesday night to see me."

"I can't sleep." She opened the purse she had been clutching, pulled out a crumpled Kleenex and began to wipe away tears. "I go to bed and dream about saving my baby."

"There's nothing you could've done." I tried to comfort her as I guided her to an outside table at Jordan Valley Café, a half block from my loft. It was twilight, and the few remaining legal secretaries from before had migrated again, this time to Jordan's, where they ate hummus and played with the hookah pipes. They tossed Big Boy a piece of pita bread, which was enough of an invitation for him to go sit by the prettiest girl of the bunch, leaving me to deal with the grieving mother.

I continued, "A few of the investigators are friends. They'll call me if anything breaks."

She gathered herself. Anger replaced sorrow. Coldly, deliberately, she seethed: "I want him to suffer as much as my baby did. I want his death to be very slow and painful."

I had nothing to say. The state attorney would most assuredly seek the death penalty, but it would be years before Lester Judson would be executed by the state of Florida for her daughter's murder.

"I know I'm not to say such things," she said. "My pastor says I need to forgive Rachel's murderer, but his children will graduate from high school, get married, and have babies. Not my Rachel."

I listened through the fog of bourbon, knowing that I needed to be a comforting presence.

"My pastor almost said Rachel's murder was somehow part of God's plan, but I cut him off and let him know I didn't want any part of a God that planned my girl's murder."

She took my silence as empathy and continued, "I won't feel safe until that murderer is brought to justice. I bought a police scanner I keep on all day at the house. We take turns listening for anything that might help."

"Ms. Townsend, these investigations take time. The police think Judson hasn't left the area—"

"Don't say his name," she interrupted me. Her face was red, blood-shot eyes blazed. "Don't ever say his name in front me until that sonnabitch is behind bars."

"Yes, ma'am," I cast a quick look for a graceful exit … none. "Ms. Townsend, why did you want to see me?"

"Today, I finally found the courage to go through the things in her room. I wanted to see if I could find anything that would tell me why my baby was targeted by this monster."

A puzzled expression flashed across my face. "You mean the police didn't search her room?"

"They took her laptop, and her journals, but not much else. They didn't know Rachel. I looked for anything out of place and found this." She handed me a yellow book of matches. "My baby didn't smoke, but she liked to collect matchbooks."

This one was from the Pizza Shack of Oxford, Mississippi, one of my favorite meal options when Dare, Mari and I were enrolled at Ole Miss. "This is odd."

Ms. Townsend looked confused. I explained, "This was a hangout that I frequented on Sunday nights when I was in college." The book still had plenty of matches in it. "How'd Rachel get ahold of this?"

She shrugged. "I'm pretty sure she didn't get it until right around when she went missing the first time. Don't remember ever seeing it. Is it some sort of clue?"

"Don't know." As if on cue, a loud clap of thunder sounded from the direction of Pensacola Bay and lightning flashed across the distant sky. "Let me hold on to it, and I'll talk with the investigators. You best be heading home before the rainstorm."

When Big Boy and I turned the corner on to Intendencia Street, he spied a familiar woman wearing a loose yellow tank top over a blue sports bra and tight washed out jeans with holes in the knees, standing outside the gate to our building. Jerking the leash out of my hand, he sprinted toward Bree, who squatted and hugged the dog while he licked her face.

"Hey, buddy. I've missed you too," she said to him.

I let the two greet each other in silence. Bree's right shoulder and arm had brightly colored tattoos of birds and flowers. She no longer tried to hide them, a testimony to her new life in the Big Easy.

Finally, "Hi, Bree. Big Boy, get down."

"No, he's fine. What have you been feeding him? His breath is garlicky."

"Hummus."

She laughed lightly. "Well, you're going to have an interesting night with him, unless you take him for a long walk."

I nodded and wanted to hug her, smell her hair and feel her warmth. Wanted, but had no clue about how to bridge the gap so I stood there like a dope.

She let go of the dog and stood there for several heartbeats, then broke the awkward silence. "You have my stuff ready?"

"It's in a box on the stairwell." I motioned her forward. "Want to have a beer before you go?"

She shook her head. "I've got someone waiting in the car and really need to get to Destin."

She opened the gate. Big Boy went through first, I brought up the tail end. Calling ahead to her, "You know we don't have to do this."

"Don't start with me," a hint of anger flashed in her voice. No longer her hero and protector, the flame that had kept us together for nearly two years had burned out.

Her temper flared. "I'm not going to stay one minute longer than I need to in a town where Monte Tatum has power. That man drugged me, taped having sex with me and tried to humiliate me."

I reminded her, "And I made sure no one would ever see that tape. He's no threat."

"Walker, he's started sending me emails at my office. The bastard keeps asking me out. Wants to know why he hadn't seen me around Pensacola lately."

"I'll take care of it." Despite my outward calmness, I felt like going ape shit on the asshole. "Until then, block his emails."

"I already have. And I've got an attorney working on a restraining order, but I'm never ever stepping foot in this place again."

"Why didn't you tell me earlier?"

"We stopped seeing each other long before Tatum's emails." That was a shot to my gut, then she followed up with a blow to my head. "Besides, you made it clear Pensacola and your newspaper are more important than me."

"I never said that."

"You didn't have to."

Almost pleading, "Give me time to make this right."

"You had your chance." Then she landed the knockout punch: "I want better, I deserve better."

Bree was right, and therefore I said nothing. She grabbed the big box at the foot of the stairs. It was heavy, but she was strong.

I offered, "Let me help."

She gave me a smirk and half laughed as she nodded at my attire. "You look like an extra from 'The Big Lebowski.' You can barely stand straight and keep from slurring your words. There's nothing you can do to help me."

I heard a male voice coming down the street. "Bree, you okay? We need to get back on the road."

"Asher, I'm fine. Help me with this box."

Asher stood three inches taller than me in a plain white t-shirt and black jeans rolled up over black, polished boots. Chest and arms muscular and very tattooed.

"Sure." He took the box from her as if it was filled with ping pong balls.

Bree surprised me with a quick hug and light kiss on the cheek. "Take care of yourself, Holmes."

I said nothing. I heard Asher say to her when he thought they were out earshot, "I thought he would be more impressive."

"He used to be."

Big Boy nudged my legs, wanting me to go after her. I sagged against the door and eased down onto the cold concrete. I heard them put the box in the car's trunk, shut their doors and drive off. I pulled my knees up to my chest and put my head in my hands. Big Boy tried to pry his way into my lap. Unsuccessful, he settled for lying down beside me.

"You never seem to have any problem with the ladies. What's your secret?" I asked him. "It must be your personality, because it can't be your looks." Big Boy growled. "I'm sorry. Didn't mean to offend. That's just like me, poor social skills."

Big Boy stood, shook himself, rattling his dog tags to show his displeasure. "C'mon, I didn't mean anything by it. You're a very handsome for a dog." Big Boy began to saunter away, still pissed. "Not the cold shoulder again. Let's go get some JD and watch the Dodgers upstairs."

The thunder and lightning had moved closer, but no rain yet. I usually slept well when it rained but didn't want to risk having any nightmares that night so the dog and I walked across the street to the RagTyme Package Liquor & Beer Store. A bottle of Jack Daniels would fight off bad dreams, at least for one more night.

Inside the small, cramped store next to the bottle club Bedlam, the salesclerk, a little, shriveled lady with an orange beehive hairdo, sat perched on a wooden stool behind the counter watching a rerun of "Criminal Minds."

"Hey, Walker, did you hear about the funnel cloud spotted near Escambia High School an hour ago?" she asked while ringing up my Jack.

I shook my head. She handed me the brown paper bag.

"Well, my bum knee is throbbing." She tossed Big Boy a pretzel, which he devoured the second it hit the floor. "I bet we'll see a lot of rain real soon."

"Stay dry." I tried to smile at her as the dog and I turned and walked out the door. The rain had just begun to fall.

2

My loft sat atop a three-story building on Palafox Street that Lum's Sushi Bar on the first floor and the *Pensacola Insider's* office was on the second. The entrance to the upper floors was off a narrow alley that separated the building from the Saenger Theatre, meaning you had to know where we were to find us.

My friend Roger Fairley left me two of his treasures in his will—the building and Big Boy. Both gave my life some measure of stability. The rent from Lum's helped support the newspaper, and the dog became an integral part of my life forcing me daily to care about someone other than myself. Big Boy also had endeared himself with the *Insider* staff and was the newspaper's star, or so he believed.

Before he died from a long battle with cancer, Roger had helped me understand the intricacies of Pensacola politics. "Remember, Pensacola is made of pirates and outcasts." His right eyebrow always inched up in a quirky sort of way each time he reminded me of this, which was often. "For centuries, this is where they hid from authorities and made themselves look respectable."

The building had been built around the mid-1800s. Before we moved in, the first floor was a liquor store, and the top two were a punk club where Weezer, the Ramones and numerous less memorable bands played on their way to better gigs in Atlanta and New Orleans.

The best way to describe my loft was to say it was functional, but always in need of a woman's touch, as was I. The Los Angeles Dodgers were two games out of first and playing the San Francisco Giants. My legs hung over the side of the armchair as I watched the game on the television. Big Boy and I split a leftover California roll that I discovered in the refrigerator. It couldn't have been there more than four days— well, that's the best I could remember. The dog appeared to have forgiven my rude remark and curled up in chair with me. I drank bourbon from the bottle while we watched the game. We fell asleep to the sound of the rain pouring down outside.

Sometime later, Big Boy and I both jumped when he heard the metal door at the bottom of the stairwell slam shut and shouting.

"Walker, it's us! Ted, Summer and me!" I recognized Mal was the one yelling. "Our car is underwater. We need somewhere to dry out."

I looked at the alarm clock: an LED red "11:49" shone. I yelled back, "Come on upstairs. I'll get some towels."

Mal's husband, Teddy, added, "We need some clothes too. We're soaked."

Teddy and Mal Taulbert were my art director and production man- ager, respectively. Summer Kay had started as my office manager two years ago and recently had been promoted to handle our sales, both print and digital. The three of them made up three-fifths of the *Insider*'s staff. I met Teddy on the second-floor landing and handed him towels, t-shirts, and shorts.

"You look like crap," he said with a half-smile. "Didn't interrupt anything, did we?"

Rubbing my eyes and trying to get my hair to lay flat, I answered, "Yeah actually. Jack and I were having another one of our long conversations."

His smile widened. "Hope you got something smaller than a 36-inch waist. Mal and Summer can't wear your shorts."

"Always something. I'll see what I have."

While they dried off and changed, Big Boy stood guard at the stairs. I found some basketball shorts from one of the youth teams I had coached years ago and tossed them down to the girls.

Walking back upstairs, I thought about putting on a pot of coffee. Instead, I found my glass and mixed myself a bourbon and water. *No need to derail my buzz.*

I turned on the local news and caught the anchor's breaking news: "Reports are trickling in of damage around Escambia County as severe storms sweep the area. The National Weather Service has extended until 2 a.m. a tornado warning for surrounding counties. A number of roads are impassable due to heavy flooding. Gulf Power reports outages affecting tens of thousands of customers from Destin to Perdido Key."

Teddy came upstairs, wearing my World of Beer t-shirt and gym shorts. He carried his and the girls' wet clothes. I looked at him, he looked at me. Then I remembered that none of the staff had ever been in my loft. "The laundry room is off the kitchen. Put 'em in the washing machine."

A minute later he was back, grabbed a beer out of the fridge, moved an empty pizza box off of the couch and flopped down. His brown curly mop was still wet. His powerful arms and legs were covered with tattoos of dragons, skulls, and axes. Preferring his photography, art and music to conversation, Teddy rarely talked, not because he was awkward around people, he just didn't always see the need to speak.

The news showed a cute girl wearing a yellow raincoat trying not to be blown away by the wind gusts. I rooted for the wind. She reported, "Interstate 10 is closed from the state line to the Santa Rosa-Okaloosa County line—"

The news anchor cut her off, "Thanks, Missy. We just received a report that floodwaters have penetrated businesses along Palafox Street, the main artery of downtown Pensacola."

Teddy grabbed the remote off the coffee table and hit the mute button. "The Garden-Palafox intersection is a lake. Rainwater's rushing down the hill at the top of Palafox, pushing cars all over the streets."

I looked away from the TV screen and toward Teddy, who had gone from a slouch to sitting upright. I said, "The rain's gotta flow somewhere. For centuries it's been to Pensacola Bay, which is what it must be doing tonight."

Built on Pensacola Bay, downtown was one of the lowest parts of the city. The business district was built over two creeks that long had been covered up, and the water table was high under normal conditions so the night's sudden downpour was sure to cause flooding in several places.

"Dozens are stranded." Teddy was excited, his voice more animated than usual. "Water's starting to get into the bars. Some customers look like they're going to stay and party through the night."

"As good a place as any to be holed up," I answered matter-of-factly like a bar and a disaster shelter were pretty much the same, at least they were for me.

Just then the girls came upstairs. Mal had tied the drawstring on the shorts as tight as possible, but they were still loose. She rolled the waistband over several times to tighten them more. She took after her great-grandmother and namesake who had been featured as the world's smallest woman in the Ringling Brothers Circus. Fortunately for Mal, Mallory Causey had married Xan Zeno, the circus's tallest man, which gave Mal the genes to grow to 4 feet 11 inches. Everything about her was petite, except her presence. Before Teddy, many men had seen her cropped black hair, pale skin, full red lips and hazel eyes and called her "cute," only to be skewered by her caustic, sharp wit.

Mal looked around the room, "Dammit, Walker, when was the last time you cleaned this dump? It smells like dirty socks, stale pizza and beer."

Summer found garbage bags under the kitchen sink and began collecting pizza boxes, empty beer cans and liquor bottles. She didn't say a word just shook her head as she moved through the room. Mal reluctantly helped while cursing under her breath loud enough for me to hear her displeasure. She picked up my Hawaiian shirt and put it in a garbage bag with the other trash and smiled at me when she did—daring me to protest.

I didn't and handed the two of them cold beers when they finished. Summer sat in the leather lounge chair stretching out her bronze dancer legs and putting her feet with her pink toenails up on the ottoman. She pulled a brush out of her purse and began working the tangles out of her damp, cinnamon-colored hair. "The band had to stop during the second set. The house manager told everyone to get to their cars as quickly as possible because the streets were flooded." On that note Big Boy curled up on her lap.

Mal sat next to Ted and added, "They should've told us sooner. When we came out of Vinyl Music Hall, our Prism had floated down Garden Street."

Summer looked up at the television. Pointing her hairbrush at the screen, she shouted, "That's my apartment complex!"

Teddy, still holding the remote, unmuted the volume to tune in to the soaked female reporter's take: "The brick retaining wall for the neighborhood's retention pond failed, sending thousands of gallons of water and mud into Woodbridge Apartments off University Parkway. Rescue crews are on-site to help with evacuations."

"Oh, no, this is horrible." Summer sat up, knocking the dog to the floor and hugged her chest tightly. "Our unit's on the second floor. We should be okay, right?"

No one answered as we stayed glued to scenes of the flooding on the television. The camera cut to the station's meteorologist, who probably never felt more important. "Tuesday's thunderstorms and heavy rain are expected to continue throughout this morning and could linger well into the afternoon. The flooding will continue."

Summer picked up her cellphone and started dialing her roommate. Busy signal. She bit her lower lip to keep her composure, sat back and patted her lap for Big Boy to rejoin her in the chair.

"This is fucking great," Mal ripped. She wasn't crying. Mal didn't cry.

"We've got insurance, baby," Teddy put his arm around her trying to keep her from going from a five to a ten on her outrage scale, a ticking meter he knew too well.

"It won't be enough. We'll be lucky if what we get pays off the car note."

—Everything went dark. We had lost power.

"Shit!" Mal turned on the flashlight app on her cellphone.

Ted and Summer turned on theirs too. I couldn't remember where I had put my phone to do the same but didn't feel like thinking that hard to find it. Then I heard my ringtone, The Beatles' "Help," coming from the bathroom off my bedroom.

"Help, I need somebody. Help, not just anybody. Help, you know I need someone, help …"

"Let me get my phone." I stood. "Oh, hey, you'll find candles and matches in the drawer to the left of the stove."

"When I was younger so much younger than today, I never needed any-body's help in any way …"

Mal got up to get the candles, and on her way announced, "I'm switching to bourbon while you still have ice."

"But now those days are gone, I'm not so self-assured …"

Jeremy Holt, our A&E writer, was on the phone. He had been covering a rehearsal of "Steel Magnolias" at the Pensacola Little Theatre. "I need a place to stay. My mom refuses to come get me because of the rain, and Yellow Cab isn't answering the phone."

Jeremy grew up in Pensacola, graduated from Boston College and moved to New York City until 9/11, which pushed him to come back to his hometown and move in with his mother and sisters. He had worked for the *Pensacola Insider* ever since. He added up to the four-fifths of the staff.

"Come on over," I invited. "Mal, Ted and Summer are already here."

"What?"

"They'll explain when you get here. I'll have a towel and spare clothes for you on the stairs."

When I walked back into the living room, candles were lit. They had all switched to bourbon and were eating chips they had found in the pantry.

"That was Jeremy. He's on his way."

"Great," Mal wasn't good at hiding her sarcasm—not that she had ever tried. "Maybe we should start building an ark."

Trying to help Teddy keep Mal calm, I said, "We won't know much more until daylight. Y'all can sleep here tonight."

Summer stroked Big Boy, but the candlelight had enough glow to show she was worried. "Is this what a hurricane is like?"

I had forgotten that she had moved to Pensacola from Michigan and wasn't around for hurricanes Ivan, Dennis and Katrina.

"A little, except the wind would really be howling louder, like a train," Mal answered, taking over the conversation.

"Roofs, branches, trash cans also would be flying in the air." Talking about something other than the current disaster did bring down a notch on her outrage scale. "The destruction is hard to fathom. Hurricanes wipe out the beach, pushing sand into every building on Santa Rosa Island not on stilts, and tourism disappears for months. Homes and businesses, even those off the coast, are destroyed as hundred-mile-per hour winds rip off roofs and crash towering oak trees down on them."

Just then Jeremy walked in, dressed in my clothes. He looked almost as fit as the rest of the staff. His new boyfriend was a personal trainer and had helped him lose twenty pounds. I looked down at my belly and at the tightness of my tattered red Ole Miss t-shirt and realized his twenty somehow got passed over to me. I tossed him a towel to continue to dry off.

Jeremy joined the discussion. "The paper barely survived after Hurricane Ivan. Walker's credit cards kept the *Insider* on life support since our advertisers were struggling to open for business."

Teddy added, "I became art director after Hurricane Dennis hit the following year because the old one split, unable to deal with another rebuild effort." He squeezed Mal. "Thank God."

I said, "But we survived and became a better paper because of it."

"Yeah, I started as receptionist fresh out of Loyola four months after Ivan," Mal agreed. "We'd already cut most of the bullshit columns and were focused on how to help Pensacola recover. We were truly the underdogs."

"Wow," said Summer, as Big Boy burrowed himself deeper into her lap. "Almost sounds heroic."

Jeremy did one last rub of the towel over his clean-shaven head. "It wasn't, but I agree we became a better paper." He lifted his towel, and we silently toasted the *Insider*.

I gave Teddy and Mal my bed. Summer claimed the couch, then Big Boy jumped in with her—the dog had a thing for Summer. Jeremy made the lounge chair his bed with the help of the ottoman.

I left the bourbon with them, but not before I made myself one more and headed downstairs to sleep on the couch in the *Insider* office. I stood in the dark by the windows facing Palafox. The wind rattled the glass, thunder crashed, and I saw lightning on the horizon over the Gulf of Mexico. Sirens could be heard faintly in the distance. I reached into my pocket, pulled out the Pizza Shack matchbook and placed it next to my computer. *Another problem for another day.*

I sipped my drink. Alone. Tomorrow would be a long day. Dare was right. I needed to get my shit together.

3

I didn't need an alarm clock. Big Boy woke every morning and demanded a walk before the sun rose. Wednesday was no different, even though he sacrificed his time next to Summer still sleeping upstairs. The wind was blowing, and rain was falling, but not as hard as last night.

I grabbed my running shoes, Dodger cap and windbreaker. Upstairs, the television was on but the sound was muted, and Summer had a pillow over her head to block out Jeremy's snoring. The sink was empty, and the dishwasher flashed a light showing clean dishes were inside. The last time the apartment looked that tidy was when Bree had spent a weekend with me.

Big Boy and I sneaked out the back door. The alley had a few puddles, but no water had made its way into the building. Our routine was to head south on Jefferson Street toward Pensacola Bay, but instead we jogged east toward Dare's house in Aragon, a trendy downtown neighborhood built on the site of a former housing project.

After jogging two blocks, we found it impossible to go any further unless I waded through knee-deep water while carrying Big Boy so we turned back. Waterlogged people were helping the road crews clear debris from the storm drains. The rain and wind picked up soaking the dog and me.

Back at the loft, Summer, our mother hen, was pouring coffee for Mal and Ted. She had found a roll of biscuit dough in the back of the refrigerator and had popped them in the oven. The smells were comforting. Jeremy was singing something from Les Misérables in the shower, and I pulled on a Sandshaker Lounge t-shirt and a pair of jeans that I got out of the dryer and joined the staff around the television.

Mal was glued to the news. "This is bad. In the past twelve hours, we've received over twenty-one inches of rain, and it's expected to continue until mid-afternoon."

On the television, reporter Misty had been replaced by reporter Kimberly—both were pretty confirming my suspicion that was a required skill set for local female TV journalists—who stood in a yellow raincoat interviewing the exhausted county public information officer. Government officials were still trying to determine the total scale of the flooding. Standing in the rain with the Emergency Operations Center in the background, the PIO said, "Our biggest concerns are three disabled bridges because they're limiting emergency response personnel's ability to access individuals in those areas."

Kimberly ended the segment, "Empty cars dot roadways all over Pensacola after drivers were forced to abandon them in the face of rising flood waters. Law enforcement has requested everyone stay in their homes until the roads are clear."

"That's if you have a home," Mal snapped, then got up, looking disgusted, to find some creamer for her coffee. "We lost our car, and the fucking, smiling TV news people said the houses in our Long Hollow neighborhood have three feet of water in them."

Teddy, having lost the battle to keep her agitation level to a five, was now trying to keep it from going to eight, added, "Baby, I left a voice message with the property manager. They'll take care of the carpets and dry us out."

"Yeah, but where do we live until then? It could be weeks before they get to us."

Summer weighed in, "My roommate told me they don't know when we can return to our apartment. She's moving in with her boyfriend, but I don't have a boyfriend, at least not one I want to live with."

Jeremy walked out of the bedroom dressed, sat down on the otto-man and began putting on his socks and shoes. He offered, "Y'all can live at my house until everything settles. I'm sure Mother won't mind as long as you contribute something to the bills."

Mal glared at Jeremy. I was amazed that he didn't burst into flames.

"Just a thought," he lowered his head, as if trying to duck any more of Mal's incoming fire.

"Why don't you three stay here?" I couldn't believe what was coming out of my mouth. I wasn't known as a warm host, or a host of any kind. "Get your clothes. We can store any belongings you retrieve in the conference room."

"Are you sure?" Summer asked. "It might work. I mean I don't really have that much stuff. A laptop and some clothes."

Teddy liked the idea. "Our furniture, well the insurance company is going to have to replace all that I'm sure. But we can bring our computers, clothes and a few other things."

Mal wasn't as confident it would work. "I don't want anyone going through my shit," she emphasized with a hard stare at every one of us.

"I'll sleep on the couch in the office," I suggested. "The loft will be for you, Teddy and Summer."

Damn, this was getting complicated. Too late to change my mind. Big Boy sat by Mal and put a paw on her leg. *The dog might actually be a service dog*, I thought. She touched his paw for a second and began stroking him absentmindedly as she formulated a plan. "Ted, let's go check on our car and get a tow truck. Then we all need to get to our things and bring them back here."

I reminded them, "Guys, we've got a disaster to cover."

"What?" Mal pushed Big Boy's paw off of her leg but he didn't seem to care. Summer was his girl, not her. She gave me the same stare that had crushed Jeremy a minute earlier. "Now you want to be newspaper publisher after spending the past three months drunk."

I ignored her barb. "Let's compromise. Mal and Teddy, you go check on your car. I'll call my friend at Ace Towing and make sure you're a priority. Summer can monitor the local government websites, and Jeremy will track Facebook and Twitter. We post updates on the blog."

I turned to Mal, "Once the police open up the streets, I'll give you the keys to my Jeep Cherokee. It's in the parking deck behind the courthouse. Take Jeremy home and check on your places."

Teddy bobbed his head in agreement, but Mal wasn't conceding leadership to me. She commanded the staff, "Everybody keep your cellphones charged and close. I'll call Pantoni and tell her to stand by for instructions on where she should go."

Tessie Pantoni was our news reporter and rounded out the paper's entire team of five. She lived in her parents' condo on the Scenic Highway bluffs. She had been Mal's roommate at Loyola and had moved backed to Pensacola last year to help her father take care of her ailing mother.

I left the staff to work out the details of our new living arrangements and walked up Palafox Street to better assess the damage. The rain had slowed to a light drizzle, and the flood waters had subsided to the curb thanks to diesel pumps sucking up the water and depositing it into the drains on the much dryer side streets.

I ran into a weary bartender who was sweeping water out of Hopjacks. "Asshole, this is a goddamn no wake zone," she yelled at a city truck as it drove down Palafox sending waves of water back into the pizza joint. When she spied me, her disgust turned to a grin. "Hi, Walker. How'd your office come out?"

I was embarrassed to say the flooding hadn't reached our end of the block. "For some reason, the flooding stopped at the post office."

"That's good. What happened to your arm?"

"Crushed it in a car door trying to help a couple last night."

"Does it hurt?"

I said smiling, "Only when I'm sober."

She laughed. Surveying the street, she motioned for me to come inside. "This is screwed up." A couple inches of water puddled in several spots in the front half of the narrow restaurant. Watermarks on the tables, chairs, and bar indicated that the water had risen to at least a foot. "People were trapped downtown last night," she kept talking as she directed me to the dry end of the bar where poured herself a beer from the only tap that didn't have a plastic cup over it and took a sip.

"Jack?" she asked and then added, "For your arm."

I didn't answer. I knew she knew. The Hopjacks staff didn't wear name tags which forced me to search my brain for her name. After last night, that was going to take more neurons than I had firing. Tall, fit, twenty-something, straight auburn hair, tattoo of R2D2 on her right arm. *Alice, no. Betty, no. Damn, nobody uses the name Betty anymore.*

"You were here through the night, Mags?" I asked, took a swallow of the bourbon to be sociable and waited to see if I had correctly guessed her name.

She smiled, "I didn't think you remembered my name."

"It's one of my gifts," I grinned and pulled out my notebook and Pilot pen. Mags hesitated when she saw my reporting tools. "The manager went out to find some dryers and wet vacs. Mr. Holmes, you really ought to talk with Mike."

"It's Walker, not mister," I insisted and walked behind the bar and topped off her beer from the tap. "I'll talk with Mike, but we need to get something on the blog now."

She pulled back her hair that had blue tips. Out of nowhere, she made a hair band appear. "Around ten, we noticed the water rising in the street. When Vinyl let out its customers, the place filled up quick. No one could leave. They couldn't get to their cars."

"Were people angry? Scared?"

"They took it as a joke at first. Ordered pizza, drank beer. I remember seeing your staff in here for a few minutes, but when I looked around later, they'd already left."

"Mal, Ted and Summer ended up in my office." I looked around for two more ice cubes. Found them floating in the slush in the bar's well, then plopped them in my glass and added a little water to my Jack since I was on duty.

Mags nodded. "But the rain kept coming down and the water kept rising. We didn't have anything to stop it." She closed her eyes and took a big swig of beer. "It went on and on and on. I was scared. I used to like the sound of rain, but this was like Chinese water torture."

She told me that people began to sit on top of tables and on the bar. When the power went out around midnight, people began lighting up joints and those who didn't get high switched to hard liquor.

"The longest damn night of my life." Another swig of her beer. "When the power came back around three, a lot of people started going home. When the sun came up around six, a guy in a fishing boat took those still here to the Red Cross shelter near the library."

I nursed my drink, twirling the ice cubes with my finger, then looked back up at her. "Why did you stay?"

"Because I live with Mike. Couldn't leave him to deal with this alone while the owner's off in India on some spiritual journey."

The wooden floor was ruined. Hopjacks would be out of commission for weeks. I took a few photos with my cellphone, finished the last of my drink and thanked Mags. On the way back to the office, I talked with shop owners looking over the damage to their places. New York Nick's, across the street from Hopjacks, had fared better than others because its floor was slightly higher, and the owner had placed sandbags outside his door.

At the *Insider* offices, Big Boy crawled out from under Summer's desk and greeted me at the door. Jeremy was focused on his computer. Ted was editing his photos of flood damage.

Mal peered around her Mac as I reached down to pet the dog. "The police are allowing people on the streets. We're heading out to survey damage to our places around eleven." She refilled her Hello Kitty coffee cup while I poured my first. "Dammit, you smell like a goddamn saloon. Have you been drinking?"

Quickly taking a sip of coffee to wash out the taste of bourbon, I protested, "No, Mal. Come on, it's still morning. I was interviewing Mags at Hops. Pretty damn good interview too."

She didn't buy it, huffed and stomped back to her desk.

Summer finished up her phone call and looked to me. "Escambia County was placed under a local state of emergency at midnight. This morning, the State Emergency Operations Center activated to Level Two in response to the severe weather and flooding."

"Put all that on the blog."

"Of course. Also, Governor Wilson earlier this morning held a press conference in Tallahassee and said he's coming to Pensacola."

"Mal, have you reached Pantoni?" I asked.

"She's already sent us photos of where Scenic Highway collapsed, south of the Gaberonne subdivision," Mal replied. "And she's got an interview with the owner of the pickup truck that slid into Escambia Bay. Now Pantoni's riding her bike over to Cordova Park. We're hearing it's even worse there."

Pantoni didn't own a car. How screwed up was it that our investigative reporter depended on public transportation and her bicycle to cover news?

Summer confirmed, "The *News Herald* already has photos of Cordova and a dozen other trouble spots up on their website. The retention pond at the airport must've burst. The streets leading down the hill to Bayou Texar look like rivers washing asphalt, trees and cars into the bayou."

"Damn, how we can compete with their coverage?" Mal challenged me, still unhappy with my interview technique at Hopjacks. I chose to bob and weave and took a reassuring tone, "Let's stay in the game. We can pull it together for a much deeper piece in next week's issue."

Summer jumped in, "I just got an alert that the governor should touch down at the airport within the hour and will tour the Cordova Park area."

"Pantoni will be there by then," I continued, avoiding using my reporter's first name. She was talented and had worked for the *Chicago Sun-Times* before returning home. It wouldn't long before she would be moving on to bigger publications once her mother's condition stabilized, no need for me to get attached. "Text her. I want her to be our person in the field."

"I'm going on the roof." Teddy pushed away from his desk while grabbing his camera, all in one motion. "Can get a better shot of the flooding."

Mal and I climbed through the window in my laundry room and followed Teddy on to the fire escape. Jeremy was afraid of heights, and Summer didn't want him to feel bad so she stayed with him. Once we got to the roof, we saw that most of the water at Palafox and Garden intersection had receded. However, to the east, a lake had formed that covered most of Aragon and stretched to the Veterans Memorial Park.

Ted started snapping photos while Mal served as a spotter for those she wanted for the paper and blog. They made a good team.

I called Dare. She picked up on the first ring. "Hello."

"How do you like lakefront living?"

"Funny," she answered in a deadpan voice.

"You okay?"

"Yes, thank God," Dare replied with a little more warmth. "The water came up to my steps, but not in the house, thank goodness, though I probably have a little water damage in the garage."

"Do you need anything?"

"Yeah, for you to be sober."

She annoyed the hell out of me. "Besides that."

"No, I'm good." She paused, then took another swipe at me. "Well, what about it?"

"I'm getting there."

"Good," and with that she hung up.

When we climbed back down the fire escape and into the building, Summer handed Mal a note. "The towing company took your car to Carver's Garage. The mechanic thinks he can dry it out and have it working by Monday."

"Did he give you an estimate?"

"No, he said he'd work it out with Walker."

Mal looked at me. "Does every person in this town owe you favors?"

"Mostly the good ones."

"Mostly the good ones? What does that mean? Bad ones owe you too."

I knew better to answer, and she knew better to press me. They posted more photos and notes to the blog, then took my Jeep Cherokee to look in on their homes.

Lum called. He was opening his restaurant and asked if I would post it on the blog since he might be the only place in the downtown area serving lunch today. His nephew brought me a Dragon roll, miso soup and some wontons ten minutes after the post went live. Lum also included some chunks of grilled chicken for Big Boy, which the dog immediately began scarfing down. The restaurant owner understood how the system worked.

I said to the dog, "See, there are some perks living with me." Big Boy burped and crawled on the couch and began to doze. While I ate, a few carpet cleaning companies and one disaster recovery firm made inquiries about web ads. *Free Chinese food and now this—we might make some money on this.*

As I was polishing off the Dragon roll, James Harden called. He was a private investigator who had helped me in the past and spent most of his life on the fringes, having lunch meetings at gas stations with people who contacted him via notes shoved under the door mat of his office in a bad part of town.

"Holmes, you need to pay attention to the jail." Harden never had time for "hello," assuming I had checked caller id before I picked up.

"Not sure I can today. My staff is assessing the damage to their places, and I've got my one reporter in the field following the governor around. It's just me holding down the fort at the moment."

"You hung over or drunk?"

"Screw you!" After a pause, "In-between."

He laughed. "The county jail is powered by diesel generators and has no air conditioning running water or sewer. Prisoners in the Central Booking and Detention Center are pissing and shitting in garbage bags."

"Dammit, Harden. I'm eating." I crunched down loudly on a wonton hoping it would startle his hearing and push him back.

It didn't. "The CBD basement is flooded. Only a handful of correctional officers showed up for work, and the prisoners are getting restless."

"Didn't the county just renovate that building after its basement flooded two years ago?" Then another wonton, but this one for taste. I wasn't going to waste them on Harden.

"Yeah, I'm hearing the pumps that were supposed to deal with heavy rains still sit in crates waiting to be installed."

"Okay, I'll try to get someone over there early tomorrow morning."

Harden wasn't satisfied. "Do more than try."

I laughed. "Since when did you become my boss? Besides, what's your play here? Why call me?"

"My sister's son, Jimmy Low, is in the CBD waiting for his arraignment. Got in a bar fight and was arrested last night. Maybe you can put some pressure on Frost and get him to pay attention."

Sheriff Ron Frost was the most powerful man in Escambia County. We had done battle several times during his first two terms. The chances of anyone stopping Frost from winning a third term were slim. My sore stomach was as reminder of what our lives would be like under the Frost regime for another four years, but there were only two people who could derail his political machine—my friend Alphonse Tyndall and me.

Tyndall had headed the Florida Attorney General's Child Predator Cyber Crime Unit and earned kudos for his task force's sting of an international child porn ring operating out of Pensacola. Captain Amos Frost, the sheriff's brother, had gotten caught up in the ring and was blackmailed by its operators. Amos Frost swallowed his service revolver after the *Insider* reported on his unprecedented rise in the Escambia County Sheriff's Office and as Tyndall's task force was closing in on the porn operation. Sheriff Frost blamed Tyndall and me for his brother's suicide.

Tyndall had leveraged his success to become a partner with Rockwell Theisen, one of the top trial law firms in the state. With the firm's consent and support, he filed to run as a Democrat against Frost. The polls had the incumbent sheriff fifteen points ahead, and the general election was little more than six months away.

I said to Harden, "If I apply pressure, it could have the opposite effect."

"Not if you're clever. There's no one more clever than Walker Holmes when he's not hammered."

I was going to say, "not you too" but let it slide.

"Walker, Jimmy's twenty-two, never been in trouble. "

"I'll do what I can."

Next Pantoni called. "The Cordova Park story should be in your inbox. Governor Walters is talking with reporters. Your buddy Tyndall is here to take the entourage to a flooded apartment complex near NAS Pensacola. Can you get me in one of the press vans?"

"Stand by."

I texted Alphonse, "Have a reporter on scene. Can you get her in the press van?"

Two minutes later my phone pinged with his texted answer: "Better, she can ride with the governor and me. What does she look like?"

"Purple hair, nose ring."

"LOL. Of course she does. Tell her to come to me."

I called Pantoni back. "You're riding with the governor."

"Really? Are you serious?"

"Yeah I'm serious. Find Tyndall. He's expecting you."

"Cool. I'll keep you posted."

Governor Bobby Joe Walters was the first Democrat elected to the state's top post since Lawton Chiles beat Jeb Bush in 1994. He had been trying to rebuild the party and did everything he could for his fellow Democrats seeking office. Walters would take advantage of this visit to help Tyndall in his race against Sheriff Frost.

Pantoni's piece on the Cordova Park damage was good:

Cordova Park Washes Away
By Tessie Pantoni

Residents of the Cordova Park area are digging out this morning after floods turned streets into rivers of mud, destroying homes and sweeping vehicles into Bayou Texar.

Randy and Mary Thomas barely escaped being swept away in the bayou last night. The two had left the movies at 11 p.m. When they came to their street, they found the water already knee-deep. Randy Thomas tried to negotiate the stream to get home to their children, but the water picked up their car.

"We just started spinning," he told the Pensacola Insider.

When the car became wedged against a tree, neighbors waded in and managed to pull the couple to safety.

Nearly all the infrastructure in the Thomas' neighborhood is exposed, a tangled mess of gas, water and sewer lines. All utility service has been shut down. City officials have promised to put porta-lets on the street and have been handing out bottles of water.

"I have no idea how long it will take to fix this mess," Thomas said. "I mean, my road is a river."

This blog, a web journal that I created no long after I started the newspaper, was how our weekly stayed relevant on a daily basis. Called "The Holmes Report," I fed it news, viewpoints, and political buzz three or four times a day. The public loved it, making it one of the most popular political blogs in the state, but its popularity required—no, it demanded—perpetual attention. Readers wanted more and more. With the help of the *Insider* staff, I tried to satisfy them.

Mal called, "Couldn't get to our duplex. Ted parked at Greater Union Baptist Church and waded to our place. There's a freight train stuck on the tracks. Manna Food Pantries has lost most of its food stock to flood waters. This sucks big time."

4

A little after two, Pantoni texted that Governor Walters, Frost and Tatum were headed downtown to hold a press conference on the steps of the old courthouse, a block south of our office, but the sheriff and county commissioner weren't riding with the governor, which really wasn't a surprise.

Tatum had sold his hipster dive bar, The Green Olive, and invested in a technology startup that was bought for millions by a Silicon Valley giant. He became a big contributor to the Democratic Party so when the District 4 county commissioner died last year, the governor appointed Tatum to fill the seat until the current election cycle.

Once in office, Tatum surprised everyone when he switched parties. He made the decision not based on a shift in his political ideology but because two-thirds of his district were registered Republicans. The governor still held a grudge over the political betrayal, and he wasn't about to let the turncoat commissioner make headlines.

"I'll handle the presser," I told Pantoni. "Come to the office and man the phones until Summer gets back."

At the press conference, Commissioner Tatum spoke first. His official commissioner polo had sweat stains under his armpits. Trying to identify with the blue-collar voters, he wore camouflage hunting pants and some flimsy looking rubber boots, though the man had never been hunting. The left boot still had an orange price sticker on it—even from where I stood ten feet away I could make out the lettering: CLEARANCE. He probably charged them to the county.

"First, I want to thank Governor Walters for being here. It's important to have a friend in Tallahassee."

Everyone clapped, except the governor and his staff.

Tatum said that 911 dispatchers had handled more than four thousand calls in the last 24 hours, and fire rescue teams had worked tirelessly since the first one came in. He rambled on some more about how "we're in this together" and other bullshit. He just needed to be seen on camera and in the *News Herald* standing beside Governor Walters and Sheriff Frost. Being the one-time owner of an infamous dive bar and a former Democrat made Tatum vulnerable, and he faced stiff competition in the GOP primary, the chairman of the Escambia County Tea Party. Tatum needed as much help as he could get to win the primary.

The tall, cadaverously thin Sheriff Ron Frost took the podium next. He had substituted his trademark Stetson for a green baseball cap with the sheriff's office logo in the spot where I assumed he had a brain. He wore a green windbreaker with the sheriff's office logo in the spot where I assumed he had a heart. Cameras clicked, videos rolled as the top lawman in Northwest Florida bent over the podium to speak into the microphones.

"Several bridges and roads remain impassable," he said. "Governor Walters has used his influence to get more road barricades for our deputies to block off the flooded streets, and they're being deployed as we speak."

He stressed the importance of the public not going past any of the barriers because some roads had no soil supporting them and said that the freight train blocking several intersections in downtown couldn't be moved until the floodwaters subsided in the Long Hollow area.

I yelled, "Sheriff, what about the jail?"

Frost hated to be interrupted. If he could have strangled me, he would have. Tatum, coming to the aid of his political ally, shouted back, "We'll take questions after the governor speaks."

I ignored him. "We're hearing the CBD has no water or sewer. Prisoners are forced to urinate and defecate in garbage bags. They're fighting over bottled water."

"Holmes, we're under a state of emergency," Sheriff Frost said, turning to face me. I returned his glare with what I imagined said: "and your point is?"

He revved up again, "We've got good people stranded all over the county. Many are struggling to find dry places to sleep tonight. A few inmates being inconvenienced don't concern me."

A female reporter from one of the television stations followed up: "We have reports of a natural gas leak in the neighborhood near the jail."

Showing some exasperation, Frost answered testily, "Our facilities chief toured the area and found no problems. Thank you." He stepped back making room for Governor Walters to take the podium.

The governor appeared to be visibly touched by the destruction he had seen. "I want to make sure that every resource at my disposal is available to help this community." He thanked the sheriff and county commissioner for accompanying him without using their names—he had no desire to help the Republicans with their campaigns. He then reiterated to be careful walking around neighborhoods. "We walked up to a house and the sheriff suddenly sank in three feet of water so every citizen has to be careful." Frost grimaced, hating to be seen as anything less than perfect.

After the press conference, Tyndall grabbed me. "Would you like to talk with the governor?"

"Sure."

The governor, silver-haired and tanned, was conferring with his aides. When Tyndall tapped his shoulder, he turned, smiled and reached out his right hand, all in one gesture.

"Governor, this is the newspaper publisher I told you about, Walker Holmes."

Alphonse enjoyed introducing me to the governor. Tyndall had been my friend for two years. He was an imposing figure—a former college athlete that chose to build a career on his intellect, rather than his physical talents.

"Governor, thank you for coming to Pensacola," I said, shaking his hand. He smiled—kudos to his dentist for perfect white veneers.

"Mr. Holmes, I enjoy your blog."

"Thank you, sir."

"How'd you hurt your arm? Typing your blog?"

I laughed. "No Governor, though blogging can be hazardous. I slipped trying to help a mother get her baby out of a flash flood."

"Are they okay?"

I nodded and thinking, *Lying was becoming too natural for me.*

Putting his arm around Tyndall's shoulders, Governor Walters said, "Alphonse says your newspaper is supporting his campaign. What do you think of his chances?"

"The election is months away, and he's closing the gap. But I don't know how this storm will impact the vote." There was a silence waiting to be filled so I added, "I mean disasters tend to help the incumbents."

Walters nodded in agreement. "What if I make him my liaison with local officials in the recovery effort?"

"Frost won't like it."

"That's not what I asked."

"It wouldn't hurt, especially if Alphonse can get on TV."

"That's what I thought," the governor said. "Alphonse, I'll talk with my team and the White House. We'll figure out the details and call you as soon as we have them worked out."

Tyndall thanked the governor.

I asked, "Governor, can I post this as a buzz item?"

Walters smiled, "That would be nice."

As I walked down the courthouse steps, Chief Deputy Krager blocked my way.

"What were you and Tyndall talking with the governor about?" He had his hands on his hips near his gun and Taser.

"Jesus," I said as I tried to sidestep him but Krager boxed me in. "This dance is getting tiresome. Maybe we should take lessons at Fred Astaire. Are your Mondays open?"

"Funny," but he wasn't laughing. "What happened to your arm?"

"My arm?" He didn't seem to remember stepping on it last night. Actually, it seemed like ages ago to me too.

"Never mind about that." Maybe he did remember. "The sheriff didn't appreciate you interrupting his speech."

"Peck, it was a press conference. Asking questions goes with the turf." Again, I tried to get past him, and he blocked me again, flexing his muscles and puffing out his chest. I could see the veins in his neck swell. He definitely wanted another excuse to hit me.

"What weird game are you playing here, Peck?"

Standing as tall as he could but still only reaching my chin, he hissed, "When we win re-election, we'll crush you."

"Peck, didn't your momma tell you about not counting your chickens until they hatch?"

"Oh, come on, Holmes. You can do better than that. Isn't there a happy hour you're late for?" His laugh was high-pitched and irritating and bounced off the marble walls of the courthouse's atrium. Even when he was out of range, it still rang in my ears.

Back at the office, the staff had reassembled, except for Jeremy who had been dropped off at his mother's house. More articles and photos had been posted on the blog. I added the buzz item about Tyndall's possible appointment.

Teddy, Mal and Summer had returned with their televisions, computers, clothes and miscellaneous boxes that were stacked in the conference and corners of the office. Mal also brought her domestic longhair cat, Liza. Big Boy and the cat appeared to be avoiding each other, and neither could figure out why the humans cared about the other animal.

We held our staff meeting in the loft's kitchen and walked through all the interviews and stories of the day. I shared what Harden had told me about the conditions in the county jail, my conversation with the governor and the possibility Tyndall would be his liaison for the recovery effort. The staff debate was how to pull all of the stories and rumors into an appealing cover story for next week.

While Summer refilled our coffee mugs, Mal glanced over her notes and tapped her pencil on a legal pad. She took control, "We should focus on the recovery effort. By the time our next issue comes out, most of the damage will have been reported."

Pantoni agreed with Mal, as she usually did. The college roommates stuck together. She had changed out of her wet clothes and was wearing the shorts I had given Mal last night and one of my white t-shirts. She filled them out well.

"I'll talk with Tyndall after his appointment is announced," she said, sitting with legs crisscrossed underneath her as she took notes on her laptop. "He should be able to hook me up with FEMA and other agencies."

Mal continued laying out her editorial plan. "That sounds good. We can put out a flood recovery guide and make it available online for readers to download."

Teddy put down his Incredible Hulk mug and added, "I'll design the pages so they can be cut out and placed on a refrigerator."

The staff was getting into a flow. I sat on the sidelines admiring my team. Mal added, "Jeremy can work on all the phone numbers and websites for a recovery directory. He'll bitch, but A&E can take a break for a week."

Summer attempted to draw me into the conversation. "I called the prospects you emailed me, boss. They're coming in for four weeks. I'll make a few more sales calls in the morning."

"Informative and profitable," I said raising my coffee cup. "The perfect issue."

Flashing a rare smile, Mal adjourned the meeting, "We can finalize all the assignments in the morning."

I suggested we order takeout from Lum's—egg rolls, chicken lo mein, egg foo young and pork fried rice. By nine, everyone was full and starting to nod off as we watched CNN recap the flood damage one more time. Since it was dark and the roads back to her parent's condo were questionable, Pantoni accepted Mal's offer for her to stay with the gang upstairs for the night. I had completely lost control of my loft.

I headed downstairs and sat at my desk. On my right, I overlooked Palafox Street, where several shops had their doors open, furniture stacked on the sidewalk under balconies and awnings as their managers and owners stood guard while the roaring of portable dryers inside their shops drowned out most other sounds. A cop on a bike patrolled the street.

Out the left window, I could see World of Beer had chosen not to open. The bar had replaced Blazzue's, which had closed after failing to build a jazz-loving clientele. Half a block further south stood Intermission, an older downtown bar that held its own against flashier competitors. Smokers standing in the street in front of it signaled the bar was pouring drinks, as usual, come hell or high water—knowing the owner he'd be open for either.

I saw the Pizza Shack matchbook and remembered I needed to check with State Attorney Clark Spencer on the latest developments in the Townsend case. Former State Attorney Hiram Newton had retired at the first of the year and had made a deal with the governor that his chief assistant, Spencer, would be appointed as his replacement until the next election. Most attorneys viewed Clark Spencer to be a politically powerful incumbent—the final deadline for filing was the first Friday of May, and none appeared willing to challenge him.

I eased out from behind my desk, having decided to visit Intermission for just one drink. Then I'd come back and sleep. Well, that's what I told myself.

Tom Petty's "American Girl" played on the jukebox as I walked in. I grabbed a stool at the bar, and Eva Johnson gave me a generous pour of Jack and Coke. A retired stripper, Eva understood men better than most so she already knew to leave me alone.

The bar, which the owner claimed was the longest in town, stretched the length of the narrow front room. Small tables with two or three chairs were arranged in no particular pattern on the tiled floor, with a dartboard, Golden Tee and other video games along the far wall. A few stools away sat three of the legacy boys, bragging loudly about how much money they would make on the flood recovery. Their families had run Pensacola for decades.

When the 1900 census count was taken, the city was predominantly black and on track to be the next big Southern enclave, rivaling New Orleans in diversity. However, the more prosperous the community became, the more rednecks it attracted from Mississippi, Alabama and Georgia. The crackers brought with them a hatred for blacks and Jim Crow laws that mandated the racial segregation of public schools and public places, as well as restrooms, restaurants, and even drinking fountains. Long-standing black businesses were forced out of downtown. Black families were evicted from their homes, and job openings for people of color evaporated, as did their right to vote. Pensacola's black population decreased by half by the end of World War I.

The legacy vultures seized the businesses and homes left behind and built their own fortunes dividing up the town among themselves and helping each other amass power and wealth. They created the Chamber of Commerce, Country Club and Yacht Club, handed awards to family members and fought any development or change that didn't make them money. Legacies only married legacies. The gene pool must have gotten shallow because the current brood was worthless.

After my third drink, a short, blubbery legacy kid—he reminded me of a baby whale—in a wrinkled Polo dress shirt and tight plaid pants noticed me. *Damn, here we go.*

"Walker Holmes?" he razzed. "Is that the great Walker Holmes in the flesh?"

I didn't take my eyes off the TV. The Dodgers were closing out their series with the Giants and had a chance for a sweep.

"It is you." The privileged punk and his two sidekicks moved closer. "You have a problem with us?"

"Boys, not as long as your daddies are proud of you."

The baby whale stepped inside my personal space, while the tallest of the gaggle, a pencil neck, blurted, "What the fuck do you mean by that?"

I waved to Eva to bring me another drink. She poured and stepped away. This was NASCAR—she wanted to watch the crash without getting hit by flying pieces of the wreckage. I took a sip, smiled with satisfaction, and went back to watching the game.

The third goon, a freckled-face redhead in a bright blue Ralph Lauren blazer that was one size too small over his maroon gingham shirt, closed on the other side of me. "You find us amusing?"

Another sip, another smile with satisfaction. The Dodgers were bringing in a relief pitcher.

"What happened to your arm?" His second question got an answer.

"I cut it on a beer bottle."

"Too bad, looks like it hurt," mocked Pencil Neck as he moved closer, completing the circle around me.

I kept my back to the trio. "Only when I'm around assholes." I paused to take a long drink from my glass. "So yeah, it's starting to hurt right about now."

The whale asked, "You think we're funny?"

The Dodgers retired the side in the ninth and clinched the series so no worries there. I wiped my mouth, stood up and faced the hipster crew. They tightened the loop around me, forcing my back against the bar. I moved toward them as I spoke, silently willing them to step back, "Yes, I do. You think you own this town because you think your grandfathers gave it to you. Unfortunately, you aren't as smart or ambitious as them or your fathers."

Freckle face poked me with his bony finger. "Shut the fuck up."

"Carrot top, it doesn't work that way. I'm your worst nightmare. A newspaper publisher that doesn't give a shit about your ancestry."

"Shut up or we'll beat the crap out of you." The punk ass baby whale had balls, I had to give him credit for that.

I laughed. "Been done before. Go back to your stools."

"Motherfucker!" The baby whale hit me below the waist, and as I doubled over, he slammed his elbow into my back. After I hit the floor, Freckles and Lurch each gave me a kick. I curled into a ball—a tactic I had learned long ago—and protected my ribs. A familiar voice yelled at the trio to get out, and they scattered like cockroaches.

"Dammit, Walker. Why do you always end up on the floor?" He helped me to a chair at one of the tables.

"Gravy, I thought we weren't talking," I said between short gasps for air.

Dressed in a starched white shirt and olive-green khakis, my attorney smiled and shook his head. "I charge by the minute so shut up and work on catching your breath." He grinned wider, "If you feel something in throat, I suggest you swallow. It's probably one of your balls."

Eva chuckled and brought me a fresh drink and a glass of white wine for William "Gravy" Graves Jr. *Hmmm, Intermission carried wine.* I stored that nugget right next to the team ERA of the 1978 Dodgers—3.12—as I thought about reaching for my glass, but the agonizing pain in groin overruled my motor functions. "Why are you here? Don't you have to help some rich insurance firm screw their customers?"

"Screw you, Holmes," though said without anger. "That was one case and one case only. Goddamn, can't you let go of anything?"

He knew the answer: no, I couldn't. "Why are you here, Gravy?"

"Eva texted me you were here."

"What? A journalist can't get a drink without the bartender tattling?"

"The better question is why can't you drink without getting your butt kicked?"

"Good point." I tried to straighten up, but my body still refused to cooperate. I struggled to turn my head toward Eva. "Who the hell was that?"

She wiped down the bar and put the towel on her shoulder. "The one who decked you was Tony Willis, his family owns a big construction company. Damn, you got under his skin quick."

I half-smiled at the backhanded compliment and tried to store that name away in my foggy brain. Gravy was talking to me.

"What's up with your arm?"

"Cut it in the kitchen, slicing a pineapple."

"Does it hurt?"

"Only when I cut fruit."

He laughed. "I miss talking with you."

I looked around, playing like I was hallucinating. "Remind me again, who are you?"

"Man, you're drinking has gotten out of hand." He reached for my arm to steady me as I was still wobbly.

"I could stop but haven't found a reason to." I made another stab at straightening up in my chair and succeeded.

"Shit, man! You aren't looking hard enough. Let me help you back to the loft."

Getting up, I grabbed my drink off the table and downed it. "I don't need help."

He sighed, "Of course you don't. You're Walker Holmes. Let's have breakfast in the morning."

"Sure," but we both knew I wouldn't show. "Hey Eva, give me a double for the road." She shook her head like a mother disapproving of a spoiled child.

Gravy piled on, "Your drunk Hemingway imitation isn't doing anyone any good, man."

I nodded my head, put my empty glass on the bar, left Eva a generous tip though thought of stiffing her for telling on me, and walked the half a block back to the couch in my office.

5

From the bottom of a dark well I must have fall into, I heard Summer's voice: "Boss, what was that?"

"What?" I was still a little buzzed but tried to sit up despite the room spinning.

"A loud boom," Mal answered.

I tried again to clear my head and make sense of their words. Mal yelled, "Son of a bitch, you've been drinking again." She went to her desk and powered up her Mac. "Why do I put up with this shit?" Summer, Teddy and Pantoni followed and looked over her shoulder at the monitor. "Several people are posting on Facebook about hearing an explosion, but no one knows where it came from."

My phone vibrated. It was a text from Harden: "Jail explosion. Where are you?"

I called and put him on speaker. "Harden, what's happening?"

There was shouting and screaming in the background. "CBD exploded. SWAT is here trying to control hundreds of prisoners. People everywhere. Hadn't seen anything like this since Iraq. Get here." The phone went dead.

I looked at my watch: 1:17 p.m. I had slept less than three hours, but his call was like a Red Bull. "Ted and Pantoni. Let's go. We're heading to the county jail."

Mal demanded, "I wanna go too. Having two cameras will come in handy. Besides, one of us will have to hold your drunk ass up."

"Fine," I grumbled as I tried to find my windbreaker. "Summer, monitor social media. We'll text you what we find out. Set up an open thread on the blog and add everything as it comes in."

She slipped me a couple Tylenols that I downed with the dregs from a stale Diet Coke, then I tossed the keys to Teddy. "You drive."

The rain was falling again in heavy sheets. The working street lamps decreased as we moved closer to the blast, and orange and white striped traffic barrels were everywhere, marking the streets that were still flooded. Several ambulances and deputies' cruisers passed us. When we turned down Leonard Street, it was Armageddon—sirens blaring, people screaming, bedlam.

We had to park in front of a bail bond office and walk the rest of the way as people were running from all directions to find out if their loved ones were alive. The nearby Platinum Club had closed at 1 p.m., and its inebriated patrons added another layer to the pandemonium. The scene was seriously out of control, and the chaos was intensifying by the minute.

Pantoni put her hand on my shoulder, pulled me close to her and shouted in my ear, "Looks like they're gonna riot. Where are the deputies?" I leaned into her, "Must have their hands full with inmates. Stay close."

I put on my "don't screw with me" face and plowed ahead. If I was smart, or sober, I would have had on my "let's get outa here" face. But then again, I concluded long ago that being smart was setting the bar too high for me. Pantoni squeezed my arm and pressed her lips tight. She had every reason to be frightened, but I had no such luxury. Just ahead were yellow crime scene tape and two cruisers in a makeshift barricade blocking our march.

We edged up to the tape. Chunks of cement and broken bricks littered the street about ten yards into the barricaded zone. A Mobile Command Unit parked a little further away stood in the way of our view of the Central Booking and Detention Facility.

"Ted, put your telescopic lens on your camera and give it to me." Through the camera's viewfinder, I saw Mac Reedy, the jail director, sitting on the steps of the unit looking like every nightmare he'd ever had in his entire life had come true. This was bad, very bad.

Someone shouted, "There they are! Over there!"

A caravan of buses, their diesel engines pounding, their gears grinding, slowly drove from the direction of the CBD, past the Mobile Command Unit, and approached the intersection beyond the barricade. The lights in the buses exposed their passengers, all dressed in orange jumpsuits. About twenty yards behind the buses, SWAT, carrying assault rifles and geared up, marched more inmates. Dozens of prisoners, males and females, walked like zombies, their jumpsuits soaked, heads down, many shoeless, several shaking and silently crying. The mob around us shouted names, but none of the prisoners looked up.

We could see in the distance the lights of ambulances as they shuttled in and out, likely offloading the injured at Baptist Hospital a half a mile away. "Teddy, take the girls back to the Jeep," I yelled. "Mal, you and Pantoni go to Baptist Hospital. Get whatever you can."

An onlooker under a half-collapsed umbrella shouted that Facebook had reports of rows of body bags. Another one, an elderly, heavyset woman in a soaked pink robe, prayed at the top of her lungs, "Jesus, Son of God, our Savior, watch over me in this end of days! Thy will be done, on earth as it is in Heaven!"

At the barricade, a deputy used a megaphone to direct the crowd to an information tent being set up at nearby Town & Country Plaza. I texted Teddy to go there while I stayed near the yellow tape that stretched from the cruisers to barrels on each side of Leonard Street, looking for an opening to get closer.

More buses flowed past me. Suddenly something appeared to go wrong inside the second to last one as it approached. The prisoners inside began to rock the bus. SWAT descended on it and swarmed the inmates. Within five minutes, the incident was over, but it was long enough for me to take advantage of the commotion and run behind the administrative building towards the CBD.

Across the parking lot, I saw the back wall of the first three floors of CBD had been completely blown out. The first floor, which was below

Leonard Street, was flooded with several feet of water. On the hill beside the CBD, a triage area had been established. So many people were milling around that my dark windbreaker helped me blend in.

Near the triage area, I thought I saw a row of dead bodies, but then one moved, and another, and another. They weren't dead, just injured. They laid on stretchers, covered with blue sheets to keep the rain from soaking them. Not sure who came up with that bright idea.

A deputy bumped into me. The shock on his face was unmistakable. The poor guy was a poster child for PTSD. He mumbled, "I was inside."

"Really?" He didn't question my presence and must have thought I was with the county or EMS.

"I arrested some guy and was bringing him in the sally port in the basement." He placed his hands over his ears. "I can't stop this damn ringing."

"You should check in with the paramedics up the hill."

"There ... there was a young cop also bringing in an arrest." He stopped and stared past me into space, then came back to earth. "They told him to move his vehicle because others were on the way so I said to him I'd ... I said I'd watch his collar."

He wiped his eyes, "Then it was like ... suction in ... ftttp! It all just sucked in ... then a second later it was black smoke and crap flying everywhere. I got out as fast as I could."

"Buddy, you really need medical attention," I said trying to coax him up the hill. He muttered, with pain and guilt in his voice, "But I've got to find that cop. He should've been out moving his vehicle like they said but I think ... I think ... he was crushed under the rubble. The whole damn building's on top of his cruiser."

"Maybe not," I tried to ease his mind.

He shook his head. "Either he is, or I'd have seen him by now."

The rain began to fall even harder, which seemed to trigger him to lose his grip faster. "Can I go home? My second shift ended long ago."

"You need medical attention." I thought about it for a second. Maybe being with his wife and kids would help him. He could see a doctor later. "Go ahead. Go home."

"You sure?"

"Yeah. We got it."

I watched him pull away in his cruiser. Then he put his brake lights on and put it in reverse. He called out to me: "What's your name? I owe you!"

"We're good!"

"But what's your name?"

"We're good!"

He shook his head, not sure he heard me. Gave a quick wave with two fingers and sped off.

6

Back at the office, I took the bandage off my left forearm and traced the edges of the wound with my fingertips, checking the stitches. The week before I had been attacked in the alley behind the office by someone who must have thought I would be an easy target to slash and run, but I surprised him with an elbow to his chin that forced him back against the brick wall. He slashed my arm as he fell back, but fortunately, Lum opened his alley door scaring off him before he could make another charge.

I spent the next two hours in the ER having my arm stitched. I reported the incident to the Pensacola Police since they had jurisdiction, but the officer gave me no hope of catching my assailant since I couldn't give a description of him. Also, it probably didn't help the *Insider* had published last year an article on Taser abuse that had led to several officers being suspended.

The next day I got a text from an unknown cellphone: "You were lucky this time - Lester Judson."

I applied an ointment the doctor had given me and wrapped my arm with fresh gauze. Then laid down to get some Z's:

> Out from the dark I saw Rachel Townsend wake up. The sixteen-year-old was naked on a mattress. Her arms were stretched above her head and tied to the bedposts. A man was on top of her, penetrating her. Others stood around the bed and watched. She could smell their sweat as they panted in excitement and anticipation.
>
> Rachel yelled for them to stop, to leave her alone. Instead, she got a gun pressed to her head.

"Want to see your brains all over that wall?" Lester Judson growled. She went quiet and eventually blacked out.

Rachel woke up to the same nightmare again and again. Each time a different man was on her, in her. She screamed to block out the pain. She didn't know if the ordeal lasted hours or days. As she faded in and out, she heard, "We have to stall longer … three hundred thousand in cash … man in Texas."

I woke up to the sound of Rachel's screams. I looked around the room, trying to orient myself. It was a dream, but that didn't mean it wasn't true. In fact, that's how Rachel had described it to me when her mother and pastor brought her to see me.

Rachel was tall, skinny with a wheat-colored bob. She had done child modeling when she was in elementary school, appeared on a couple billboards for one of the malls and won a few pageants in middle school. She had the figure to pursue bigger modeling jobs but got burned out by the time she hit high school and wanted to be a nurse instead.

She was somber, honest and direct as she stared out our conference room window and recited the facts, facts that Sheriff Frost, Chief Deputy Krager and the investigators had made her repeat over and over again. But in the end, they didn't believe her. I did.

"That doesn't happen in Pensacola." "She must have deserved it." "She asked for it." "That doesn't happen to girls who don't want it." "That's too unbelievable." Rachel had heard it all.

Young Rachel and motherly, but also young, Gina Judson had met at adult high at Pensacola State College. Rachel enjoyed helping Gina take care of her toddler so she was excited when Gina invited her to hang out at her dad's home. Rachel got her mother's permission under the condition that she would be home by 10 p.m. Gina's "dad," Lester Judson, had bought the girls pizza and cola. After a few sips, Rachel began to feel woozy. She remembered five men walked in from the back of the house before she blacked out.

When she woke up, she was laying in a pool of vomit in an unfamiliar bathroom. But Gina was there so that made her feel better. Her friend told her to take the pill resting in an open palm. It'd make her feel even better. The next time Rachel regained consciousness she was on a mattress, being raped.

At around 10:30 that night, Rachel's mom called Gina trying to find her daughter, but the phone just kept ringing. She kept calling, and still it kept on ringing. About an hour later, she couldn't wait any longer. The hundreds of rings going unanswered had made her get in the car and drive over to there. Lester Judson told her Rachel had left to be back home by ten just as she told her mother she would. It was along twenty-four hours before law enforcement considered the girl's disappearance a missing person case. Once they did, everyone rallied and distributed flyers with Rachel's photo.

Rachel continued telling me about her ordeal. "Mr. Judson and Gina must've panicked or something because they carried me out to a car, laid me on the backseat and covered me with blankets. I'd run out of fight and could barely hold my head up. I thought I'd be sold. But something else happened. The car stopped, and they dragged me out. Mr. Judson said, 'If you say our names or what happened to you, we'll kill you and the rest of your family.' All I know is they sped off, and I was lying on the asphalt of a Circle K parking lot near the Interstate."

Fortunately, the pastor was inside that Circle K passing out flyers at that very time. When Rachel staggered toward him, he was shocked, in relief and in horror. No one thought she'd survive. She had lethal amounts of crystal meth and roofies in her system. Her mother, in a choked voice, added, "She had internal bleeding that went on for days. Those animals infected her with chlamydia and gonorrhea."

Talking to law enforcement didn't ease her pain. She wasn't offered a victim's advocate or a female detective. Instead, she was put alone with a male investigator. "I could tell he wasn't on my side the moment he walked into the hospital room." They closed her case shortly after.

For weeks, back home, Rachel suffered nightmares and night terrors. She felt always in danger and distrusted anyone other than her immediate family. She couldn't be alone in the dark. She panicked one morning when her brother smelled liked the same cologne as one of her attackers.

"We came to you, Mr. Holmes, because they say you aren't afraid to take on anyone," Rachel looked me in the eye—I sensed that wasn't something she did much of anymore, and as if on cue she turned her long gaze out the window again. "I need someone to believe me and tell my story so no one else gets hurt by them."

"I'm always afraid, but I refuse to give into the fear," I answered quietly.

Dignified but with a hint of desperation, she pleaded: "We've nowhere else to go."

I released a big breath and looked in the faces of Rachel, her mother and their pastor. I needed to explain that I wasn't their savior, but the best I could come up with was: "We could make it worse."

"Do something. Anything. Please."

"We can write your story and tie it into a larger one about human trafficking. That might put enough public pressure on Sheriff Frost that he'd be forced to reopen the investigation, especially since he has an election coming up."

Rachel nodded her head giving consent. I felt a gnawing in my stomach. This wasn't going to turn out well. "Rachel, we'll need to publish your name—"

"I don't care."

"—because it'll draw readers to your story," I continued. "If I use a pseudonym, it might hurt us building sympathy for your ordeal and the plight of others caught up in human trafficking. Some would question its authenticity."

She didn't hesitate, "Let's do it."

"I can't do anything about Lester Judson." I squirmed a little in my seat. "I might draw more of his ire away from you and toward me, but, Rachel, you're still his accuser. That puts you in danger while he's still out there."

Her mother had an answer. "She can move in with my brother and his family in Jay. No one will find her there."

"Okay, but for how long? I don't know what it'll take for Frost to reopen the case, or if he'll even ever do anything about it at all."

Rachel was unwavering, "We have to try."

The next week we published her story, "Justice for Rachel." The issue flew off our stands, and Frost reopened the case. A week later, warrants were issued for the Judsons. Soon after, Gina was found dead in a Pascagoula motel. The Jackson County coroner ruled the death of Gina Touchant—her real last name—was either an accidental drug overdose or a suicide. No signs of Gina's toddler or Judson were found in the hotel room.

Then Rachel vanished. Three days after Gina's body had been found, Rachel attended her nephew's baseball game. Her uncle said she had gone to the concession stand alone to buy drinks and never came back. Seven days later, her nude, severely beaten body was found floating in Coldwater Creek, and I received a phone call.

"There goes your Pulitzer," a man's voice drawled, and then the line went dead.

I got shit-faced drunk that night.

7

The Beatles woke me a little after seven with the "Help" ringtone: "When I was younger so much younger than today, I never needed anybody's help in any way." It was Alphonse Tyndall: "Walker, have you been to the jail?"

I sat up and ran my left hand through my hair, trying to shake out the cobwebs. "Yes, it's a mess. Looked like the world was ending."

"I almost missed it, was dead asleep and didn't hear the explosion. Then people started knocking on my door around four a.m. Screaming about a terrorist attack or something. I got in my truck and went to sort things out."

While he was talking, I sat up and nudged Big Boy off the couch. He shook himself, stretched and headed downstairs. I smiled at the theatrics of his departure and returned to Alphonse, "We must've just missed you."

"Fortunately, Frost and Krager weren't around so several of the deputies I know let me past the barricade and filled me in." His friends had believed the explosion was most likely a natural gas leak in either the laundry or kitchen in the basement. He told me one guard was killed in the explosion. Another was paralyzed. Dozens more of the staff were injured.

I teetered, struggling to put on my jeans with one hand while the other hand held the phone to my ear so I could keep talking. "How about the prisoners?"

He sighed, "That's the problem. The network servers were in the basement, which has made it hard to come up with an accurate head count in the CBD. Like you said, it's a mess."

Cirque du Soleil would have thrown me out on my ass if I'd ever tried to audition. Wedging the phone on right shoulder, I fell over zipping up my jeans, then crawled on the floor looking for my deck shoes. I could hear Summer singing in the shower and smiled again to myself, *what a crazy world I lived in.* I asked Alphonse, "Have you heard from the governor's office?"

"I filled them in on the explosion, and I'm still waiting for their decision on my role."

"As soon as you hear, let me know immediately. Pantoni wants to interview you."

"The blue-haired reporter?"

I smiled, "Eggplant, man. Know your colors."

I was about to end the call, but Alphonse wasn't ready to. "I've got someone who wants to talk with a reporter. Her son was in the CBD when it exploded. Can you come to my campaign office?"

We agreed to meet in forty-five minutes. Downstairs, Mal, Teddy and Pantoni were at their desks. They hadn't gotten much sleep and looked haggard, running on coffee as they edited photos and keyed in their notes. Teddy was close to nodding off.

"Guys, go lay down for a couple hours. Let the calls got to voicemail." I poured a cup of coffee and sat down at my desk.

Mal and Teddy headed upstairs, but Pantoni waved me off. Staying in her chair, she filled me in on the latest developments, "The presser is gonna be in front of the CBD at noon. We still haven't gotten good numbers on those killed and injured. I've got a call out to a deputy, someone I used to date. Maybe she has some information."

"She's still talking to you?"

"Yeah Walker, my exes don't wish me dead like yours do."

She had a good point. "Fair enough." From my desk, I watched the owner of the art gallery down the street cuss out his young assistant for leaving expensive artwork on the sidewalk overnight. Last night's downpour had ruined several pieces.

When Summer came downstairs, I drove to Tyndall's campaign headquarters in the middle of a strip center sandwiched between a tattoo parlor and a Vietnamese market. A frazzled Reshanda Green sat with Alphonse at a card table in the back, surrounded by VOTE TYNDALL FOR A BETTER TOMORROW yard signs. She clutched a box of tissues, and through sobs, accused the sheriff's office of ignoring the inmates' complaints, particularly her son's, who she said had called her yesterday morning about the gas fumes and complained of feeling lightheaded.

"They didn't do nothing," she complained. "Malik was on one of them floors that exploded. Haven't heard one thing since. I need to know where my boy is." She began sobbing prompting Alphonse to put his arm around her shoulders. "I need to know if he's alive or hurt."

I leaned in to get closer to her. "I'm sorry you're going through this, Ms. Green, we're still waiting for Sheriff Frost to release the names of inmates and where they've been taken. The hospitals aren't sharing any details."

"It's not fair that the county hasn't told me where my baby is."

I nodded, then opened my notepad. "I'd like to take a few notes, if that's all right." For the next fifteen minutes or so, I interviewed Ms. Green. Wringing her hands and weeping, she gave me more background on her family and Malik and told me about conversations she'd had with her son and her thoughts about the nightmarish scene the night before.

Overcome with worry, she broke into tears and buried her face in her hands. "I don't know what to do." She lifted her head and begged, "Please, please help me find my baby."

I moved closer and squeezed her hands. "We're doing everything we can to locate all of those trapped and get the facts out. We'll get answers."

Alphonse gathered up Ms. Green and started walking her out to her car. She looked over her shoulder when she reached the door: "Thank you both. Bless you."

When he came back, Alphonse grabbed two bottles of water from a small refrigerator. He still moved like an athlete, even though it had been twenty years since he'd played linebacker at Howard University. He kept his coal-black hair cut close to the scalp on purpose, because it required zero maintenance. His mustache was well-trimmed and grew in perfect symmetry around the sides of his mouth. His vanity showed only through a silver Rolex Submariner watch that he had bought when he went to work for Rockwell Theisen.

Alphonse looked like he was carrying the weight of the world on his shoulders as he slumped into a metal folding chair. He wore on his face the worries of all the families with loved ones caught in the explosion. The strain of the sheriff's campaign also weathered him, but still he put others ahead of himself, which was one of the main reasons we were friends.

"She was much more upset when I first brought her here." He paused to swig from the water bottle. "When I got to Leonard Street, she was standing in the rain, crying, under a rickety umbrella. She had walked the seven blocks to Baptist Hospital and back to the county jail, but no one would help her."

I sat back in a matching folding chair and shared what I had seen. "A large section of the third floor collapsed during the explosion and fell onto the lower floors. I didn't say anything because I don't know where exactly her son was housed."

Alphonse nodded and guzzled another throatful. "Rumors are flying all over the place, and Frost has done nothing to settle them."

"Well, he's got a press conference at noon."

"The governor's office is saying it may be closer to two. The state fire marshal is coming over."

I got up and walked around the office, trying to shake off last night's kicks at Intermission. My forearm ached too as I went to look out the front window. Very few cars were on Pace Boulevard.

Alphonse joined me at the window, then sighed, "The deputies were dog-tired, having already worked double-shifts. They were operating on automatic pilot."

I nodded in agreement, "The shock of the explosion hasn't fully set in yet. The press conference should be very informative."

As I drove back to the office, Summer called. On speaker phone: "Jeremy can't get a ride in. He'll work on the flood recovery directories from home."

"Did you get any rest?"

Ignoring my detour, she kept to her highway: "The printer hasn't delivered the papers yet."

We printed our newspaper in Panama City and had it delivered to a storage unit off of Fairfield Drive. Summer had caught up with the driver on his cell and found out that he was having trouble finding bridges that the Florida Highway Patrol hadn't closed. The papers probably wouldn't arrive until after five.

I swerved to avoid a man in a LA Lakers ensemble—dirty purple and gold jersey with number "23" and "BRYANT" in black letters across the back and matching dirty purple sweatpants—pushing a shopping cart filled with crap across Pace Boulevard. I blew the horn, and he flipped me off. A perfect west Pensacola exchange. "Put a notice on both our websites that we'll have the issue out by tomorrow morning so we'll have a buffer if something goes wrong."

As soon as that conversation ended, my phone rang again. Through the speaker came Gravy's chiding voice: "You missed breakfast. Looking at your blog, it doesn't appear you got any sleep."

"I got enough."

"I've got a client that was housed in the CBD when it exploded." Gravy had built his law firm on criminal defense and personal injury cases. "He's sitting in the work release center with a bulge in his abdomen and maybe a broken bone in his foot. The guy needs to see a doctor."

He asked if I would put something up on the blog to pressure the county to give injured inmates medical attention.

"I've families calling me, and I can't give them any answers."

"I'll see what I can do," was my best offer.

Back at the *Insider* office, Teddy was editing photos from last night. Mal and Summer had gone grocery shipping. With Mal's cat in the loft, Big Boy refused to go upstairs and sat on the couch near my desk, looking out the window. Upset about his place being crashed, he glanced my way for only a second before turning back to the window. He was probably plotting to throw me out the window.

Tessie hadn't slept, she thrived on excitement. Her purple pixie cut was disheveled as were her "My Chemical Romance" shirt and black jeans. Hunched over her Mac with her face inches from the screen, her naturally droopy eyes—that some found sexy—were nearly shut, but she had upgraded from coffee to Red Bull to make sure they didn't. I walked over to her desk. "Why aren't you upstairs sleeping?"

She rubbed her eyes and looked up at me. "I'll sleep later." Reading from an email on her Mac, "Listen to this: 'The male prisoners have been divided between work release center, road camp and main jail. The females have been sent to jails in Santa Rosa and Okaloosa counties.'"

"Any more info on deaths and injuries?"

She shook her head. "The sheriff's office is working up a list." She drained the Red Bull, tossed the silver can toward the trash basket and missed; the bull's corpse rattled across the wood floor. "FYI, the press conference has been moved to two o'clock. Maybe you'll learn more then."

"Pantoni, get some sleep."

She didn't move. Just looked at me, cuddling her arms around her body and rubbing her biceps. "Last night was intense. I was scared shitless, but none of it seemed to phase you. Even half drunk, you kept walking into that chaos."

"Here's my secret. I was plenty scared, but sometimes you can't give into the fear. The world doesn't need to know what's inside your head."

She leaned back in her chair stretching her arms and yawning. "At the *Sun*, I mostly did puff pieces. This is really different."

"You're a real journalist now."

She mulled over my compliment with her eyes shut. The natural beauty of her smooth olive skin and aquiline nose on her round face softened as her hyperdrive finally subsided. I thought maybe she had dosed off. "Pantoni, get some sleep."

She got up and headed for the stairwell. "You know I have a first name."

I chuckled, "My editor at the *Commercial Appeal* never used my first name, just called me 'Hotty Toddy.' We're fine, Pantoni."

She smiled, then pulled herself up the stairs.

By that afternoon the rain had stopped. Teddy and I joined the sweating reporters and camera crews that lined Leonard Street. Many of them were tired and irritable after milling around, baking on the hot asphalt since noon. The fact that we arrived five minutes before the press conference and assumed positions near the microphones made them even more irritable.

Dressed in his standard uniform—brown suit with a star on the lapel, cream-colored shirt, Bolo tie and Stetson, Sheriff Frost had set up the perfect backdrop for his press conference. The podium stood in front of the damaged CBD with its main entrance blown apart, nearby windows were shattered, and chunks of concrete obliterated leaving huge holes in sections of the walls.

In his gravelly voice, he commended his deputies for their quick response to the emergency. He explained that rapid triage had been done on site. One hundred eighty-four victims were transferred to two area hospitals for treatment. The whole operation of treating and transporting the inmates took two and a half hours. The sheriff exuded confidence and professionalism in assuring the residents of Escambia County that he had everything under control.

Jail Director Reedy, who probably had gotten no sleep, lumbered in his rumpled uniform to the podium as if he was headed to the gallows. He told reporters his staff had accounted for all inmates. Three inmates, a correctional officer and a law enforcement officer were killed in the blast, and their names would be released after their relatives had been notified.

Wanting to break up his prepared presentation, and because I was jerk, I shouted, "When can we get a list of the surviving inmates and where they're being housed? Families have a right to know." Reedy hesitated, looked at Frost and cleared his throat. "The sheriff's office communications department is working on that list now."

Frost's PIO, a serious woman in her thirties with dishwater-blonde hair in a ponytail tucked underneath a baseball cap with the sheriff's office insignia emblazoned across it, and a green polo with a matching insignia, stepped up to the microphone. Her confidence and bravado mirrored the sheriff's. "We'll have the list available no later than Saturday morning. The CBD roster information was lost in the blast. We're recreating it from a backup that was done the morning before the explosion. Once we've double-checked the data, we'll post it on our website." Another reporter tried to ask a question but was cut off by the PIO: "We ask everyone to hold their questions until the end. We have a lot of information to cover."

She then introduced State Fire Marshall Bingham. Florida law gave the state fire marshal the power to look into any explosion or fire occurring wherein property had been damaged or destroyed to determine if the incident was the result of carelessness or design.

"The Bureau of Alcohol, Tobacco, Firearms and Explosives will handle this investigation," said Bingham. "The explosion is believed to have originated in a rear laundry room in the basement. It mostly likely was due to a natural gas leak and not a bomb, but we need to be sure. ATF will determine how the blast occurred and advise on next steps."

He stated the obvious—the detention center had suffered significant structural damage; confirmed what I already knew—the police officer who died had been crushed in his vehicle that was parked in the sally port at the time of the blast; and refused to offer any new details—the causes and manner of the other deaths were still under investigation.

"The National Response Team will be slow and methodical," he continued. "It may take several weeks to complete."

Sheriff Frost took back the microphone to bring the press conference to a close. His demeanor showed that he clearly wasn't happy that the state fire marshal was investigating the explosion, but *tough shit* I said to myself. Reporters pressed him for more details about the gas leak. Frost denied that there had been any official reports of natural gas in the CBD prior to the explosion. "Our 9-1-1 dispatch received no calls concerning a possible natural gas leak at the facility. Thank you all."

WTF? I thought, *how would a prisoner call dispatch to report a gas leak? Can they order in pizza too?*

He and Bingham started back toward the administration building. I hollered, "Sheriff, how could a prisoner call 9-1-1? We've heard they weren't allowed to use the pay phones after lunch yesterday."

Chief Deputy Peter "Peck" Krager jumped to the microphone, wanting so badly to get on camera. "This press conference is over. Unfortunately, the sheriff and fire marshal don't have time to take any more questions."

"Come on, Peck," I yelled. "Some of these reporters have been standing here for hours, and this is all we get? How much water got into the basement?"

"No more than two feet."

I came at him again: "Where was Sheriff Frost after the explosion? Where were you? Why weren't the two of you on the scene last night?"

Several reporters shook their heads in disbelief and began to shout their own questions. A *News Herald* reporter first: "Weren't the kitchen and laundry areas recently renovated?"

Another jumped in, "Was the video from the cameras inside the building salvaged?"

Peck had lost control of the situation. Flustered, he blurted out, "We'll release more information as we get it," then turned and ran to catch up to his boss.

Our Thursday afternoon staff meeting was important. The print deadline for the next issue was five days away, and we only had a general idea of what it would look like. We had covered on the blog the flooding and explosion, but so had the *News Herald* and other media outlets. The *Insider* had to be unique, more provocative in its coverage.

A dozen years ago, when I quit my job with the Fort Walton Beach daily newspaper and cashed in my 401(k), I found a couple investors and started the *Pensacola Insider*. My goal was to capture a large enough share of the advertising market to force Barnett Press to buy me out. I'd pay off my investors and pocket a cool five million. Well, that was my plan, but it went to shit after three hurricanes, a real estate crash and a recession during the *Insider's* first five years. All of which forced me to beg, borrow and nearly steal to keep the paper alive.

I should've just walked away. But didn't partly because I wanted to honor Mari's memory and prove that I could be a great journalist and partly because I believed in small town, locally owned newspapers. The *Insider* promised its readers that it would fearlessly follow the facts wherever they led, hold politicians and community leaders accountable, and fight for a better life for all aspects of the community, not just a chosen few.

Pensacola looked forward to each issue to read our perspective on issues and see how we connected the dots. We had woven ourselves into the fabric of the community, become a voice for the voiceless and made the comfortable uncomfortable.

With Mal, Teddy and Summer losing their residences, the flood had touched us personally. We understood the fear and anxiety of our readers, because, hell, we had experienced those emotions ourselves over the past two nightmarish days. The jail explosion, with its death and mayhem, added another dimension that we had to figure out how to cover.

Everyone was ready for the editorial battle as we tried to rein in all the story lines into a coherent issue. After I filled them in on the press conference, Mal tossed out the first grenade: "Do we still want to do the recovery guide?"

Looking more than a little worried, Summer fought for her clients, "That's what I sold our advertisers. We can't change now."

"We don't need a puff issue. The jail explosion changes everything," countered Pantoni, nodding toward me. "With Walker's relationship with Tyndall, we've a chance to give readers more unique insights into the flooding and the blast. We gotta capitalize on it."

"Hell, I've got good photos either direction we go," injected Teddy, who leaned back, folding his arms. He had decided to be Switzerland.

Jeremy was there via speakerphone as we sat around the kitchen island in the loft. He complained, "I spent all day on the lists of charities and government services available. We can't waste it."

They turned to me wanting to know which direction to take. Since Rachel's body had been found, I had avoided most staff meetings, letting Mal run things. Plus, my drinking binge had cost me their respect. Still, they looked to me, wanting to know if I was ready to take on the challenge. I put my elbows on the table and rested my head in my hands and massaged my eyebrows. The room was quiet. Running my hands through my thinning hair, I lifted my face, "We'll invest in the extra pages and do both the recovery guide and the expanded coverage of both the flood and the jail explosion."

"Welcome back, man." Teddy grinned. The art director had done two tours with the Air Force in Iraq and Afghanistan. He rarely talked about his military service other than to say he flew drones. Very little phased Teddy. No matter what happened at the paper, I always sensed he had been through worse.

Not quite ready to accept my decision, Mal lobbed another grenade, "Can we afford the additional printing costs?"

Some described my production manager as a pessimist, but she thought of herself as a realist. In the months after Hurricane Ivan, I had hired Mal as our receptionist, and she gradually learned more areas of the newspaper and took on more responsibilities. Then when Teddy joined the *Insider*, she had finally met a man who was as intelligent and talented as she was. It didn't take long for the two of them to move in together, get engaged and married. Mal handled the layouts of every issue, managed the writers and dealt with the ads. Teddy designed the covers and laid out the articles with her help.

We all looked at Summer for the answer to Mal's question. She flipped her hair back and nodded affirmatively, "Our cash is okay and should improve, especially with the ad sales I've made this week."

Summer had moved to Pensacola with her boyfriend who was in flight school at Naval Air Station Pensacola. But when he got his wings, she decided she wasn't meant to be a Navy wife and couldn't follow him to San Diego. She came to work for us as our office manager and book-keeper and then moved into sales when our sales director left for some millennial type commune in Sedona, Arizona with her artist husband. Her easygoing manner had won over clients, and advertising sales had steadily climbed ever since.

I was tempted to take over the conversation, but held back because I didn't want to undercut Mal. I had already planned on naming her editor by the end of the year after we got through the election cycle and all its ugliness. It wouldn't have been fair to put her through that hell her first year as editor.

Mal divided the labor. "Jeremy and I'll focus on the recovery guide. Summer, I need your help to run down ad copy. Pantoni, you work on recapping the flood. We need to reach out and take advantage of every source we've got to find out what happened in the hours before the blast."

Pantoni gave a mock salute. "I'll also retrace the steps of the governor's tour and let you know if I uncover anything."

I got up from the table and went to the refrigerator. Grabbing a bottle of water, then turning around, I said, "I'll focus on the jail explosion and take on Frost. Might as well poke the bear."

"No one does it better," laughed Teddy.

Mal didn't. "All copy needs to be sent to me by Saturday night. We've got some long days facing us." The only protest came from Jeremy. He grumbled about not having any A&E in the issue. "My god, we've won awards for our music coverage. Bands will be playing next week."

"And they'll be playing the following week too," Mal shot back—no time for his or anyone else's insubordination.

As the meeting broke up, Pantoni offered to take Big Boy for a walk and gather a few more quotes from downtown business owners. After they left, I brought up the rest of the staff's living arrangements. "Y'all are welcome to stay here as long as necessary."

"The bad news is we could be out of our townhome for months," said Teddy. "The landlord's working with FEMA and his insurance company, but it'll take time."

Summer commiserated, "My unit is fine, but the complex is a wreck. They won't give us a date when we can return."

"Apartments and condo rentals will be at a premium now," moaned Mal. "Everyone will be fighting for temporary housing. We're screwed."

"We're family," I insisted. "A little dysfunctional, but still a family. You can stay here as long as necessary."

Practical Mal seemed to seize on the dysfunctional part. "We need to figure out where everyone will sleep and how we'll share meals and expenses."

I wanted to cut her off before the living arrangements got too complicated. I envisioned her coming up with spreadsheets. "Mal, you and Teddy take my room with your cat—"

"Liza," she corrected.

"Right … The utilities and other expenses are fixed and won't change much so don't worry about those. Save your money. We can split food costs."

"Mal and I'll figure out how to help Liza and Big Boy get along," offered Summer. "I've already bookmarked some articles for us."

Fat chance, I thought. "Summer, will you be okay on the loft's couch?"

She leaned back, hooking an arm over the back of the chair. "The loft's couch is fine."

"Walker, we've got an inflatable mattress," suggested Teddy. "Let's move the conference table into the newsroom and then the conference room can be where you sleep."

The *Insider's* newsroom was one large space with exposed, ancient bricks that we had covered with framed covers of old issues. A skylight and two rows of windows overlooking Palafox and Intendencia Streets gave the room plenty of unfiltered light. The space looked like what an underdog alt-weekly should look like.

"We'll move our flat screen upstairs and hook up your TV with its booty in the conference room," continued Teddy. "That way you won't miss any Dodger games."

When Pantoni and Big Boy came back from their walk, the dog sniffed all around the loft looking for Mal's cat, which fortunately was behind a closed door in what used to be my bedroom. Big Boy had been with me for a little more than two years. Many mistook the small dog for a puppy because he could be so animated and energetic, but his gray snout gave away his age. He hardly ever barked, watched over the office, and greeted the staff every morning, rotating between desks where he would nap under throughout each day. Big Boy was the star of the *Insider* and did not like sharing the limelight with a cat whose name would remain unspoken by me despite Mal's preference.

I had never been much of a pet person. Hell, I had trouble taking care of myself, but Roger Fairley knew I needed a companion. During his last days, as cancer riddled his body and shutdown his vital organs, he told me, "Big Boy will be your dog. He needs to be walked several times a day. He'll listen to your problems and watch over you and the staff."

It wasn't a request. No, it was a command. I missed Roger, and, damn, he had made me a dog lover. A reluctant one, but still a dog lover.

I looked at my staff. "Since Summer says we have money in the bank, I'll treat everyone to The Fish House for dinner. We can walk over there around six."

Pantoni looked at her watch. "I need to bug out. It's close to five and my parents want me to have dinner with them."

Teddy offered, "I'll take you home and meet the rest of you at The Fish House."

Just then my cellphone vibrated, signaling a text from Dare: "Need to see you. Can you come over to the office now?"

Evans Timber & Land Company owned Jackson Tower, which loomed at the end of Palafox Street and overlooked Pensacola Bay. In the early 1900s, the Evans family hired New York City architect James Edwin Ruthven Carpenter Jr. to design the tallest building in Florida that would serve as the home of the American National Bank, and of Southern Bell, the state's first telephone exchange that had only thirty-one telephones, six of which were owned by the Evans family.

The tan, twelve-story building mimicked the designs of Chicago architect Louis Sullivan, the "father of skyscrapers." The first-floor entrance and windows had arches, and bands of terra cotta masonry with intricate floral designs that drew the eye upward emphasizing the vertical form of the building.

Jackson Tower had stood as Pensacola's tallest building for nearly three-quarters of a century. Not because it was gargantuan, but because the city council had been so angry it blocked the view of Pensacola Bay from homes in North Hill that they passed laws limiting the height of any future buildings. That law was finally lifted in 1974.

Evans Timber & Land occupied the top floor and was the largest landowner in Northwest Florida, rivaled only by the US military whose Navy and Air Force bases lined the Panhandle. When I got off the elevator, I nodded at the receptionist and walked through a maze of cubicles past a boardroom, where I could see city and county officials arguing with Dare's construction managers. Blueprints were spread across the table.

Dare's corner office had a panoramic view of the city stretching from Pensacola Beach and the Gulf of Mexico to the Naval Air Station in the distance. One wall had mahogany bookcases filled with books, many of them first editions signed by Robert Penn Warren, Eudora Welty, Harper Lee and other Southern writers. Behind her massive desk hung a portrait of her late husband Rory, who had leveraged his family name and wealth to become Florida Senate President and had his sights set on becoming governor but died of a massive heart attack while giving a speech on the chamber floor.

The Evans' dynasty didn't skip a beat after Rory's death. His brothers chose Dare to run the family businesses. She also took his place in the Northwest Florida business community. No one trifled with Dare Evans.

Under Rory's portrait was a silver tray with an open bottle of Four Roses and a set of Waterford Crystal tumblers. Next to the tray was Rory's most prized possession, the football from Ole Miss's 1970 Sugar Bowl victory over Arkansas, autographed by Coach Johnny Vaught and Archie Manning.

We had all met for the first time at the University of Mississippi. Rory had been a second-year law student and Dare and I were freshmen. My parents drove me from our home in the Mississippi Delta town of Belzoni, the "Catfish Capital of the World," to Oxford in the family station wagon and told me they would return to pick me up at Thanksgiving break.

Dare couldn't have been more different from me. She graduated from St. Agnes Academy, a private Roman Catholic, all-girls high school in Memphis. Her father was the corporate attorney for Holiday Inn and a running back on Johnny Vaught's undefeated 1962 football team, and her mother was the Ole Miss homecoming queen that season.

We met at a fraternity pledge swap where we ducked out to eat burgers and cheese fries, and talked about William Faulkner, Ronald Reagan, Ted Kennedy, and how to change the South. She became my closest friend and remained so through college, the deaths of Rory and Mari, and the tribulations of my newspaper.

When I walked into her office, her back was to the door as she looked out her window at the bay. She had a glass of bourbon in one hand and with the other played with her strand of pearls, deep in thought. Dressed in a white polo shirt and black slacks, I still saw the coed that captured my soul at Ole Miss. I soaked in the sight a few seconds before I knocked on the open door to signal my arrival. Dare turned, smiled and greeted me with a warm hug.

"Thank you for coming over," she motioned for me to sit down. Lifting her glass, "Want a drink?"

I shook my head. "I'm the designated reporter tonight."

Her smile widened. "Impressive. Good to have you back."

I plopped in a leather chair. "I just got lost as you know I tend to do from time to time."

Dare nodded as she sat down behind her desk. I could see she wanted to talk about something, but wasn't quite ready. So I primed the pump a little. "How did your properties fare?"

"Not well." She brushed her hair aside to get it out of eyes, grabbed a pair of readers and glanced at her laptop. "My team's still assessing the damage. The city's ancient drainage system was completely overwhelmed. The building code had required everything be built to handle a twenty-year rain event. This one was a hundred-year, maybe even two hundred-year, rain event."

She took a sip of her bourbon. Dare drank her Four Roses, Faulkner's preferred bourbon, without ice. "We've got retention ponds and retaining walls that failed and created lakes in our subdivisions. The streets have turned into rivers. It's a mess."

I spied several bottles of water on the bottom shelf of a bookcase and grabbed one. "The governor has committed the state's resources to expedite our recovery."

"I've been on the phone with his office and the regional director of the Federal Emergency Management Agency," she said. "We've offered FEMA office space here to set up their command post."

"What's up with the people in your conference room arguing?"

Her temper flashed, "We had to beg those idiots to sit down and work out the ground rules for our construction teams so we can begin repairs. I'm not saying it took bribes to get them to the table, but it came darn close." Taking another sip of bourbon, she sighed, "I hate the petty politics of this place. Whenever there's a crisis, a group always finagles a way to make money from it. We've got people worried about where they're going to sleep tonight, and those sonnabitches want to talk permits, variances and fees."

Her Southern accent always became more pronounced when she pushed herself too hard. Rather than talk, I sat and waited for her to tell me what was really on her mind. She settled deep into her chair and stared at her tumbler. From our long history, I knew when Dare avoided eye contact, she wanted something that she knew I wouldn't like. The longer her eyes evaded, the bigger the ask.

She distractedly counted the pearls around her necklace, seeking the right words. I took this to mean I was in trouble and felt a trap closing around me. "Walker, did you hear the name of the police officer who died in the jail explosion?"

I shook my head. "I've been away from my email the past couple hours. Was he someone you knew?"

"Timothy Sturdevant." Dare paused and then added, "Jackie wants to see you."

I jumped up and put out my arms like I was fending off a charging animal. "No way."

Jackie was Jacqueline Sturdevant Holmes Wade, Dare's sorority little sister and my ex-wife. "She needs your help."

I began to pace the Persian rug. "Dare, some things are too much."

"Please, I wouldn't ask if it wasn't important," she pleaded. "Her brother was the only family she had."

I shook my head. "The last time I saw her was about five years ago. In the Atlanta airport, husband No. 3 tried to slug me."

"Husband No. 3 is no more, died in a duck blind in north Alabama."

"Did Jackie play a role?"

"Not funny," she reprimanded me. "Why is this such a big deal? You two were only married three years and that was ages ago."

I sank back into my chair and let out a long breath. "One year of happiness, one year of arguing about my career, and one year of nothing but hell."

"You're being melodramatic."

"Jackie's nothing but melodrama, and I don't need any more of that. We've got a city that's flooded and a jail that's exploded."

Dare refused to back down. "And her brother died in that explosion doing his duty."

I felt like a mouse caught in maze with no exit, traps at every turn. I remembered Tim being the five-year-old ring bearer at our wedding. "I didn't know he was in Pensacola."

"Neither did I. Jackie said he had moved here last summer."

"Dare, his death was one of those unfortunate incidents of being in the wrong place at the wrong time."

She showed me no sympathy. "But you're going to find out what really caused that wrong place and wrong time."

"I'm investigating it whether I meet with Jackie or not."

Dare stood up, and the mousetrap snapped down on me. "You'll meet with Jackie at my house around four tomorrow afternoon."

I made a feeble attempt to escape. "Why don't you take the meeting? Then you can relay to me what's on her mind."

"That won't work. She wants you."

I finished off the water bottle and headed for the door. Turning, I gave an inch: "I'll think about it."

"Please."

"All I said was I'll think about it."

But she knew I'd already decided. I had never refused Dare.

When I sat down at the table on the deck at The Fish House, Mal and Summer were discussing how to get Liza and Big Boy to co-exist in the loft. Teddy drank beer and sat on the sideline. Wise man.

"Liza's scared to death of Big Boy. And the dog doesn't know how to react to a cat on his turf," explained Mal, with sympathy for the Labrador mix. "We left the bedroom door open. He walked in and immediately stuck out his nose to sniff her. Liza attacked the poor thing. Had to pull her off him and got this in the process." She showed off the scratches on her arm. "She's a sweet cat. Really she is."

I had watched Mal's cat, still nameless to Big Boy and me. She was a venerable queen with eyeliner in her DNA. Her huge green eyes were surrounded by black fur. The longhair had a pink nose and tabby spots dotting her white coat. As soon as her furry paws hit the floor, she seemed to walk from room to room criticizing the furniture and looking for spots that framed her figure well. Every time she exited the room, her enormous raccoon-striped, bottle-brushed tail heralded her departure.

With Big Boy now a stranger in the loft, the cat had made the upstairs her domain. She walked—no prissed—on white and pink paws, marking everything with a flick of her long tongue.

On top of that, Mal had long conversations with her, consisting mostly of:

"You are pretty."

"Meow."

"I love you."

"Meow."

"What do you think? The Modest Mouse t-shirt?"

"Meow."

As sarcastic and cutting as she could be at times, Mal had a soft side. She loved Taylor Swift and Beyoncé and would drive to their concerts in Atlanta or New Orleans and be back for work the next morning. She was a sucker for the panhandlers that dotted Palafox and would fork over money without a second thought.

Over the years, I had gotten accustomed to Mal's endless stream of selfies with her cat on Facebook and had picked up some inside information along the way. Bree had explained to me that cats don't communicate with each other via meows. That was just how they talked with stupid humans. "Cats agree to live with people in exchange for food and pipe cleaners," Bree told me. "They have to like you, or they'll bolt at the first opportunity."

I grabbed a fried crab claw and dipped it in the cocktail sauce. "Big Boy has never been around other animals. Roger rescued him from the county animal shelter and thought his previous owner had mistreated him."

Summer sat beside me and pulled out her cellphone. "I googled this. Mal did the right thing to put Liza in your bedroom and let her establish her territory."

"I knew the move from Long Hollow would upset her," Mal offered defensively. "Cats are all about their territories."

They were tag-teaming me. I really didn't care that much, the animals would figure it out. So instead of listening, I was fighting the urge for a cold beer. The pitcher was on the table, begging to be poured in a mug for me. Summer interrupted my thoughts: "We need slow, controlled introductions." She put her hair behind her ears and read from an article on her cellphone. "The experts say Big Boy should be on a leash. We need to give Liza treats and encourage her to leave the bedroom and approach him without fear."

I began to look for a waitress. I needed a mug. Teddy kneed me under the table, signaling for me to say something. I complied, "The best we can hope for is that the two tolerate each other. Big Boy likes you and Mal but giving up the loft to another animal is asking a lot of him."

Teddy grinned. He enjoyed watching the girls drag me in and egged them on to continue. "How long do the experts say it'll take for them to co-exist?" I gave him a homicidal side-eye.

"Three or four weeks," Summer beamed, wiggling proudly in her seat. "We have to keep Big Boy at the highest level of calm-submissive behavior while allowing Liza to become calm-assertive in front of him. If we do it consistently, eventually she'll tell him what to do. Then, Liza'll feel safe around Big Boy."

Mal's pessimism kicked in as she filled her and Teddy's mugs. "None of us have the time or patience for this bullshit."

Summer insisted, "I'll make it work." She pulled at her brown hair and swirled it around her fingers as she talked. Summer had a soft voice and a wicked smile. A Michigan native, she liked to explain where she had grown up by holding out her palm, which resembled the state, and pointing to a spot a half-inch below her index finger, saying, "I grew up here." Her perennial optimism counterbalanced Mal's moods.

The waitress finally appeared, and I ordered an iced tea. *Dammit. I can be sober for at least one day.* We sat out on the deck and enjoyed the southern breeze off of Pensacola Bay. Summer ordered the shrimp and grits, The Fish House's signature dish. Mal and Teddy shared a couple of sushi rolls. I enjoyed the grilled oysters.

"We have the names of the three prisoners who died and posted them to the blog," Mal told us.

I finished an oyster and wiped my mouth with a napkin. "Do you remember their names?"

Mal didn't, but she pulled out her cellphone to find the press release among her emails. "Malik Tomas Green, Ephesians Anthony Johnson and James Harden Low."

"Damn." Low was Harden's nephew, and Green's mother was the nice lady I'd met at Alphonse's campaign headquarters. I stepped away from the table and called Tyndall. He didn't answer, but he texted back that he would call me in the morning. He was with Green's mother. I texted Harden and got no reply.

When I returned, Mal asked, "Do you want to know the name of the police officer?"

"Timothy Sturdevant"

"How'd you know?" Mal's surprise evident by her wide-open eyes.

"Dare told me," which seemed to satisfy her for the moment.

"Do you want Pantoni to contact Sturdevant's family?"

"No, Dare wants me to meet with his sister tomorrow night." I wasn't sure I could keep the truth from them for long, but I didn't want to talk about it after a long-ass day.

Teddy tilted his mug in my direction. "You no longer drinking?"

Mal laughed. "He has enough alcohol in his system that he doesn't need to touch a drop for at least two more weeks and he'll still have a buzz."

I joined in the laughter because I deserved the ribbing. We toasted my sobriety, even if only temporary. They wanted to keep drinking, but I badly wanted to crash so I left Mal the company debit card and headed back to the office. Maybe the air mattress in the conference room would be the solution to my insomnia.

As I walked back, I thought of Mari. We had begun dating the second semester of our sophomore year at Ole Miss. She volunteered at the student crisis center as a counselor for its hotline service. I was in journalism and thought I was destined to be the next great investigative reporter for the *New York Times*.

We became engaged our senior year and already had begun planning our wedding. On March 14, 1991, I covered a voters' rights rally in Holly Springs, thirty miles north of Oxford. I had promised Mari that I would pick her up at nine that night when her shift ended, but I let time get away from me and didn't show until half an hour later. She wasn't inside the crisis center. Her roommate said she hadn't returned to their dorm room either. I searched the library and the bars and restaurants on Oxford Square, but no Mari.

The next morning, I went to the university police and reported her missing. My fraternity brothers and our friends plastered the campus and the city of Oxford with flyers. Her family arrived and helped with the search. Hunters found Mari's nude body in the woods off US Highway 278 East. Her killer was never found, and her murder got filed away as another cold case involving a college coed in the wrong place on the wrong night.

Rachel Townsend's disappearance and death had resurfaced those memories. The drinking had been my coping mechanism. I liked the numbness it offered. However, the fire to help the helpless, fight corruption and publish something that made a difference still burned inside me. I still cared. Mari would expect nothing less from me. I thought to myself, *would I ever stop aching for her?*

As I approached the office, I found Tiny sitting in the alley in front of the stairwell door. The bald, chubby black man wore a Hopjacks t-shirt and gray shorts. Next to him on the concrete rested an old and patched up green duffle bag.

"Mr. Walker, the veterans group home got flooded," he said in a soft, almost childlike voice. "I need some place to stay 'til they find a place for us." Tiny lived in a group home near Mal and Teddy's townhouse. He was an Iraq War veteran, who also suffered from PTSD. He earned his meals by helping bus tables at the Bodacious Brew on Palafox in the mornings, volunteered at the Fricker Community Center most afternoons and did odd jobs for the newspaper.

"Either it's Walker or Holmes, no mister. Come on upstairs. You can shower and sleep on the couch in the office. But you have to be out by eight every morning."

"No problem, Walker. I won't be no trouble."

"I'll give you a key."

"I'll make this up to you."

"Don't worry about it. Everyone else is already living here." Tiny looked puzzled so I explained, "Mal, Teddy and Summer have taken over the loft until their landlords decide when they can move back into their places. One more person won't make much of a difference."

Tiny looked like he hadn't slept since the rainstorm. I gave him a spare pillow and blanket and placed a note on the office door for the others explaining he was sleeping in there. Then I texted Gravy to meet me for breakfast the next day before Big Boy and I fell asleep on the air mattress to the sound of Tiny snoring in the next room.

10

On Friday, I drove to CJ's Kitchen on Garden Street on the western edge of the Pensacola city limits. The smell of fried eggs and bacon covered up the hint of Pine-Sol when I walked in the little diner that had a short counter with a few stools, a row of three booths and a handful of tables. Gravy sat alone in a booth that was separated by a plywood partition from the short order cook.

William "Gravy" Graves Jr. handled most of my newspaper's legal issues. He got his nickname for his daily breakfast regimen at CJ's. No matter how late he was out the night before, Gravy could be found every morning in a booth eating a big, open-faced biscuit smothered in creamy white sausage gravy.

He sat reading handwritten notes on a yellow legal pad as he ate, occasionally scribbling out references on a printout. He hadn't noticed I'd arrived until I stood over him. He looked at my white button-down shirt and pressed khaki pants and smiled, "Walker Holmes has returned from the dead."

I slid in the booth and motioned to the waitress for a cup of coffee. "To paraphrase my patron saint, Samuel Clemens, 'reports of my demise are greatly exaggerated.'"

Gravy looked as if he hadn't slept. Though his gray pinstriped suit was crisp and red bowtie in a perfect knot, he had bags under his eyes and had missed a clump of whiskers on his neck in that morning's shave. "It's my turn to say you look like crap. You been busy?"

"It's the jail explosion. We've been overwhelmed with calls for help."

I nodded. "That's an understatement. When did you first hear about it?"

Rubbing his eyes, he took a sip of his Tab before answering. "I actually heard and felt the explosion at my house, even though I live a good five or six miles away. I was on Facebook checking on my old girlfriends when it happened. Didn't know if it was International Paper or Monsanto because it felt like a chemical plant explosion."

The waitress brought my coffee and took my order for a ham and cheese omelet, no toast, no grits. After she left, he continued, "I put on Facebook, 'Does anybody know what that is?' Somebody in East Hill posted back, 'No, but I felt it too.' A little while later a former deputy messaged me that the jail had exploded."

I nursed my hot coffee after I doctored it with Splenda and creamer. "What are you hearing from your clients?"

"Your friend Theodore's niece, Maya, was waiting to go before a judge for a violation of her parole. Nothing serious, just driving with a suspended license. She has a young baby, and I was trying to get her out of jail without having to post bond."

After the explosion, Theodore had called the Gravy's cellphone in a panic, which was unsettling because few things upset Theodore Ware. He was standing in the rain on Leonard Street with the frustrated mob. A corrections assistant had told him that none of the casualties were female, but he couldn't get specific information about his niece. Gravy was this only lifeline.

"So I texted a friend of mine—a sergeant at the sheriff's office—and asked if everything was okay. Her response was, 'It's horrible,' and then the connection went dead."

"Did you find Theodore's niece?"

"Yesterday around noon. My sergeant friend had connected with a few people and found Maya. I've got an emergency hearing before a judge this morning to get her out of custody."

Gravy slid the printout across the table. "When word got out that I found Theodore's niece, people began calling my office asking us to help find their relatives. This is a list of my new clients as of nine last night."

The waitress brought my omelet, refilled my coffee and handed Gravy another Tab. The diner kept a case in the cooler for him. No one else would drink it, but he was such a regular that it was worth their while to keep it in stock. Gravy pulled back the list so that I wouldn't spill anything on it. "I've already had some success in locating prisoners. I'll work on the rest of this list when I get out of court."

In between bites, I asked, "How are you finding them?"

"Bribery," he laughed. "I had Theodore fry up a mess of chicken thighs, wings and drumsticks, which I delivered to the jail command center. The major had his staff make calls to the county's work release center, the road camp and the jails in Santa Rosa and Okaloosa Counties where some were taken."

"How long did it take?"

"By the time I walked to my car and returned with a Tupperware container of banana pudding, they had located most of them," he grinned. "I suspect I'll be hitting Theodore up for some more fried chicken today as I keep adding more clients."

I tapped the printout. "Who on this list would you recommend we call to find out what really happened inside?"

"Let me talk with my staff. I'll email a few names and their contract info."

I nodded thanks. "Harden's nephew was one of the prisoners who died."

Gravy grimaced. "I saw he had called my cellphone yesterday but left no message. I was too busy to call him back."

I drank some of my coffee, played some with my food, the talk of the jail explosion had made me lose my appetite. "Harden called about his nephew. After we learned the names of the prisoners who died, I tried to call him but got not answer."

Gravy gathered up his papers and phone. "I'll try him again as soon as I get out of court."

After leaving CJ's, my Friday was filled with phone calls and emails from readers about the impact of the flooding on their lives. Gradually local government services returned, streets were cleared, and boil-water notices were lifted. Neighborhood streets were lined with piles of debris, destroyed furniture and carpeting heavy with water that had been ripped out of homes.

Around three, I began thinking of excuses not to see my ex-wife. Jackie and I had dated when I worked at the *Commercial Appeal* in Memphis after graduation. She was Dare's little sister in the Chi Omega sorority, but I didn't really know her. Jackie was someone I happened to run into with Dare at Ruby Chinese or Smitty's with a throng of other sorority girls. After we graduated and Dare was married to Rory and living in Pensacola, she set up a date between Jackie and me.

She was medium height with flaming red hair, round face dusted with light freckles, and jade green eyes. She had been engaged to an Ole Miss baseball player who signed with the New York Mets. After spending six weeks following his career with the Pittsfield Mets in the New York-Penn League, Jackie dumped him and returned to Memphis to work for her daddy's automotive group. She was bored, and I was trying to recover from Mari's death. Dare thought we both might appreciate some company. We did enjoy each other but not for the company. It was the fighting that attracted us.

Jackie's temperament matched her hair. She had a sharp wit and strong opinions. Our first date was over beers and ribs at The Rendezvous, a barbecue spot in the basement of an ancient building off an alley near the Peabody Hotel. We argued about how Ross Perot impacted the 1992 presidential election, national health care, grunge rock and the meaning of various X-Files episodes. We made each other laugh, but neither of us backed down from an argument. Jackie and I hadn't had sex for months. The underlying sexual tension fueled the discussion, and the night ended at her townhouse in Harbor Town on Mud Island.

When I quit my job at the *Commercial Appeal* six months later, she had agreed to follow me to Pensacola if I married her. She saw the relocation as only being temporary and that I would soon be a feature writer for *Vanity Fair* or *Rolling Stone* and we'd be living in New York City. For the first year of our marriage, she held on to that dream. Those were some of the happiest days of my life, but things soured when I quit my third newspaper job and had to trek to Panama City every day to write for its daily newspaper. She and Dare would get together, but Jackie began to resent the finer things her sorority sister had that she didn't.

Midway through the second year of our marriage, Jackie had a plan. She knew I had taken the LSAT before graduation and had done well enough to be accepted into several law schools. She harped on me to become a lawyer like Rory Evans. She first tried reason to convince me, then sex, and finally screams.

"Daddy'll pay for it!" she shouted. "You're wasting your mind working for these shitty newspapers! You can do so much better. We can do so much better!"

"I'm a reporter! I was one when we first met, and I still am. That's who I am."

"But I thought you'd be a much more successful one!"

Reaching for a beer, I admitted, "So did I."

That night I began sleeping on the couch we had out on the back porch. Three months later, she packed up all her stuff and left while I was on assignment in Tallahassee. When the divorce papers were delivered by registered mail, I signed them without a fight. Jackie had hated me ever since.

The divorce had happened fourteen years ago. Jackie quickly married a successful attorney from a wealthy Memphis family. That marriage lasted nine years, and she walked away with a nice divorce settlement. She then married a Mississippi Delta plantation owner, twelve years her senior. He was the one who tried to pound me in the Hartsfield-Jackson Atlanta International Airport. According to Dare, he had died while hunting, but I needed proof it was just an accident.

As I delayed my trek to Dare's house and the inevitable confrontation with Jackie, the smell of something baking drifted from the kitchen upstairs. A timer went off. Summer bounced out of her chair and headed upstairs with Big Boy in tow. "Those are my oatmeal raisin cookies."

Mal looked around the edge of her Mac and said with more than a little sarcasm, "She's going to get us all to eat healthy. Those cookies are supposed to be good for us."

Teddy pulled off his headphones. "Yeah, only 150 calories each, less than a draft beer."

With a deadpan face, I asked, "What's a calorie?"

The crash of a broken plate and a loud "Oh, no" came from the loft, followed by a yelping Big Boy thundering down the stairs and into the conference room. Looking at the laughing Mal and Teddy, "I guess that's my cue to leave with the dog. Headed to Dare's and then catching up with Gravy. Don't wait up for us."

Dare lived in a mauve-painted row house in Aragon. The sound of diesel pumps sucking water out of Admiral Mason Pond on the eastern edge of Dare's neighborhood could be heard in the distance. The noise mixed with the whirring ocean-like sounds of fans and blowers drying the wooden floors of nearby homes. A silver Dodge Ram pickup truck was parked in front of her house indicating Taylor, her latest suitor, was visiting. *Good, just what I needed—an audience.*

Taylor Canton, age 52, owned and operated several resort hotels on Perdido Key, Pensacola Beach and Okaloosa Island. Tall, tanned and outdoorsy, he was a good match for Dare, except he was not well-read, oh, and a Republican. Taylor understood balance sheets, not Balzac or Bronte, but he was pleasant and made Dare happy.

He greeted Big Boy and me at the door, giving me a firm hand-shake and petting the dog. The house smelled of fresh bread, pine from the scented candle on the mantle and Taylor's Polo cologne. I noticed there were fewer photos of Rory on the tables and walls than before. Their numbers had gradually diminished in tandem with Dare's social life rising.

Dare was highly sought after, not only for her wealth, which was considerable, but for her looks, wit and social graces. Men looked more handsome, more intelligent and more successful with her on their arms. She didn't date a lot and tended to hang on to a man for several months, but inevitably they'd commit some boneheaded mistake, like question-ing the sainthood of Archie and Olivia Manning and their boys. Once she stopped dating a man, Dare never looked back. She didn't have to because there was always another suitor in the wings.

I often told her, "The treasure never has to hunt, and Ms. Evans, you are the treasure."

She would blush, smile and drink her Chardonnay. Pleased.

While Dare and Big Boy were in the kitchen, Taylor settled into the brown leather chair in the corner and planted his scuffed, worn cowboy boots on the matching ottoman. I preferred to stand, bracing myself for Jackie's arrival which would be late as always, wanting to make a grand entrance before she crushed my balls.

Big Boy came out of the kitchen and sat on the maroon couch as Dare brought out a tray with slices of a baguette, pesto in olive oil and an assortment of meats and cheeses, along with drinks. Taylor got up to pour her a glass of wine. I grabbed a bottle of water. Dare smiled but didn't remark about day two of my tenuous sobriety.

She moved to the couch where she could stroke the dog. I shifted to a nearby wingback chair. The warm May sun was setting and cast an orange glow on the view from the windows facing east.

"Jackie texted," Dare announced sipping her wine and reaching for a small piece of gouda. Taylor had made a mini sandwich with slices of salami and pastrami, cheddar and two pieces of bread. He enjoyed his creation, content and pleased with himself. She continued, "She's running late, having trouble with getting the medical examiner to release her brother."

For half an hour, we waited for Jackie's arrival and passed the time talking about the storm and recovery efforts. The beaches had suffered no damage, and Taylor's hotels were fine. He let us do most of the talking and focused on his beer and the charcuterie plate. The conversation eventually turned to Jackie and her younger brother.

"I always liked Timmy," which seemed like a safe topic for me. "He stayed with us for a week when we first moved to the beach. Good kid."

Dare nodded, "Jackie's taking this hard. Both her parents are dead. Tim was the only remaining family member she had."

Taylor washed down his last bite with beer and tried to participate in the conversation. "You two were married?"

"For three years, back when we first got out of college." I wondered why Dare had invited him. *Was he here to comfort her or protect me?*

"Was it an amicable split?"

I smiled. That was probably the first time Taylor Canton had ever used the word "amicable" in a sentence, a sign of Dare's influence. "In the history of divorces, ours probably ranks in the top 10 for the most bitter. We maybe have spoken five words since I signed the papers, and none of them were suitable for—"

"Walker!" interrupted Dare. "Be kind. The woman was your wife, you loved her once, and she has lost her brother."

I reached for a small piece of bread and dipped it in the olive oil and pesto while picking up a small napkin to avoid spilling anything on the chair—as an afterthought, and on myself. Right about then a glass of wine or beer started to seem like a good idea. "What does she want from me?"

"I think answers. If anyone can figure out what really happened, it's you."

I sighed, tossing Big Boy my bread crust, which he caught mid-air. I got up from the chair and retrieved his leash. "Listen, tell her I've got this. She can read about it on the blog. We don't have to talk."

When I opened the door to leave, Jackie was just coming up the walkway.

"Leaving so soon?" she chided as she pulled me back into the house in her wake. A hot mess—with equal emphasis on hot and mess, my ex-wife didn't enter a room, she conquered it. Her red hair was luxurious and loose. Wearing a figure-fitting, black turtleneck jumper over slim cut matching trousers, her appearance was stunning and expensive. A gold-chain belt accentuated her narrow waist, the metallic look coordinated well with bracelets, necklace and dangling hoop earrings. Her honey brown round sunglasses went beautifully with the caramel Louis Vuitton Olympe handbag that she dropped on the floor as she kissed and hugged Dare and was introduced to Taylor. She instinctively knew to commandeer the chair I had occupied earlier.

"I need a drink," she proclaimed as she crowned the sunglasses on top of her head and adjusted herself to the soft lighting in the room. "Wild Turkey on the rocks."

Dare fussed over Jackie while Taylor worked on her drink order, got another beer for himself, and refilled Dare's wine glass. Big Boy observed them for a few seconds, then wandered off to lie on the kitchen floor, signaling I was on my own.

Dare and Taylor sat together on the couch, his beefy arm draped over her shoulders. I sat in the leather chair he formerly occupied and faced Jackie. *The coffee table separating us might give me the precious seconds I needed to escape if she jumps me,* I mused.

Dare and Jackie made small talk for a few minutes. Taylor joined in displaying his charm, I didn't since it was well known I had no charm. Jackie even glanced in my direction several times, and Dare tried to pull me into the conversation, but I just smiled without speaking, nodding at what seemed like appropriate times.

I never would get used to the pang of seeing Jackie. I saw her as I did on our first date, a girl not of stunning beauty but very attractive with a manner that pulled me to want to touch her, hold her, kiss her. The sly smile and warmth in her eyes had vanished, but, dammit, I still longed for them. A siren of a fire truck wailed from somewhere on the west side.

At one point, Taylor announced, "I've got to go. Told my buddies I'd join them at the hunting camp." He kissed Dare, shook Jackie's hand and nodded to me as he headed out the door. Big Boy peeked out from the kitchen, saw it was Taylor leaving, not me, and returned to his own life. I reached forward for another bottle of water sensing the battle would soon begin.

Jackie lifted her chin and challenged me, "So you showed up. I told Dare you wouldn't."

I leaned back in the leather chair and took in deep breath, slowly letting it out, steadying myself. "She asked me to come. That's the only reason I'm here."

Dare shook her head at the smoldering friction between the two of us. She had once tried to keep us on friendly terms, but the tenuous glue that held our marriage together had dissolved long ago.

Jackie wasted no time, "I need help, Holmes, without any excuses about how you don't have the time."

I took a drink of my water and said nothing, waiting for the verbal punch. Jackie didn't disappoint me. "You're supposed to be this fucking great investigative reporter, even though I still see a frightened little boy still trying to prove himself to his dead fiancée."

Dare protested, "Jackie!"

There was a time when a barb like that would have goaded me to reply in kind. She would have counted it as a victory, especially if I blew up in front of Dare. I had only one weapon that prevented Jackie from seeing how deeply she had cut me, and that was my smile. I deployed it, and added, "Give it a rest, Jax."

"Don't call me by that name!" She extended her talons. "It's Jackie, you asshole." She took a big sip from her glass.

Still smiling, I ventured, "What do you need me to do?"

Seething, because I hadn't taken her bait and Dare hadn't take her side, Jackie set down her glass, folded her hands in her lap and looked at them. She would use me, discard me without a second thought and relish it. I would let her because of Dare. I knew this and felt no desire to comfort Jackie or make the conversation any easier for her. I had neither sympathy nor empathy for her, which made me feel more than a little guilty.

She regained her composure and smiled back, but her jade eyes revealed daggers. I didn't take my eyes off of her and returned the smile, perhaps my daggers were just as evident. I could see Dare on the periphery, uncomfortable and unsure whether she should insert herself to prevent any furniture from being thrown.

Another fire truck's siren could be heard in the distance, also heading west to most likely join the other one. At that same moment Dare got up to turn on more lights, as dusk fell. Then, in a soothing voice, restarted the conversation. "Jackie, listen to me. Walker is here because you need him, and I asked him to help. That's the only reason he's here."

Dare turned to me, "Walker, you listen. Jackie lost her brother. Please keep that in mind. She wants to know why, and she and I know you can uncover the facts better than anyone."

"It's one of your two superpowers," Jackie tossed out with the flicker of a sneer, knowing my other power—pissing her off—which she mentioned often during the last year of our marriage.

Dare commanded both us, "Be nice."

Many years had passed since we lived under the same roof, but I still evoked from her a compulsive need to hurt me. Had I not been in the room, Jackie would have been bright, warm and open. I felt more than a little ashamed that she couldn't be that way around me.

Dare persisted, "Jackie, you asked Walker here to help, not to fight. If there was ever a time for you two to get along, it's now."

Big Boy came out of the kitchen. Dare patted her legs and he jumped up, curled up with his head on her lap. Jackie looked disapprovingly at the scene. "Dare, when did you get a dog?"

"I didn't. Big Boy is Walker's and he is a welcomed visitor here," letting Jackie know that any negative comments about the dog wouldn't be tolerated. Big Boy scooted closer to Dare and looked at me. I thought I saw him smile.

"Fill us in on what you know about the explosion," Dare asked me in a firm but pleasant voice. Her left hand played with her pearl necklace while her right stroked the dog. Jackie picked up her Wild Turkey, held the glass to her lips and waited.

I walked them through the chaotic scene at the CBD the night of the explosion and what I had learned from my various conversations since including that Tim's police cruiser had been crushed in the blast. "His car was nearly completely submerged. The building collapsed its roof."

"So no one checked if he was alive?" Jackie's anguish seemed to have seeped through every bone in her body.

I looked at her then Dare. "The vehicle was under concrete. There was no way to get to him."

Jackie turned angry. "The sheriff's office hasn't given me details of where his body was found. I need more information."

I felt the first stirrings of sympathy for her and immediately tried to squash them. Such emotions would only make me more vulnerable, something I could do without. However, I did what Dare expected me to do. "If there's anything I can do, I'll do it for Timmy's sake and the others with loved ones caught in the blast."

I didn't mention my odd conversation with the frightened deputy the night of the explosion. Our little talk about Tim and his prisoner. I made a mental note though to check with police dispatch.

Jackie finished her drink and set down the glass. She wasn't happy with my commitment. "Why don't you just say this is beyond you? Timmy was engaged and had bought a home that they were renovating together. He loved her. They were going to have children right away ..."

She faltered. I knew she was thinking, *just like we had planned when we were married.* Perhaps it was too much, even for her. How could people who had once laughed and enjoyed each other so dearly come to such an impasse? Yet, our lost love and passion were irretrievable.

She reclaimed herself. "I want answers! We'll sue the hell out of all of them!"

I thought about mentioning how sovereign immunity in Florida limited damages but didn't. Not the right time. "We and the other media will dig into this story. The state fire marshal's investigation will take weeks, but we'll have a pretty good idea what happened before that report's released."

Jackie nodded her head. "I'm staying in Dare's condo at Beach Club Resort. Call when you find out anything. Dare has my number." She scooped her bag off the floor, stood, nodded her thanks to Dare and looking through me walked out of the house.

"Well, that was about as pleasant as a bikini wax," Dare managed as Big Boy snuggled beside her on the couch. "At least she somewhat listened. She's really hurting."

"A lot of people are."

"Walker, she's asking for your help. You were hardly sympathetic."

"Jackie wants my involvement not because she expects me to succeed and find the truth. She wants to see me fail and have others discover what happened. Me succeeding makes her angry."

Dare could only shake her head. I rose and looked around for the dog leash.

"Let him stay with me tonight," she offered smiling. "He's sleeping and probably would be happy to get out of the dormitory that was once your apartment." I nodded okay. As I headed out the door, her parting words followed: "Watch your drinking."

11

As I walked toward downtown, my PI friend called. I answered, "Jim, I was so sorry to hear—"

"He was a mess," Harden cut me off in a drained voice tinged with anger, "but he didn't deserve to die."

"I'm meeting Gravy in a few minutes at Nick's. Why don't you join us?"

"Can't leave my sister right now. She's all torn up over this and will get worse tomorrow when we get her son's body and start making the funeral arrangements."

"Then maybe we can talk this weekend and compare notes."

"Walker, the damn building should've never exploded! We need to nail the bastards who let this happen. Text me tomorrow." He hung up.

Syracuse native and former Bruce Springsteen roadie Nicholas Strazi opened New York Nick's not long after I launched the *Insider*. Nick had strong opinions about the games displayed in his sports bar, stubbornly refusing to change the channels on his more than forty TV screens once he had their programming set. He said his refusal was out of principle, but I knew it was out of spite.

Gravy sat a table near the kitchen watching the Tampa Bay Rays while drinking a Conundrum cabernet, which I suspected he had brought with him into the bar. His suit was wrinkled, his bowtie untied, dangling around his neck—its dark colors peeking through the fairly thin paper napkin tucked into his shirt collar that served as a bib while he chowed down on messy Buffalo wings and fries. Crumpled up used wet wipes sat discarded just to the right of his drink.

The waitress put a Bud Light before me as I sat down. Behind the bar, an unsmiling Nick nodded my way. He and I had bet on the NCAA East Regional Championship during March Madness. Of course, he had chosen the Syracuse Orange and I took Ohio State, who won the game 77-70. Therefore, my first beer was free every time I walked into his establishment, which might seem unfair to some, but had I lost he would have gotten free ads in the newspaper.

"How long are you gonna make him give you a beer?" asked Gravy. "Hell, you're no longer drinking."

I took a sip but didn't fall into the temptation to down it quickly. "Until next year's tournament."

I asked the waitress to bring me a glass of water and turned back to my friend, "How are the Rays doing?"

Gravy shrugged, "We're winning, but our pitcher's struggling."

The beauty of New York Nick's was Nick played the music just loud enough that you could have a conversation without the next table over-hearing what was said, which made it the perfect bar to discuss what Gravy had learned. Playing it safe, he lowered his voice, "The day of the explosion, CBD was hell. My clients smelled gas and were getting sick from the fumes. The guards were opening up some of the doors to the exits and turning on fans trying to get some fresh air circulating."

He paused to offer me some of his wings, which I declined, and then opened another wet wipe to clean his hands. "The smell got worse and worse. The fire alarms kept going off all day, which was probably an electrical problem, would be my guess."

I changed my mind, and grabbed a couple wings, then picked them clean. They were spicy hot, pushing me to down my water. Gravy waved for the waitress to refill his glass and pulled out a legal pad from his black briefcase and checked his notes: "The prisoners were fed sporadically, mostly peanut butter and jelly sandwiches. Some soiled their clothes, which added to the stench."

He ate a fry. "And I'm sure the stress level in there was awful. There's no airflow—so you have all these odors, and then you have these alarms going off all the time."

I doubled down on my change of mind and took the last wing. "What about the prisoners that died? How'd they get on the first floor?"

Gravy removed his bib, checked to be sure no sauce got on his shirt and inched forward placing both elbows on the table. In a hushed voice, "That's where the idiot guards took them. When prisoners complained, the guards would take them down to the holding tanks above the laundry. They'd sit there for thirty minutes or an hour for short little 'mental health vacations' and then were returned to their cells. Hell, the guys thought the guards were doing them a favor. It was the only way they could get away from the stench and alarms."

"Damn, what a cluster." I grabbed a napkin to wipe my mouth and hands. "Malik's mom said that her son was on the third floor. How'd he end up in one of those holding cells?"

The attorney grabbed another wet wipe and waved for the waitress to bring me some. "One of my guys said the boy was complaining about headaches so they had moved him into a holding cell and planned to transfer him to the infirmary in the main jail the next morning."

He closed his eyes and rubbed his temple as he tried to organize his thoughts.

I prodded him, "Where are your clients now?"

"Most of them are in the main jail, but my client list grows every time I walk into the place."

I tilted my head, confused. "What do you mean?"

Gravy slowly sipped some wine, breaking from the intense conversation to savor its rich flavor. "When I meet with a new client, they say they have a friend that wants to retain me. I've probably added thirty new clients this afternoon alone."

"Are the guards giving you trouble?"

"Not yet. They're a little overwhelmed and kinda give us free rein."

Nick's was filling up by then. After a week of rain and flooding, people wanted to get out some. Gravy and I looked over the crowd, seeing only familiar faces, and listened to Golden Earring's "When the Lady Smiles" while the Rays blew a three-run lead.

I restarted, "What's the medical care like?"

"Shitty. Not enough doctors, and the infirmary is packed. From what I'm hearing, they aren't keeping good records of the injuries."

I was tempted to chug the beer, but instead stayed with the water. "Why are those records so important?"

Gravy explained, "When we go to trial, the jury assumes that people aren't gonna lie to their doctor, right? The perception is doctors and nurses take detailed notes. People, particularly jurors, always assume that the medical notes are accurate."

"What makes you think they are inaccurate? Not that I'd put it past Frost."

"A client said he told the nurse about his injury and she wrote down something that looked bogus. A couple of others told me that they watched the doctor also write down bogus stuff, but they just assumed that he was documenting their injuries in shorthand or something."

Gravy finished his glass of wine and asked for the bill. "I can see it now. The county's attorney will argue my client didn't report a certain symptom that's in our lawsuit, and the record will support the doctor not my client."

"I need to talk to your clients." I surrendered at The Battle of Sobriety and gulped down my Bud Light—*so much for my will power*. I looked at my watch, noting sobriety had lasted less than forty-eight hours. "I need their voices in my story. Can you get me inside?"

"Maybe. Meet me at CJ's Kitchen in the morning around 7:30. We'll drive over to the Escambia County Jail. Look professional, wear a coat and tie, and carry your leather satchel."

"Sure," I answered, trying to sound like *everything'll be fine*.

The next morning, over his biscuit and gravy, my attorney walked me through how he hoped our jail visit would go. My stomach was too nervous to handle food so I passed on breakfast, stoically drinking black coffee and trying to hide my anxiety.

In Sheriff Frost's eight years in office, I had never visited the county jail, even though the *Insider* had won several awards reporting on deaths in the facility under his administration. I had a secret fear that Frost and Krager would never let me out if I ever went in. Occasionally I would get a call from a mutual acquaintance who offered to serve as an intermediary and help Frost and me "patch things up." The standard line changed from time to time, but the gist was the same: "Sheriff Frost is a dedicated public servant, fighting to make our county safe. He's doing the best he can under the conditions." I never quite knew what they meant by "under the conditions." I always passed on the invitation. Since his brother Amos' suicide two years ago, reconciliation offers had stopped, I assumed because Frost blamed me for the death.

Gravy laid out his plan after the waitress dropped off his second Tab. "You stand next to me, don't say a thing, and let me do all the talking."

"I don't want to lie to get in the place."

"Neither do I. We're there to meet with my clients." He popped the top of the soda and quickly brought the can to his lips so it wouldn't slip over onto the table. "It's early on a Saturday morning. Things are usually more relaxed so the guards rarely check IDs."

Doubt gnawed at my gut. "At the first sign of any problem, I'll go outside and wait by your car."

He smiled, displaying a neat line of white teeth, "This'll be a piece of cake."

When we arrived at the county jail, only three vehicles were in the parking lot, which I took as a good omen. I followed Gravy into the jail, dutifully holding my brown satchel with one legal pad in it. We had left our cellphones in his Lexus since they weren't allowed in the jail.

Gravy walked up to a rotund sergeant sitting behind a bulletproof glass partition while I stood behind him, looking ahead without making eye contact. The attorney mentioned the clients he wanted to see while the sergeant asked for our names and photo IDs.

"William Graves Jr. and Walker Holmes," announced Gravy as he slipped the IDs through the slot. The sergeant scanned a list on a clipboard, found Gravy's name and put his driver's license back in the slot. Tapping the clipboard with his pen, he said, "Walker Holmes is not on the list of attorneys."

"Mr. Holmes isn't a lawyer," Gravy tried to explain. "He's my associate whose help I need interviewing my clients."

"Mr. Graves, the word from 'The Tower'," he said nodding towards the sheriff's administrative building across the street, "is only attorneys on this list are allowed in the jail. There ain't no Holmes on it so he can sit in that waiting area over there 'til you finish with your clients."

He slid my ID back through the slot. Gravy started to argue with him, but I tapped him on the shoulder. "I'll be fine, go ahead. I'll wait for you."

The waiting room smelled of sweat and dirty socks that a lemon disinfectant had failed to mask. Its walls were lined with cheap wooden chairs with well-worn lime green cushions patched with gray duct tape. A table in one corner had old magazines on NASCAR, hunting, fishing and weight loss, and several of the overhead fluorescent lights were out while one flickered, struggling to fight the darkness. I sat under the one panel that held its brightness, draped my blazer on the back of a nearby chair and began to work on my to-do list for the weekend.

Not long after I sat down, a loud, aggressive voice crashed my peace: "Get up, face the wall and put your hands behind your back." I looked up to see standing at the entrance to the waiting area two deputies. Each stood over six and a half feet tall and had huge forearms, thick necks and shaved heads. *Twins?*

I put my legal pad back in my satchel and rose slowly, realizing my fears were coming true. In a firm voice that was loud enough for anyone nearby to hear, I demanded, "What's this about?"

They walked closer and got in my face. "It's a crime to try to gain access to a jail under false pretense. You're under arrest, Holmes."

"That's bullshit. Get my attorney William Graves. He's talking to his clients down the hall."

As I grabbed my jacket and satchel, the slightly larger deputy slapped me with an open, beefy hand, forcing me to reach out to a wall to steady myself. The blow wouldn't leave a mark, but it stung like hell. His partner spoke gently with an undercurrent of malice, "Wallace, don't let him get under your skin. The chief said this pecker is a smart-ass."

Wallace yanked my belongings out of my hands, spun me toward the wall and smashed my face against it. He pulled my arms behind me and cuffed me tightly. In my ear, he whispered, "You follow my partner down the hall. I'll be right behind you with my Taser. Say a word or make any quick moves and 50,000 volts will shoot through your body."

The deputies took me to a windowless room and handcuffed me to a table. The lights were so bright I thought about asking for sunscreen. My chair faced what must have been a two-way mirror, while the deputies loomed from behind. There was a knock, and Sheriff Frost entered. A wry little smile formed at the edge of his mouth, "Mr. Holmes, impersonating an attorney is a crime, especially when you're trying to get into a correctional facility during a declared state of emergency."

"Bullshit, I—"

Someone, probably Wallace, slapped the back of my head. "The sheriff's talking. Mind your manners." I shook my head to fight off the haze closing in on my consciousness, then started over keeping my voice calm but forceful. "Sheriff, I never said I was an attorney. When I was told I couldn't go in with Mr. Graves, I sat in the waiting room. I didn't cause any trouble."

Frost slowly shook his head, as his smile stretched across his wrinkled face up to his eyes. "You made a mistake trying to sneak into my jail. Thought you'd get some sort of scoop to help your friend beat me in November."

I looked him straight in the eyes and swallowed back a quick one-liner. This wasn't going to go well, but eventually Gravy would start looking for me, or so I hoped. I needed to buy time.

Breaking the silence, the sheriff pointed to bandages peeking out of my sleeve. "What happened to you?" He gave a small derisive laugh. "Failed suicide attempt?" The deputies found it funny too and laughed along with their boss. *Kiss asses.*

My temper rose. "Never mind my arm. I'm here because of the explosion. Your people aren't giving us many details so I wanted to talk to your prisoners and find out the truth."

His cheeks burned as his eyes looked down on me. "Truth? Truth you say. Like the truth that you printed about Amos? Truth that drove him to blow out his brains."

I softened my voice but kept it firm. "I'm sorry about his death. I really am. But we both know that the article didn't cause his suicide. He was battling other demons."

The sheriff reached across the table, grabbed me and pulled me in. I fought back a scream as he squeezed my injured arm. I smelled the cigarettes on his breath. He shouted, "Your reporting was the last straw that put him over the edge! We could've handled the porn thing! You killed him, Holmes, and I'm gonna make sure you pay!"

I wrestled free of his grasp and pulled back as far as the handcuffs would let me. "I'm not asking for your forgiveness."

I was struck with another slap to my head by one of the goons behind me. That one had a lot more power, and only the handcuffs kept me from being knocked off the chair. I barely held on to consciousness while dots danced before my eyes. I felt a knot on my head already forming. "Sheriff, please tell Wallace that we're just having a friendly conversation."

"My deputies are loyal and don't like you disrespecting me. Isn't that right, Wallace?"

"Yes, sir."

Frost began pacing the floor. "You're a smug little pissant that has no understanding of what it took for me to reach this position and how hard it is to maintain order in Escambia County." He pounded his right fist into his left hand. "I worked my way up through the ranks doing whatever my bosses asked. I helped four sheriffs get elected and stay in office. I never wavered. The goal was always for me to become sheriff one day." He stopped and pointed a long finger at me. "I'm not going to let you destroy what I've built."

I knew I should stay quiet, but I know a lot of things that I don't bother with: "What have you built?"

His mouth hardened. "An empire." I felt the deputies move closer to me so I knew it wasn't the time for a wise crack. At least this time I listened to myself. Frost explained, "We are one of the poorest counties in Florida. The Blacks are animals that fornicate and kill each other. My job's to keep their crimes out of white neighborhoods, protect our wives and daughters, and provide a safe haven for good Christian families and business owners."

I started to shake my head but was stopped by a slap to the head. Wallace grunted, "Listen to the sheriff." Frost let Wallace's words sink in before he continued, "You don't understand any of this. A black man can never lead this community, can never be sheriff. The fragile balance in this place would fall apart. People would be put in danger."

He put his hands on the table and leaned toward me. "That's why your friend Tyndall will lose the election, and it's why he won't be the governor's liaison for the recovery effort."

I must have shown surprise because Frost pulled back and cackled, "You two thought you outmaneuvered me. Well, the governor needs to pass an education bill. I made calls to the House speaker and Senate president. The bill won't make it out of conference committee on Monday if Tyndall is given any role in the recovery. My friends in the legislature agree that it'd give him an unfair advantage in the election."

"But you're the incumbent sheriff and have all the advantages."

The expected blow didn't come.

"As it should." Another one of his creepy smiles perverted his face. "Tyndall and you are finished in this town. He'll be humiliated in the race and his legal career obliterated unless he drops out. If you were really his friend, you'd tell him to withdraw and take a job with the governor. Your newspaper is finished, especially if you continue to make up stories about the explosion."

I glared back. "We'll see."

He stood and walked towards the door. "Yes, we will. Boys, take Mr. Holmes to his cell."

"I haven't committed a crime! This is ridiculous! What are the charges?"

"We'll think of a few," Frost answered and then pointing to my left arm, told the deputies, "Be sure to make a note in your report that his arm was bandaged before he walked into our jail. We don't want any claims of police brutality."

The deputies laughed, freed me from the table and escorted me past smiling correctional officers, through a series of gates and up two flights of stairs. I discreetly scanned the hallways, cells and side rooms praying I would see Gravy or a familiar face. No such luck. They stopped me in front of a cell and motioned for the floor supervisor to open the bars. A man taller and bigger than either of my escorts stood, "assumed the position"—face to the wall and hands leaning against it, legs spread apart.

Wallace said, "Kong meet your new roommate, Walker Holmes." He took off my cuffs, pushed me into the cell and said to me, "Kong killed a man last night in a bar fight. Another guy is in the hospital in critical condition." The cell door closed, and the deputies laughed loudly as they walked away.

My cellmate turned and sat down on the bunk bed that creaked under his bulk. "You the newspaper man?" He had his eyes fixed on me and his balled, cantaloupe-sized fists in his lap.

I nodded.

His voice was soft. "I used to be the cook at the H & O Cafe. Mr. Curtis always talked about you. I don't read so good, but Mr. Curtis would read your stories to me. He said you ain't afraid of nothing."

I reached out my hand, "I'm Walker Holmes. Sorry to meet you under these circumstances."

"I'm DeSean Conrad." He shook my hand firmly but not tight enough to break any of my fingers. "The guards call me 'Kong' to rile me."

I sat on the floor opposite the bed. "Forget those racist bastards. How's Curtis?"

Conrad shook his head. "Not good. His health has been slipping ever since he closed the cafe. I ain't been doing so well either. Can't find no job."

H & O Cafe was one of the first black-owned restaurants in Pensacola, started by Hamp Lee and his brother Booker in 1922. Named after their wives, Hattie and Ola, the brothers had earned a reputation for their soul food. Their great-grandson, Curtis, had kept up the tradition for more than a decade, but the East Hill neighborhood began to decline. Younger customers preferred the restaurant chains, and the health department inspectors no longer looked the other way at the numerous code violations. Curtis had closed H&O Café the year before.

"I'm sorry to hear about Curtis and you."

"Mr. Walker, I didn't mean to kill nobody," he put his head in his hands. "It was self-defense. They jumped me. They got upset on a count of I was dancing with a white woman."

He looked up with bloodshot eyes. "Ain't never been in trouble before. The guards say I'm headed to death row and should plead guilty and beg the judge to give me a life sentence."

"Don't pay attention to the guards. They're screwing with you. Do you have a lawyer?" He shook his head. "I've got a friend, William Graves—the best criminal attorney I know. If you'd like, I'll ask him to come see you."

"Please, Mr. Walker."

"It's okay but drop the mister."

He looked relieved and relaxed for the first time since he had been arrested. I told him, "Don't talk to anybody else about your case. Tell the guards that you have an attorney."

He nodded his head in agreement. "You mind if I lay down a bit? Haven't been to sleep much since they locked me up. Top bunk is yours."

I stayed on the floor, pulled my knees up and rested my head. It didn't take long for Conrad to start snoring. I closed my eyes and wondered how long it would take for Gravy to get me out of here, before dozing off myself.

"Well, isn't this a Norman Rockwell moment?" Gravy's voice startled me awake. I had no idea how long I'd been napping. I stood and stretched. Conrad got up and started to face the wall and assume the position. I stopped him, "DeSean Conrad, meet your attorney, William Graves. Gravy, my friend here needs legal counsel."

They shook hands through the bars. Gravy gave him a business card and he told him not to speak with anyone else about his case—just show the guards the business card. He said he'd be back soon so they could talk more.

Gravy and I walked out of the jail into the Saturday noon sunshine, and I vowed to never visit it again. But Frost was coming after the newspaper and me. Only a fool would pick a fight with the sheriff, the most powerful man in Escambia County.

No question, I was that fool.

12

Ron Frost was dying. He had smoked cigarettes since he was 11 years old and had never tried to quit. Hell, he figured he'd never live past fifty since the males in his family rarely did, mostly succumbing to heart disease or gunshot wounds.

The night of the explosion, Frost was exhausted because his stamina had been zapped by the experimental drugs his Houston doctor had given him. He needed to do radiation treatments and chemotherapy but was holding that until after the November election. The drugs had halted the cancer's growth, but they wouldn't keep doing it for much longer.

The night of the explosion, he had turned off his cellphone and sent his wife to visit their daughter in Birmingham. He didn't know how long the deputies had been knocking at his door before he finally heard them.

He shouldn't have run for a third term, but he owed it to Peck. His chief deputy would never win an election for sheriff on his own, but Frost could, and then work out a deal for Peck to get appointed to finish out the term. Once in office, Peck would easily win re-election, at least for one more term, which would be enough to satisfy the boys in Biloxi. Peck would protect Frost's legacy and make sure the gambling and prostitution money still flowed.

When he was a teen, Frost loved to paint landscapes and was smart enough to have become a lawyer or doctor, but his father and uncles had other ideas. Instead, he would become the first county sheriff in the family. He didn't fight the decision because he liked the authority and respect that came with the badge. It wasn't until he had spent a year or so on the job that he realized law enforcement could also be profitable.

The first sheriff that Frost worked under was Bud Long, who took a liking to the tall, lanky, nineteen-year-old deputy that he had assigned to be his driver on his trips to Biloxi, the vice capital of Mississippi. If the crooks had been a little more organized, Biloxi might have rivaled New Orleans when it came to gambling, prostitution and bootlegging, but the Biloxi Boys knew their limits and gave a cut to the Louisiana mafia.

Frost would pick up Sheriff Long at Martel's Restaurant in Brownsville in a Pontiac Bonneville that the sheriff's office had seized during a drug raid and drive him to the Broadwater Marina where they would board a gambling boat with the Harrison County sheriff, Biloxi mayor, a couple of state lawmakers and a passel of beautiful young girls.

On his first road trip, Frost stayed on the deck, drank coffee and listened to the laughter, moans and other sounds that came from the cabin rooms. A petite blonde in a see-through negligee strayed away from the group and rubbed up against him.

"Why don't you join us, sugar?" she whispered, as she stretched on her toes to reach his left ear. "I'm tired of old men pawing me. Me and you could have us some fun."

Frost gently, respectfully, pushed her away. "Thank you, but no. I'm married and have to drive my boss back to Pensacola tonight."

She rubbed her breasts against his arm, then shrugged her shoulders as she walked away. "Your loss."

After what seemed like an eternity, the boat returned to the dock. Sheriff Long came on deck carrying a brown-paper grocery bag, which he handed it to Frost and told him to put it in the trunk.

On the drive back to Pensacola, Long slouched in the passenger's seat with his cowboy hat tilted over his closed eyes: "Frost, Harrison County has over three thousand slot machines, organized blackjack games, poker games, craps tables, bookmaking services and roulette wheels. The sheriff's paid an eighteen-dollar monthly protection fee for each hookup. That protection wards off police raids and any competition moving into the area."

Long estimated the Harrison County sheriff would take in about two hundred-ninety thousand dollars a year, which was a lot of money in 1966. "He also gets a piece of the prostitution and strip clubs, but that fluctuates depending on how the Keesler base commander is feeling any given month."

He continued, "Our gambling and prostitution aren't so big, but I get a piece of what happens in Lillian, Gulf Shores and Orange Beach because we provide safe passage to and from Pensacola. I don't take the money directly from the clubs and juke joints. Every couple weeks I come over here, let off some steam and drive back with a bag of money."

When they drove across the Alabama State Line, Long pointed to an exit, "Pull into that rest stop. Need to piss."

After he relieved himself, the sheriff shouted to Frost to toss him the car keys. He walked to the back of the car and opened the trunk. When he climbed back into the car, Long tossed the deputy an envelope that held five hundred-dollar bills.

"Your daddy and uncles say you can be trusted to keep your mouth shut, Deputy Frost. Can you?"

"Yes, sir," answered Frost nodding his head.

"Remember this son, always reward loyalty."

Frost began to regularly drive Long to Biloxi. Each time the petite, half-dressed girls that came on to him bothered him a little less, and the payouts grew larger. The young deputy had a folksy charm that ingratiated him with his boss and the money made it a lot easier to look the other way, grant favors and kiss ass. It didn't take long for Frost to prove his loyalty to Sheriff Long.

When the sheriff was investigated for drunken, lewd behavior with high school girls while at a safety patrol conference in Montgomery, Deputy Frost testified on the sheriff's behalf, which earned him a promotion to sergeant after the state attorney dropped the charges.

Then Long won a third term, but his vices prevented him from completing it. He was caught gambling—actually it was strip poker—in an FDLE raid of a bottle club in Okaloosa County. The governor removed Long while he awaited his trial, but the sheriff never had his day in court. Not because of the judicial system, but because he was having an affair with his chief deputy's young wife, a former safety patrol cadet. The chief deputy fatally shot his boss when he caught him with his pants down climbing out of the couple's bedroom window. The man claimed he thought the sheriff was a burglar breaking into his home.

Sergeant Frost also worked for Long's successor, Dana Sota. He not only introduced Sota to the Biloxi Boys but also came up with a scheme to establish a stronger law-and-order reputation for his new boss. He told his friends running illegal gambling in Escambia County to suspend their operations for a couple weeks while Sheriff Sota pledged to clean up the illegal gambling, prostitution and other illicit activities. The Escambia County Sheriff's Office raided poker rooms in a few black clubs and arrested several freelance prostitutes in Brownsville. Sergeant Frost made sure the press got full coverage of the arrests. The downtown Rotary Club gave Sota an award for his efforts, and as soon as the media proclaimed the gambling and prostitution problems solved, the illegal operations under Frost's protection returned, bigger and better than ever.

Understanding the fickleness of Escambia County politics, the Biloxi Boys began to depend on Frost to protect their operations and keep the money flowing. Whoever wore the sheriff's badge became less important as long as Frost was part of the administration. Frost made the trips to Biloxi and split the proceeds with the sheriff, but only the Biloxi Boys and Frost ever knew the total payouts.

Sota lasted six years in office. He was linked to a plot to kill County Solicitor Jim Reilly, who had filed to run against him. The sheriff narrowly won a second term but was removed from office after Reilly's cousin in the Pensacola Police Department arrested him for DUI. Fortunately for Frost, he was promoted to lieutenant before the arrest.

During the nineties, Frost rose to the rank of captain and served as the public information officer for the next two sheriffs, which helped him build a name for himself with the public. When Mississippi legalized casinos, many of the Biloxi Boys relocated to south Alabama and the Florida Panhandle. Frost continued to protect their gambling, prostitution and countless other illegal operations. He was well paid and didn't lose a minute of sleep, believing prostitution, gambling and drugs were going to exist anyway, and that they mostly preyed on tourists,

Blacks, Hispanics and dumbass politicians. He was the only one who could keep it out of the good white neighborhoods. Frost maintained order and deserved to be rewarded, or so he thought.

Sheriff Frost admitted that he had his doubts about whether Peck could handle the operations. He had given the chief deputy a small taste of the prostitution business to prove his value to the Biloxi Boys. Peck had increased profits but had also brought in a cousin to help run an escort service in Orange Beach. The little bastard had a fuse even shorter than Peck's and was too rough with the girls. He had cut a few that had mouthed off to him and sent those troublemakers to Texas to service the oil field hands.

Then, there was the Townsend girl. The Biloxi Boys expressed concerns that her ordeal would attract unwanted attention. So when she went to the sheriff's office, Peck made sure the investigation went nowhere. He shot holes in her story, and the Biloxi Boys' relaxed with the girl's homicide. Peck had seen the girl's death as the best thing that ever happened because it not only killed the story, but for all practical purposes it had also killed off the nuisance *Pensacola Insider* publisher, and in a year or so, the chief deputy thought people would forget all about the Townsend girl. But the flood and explosion happened. Holmes began to regain his fire, and Peck's steroid habits were making him more erratic and dangerous.

Frost was tired. He had the money to pay for cutting-edge cancer treatment and live another twenty years on some Caribbean island. However, he needed to win the election and hold on to the office for a couple more years.

13

As we got into his Lexus, Gravy fussed, "I can't leave you for five minutes without you getting into trouble. What was that all about?"

"Attitude adjustment, but I don't think it went how they planned." I rolled down the window to soak in the fresh air, never appreciating my freedom more.

Gravy grumbled, "He had no right to hold you in a cell."

I tried to lighten the mood and not dwell on how badly the jail visit had gone. "Yeah, but I did get you another client, DeSean Conrad."

"Who probably won't be able to pay."

"Money isn't everything."

Gravy countered, "Wise words from a man who gives his paper away for free."

We both laughed. He asked, "Really, what was that all about?"

"Frost is going to crush Tyndall, the *Insider* and me. He wants me to deliver a message to Alphonse that he should withdraw from the race or he'll be destroyed."

"And you?"

I rolled up the window as Gravy put the Lexus in gear. "Oh, I wasn't given an option. I'm done if Frost wins a third term."

"Did his men rough you up?"

"A few slaps to the back of the head."

Gravy looked concerned. "I'm sorry. I thought this wouldn't be a big deal."

I shrugged my shoulders and grabbed our cellphones out of the glove compartment. "Anything involving Frost and me is a big deal." I handed him his phone. "I don't blame you. I accepted the risk."

"What's our next step?"

I liked that Gravy said "our." "Let's see if our sheriff's candidate is available. I'd like to talk with you two together. That way I don't have to repeat myself."

I reached Alphonse, who told me he'd just been notified by the governor's office that he wasn't going to be recovery effort liaison. He wanted to meet us at Five Sisters Blues Cafe. Gravy texted Maya, who replied she was working at the restaurant and would talk with us. On the way to the café, Harden texted and said he was also available and would join us but might be a little late.

Five Sisters sat in old "colored downtown." The Jim Crow laws had forced African American businesses and customers off Palafox Street to West Hill, which eventually became known as Belmont-DeVilliers. Five Sisters Blues Cafe opened during the twenties and had survived depression, segregation and a new wave of street thugs. The youngest sister's great-grandson, Theodore Ware, had taken over the restaurant after Hurricane Katrina. Theo was so tall he had to duck through every doorway he entered. His callused hands from his years as a brick mason swallowed up mine when we shook hands. His face always had a smile. But if he wasn't smiling, it was best to run.

Alphonse and Theodore were talking at the bar when Gravy and I walked in. B.B. King's "The Thrill is Gone" played over the speakers, and we could smell chicken being fried in the kitchen. After handshakes and hugs were exchanged, Theodore suggested, "Why don't you use the meeting room upstairs? Maya'll bring you sweet tea, fried chicken, collard greens and cornbread. You can talk without interruptions."

As the others headed upstairs, I pulled him aside, "How's Maya doing? Is she up to talking about the explosion?"

In a deep voice barely above a whisper, he replied, "Your friend Gravy got her out. She's shaken, but she's like her momma, resilient. Already told her you'd want to hear her story."

I stepped closer to the gentle giant, "It'll help, but don't force her to do anything she's not ready for." He chuckled, shaking his head side to side, "We're tough people. We've been told to shut up and be quiet too long. Maya'll help."

When I caught up to the group, they were already seated at a round table. On the rustic brick walls were posters from the Five Sisters' musical past—Bobby "Blue" Bland, Gwen McRae, Clarence Carter and Muddy Waters.

Soon after, Maya came in and poured us iced tea. Then the food was brought in. It was still covered with aluminum foil because she figured we would want to talk with her first, and didn't want the chicken, collards and cornbread to get cold.

Maya did as her uncle had instructed and shared her experiences. "There's pictures I can't get out of my head no matter what I do." She fidgeted with a turquoise ring on her left hand as she talked, twisting it back and forth. "Flames shooting up from holes in the floor. Everyone yelling at the guards and not getting answers. Stumbling outside and seeing bloodied, battered people collapsed on the lawn."

I asked, "Did you smell gas beforehand?"

Maya nodded her head. She was sort of in a daze, starring at the Bobby Bland poster on the wall. Concerned, Alphonse suggested that maybe she shouldn't share anymore. Then she snapped back, sat upright and looked at us. "No, Uncle Theodore says we need to talk about this and not bury it. I have to help."

I tried a softer approach. "Let's talk about the natural gas."

"My floor smelled like rotten eggs." Maya pulled a handkerchief out of her apron and absentmindedly rubbed her nose. "The other girls that worked in the laundry said the stench down there was overpowering, but the guards ignored their complaints; said it was from some diesel generator. It wasn't no diesel smell."

Gravy urged her to keep talking, "Maya, tell 'em what you told me about the night of the explosion."

She looked down at the handkerchief she clutched in her lap. I poured her a glass of iced tea, which she took and nodded thanks. "For some reason, when the lights went out, the odor got really, really strong. Told the CO that my head ached and felt like I was gonna throw up. When we went to bed, I heard inmates retching and prayed that I'd see my babies again."

I asked, "What do you remember about the blast itself?"

She shut her eyes and a tear rolled down her cheek. "I was almost thrown out of bed. My cell was two floors above the laundry. The whole floor just busted out, and my bed began to slide into the hole. I screamed and screamed for help." She opened her eyes, wiped them and took a big gulp of iced tea. "I thought we were going to die. We had no way out."

Maya said guards unlocked the door and led the inmates down the stairs. They were able to climb through a blown-out window and wait in the yard. Prisoners and jail personnel helped one another during the ordeal. "We were all in the same mess and had to depend on each other. Once outside, we were too stunned to run away. Just stood in the rain and waited for them to tell us where to go."

Reaching out to hold her hand, Alphonse said, "Maya, we know talking about it isn't easy."

"I'm grateful Mr. Gravy got me out and back with my babies." She stood and straightened her apron. "What the sheriff's saying ain't true. You need to tell the real story and make sure those responsible are punished. No one should ever go through the hell I did. No one."

We sat in silence for few minutes after she had left. I ran my fingers through my hair, skimmed across my scalp to feel the knots where the goons had stuck me. Alphonse finally broke the silence, "I wonder how many Mayas are out there? Both prisoners and correctional officers."

Gravy replied, "From what I'm getting, we've got many more people much worse off than Maya. She may be among the lucky ones."

I got up and pulled the foil off the food and handed out the plates and silverware. The fried chicken platter was passed around the table, followed by the collard greens and cornbread. The chicken was hot and moist, and the cornbread sweet, complimenting the greens perfectly. The food held our attention for several minutes as butter and pepper sauces made their ways around the table.

Just then Harden walked into the room and grabbed a Bud Light from the bucket before saying anything. He wore a charcoal-colored suit, and his gray eyes were raw and red-rimmed. He raged, "I left my sister at the funeral home after helping her with the arrangements for her only child. He died because of a bogus arrest!"

He drained his beer. I had never seen him so unhinged. He demanded, "The sonnabitches will pay! Someone's going to jail for this!"

"We need to gather as many facts as possible." I passed him a plate. "Frost doesn't want anything to derail his reelection, but this explosion could be key to doing just that."

"Hope so 'cause all those poor souls in the CBD will never be the same. They're too messed up."

Harden said on Friday night the county administrator had requested any emails or reports regarding gas leaks at the Escambia Central Booking and Detention Center, however none were found except one about the county's facilities manager having been told about a complaint of a possible gas leak; he'd walked the property the afternoon of the explosion and reported he smelled only diesel fumes from the generators.

Gravy and Alphonse nodded and encouraged the private investigator to continue. I took notes as he talked. Harden's account matched with what Maya had shared: power outage, noxious gas odor, basement flooded and guards ignoring the prisoners' complaints.

"When you called me on Wednesday—damn, which seems like years ago—you mentioned the pumps that were supposed to deal with heavy rains hadn't been installed," I reminded him. "Have you found out any more about that?"

"Haven't had time, but it's high on my list." He paused to take a bite of a drumstick. I grabbed beers out of the ice bucket and handed them to the guys, then refilled my iced tea.

Alphonse screwed the cap off his beer, took a sip and turn toward me, "Gravy says you have a message for me from the good sheriff."

"Yeah, drop out of the race or Frost will destroy you."

"He's in for disappointment. We'll see this through to the end and just maybe we'll knock him off in the process."

Harden added, "I want to deal the death blow."

We toasted our new partnership with beers and my iced tea, then dove into working on a plan of action. Gravy would continue to sign-up clients and pass along their stories. If any were particularly significant, he would set up an interview with the *Insider*. The more clients he had, the more leverage he had with the county to get services for those injured.

Alphonse would make the jail explosion a campaign issue and openly challenge Frost's management of the facility. He would push the sheriff's office and county to release more information about the blast and would use his political connections to get the state attorney to take any findings to a grand jury.

Besides looking into the pumps and renovation of the CBD basement, I asked Harden to check into where Sheriff Frost and Chief Deputy Krager were the night of the explosion. "Neither of them was on the scene when we arrived. No one saw them until the press conference, and they haven't been forthcoming about their whereabouts."

Harden corroborated, "I heard his staff repeatedly tried to call their phones, and they kept going to voicemail. I'll ask around."

Gravy asked, "And what will you be doing, mister newspaper man?"

"I'll do what I do best ... turn up the pressure."

14

When I got back to the office, Teddy was out taking more photographs for the next issue. Mal and Pantoni worked on the editorial, huddled over at Mal's desk—her workspace the most organized and orderly in the office. Ad requests were kept in clear plastic project folders that were stacked on a corner of her desk and later would be placed in the production file cabinet once the issue was sent to the printer. Even her Post-it notes were color-coded and neatly organized on her monitor. The only personal touches were a miniature porcelain cat figurine and bobbleheads of Barack Obama and Taylor Swift.

I heard the Eurythmics' "Sweet Dreams" coming from the loft while Summer was rearranging the space to better accommodate her, Mal and Teddy. Mal handed me a cup of black coffee as I sat down at my desk and powered up my Mac. Normally she wouldn't do such a thing, but I think she was checking my breath to see if I had been drinking. She smiled and didn't say a word indicating I had passed her test.

She and Pantoni pulled their chairs over to my desk to get an update. I told them about my attempt to interview inmates at the jail but left out the part about my arrest and confrontation with Frost, seeing no need to worry them about personal grudges. I also shared what Maya and Harden had said about the conditions of the CBD, which matched what Pantoni had gotten from her sources. Mal said she had heard the *News Herald* would have a big feature on the jail explosion in its Sunday edition.

Hating to be bested by the daily newspaper, Mal's competitive side sparked, "Maybe we can get Frost's response to inmates' accounts in the next issue."

I agreed. "I'll post on the blog a little of what I learned today to push Frost. He'll have to respond if both the *News Herald* and *Insider* are reporting on the chaos."

Seeing a way to beat the *News Herald*, Mal added, "The ideal would be for the sheriff to issue a statement or hold a press conference by Monday afternoon. That'll give us enough time to fact-check his comments with what you and Pantoni have gathered, complete the issue and get it to the printer by our Tuesday deadline."

When Teddy returned a little after six, we loaded up the Jeep Cherokee to reward the staff for working on a Saturday. Our destination was The Elbow Room, a Brownsville neighborhood bar next to one of Pensacola's few remaining strip clubs, Benny's Backseat Lounge.

In 1963, Jimmy Flynn, a former Navy aviator, convinced his mom to convert her popular eatery, Maggie's Café, into a pizza pub. The pub later burned down, and Jimmy rebuilt as a cinder block, windowless building lit with red lights on the inside like a bar he had recalled from his days stationed in France in the late 1950s. I suspected that Jimmy was remembering a brothel, not a pub, but who was I to doubt a war hero?

When I asked him about the red lights on my first visit over a decade ago, Jimmy smiled and said, "Everybody looks better in red."

Patrons could play Pac-Man, an arcade bowling game, electronic darts and a Dolly Parton pinball machine. The place had a bookshelf stacked with old board games like Life, Sorry and Battleship. The pizza was hot with fresh ingredients and the beer ice cold.

When we walked into the place, I waved to Jimmy and moved to the back to sit at the "Godfather table," a round table that accommodated eight people under an Old Milwaukee light fixture that hung from the ceiling. Next to the table was a life-size cardboard cut-out of Seven from "Star Trek: Voyager." A huge Star Trek fan, Jimmy wore a Star Trek Command Badge on his vest. Cardboard likenesses of Captain James T. Kirk and First Officer Mr. Spock stood near the front door. Some might have called The Elbow Room a dive bar, but Jimmy didn't care. He had his loyal patrons—a mix of blue and white collars, aging hippies and young hipsters.

Summer didn't initially join us at the table and instead went to pump quarters into the vintage jukebox, which meant we would listen to A-ha, Culture Club, The Human League and Howard Jones for an hour. Del came over to get our drink orders. When she returned with our beers, I nodded towards the owner and asked her, "It's good to see Jim behind the bar. How's he holding up?"

He had turned seventy-two in March and spent most of his time hooked up to a portable oxygen tank because he suffered from emphysema and chronic bronchitis, thanks to a lifetime of smoking Lucky Strikes.

Del brushed back her bangs and smiled, "You didn't hear what he did the night of the flooding?" She sat down at the table and came closer so that Jimmy couldn't hear our conversation. "Customers came in talking about how downtown had flooded. Jim had to see it for himself. Wouldn't let anyone drive him. Well, his car got stuck, and being stubborn, he didn't call any of us. No, he walked the five miles back to his home in Myrtle Grove dragging his oxygen tank."

It was hard not to laugh, even though the idea of him doing that was pretty pathetic.

Del nodded. "He's a tough one."

She pulled her order book out of her flowered apron and asked what we wanted. Teddy and I decided to split a "Works" pizza. Mal ordered the Enterprise, a baked, breaded eggplant hoagie made with goat cheese and marinated tomatoes. Summer and Pantoni got pub salads.

We eat, drank, relaxed and talked about everything except the newspaper. As Howard Jones' "No One is to Blame" began to play, Mal ribbed Summer, "Why do you make us relive the early years of MTV every time we come here?"

Summer blushed—though it was difficult to tell under the red lights. "This is what my mother played all the time when I was growing up."

Pantoni came to her rescue. "I like it. The problem is the limited selection on the jukebox, not the genre."

"Whatever," sighed Mal as she sat back and nestled in the crook of Teddy's right arm. "It feels great to get out of the office and away from downtown as long as Walker doesn't make us go over to the strip joint next door."

"Hey, Benny's a friend. I may walk over to check on him. It'd be rude not to."

"Sure, that's all you'd be doing," grinned Teddy. "You'll completely ignore the dancers."

Mal elbowed her husband in the ribs. "Only losers go to strip clubs. They exploit women."

Summer resisted, "Several of my college classmates paid for tuition dancing in clubs."

Mal smirked, "Of course they did."

I took a sip of my PBR. "Benny treats his dancers better than most. He isn't a saint, but few of us are. Plus, he has sources of information none of us would get any other way."

"He's your source, not mine." Mal dismissed me as she waved for the waitress to bring the table another round. "Go ahead and visit him. We're staying here."

I picked up a slice of pizza and took Mal's cue to walk next door to Benny's Backseat. Five years ago, Benny Walsh's third wife, by then ex-wife, was in a terrible car wreck. I had investigated the county road where the accident took place and found out the road contractor hadn't followed the construction documents and had built the road's curve too tight to handle the posted speed. She sued after we published our investigation, and the road contractor settled for five million dollars. Benny no longer had to pay alimony, I got a lifetime friend and news source.

When I walked into the Backseat, the doorman waved me in without paying the cover. Benny sat in his usual table off to the side of the stage where he could watch the dancers, front door and cash registers.

"Holmes, what the fuck are you doing here?" Benny yelled as my eyes adjusted to the dark room. He wore a pink polo shirt. The stage lights reflected off his bald head and made his gold tooth glisten when he smiled. He didn't shake hands, he bumped fists. Motioning to a shapely waitress in a black corset, fishnet stockings and red stilettos, he said to me, "How 'bout a drink?"

"Diet Coke please. Was at Elbow and just wanted to check on you."

He smiled, "I heard you were on a pretty big bender for a while."

"Well, I was screwed up but worked my way out of it."

Benny nodded, "Good."

The waitress brought my soda. She smiled and winked. She looked vaguely familiar. Then it came to me—it was Catelyn from End O' the Alley. I thanked her and admired her butterfly tattoo as she walked back to the bar. Then I asked Benny how he and his mother did in surviving the flooding.

"I'm fine. My condo on the beach had no problems. Mother had some flooding in her carport in East Hill, but she's okay too. Thanks for asking."

Sailors surrounded the stage as a lithe platinum blonde twirled around on a polished brass pole to Theory of a Deadman's "Bad Girl-friend." The bouncers edged closer to the stage to protect the girl as the boys got bolder and bolder. I nodded towards the stage, "Somebody might get hurt if they get out of hand."

"Nah, Leo and Matt will keep 'em in line. Shellie's a pro. See all the bills on the stage. She'll coax another two hundred out of them before she finishes."

I took my eyes off the stage. "I spent most of today trying to find out what really happened in the jail explosion. Can't figure out where Frost and Peck were when it happened."

Benny drank his ginger ale. "I don't know anything about Frost, but I do know where Peck was."

"Do tell. I hate that asshole."

Benny laughed. "And he's not too fond of you either, but who is?"

He had a point. "Tell me what you know."

"Peck was with one of my former dancers Wednesday night—Cindy ... Coplin."

He let the name linger. Then it dawned on me. "You mean Rebel Yell."

Cindy Coplin, aka "Rebel Yell," had danced for Bennie in the late nineties right when she got out of high school. She earned national attention when she posed for a series of risqué photos. Baring her breasts in three of the two dozen photographs taken outside a fire station with its crew led to several of the firefighters getting reprimanded by the county and their wives. Coplin and her triple D's later left Benny, did a series of porn films and even appeared once on The Howard Stern Show. Last I heard she was on the strip club circuit in the Carolinas.

Benny nodded. "She's back in town to see her family and hooked up with Peck. Apparently she likes his new strongman look, and likes that he's now chief deputy. You never know when you might need a friend in the sheriff's office."

I laughed. "Peck and Rebel Yell? Who would have thought of that one? Think she'd talk to me?"

"Not on your life, but you'll figure out a way to use that nugget."

Indeed, I would. I thanked Benny, waved goodbye to Catelyn, and returned to The Elbow Room to gather up my crew. When we got back to the office, Tiny was sweeping up shards of shattered ceramics—it was my "Morning Joe" coffee cup all shattered. Tiny was panicky. "Big Boy and Liza got into another fight. Started chasing each other all over the place. I got 'em separated but not before they broke your mug. Sorry, Walker."

Summer sighed, "They were doing so well."

"It wasn't my fault, Ms. Summer," pleaded Tiny, worried that he would be blamed.

She hugged him. "No one's blaming you. I've just got more work to do with those two."

Relieved, Tiny finished sweeping and went to make his bed on the office couch. Mal headed upstairs to sooth Liza, followed by Teddy and Summer. Pantoni not far behind them—she'd made the decision to sleep over. I found Big Boy under the covers on the air mattress in the conference room. He wasn't happy.

"Come on, fella. Help me pick out some shorts and we'll go for walk." He perked up when he heard the word "walk," jumped off the mattress and began doing his doggie yoga-like thing.

As we neared Pensacola Bay, my cellphone vibrated. I didn't recognize the number. A second later a text message flashed: "How's your arm? Too bad Frost let you escape from the jail. Your ass is mine—Lester Judson."

I replied, "Screw u."

15

On Sunday, we all needed more downtime so we went our separate ways. Summer had planned a day of kayaking and took Big Boy with her. Mal and Pantoni headed to the cinema to watch *Belle,* a film that had a Pensacola connection—Dido Elizabeth Belle was the daughter of British Admiral John Lindsay and his slave Maria Belle, who had lived in colonial Pensacola in the 1760s. Teddy was shooting a wedding at Seaside, and Tiny went to open the gym at the Fricker Center.

Fortunately, Dare rescued me from a day of solitude when she texted if I would join her for brunch at her home. Before Rachel Townsend's murder, we ate together nearly every weekend when my then-girlfriend Bree wasn't in town. Then I went on my bender, and she started dating Taylor. When I walked into her house, I smelled beignets and chicory coffee. In the past, we had mimosas and Bloody Marys, but Dare wasn't going to tempt my tentative sobriety.

She wore tight designer jeans and a baggy red Ole Miss sweatshirt that must have been thirty years old and displayed the politically incorrect Colonel Rebel. She was barefoot, but still wore her pearls. We hugged and sat on her deck. She looked disappointed that I hadn't brought my canine companion but was happy that he was playing with Summer and her friends. She admonished, "Big Boy needs more playtime than you give him."

I agreed and dipped a beignet in my coffee. "For a multimillionaire, you're a hell of a cook."

Dare laughed, "Not much of a compliment from a guy who lives off of pizza, burgers and wings."

I smiled and enjoyed the morning sun that gave every indication the day would be a hot one, but at that moment we had occasional breezes. Halfway through my first cup of coffee, I filled Dare in on the events of Saturday, giving her the blow by blow of my confrontation with Frost.

"You're playing with fire. Frost has been bashing you all over town. He's serious about shutting you down."

I didn't respond immediately, and instead drank my coffee and listened to the smooth vocals of Al Jarreau's "Glow" playing on her sound system. "He wouldn't go after me unless he's afraid of our newspaper."

"Or blames you for his brother's death."

"Well, and that too." I closed my eyes and tilted back my head to soak in the sun.

"Walker, this is serious. He might win this time."

Not opening my eyes, I replied, "He won't. Pricks always underestimate me."

She refilled my cup. "Walker, if only you were as confident as you sound." She nudged me. "Let's move to the living room. We're losing our breeze, and it's getting hot out here."

As I picked up the tray of beignets, I said, "Frost and everyone else wants to control me and the *Insider*. They want applause, not criticism."

Dare changed the subject once we settled on the couch in the living room. "Have you talked to Jackie since Friday?"

I shook my head. "She's texted me several times. I don't have time for her crap."

"Walker, she lost her brother—"

"And she doesn't want my help! She's out to somehow blame me for Tim's death."

"No, it's not about you. She's lost her brother and trying to understand what happened. Tell her what you've learned. Please."

The "please" got me as it always did. "Yes, ma'am."

As if on cue, my phone vibrated. I showed Dare the text from Jackie: "Need to meet TODAY. Come to beach."

I shrugged, smiled at Dare and texted, "Can't."

"Jeep repossessed?" she replied.

"C'mon Walker," Dare nudged my shoulder so I texted back: "NY Nick's on Palafox @3."

I looked at Dare, "Happy?"

Pleased, she went into the kitchen and brought back a carafe of coffee. I shook off her offer of another refill, and, for the first time, noticed the fatigue in her eyes. I had been so absorbed with telling my tales that I hadn't paid much attention to the toll the flood had taken on her. "Is there a reason you wanted to see me?"

She sat in the leather chair and folded her legs underneath her. "We've been blocked from getting any contracts for the road repairs."

Two years ago, Dare had bought the paving company that was owned by Bo Hines, a guy who had stolen funds from the local arts council, was suspected of killing his wife, Dare's best friend, and nearly murdered me. He had died on his yacht, and the town blamed me for the homicide, not knowing that his niece had pulled the trigger. Dare bought Hines Paving Company and reimbursed the arts council. Proceeds from her purchase of the company went toward establishing a trust fund for Hines' niece. The enterprise had thrived under Dare's management and remained the top road contractor in Northwest Florida. She should at least have some of the emergency repair work.

"Under the emergency order, the county administrator has the authority to give contracts to whatever company he wants." She rested her mug against her chin. "We haven't even gotten a phone call asking for a quote."

"What does the county administrator say?"

"Not much, other than he's getting pressure from his commissioners to give the business to other contractors."

"You usually have influence over the board." I finished off my coffee. "You've contributed enough to their campaigns."

She put her mug on a coffee table and stretched out her legs. "You'd think, wouldn't you?"

"Are Frost and Tatum behind it? Somehow punishing you for being my friend?"

She gave me a bemused smile. "You don't have any friends."

I conceded her point. "I'm serious. I can go nuclear on the bastards."

"Settle down, cowboy. What I need you to do is put out some feelers and let me know what you learn." Dare stood, signaling that she didn't want to talk about it anymore and that it was time for me to leave.

"Do you have any indications of kickbacks?"

She shrugged. "There's always rumors. Maybe your sources have some useful information. Meanwhile, I'll continue to work things through my channels." She kissed me on the cheek, and I left for my rendezvous with the ex-Mrs. Holmes.

When I walked into New York Nick's a little after three, Jackie was already drinking. Bruce Springsteen's *Nebraska* played overhead, and about a dozen customers sat at the bar watching baseball, complaining it was too hot to go to the beach.

"I thought you'd given up and run away," she remarked, looking up from her cellphone.

"Walker doesn't run away," said the approaching waitress—chunky, in shorts, tank top and knee-high tube socks as she put a Bud Light in front of me the instant I sat down.

Jackie didn't miss a beat. "I meant staggers away."

I took a swallow of the beer wishing it was straight Jack Daniels, longing for the kick into oblivion that bourbon offered. I remember Roger Fairley telling me once, "Sobriety and ex-wives aren't compatible."

Thinking of the quote, I smiled, which upset Jackie because she thought I was laughing at her. Her displeasure bubbled up: "I wanted to meet 'cause I don't need your assistance anymore. Sheriff Frost has offered to help me find out what happened during the explosion."

"Really? Frost's a crook and will only use you to get to me. Stay away from him."

"He told me that you had some conflict with him, but he wouldn't let your pettiness get in the way of him doing his job." Jackie pulled out a pack of Virginia Slims from her purse, but then remembering she couldn't light a cigarette inside the restaurant, dumped it back in her bag. She turned her focus back to me and decided to drive a dagger into my heart.

"I heard your tattooed New Orleans artist dumped you."

I didn't reply.

"She got tired of your obsessive compulsiveness and self-absorption just like I did?"

"Stop it, Jackie."

"It's always your writing and Mari," she jabbed. "You can never let go. You're compelled to prove yourself to some ghost you only knew for two years."

"Stop it, Jackie."

She drained her drink. "You'll never grow up."

"Probably not."

She lifted her chin and bowed back her shoulders. "Journalism first. Always fucking journalism. Fearless, obsessed, relentless pursuer of headlines. No room for me or anyone. We'd still be married ... you could've been an investigative reporter for *The Washington Post* or *The New York Times* ... won awards, had book deals ... if you looked at the bigger picture ... if you had loved me, not a ghost. I could've made you somebody."

I put down my beer. "We had this conversation a hundred times before the divorce."

"And now you've got this worthless rag of a newspaper that the sheriff and your creditors will shut down before Labor Day. You'll end up with nothing. Nothing at all."

I folded my arms and began counting the freckles on her nose, not saying a word. When we divorced, the few couples that were our friends took Jackie's side. Our divorce was seen as my failure, and I never fought that premise, which irritated her even more. Then she had a second divorce, which chipped away at her argument that only I had commitment issues and further fueled her antagonism toward me.

"And you don't care! You've put a decade into this paper and have nothing to show for it!" The music wasn't loud enough to drown out her yelling at me.

I cared plenty, but there was no point in fighting. She wanted me to respond with similar barbs and prove to her fragile ego that I deserved her scorn. Instead, I stared at her, said nothing and rode out the storm.

She gathered up her keys, cellphone and purse in a huff, pulled her sunglasses down from their resting spot on her head and moved toward the front door. Then turned toward me: "Sheriff Frost said he let you off for trying to get into his jail under false pretenses. Something about trying to pass yourself off as a lawyer. Told me to tell you he won't be as charitable next time."

"Jackie, I'm serious. Stay away from him. He's evil."

She laughed. "I think I might contribute to his re-election campaign."

She left, and I fought the urge to order bourbon shots. Frost had found a chink in my armor, a way to get at me. I needed Jackie to leave Pensacola.

16

Pensacola continued to dry out and clean up. Governor Walters fulfilled his promise and state agencies poured resources into the area to help with the recovery while "Legacy Boy" Tony Willis and his buddies received a lot of no-bid contracts thanks to the emergency order.

The *Insider* published its recovery guide. Ad sales, and more importantly, deposits were steady. The living conditions in the loft settled down as Big Boy and the cat whose name would remain unspoken by me maintained their distance from each other. Tiny became our unofficial maintenance man and janitor. Every morning he emptied the trashcans, swept the floor and took the dog out for a walk. The girls even let him straighten up the loft and take care of the cat's litter box.

The week was also dotted with funerals. The Pensacola Police Department held a memorial service for Officer Timothy Sturdevant outside of its headquarters. Jackie and Dare sat under the tent with his widow, a petite, blonde, young woman who hid her tears behind dark sunglasses. The mayor and police chief stood at a podium next to a large portrait of a smiling Timmy and a large wreath. After the speeches, a folded flag and service medal were given to the family, and the honor guard gave the fallen brother a twenty-one-gun salute. I stood on the edge in the back, alone in the hot sun. They were taking his body to Memphis for burial. Dare had wanted me to fly with them, but I refused because Jackie would have hated me being there.

When I left the memorial service, I went to Greater Union Baptist Church for the funeral of Malik Green. I was a snowflake in a coat and tie sitting in a sea of hurting black people. Tyndall sat in the front pew with Ms. Green and a host of children, aunts, uncles and grandparents. In a brown suit that hung loosely on his slight, wilting frame, Malik's grandfather gave the eulogy, speaking in a rich voice that carried through the church.

Malik was a gifted high school basketball player who was too short to play at the college level. His grandfather talked about how the young man was learning to be a brick mason to help support his mother and younger siblings. "He was growing into a fine man," he said with tears running down his cheeks. He called for the male members of the family to stand in front of the congregation as he spoke. "We are a family of strong men and will remember and honor Malik for the rest of our lives." When he concluded, the men and boys joined him in singing "Just the Two of Us," which the grandfather described as a tune he sang to Malik "every time we rode in my pickup truck from when he was so little that he sat on a telephone book to see over the dashboard."

The pastor told his flock that it hadn't been too long since he'd stood before the congregation to pray for the futures of Malik and his fellow high school graduates. "His brief life will forever be preserved by the memory of his loving dedication to God and family. Malik touched all our lives. What do you do when these awful days come? The first thing we need to do is recognize we have a loving Father and that we're all together. We need to support one another. We need to rally together."

The pastor looked directly at Tyndall, "We need answers, and we need a sheriff that will care about us."

Around the same time as Malik Green's funeral, James Harden buried his nephew in a quiet graveside service without much fanfare. I texted him several times but got no response, which worried me. Two days later, on Saturday morning, he finally answered with a text asking me to meet him at Nick's at 11:30 a.m.—a place where he and I could drink beers and eat wings and burgers without anyone hearing what we discussed, thanks to the Rolling Stones. The PI arrived and smiled for a brief second when he spied me sitting in the middle of the restaurant. He joked, "No better place to hide than in plain sight." He ordered a

Corona. Seeing the Bud Light in front of me, he said, "You still holding Nick to his bet or has the pressure gotten to you?"

"A bet's a bet."

We put in an order of twenty grilled wings and a side of fries. Harden's eyes gave away his exhaustion. He was still on edge, and his eyes kept darting around the room to make note of who else was in the bar.

"You look like you haven't slept for days," I said after the waitress walked back to the bar.

"I buried my nephew. The boy was a screw-up, but he didn't deserve to die. I'm calling in all favors. Someone's going to prison for this."

I nodded, "Gravy and his staff are gathering the statements of hundreds of prisoners. We'll have a pretty good picture of the hours before and after the blast."

"No one gives a damn about the inmates, except for their families."

"We've started making public record requests for contracts, change orders and all documentation concerning the renovation of the CBD basement." A young couple with a crying baby sat down two tables away. "Dare's road company has been locked out of the road repairs. The county will drag out fulfilling our request, but eventually we'll get the records."

Harden looked at the crying baby, not hiding his disapproval of having an infant in bar. "I know where Peck was the night of the explosion."

"With a stripper."

He shook his head. "That's what he wants people to believe. The chief deputy was at a Klan meeting."

Not sure I had heard him correctly, "Did you say Ku Klux Klan?"

"Right here in Pensacola."

"Are you talking about that small group of breakfast buddies and their secret society?"

"Might not be so small or so secret." Harden paused to let his words sink in and to drink his beer. "Peck's apparently the Fury for the Panhandle." He pulled out a small, battered notepad from his back pocket to refresh his memory. "The Exalted Cyclops runs the Northwest Florida province. Under him are the Furies. Peck is the Fury in charge of the Wrecking Crew."

"Wrecking Crew?"

"It's the muscle that goes after the Klan's enemies and any wayward members. Pioneered by your fellow Mississippians, they investigate foes and suspected leaks."

It was my turn to drink my beer. "Perfect role for the chief deputy sheriff."

"Peck was sitting in on a meeting of the Kaliffs, a sort of advisory board from best I can tell."

Our waitress delivered the grilled wings and fries to our table, Harden ordered another beer from her. Meanwhile, the couple gave up on trying to quiet their infant and moved to an outside table.

"Damn, Jim. This's right out of the 1920s. I've always thought Pensacola was five years behind the rest of the world, not a century."

"This is real," Harden said. "You have to take it seriously. I checked with my friends at the FBI. They're aware of the local Klan but have chosen to focus on drug dealers and tax fraud instead. A lot less headaches because no one wants to admit racism exists."

"Do you have any idea what Peck discussed?"

"That's what I need to find out." He picked up a wing and dipped it in ranch dressing. "Though I heard you and Tyndall were mentioned."

"What's the Klan's issue with me, other than I'm a fallen Roman Catholic?"

"Being a fallen Roman Catholic might work in your favor if you attended a local Baptist church occasionally."

"Not likely," I smiled.

"Walker, they believe you and your newspaper threaten their control of Escambia County, and, let's admit it, you do." Harden grabbed another wing. "Heck, you got your best friend arrested. What chance do they have of ever changing you?"

"Hines deserved to go to jail."

"And you killed him."

"It was self-defense."

"Yeah right," Harden replied. "They're afraid of you, and these guys kill whatever they fear."

The waitress checked on us, and I asked for water. After she left, Harden continued, "While it's still a long shot, Tyndall might get elected. Just the possibility of a black man taking over the sheriff's office has 'em rabid."

"Will your source sit down for an interview?"

"Not a chance. My guy's worried Peck and his crew will find out he talked to me."

"Why did he talk to you?"

"Butch is married to my sister, and is angry Frost let his son stay in the CBD. Said neither the sheriff nor chief deputy would return his calls after the arrest. Later Peck told him that he would've done something but had to attend the Klan meeting. Peck even shared some of the details of the meeting to defend why he couldn't pick up the phone. Dumbass."

"Does Butch know who the leaders are?"

Harden shook his head. "He isn't a Klan member but got to know Peck through softball. After a few beers, the chief deputy likes to brag about his powerful connections. Butch never asked a lot of questions because he didn't want to get involved in that crazy shit."

"Is Tyndall in danger?"

Harden nodded, "Most likely, as are you."

We ate our wings and fries in silence, glancing at the baseball games on several of the big screens. Harden spoke up, "There's another thing. Sturdevant was your brother-in-law, right?"

"Ex-brother-in-law. I didn't have any relationship with him. Didn't even know he was in Pensacola."

"But you went to the memorial service."

Harden did have good sources. "Yes, I'm a jerk but not completely heartless."

The PI didn't smile. "The prisoner that Sturdevant was booking at the CBD was Lester Judson."

I pushed back from the table. "What?"

"Sturdevant had caught him in a routine traffic stop for running a red light."

"But Judson isn't listed on the prisoner reports. How can you be sure?"

"Somehow he slipped away in all the confusion. A friend at police dispatch saw you at the memorial service and wanted me to pass on that she talked with Sturdevant when he made the arrest."

Stunned, I asked, "Why am I just hearing this? Why hasn't PPD said something?"

"I'll give you one guess."

"Peck."

"Stay focused, Walker," Harden advised. "At least we know Judson's around. Maybe he's hurt. We'll get him and Peck."

"I want to see that perp walk."

"Me too," Harden assured.

I drove over to Tyndall's campaign headquarters after we finished lunch. His campaign had begun to gain momentum. While Governor Walters wasn't able to make Alphonse his flood recovery liaison, he did him an even bigger favor by loaning his communications director, Jen McLean, to help organize his campaign.

A Georgetown University Law graduate, McLean had worked for Senator Bill Nelson and President Barack Obama before moving back to rein in Walters' administration, where she quickly earned the respect of department heads, lawmakers and the capital press corps. Since her arrival in Pensacola, McLean had quickly developed a social media campaign on Facebook and Twitter that Frost and his team were clueless on how to match. Alphonse's handsome oval face and bright smile were everywhere. Frost had no counterattack, at least not initially. Since the jail explosion, the sheriff's race had tightened. According to the latest *News Herald's* poll, Tyndall had pulled to within eight percentage points of Frost.

Even though it was a Saturday afternoon, the campaign office was filled with white and black, young and old volunteers manning a phone bank. On the wall, a dry erase board listed the neighborhoods the campaign would target up to the general election. By each neighborhood were numbers that detailed the houses visited and how many voters had committed to vote for Tyndall.

"Impressed?" Alphonse asked me. He was dressed in an orange polo shirt with "ELECT TYNDALL — It's Time for a Change" boldly across the front. The orange color was the same as that of the jumpsuits worn by the jail inmates, which wasn't a coincidence.

"Very much so," I replied. Alphonse introduced me to the volunteers. They smiled and returned to the phones. They had a mission to accomplish and wouldn't let in distractions.

"Let's go see Jen," he said as he escorted me to a back office where McLean sat at a desk behind two monitors. Tall, fit and tanned, the former shooting guard for the University of Florida Gators women's basketball was leaning back in a chair. She twirled a gold hoop earring on her finger while she argued over the phone with the Channel 3 station manager whom she had reached on the golf course. Jen wanted Alphonse on Monday night's six o'clock broadcast.

It sounded like she would get her way: "We both know Sheriff Frost represents the past, and Alphonse is the new face of Escambia County. You want to be on the right side of progress. Besides, Frost's never done you any favors."

When she hung up the phone, Jen took a swallow of her Coke Zero. She smiled, which lessened the sharpness of her features, and reached out a hand without getting up. Her handshake was firm, but brief. "Walker, good to see you."

Jen didn't like me, though she hid it from Alphonse. She didn't trust reporters, particularly those who had close relationships with her candidate. She preferred the media went through her to get to Alphonse

Even so, I extended an olive branch. "In less than a week, it looks like you got this raggedy-ass operation actually looking like a real campaign."

She brushed aside her bangs off of her eyes and smiled at Alphonse. "It helps when you have a winning candidate."

Alphonse smiled, "Jen has been a godsend, and the state Democratic party has given us enough money to mount a serious fight. We're closing in on Frost."

I agreed, "He has to be getting nervous."

"Damn right," boasted Jen. "The bastard has plenty to worry about."

I motioned to Alphonse to shut the door. "There's a new wrinkle. A reliable source tells me the Klan may get involved in this race. Your life could be in danger."

Alphonse laughed. "The Klan, really? Frost's a sick, racist son of a bitch, but a Klan member?" Jen looked at me like I had said the tooth fairy was real and working the afternoon shift at Circle K and added, "This isn't Mississippi or Alabama in the sixties. The Klan no longer exists."

"It does," I replied. "You don't have to believe me, but it doesn't hurt to take precautions."

Alphonse and Jen asked simultaneously, "Precautions?"

"Travel with protection big enough to ward off attackers and sharp enough to keep an eye on the room for you. Mention something to your buddies in the Florida Attorney General's office about concerns over the growth of the Klan's influence in Northwest Florida. Word will get back to Frost."

"And he'll call off the dogs?" asked Tyndall.

"Maybe. But at the very least Frost will know you suspect something. He might not risk an overt attack."

Jen stood up with her hands on her hips. She and I were probably the same height, but her better posture made her appear taller. "Wait, wait. We've got a racist cabal that's out to stop an African American from being elected to the most powerful position in Escambia County. That's a national story. I can pitch it to *The New York Times* and *The Washington Post*. Get you on the network news shows."

"Too early, we don't have hard evidence," I tried to dissuade her. "Your candidate will look like a conspiracy nut without proof."

Jen countered, "Or do you want the story for yourself?"

Alphonse gave her a sharp look. Jen wasn't going to fight with me in front of him. She sat back down with her arms folded, not pleased that I was advising her candidate. Alphonse chose to overlook her body language and turned back to me. "Will your source go public?" I shook my head. "What do you recommend we do?"

"I say you draw them out. Continue to run your campaign and put them on the defensive. They'll make a mistake, and we'll pounce on it."

Jen asked with more than a hint of sarcasm, "And how do you suggest we draw them out?"

I ignored her tone. "I'm working on it. Give me a couple days."

I left the two of them huddled in her office laying out the schedule for the next week. Jen would get in her knocks against me after I left.

17

started my work week with breakfast with Gravy at CJ's Kitchen. After the waitress poured my coffee and took my omelet order, I looked at my attorney and asked, "Why is it that she always knows your order, but she can't ever remember mine?"

"Maybe you aren't as popular or as important as you think," he laughed.

Having no counter argument, I pointed to a manila folder by him. "What do you have that's got you so excited?"

Amped on Tab, Gravy smiled and shoved it across the table. "This'll get Sheriff Frost's attention."

The folder contained a Notice of Claim to Sheriff Frost on behalf of Kendrick Roder and stated he had "suffered injuries as a result of medical malpractice and other negligence by the Escambia County Sheriff's Office and the Escambia County Jail and/or its employees and agents." Gravy's law firm had also requested the notice be sent to the county's insurance carrier.

Bending forward and reaching across the table, he tapped the document. "The sheriff and board of county commissioners will be served with a dozen of these today, and I'll follow up with a press conference outside the federal courthouse."

Puzzled, I asked, "Why do this now? The explosion was only two weeks ago. The fire marshal hasn't completed his investigation."

"My clients aren't getting the medical care they need and when they do see a nurse or doctor their injuries are not being properly documented. The county attorney will quickly realize I don't plan to fight this in state court where sovereign immunity limits the damages to two hundred thousand dollars. He'll figure out that I want to try this as a federal class action suit where the damages could be in the millions."

Gravy sat back and rubbed his hands together. "Then, I'll have a chip to bargain with for better care for the inmates."

"How many more notices do you plan to file?"

"About two hundred," he smiled. "We'll send them in batches of twenty-five every few days."

"And the press conference might help you sign up a few more clients and give Alphonse's campaign a boost by calling more attention to the jail tragedy."

Gravy folded his arms and nodded, "We've got about a dozen law firms that are representing prisoners. I'm the first to submit a Notice of Claim and have the largest number of clients, which should guarantee that we'll be at the table when the county wants to talk settlement."

As the waitress delivered my breakfast, he pulled the folder back to avoid me getting cheese or salsa on it. Gravy always complained that I was a messy eater, and he was right. He beamed, "This gives me more standing during any negotiations with Frost and the county."

"And when the fire marshal issues his report on the explosion, you'll be all set to go to court," I added, admiring my friend's legal strategy. "Frost isn't going to be happy."

He took a sip of his Tab. "The sheriff's happiness isn't my concern. The explosion was avoidable. Men and women were hurt, some died."

After I cut into my omelet and took my first bite, I asked, "What do you know about the Klan being active in the area?"

"Not much." He didn't seem surprised that I brought it up, but he was part of old Pensacola and few things phased the legacy families. "It's possible a few idiots might still be calling themselves Klansmen, but no one has had a burning cross in their yard for decades." He loved to share bits of Pensacola's history. "In the mid-seventies, when I was in St. Michael's Elementary School, I remember seeing men in white robes and hoods marching down Palafox Street. The Klan was pushing back against the black ministers that had led protests against the Escambia County Sheriff's Office."

Pulling his cellphone out from the breast pocket of his suit, Gravy said, "*The New York Times* did an article about the protests and the Klan in Pensacola, I think. Let me see if I can find it."

The article opened with a C.B. Krager holding a Klan meeting of about two dozen members in a little auto repair shop in Warrington. Krager was quoted as saying the Klan needed to help protect law enforcement against the "unruly coloreds."

I stated the obvious, "This C.B. Krager has to be some kin to Peck."

Gravy didn't disagree and had more to share. "A couple years ago, an attorney friend was renovating his office that was once owned by a county judge who had died, over on Baylen Street—knocking out a few walls, adding a couple windows, replacing the floor, those kinda things. The contractor called my friend one morning and told him to come to the site as soon as possible because the workers had uncovered a secret room that contained several Klan robes and ceremonial items."

"What did he do?"

"I think he might have burned them."

"Will you give me his name?"

Gravy shook his head. "He'll know I told you, and anyway he'll deny it."

We finished our breakfast, and I committed to having the *Insider* at Gravy's afternoon press conference.

At 3:30, Gravy, his legal team and the families of his clients stood on the steps of the Winston E. Arnow US Courthouse on North Palafox Street. Appointed by President Lyndon Johnson, Arnow had changed the political landscape of Northwest Florida during his twenty-seven years on the federal bench, including ordering the desegregation of the Escambia County School District and later paving the way for black representation on the county commission, city council and school board by mandating single member districts be drawn so that at least one district had a majority of black voters.

Gravy's paralegals handed out a press release on the notices filed and gave brief summaries concerning five of his clients most seriously injured in the blast. Before Gravy took the microphone, police sirens were heard in the distance coming down North Palafox past the "Our Confederate Dead" monument in Lee Square. Four Escambia County Sheriff's Office cruisers drove the wrong way on the northbound side of the street, then stopped and blocked off the street in front of the courthouse.

Waving a document, Chief Deputy Krager, accompanied by two deputies, approached Gravy shouting that the attorney was under arrest while other officers surrounded Gravy's staff and his clients. Television cameras and newspaper photographers captured the entire spectacle.

Gravy kept his cool. "What am I being arrested for?"

Krager boomed for the press, "For fraud and extortion of Escambia County. Put your hands behind your back, Graves."

Gravy took the arrest warrant from Krager and said, "What? This is ridiculous!"

However, the attorney didn't resist when a deputy pulled his left arm behind his back and began to handcuff him as he was read his rights. I pushed through the crowd and shouted, "Peck! What fraud?"

"Step back, Holmes, or we'll haul you in too."

A television reporter jumped in, "Chief, we need more facts. We've got to get something on the air in a little over an hour."

The chief deputy stuck out his chest, enjoying the arrest way too much. "Sheriff Frost will hold a press conference tomorrow morning."

While deputies placed Gravy in a cruiser, two of Gravy's senior attorneys were ushered into another vehicle. Pointing at them, I yelled, "Where you taking them? They under arrest too?"

Krager shook his head but with a smile on his face. "We've a search warrant for the premises of the Graves Law Firm. We need firm representatives available since Mr. Graves will be detained for a few hours."

The reporters got in their vehicles and followed the cruisers to Gravy's offices for more photographs and video. The families of Gravy's clients stood silently in shock while the remaining secretaries and paralegals of his firm tried to comfort them. More than a few fought back tears. I called Mal and filled her in on the aborted press conference and Gravy's arrest. She said, "I'll send Teddy over to the law firm to take photos."

"Okay, I'll walk back to the office and work up a blog post after I make a few phone calls."

She warned, "Maybe we should assign someone else to this since you and Gravy are so close."

"Mal, I know Gravy. Frost has set him up."

Mal objected firmly, "Walker."

I conceded, "We'll take it slow and report the facts as they're revealed."

She didn't give in. "We need to discuss each post and article before it's published, even yours. Agreed?"

"I'm losing you … must be a bad connection. We'll talk when I get to the office," I said as I hung up the phone. I called both Harden and Tyndall. Jim didn't pick up the phone, but Alphonse had seen news of the arrest on the *News Herald's* Twitter feed. After I filled him in on the details, he said he would make a few calls to try to help. We agreed to meet at The Elbow Room around nine to compare notes. With any luck, Gravy would be released and would join us.

I called State Attorney Clark Spencer. "Holmes, I was blindsided by this as much as Gravy. Frost didn't present his case to us for review before he made the arrest."

"Can he do that?"

"Yes, but it's rare. Normally, the sheriff's office wants some cover on a controversial arrest like this. My guys are telling me he got Judge Waller, one of his hunting buddies, to sign the warrants. Frost did an end run around us."

"Will you prosecute?"

"On the record, we need to review the evidence and determine if it's sufficient for a grand jury to indict him. Off the record, this is a bunch of cow manure."

"Will Gravy have to spend the night in jail?"

"Negative, we aren't asking for bond. He'll be free as soon as Frost's investigators are finished with him, and I've got an assistant attorney observing the interrogation to make sure Frost and Peck don't try anything." I paused to think for a moment. Spencer tapped the receiver: "Walker, you still there?"

"Yes, the notices were only filed a couple hours before Gravy's press conference. How'd Frost know some were suspicious and have time to get the warrants?"

"Good question. Judge Waller isn't returning my phone call."

"This is insane!"

"My thoughts exactly," agreed Spencer. "I can't say any more until we have delved into Frost's documentation."

On the six o'clock television news the reporter said, an official familiar with the investigation speaking on the condition of anonymity, had stated that the notices had discrepancies on whether the purported clients were actually in the county jail when it exploded. One alleged victim, who supposedly was a bus driver arrested on the eve of the event, was actually a dog. State Attorney Clark Spencer refused to comment on camera citing the ongoing investigation.

When I walked into The Elbow Room later that night, Gravy was sitting at the Godfather table drinking PBR. His charcoal gray suit jacket was gone, the collar of his wrinkled white shirt was open, and his sleeves rolled up, while he plotted his next moves on his ever-present legal pad.

"This is bullshit," he said as our tattooed, dreadlocked waitress poured my beer into a frosty glass. "They're asserting the notices were criminal acts."

"Was one of your clients a dog?" I asked. Someone had put quarters in the jukebox, and Elvis Presley's "A Little More Conversation" began to play.

"Hell, I don't know." He massaged his temples with both hands. "The notice is simply a requirement under Florida law that we notify the government we intend to sue them. The state will then investigate the claims and determine if they want to settle or go to court."

"But do you have a dog as a client?"

"Maybe." He took a sip. "Probably." And another one. "Listen, we had so many people calling into the office that my staff was overwhelmed. We didn't have time to run down every name, but it doesn't matter because we have months to sort through the documents and determine our best cases, before we actually file any lawsuits."

"What were the dog's injuries?"

"Erectile dysfunction." We both laughed.

Alphonse walked up and joined us. The jukebox switched to Patsy Cline's "Crazy."

"I'm glad to see you two have found humor in Mr. Graves' situation." The waitress brought him a Michelob Ultra with a glass of ice. Alphonse loved beer, but Jen had warned him that he couldn't afford to have an overly ambitious deputy pick him up for a DUI. The light beer over ice was the compromise they had reached.

"Walker was telling me the joke about the lawyer who got arrested at his big press conference," Gravy shared. The waitress brought him another beer. I guessed I was giving him a ride home.

Alphonse said, "The arrest was bullshit—a show to humiliate you and send a message to the rest of us that no one's safe."

Gravy nodded in agreement. "The state attorney's office isn't going to prosecute. The big question is how did Frost know so quickly that some of the names weren't real."

We drank our beers and listened to Patsy sing, "I'm crazy for trying and crazy for crying, and I'm crazy for loving you." As the jukebox began to switch to another song, I said to Gravy, "You were set up, man."

"They must've had operatives ask for representation over the phone and then looked for their phony names in the notices we filed today," replied Gravy.

"What's the impact of your arrest?"

"My biggest concern is what this'll do to my firm's reputation. Few people remember the follow-up to a major story." Gravy pointed to his pad. "My staff and every other law firm with jail explosion clients are double-checking their names and verifying the injuries, which will slow us down and delay more notices being filed."

He drank some of his beer. "My firm will have to fight to keep the clients we already have signed up. I expect our phones will be ringing steady tomorrow, and I've gotta have my staff ready to answer all the questions."

I tried to comfort him, "Mal will set up an interview to let you tell your side of the story."

Alphonse smiled, "Be sure she talks to the dog first."

"The *News Herald* beat us to the punch," I teased. "That's the sidebar to Gravy's arrest."

"Great," moaned Gravy. "I came here for support, not grief." He put his face in his hands. "We've got to fight to get back our computers and files. Shit, this'll tie us up for days. Hell, maybe weeks."

Alphonse wasn't going to let the attorney play the victim. "Dammit, you rushed the notices to put pressure on Frost and he outmaneuvered us."

Gravy lifted his face and objected, "We needed to get the notices sent to start the statute running under Florida law."

I finished my beer and shook off the waitress bringing me another. "What will you do now?"

"Gimme a couple weeks to get back our records, stem the loss of clients and sort through our case files," answered Gravy. "We'll file a civil rights lawsuit against Frost in federal court where he can't hide behind sovereign immunity."

As I ordered a pizza to help offset Gravy's alcohol intake, Jen McLean walked into the bar. She was dressed in what must have been her version of casual—a grey UF shirt over tight orange slacks, a white headband held back her raven-black hair. Once her eyes adjusted to the red lights, she spied us at the backend of the bar. Ignoring Gravy and me, she handed a printout to Alphonse. "We've got a problem. The black pastors were emailed this tonight."

He looked at it and passed the piece of paper to us. He was upset and his voice reflected it: "Frost and I agreed to run positive campaigns."

The paper had a picture of Alphonse and Jen kissing in what looked like the hallway of either an apartment building or hotel. The photograph was grainy, but it was clearly them. The caption read: "Black sheriff candidate sleeps with his married white campaign manager. Family values?" It told readers to check the website AlphonseAffair.com, which would go live in the morning.

Sitting down at the table next to Alphonse, Jen pounded the table once with her fist. "My personal life is no one's damn business. The bastards know that I'm separated from my husband and have filed for divorce."

"It's Pensacola," I countered. "Your personal lives are everybody's business, and you're naïve if you thought this wouldn't come out. How stupid can the two of you be?"

Gravy pulled back a little from the table to make room for the battle between Jen and me. I was upset with both her and Alphonse. "You're supposed to be the campaign guru, and you thought this wouldn't come out. Really? I'd be worried what other photos they have of you."

Jen glared back, but before she could tear into me, Alphonse put his hand up and spoke. "This is bullshit. Our personal lives aren't relevant to my campaign. We're consenting adults. She's married in name only."

Trying to defuse the tension, Gravy asked, "Have you checked out who owns the website?"

"They're clever," replied Jen. "They paid to keep ownership anonymous. It'll take a court order to undercover who's behind this. We know it's Frost, but proving it is another thing."

Alphonse put his arm around her shoulder, comforting her. "We'll get through this. We've nothing to be ashamed of."

I wouldn't let them off the hook so easily. This was bad—crippling "throw in the towel" bad. Even if Jen wasn't married, Escambia County voters still weren't fond of interracial romances, especially if one of the parties was running for office. "What were the two of you thinking? You may have handed the election to Frost."

"Lay off!" Alphonse pushed back. His muscles tensed. My words hit Jen hard, and her voice filled with emotion as she said to Alphonse, "I don't want to be the reason you lose this race. I dread seeing what's on that website."

Being an asshole, I refused to let up. "I assume the photograph is genuine."

Alphonse nodded. "We began dating quietly before Jen moved to Pensacola. We met a couple years ago when I was working in Tallahassee. When she separated from her husband, we reconnected during the Christmas holidays, and things got serious before the jail explosion. I just wanted to wait until after the election before we openly dated."

"So your story that Jen was loaned to your campaign by the governor was bullshit." I could see Del out of the corner of my eye. She wanted to check on us but had made a decision to stay out of the line of fire. "Jen was coming over here to work on the campaign no matter what."

Alphonse countered, "It wasn't that simple. Jen had been helping me behind the scenes for months. When the liaison role fell through, she saw the opportunity to convince the governor to help me in an official capacity."

I said, "Somehow Frost's campaign got wind of your relationship, probably because you two weren't as secretive as you thought back in Tallahassee. They must've been watching you for some time—either to discredit you or hurt the governor."

Just then, Alphonse's cellphone vibrated. He showed us the screen: "Frost." He got up and took the call outside of earshot of Linda Ronstadt's "You're No Good." Del came over to the table then and Jen ordered a glass of wine. We sat in silence, checking our phones.

When he came back, Alphonse was seething. "The sheriff wanted me to know that he's as upset about the email and website as I am. He said his investigators are trying to find the culprits. He reminded me of our pledge to not run dirty campaigns."

Jen blurted out, "Bullshit!"—which apparently was the word of the day for all us.

I agreed, "Frost wants you to know that he knows about this AlphonseAffairs.com."

Alphonse looked at me. "What do we do?"

Jen sat upright and threw back her shoulders. "We can figure this out without the help of someone in the media."

Alphonse defended me, "He's my friend."

Ignoring Jen's displeasure, I recommended, "Embrace your relationship. Don't shy away from it."

Gravy nodded in agreement. "When you can't disprove or discredit your opponent's argument, steal his thunder by admitting it and move to your strengths."

Jen nodded her head slowly. She was thinking of options.

I added, "Make your relationship public. Don't explain or defend it unless you're asked. Try to expedite the divorce."

"Will your ex be supportive of your new relationship?" asked Gravy.

Jen thought he would help. "Our careers took over our lives. Thomas took on several international clients and traveled weeks at a time, and I worked long hours in DC and Tallahassee. We grew out of love. There are a few assets that our attorneys have been wrestling over, but I'll concede on them so that we can finalize the divorce."

I pushed her to act quickly. "You need to call him, tonight if possible."

Gravy saw where I was going. "Give him all the details and ask if he'll help when reporters call."

Alphonse said to her, "Don't do anything you don't want to do. We can ride this out."

Jen reached out and held his hand. "No, they're right. Thomas will be positive, especially if he gets the Marco Island condo."

The pepperoni pizza was delivered to the table. Jen had downed her wine and ordered another glass. Another round of beers was delivered to the rest of us as Jen stepped outside to call her soon-to-be ex-husband.

"Frost has screwed with you two and Gravy," I said after Jen returned to the table and told us Thomas had agreed to help. "And Harden has stop answering my text messages. I'm worried."

"Bad news always comes in threes," Gravy pointed out as he reached for a pizza slice. "The next attack will be against you or Harden."

We talked strategy for an hour and how the couple could answer the inevitable questions. Alphonse and Jen made a list of black ministers he needed to call. Gravy and I offered to help, but the calls needed to come from Alphonse, not two white guys.

Alphonse, Jen and Gravy left together. Jen was renting a Sans Souci condo near Gravy's house on Pensacola Beach so I didn't have to drive my attorney out there after all. When I got back to the office, Tiny was asleep, snoring on the couch. I could hear the television upstairs and decided not to check in with them. Big Boy joined me on the air mattress.

My cellphone vibrated. It was a text from Jackie: "Gravy arrested. U next?"

I didn't reply.

When I had first met Jackie, we couldn't keep our hands off each other. Our courtship had been sensual and passionate, filled with laughter and fun. We married three months after our first date. The first year we were so in love that I would drive hours when I finished an assignment to be in bed with her. I couldn't bear the thought of sleeping without her in my arms.

I couldn't say when it first began to fall apart. Some of it was her jealousy of Dare and Rory's wealth, but that wasn't completely fair to Jackie. She wasn't as shallow and superficial as she sometimes appeared, but she didn't understand my drive to uncover corruption regardless of the personal risk. In our last year of marriage, she had started using her maiden name because she didn't like mentioning she was Mrs. Walker Holmes and have people turn their backs on her because of an article I had written. It wasn't until two years after our divorce that she called me drunk late one night, and finally shared what she had been keeping bottled up for so long. "A wife wants to feel needed," the alcohol slightly slurring the word "needed." "There's no room for anything or anyone in your life. I'm tired of the nights sitting alone with a dinner I've cooked for us, not knowing where you were or if I'd see you again. And you know what's worse—you don't even care what I'm going through."

I didn't know what to say so I didn't say anything. I didn't blame her. I owned the failure. Was I wiser and better at love since the divorce? If my breakup with Bree was any indication, I had to answer in the negative.

My phone vibrated again. The text read: "Your days are numbered—Lester Judson."

I replied, "No, yours are. You SOB."

18

The website AlphonseAffair.com was garish and looked like it had been designed by a drunk sixth-grader on a Commodore 64, but its content was brutal and gave the impression that it was the work of a private investigator, complete with video clips with date and time stamps showing Jen and Alphonse entering and leaving each other's places at a well-known condominium complex in Tallahassee, along with posts that gave more details about the encounters.

The site had a page entitled "Seventh Commandment." It was dedicated to Jen's marriage and showed a marriage certificate, wedding photos taken from Facebook and Bible verses about the sanctity of marriage. The "Two-faced Tyndall" page had photos of him speaking at various churches followed by more with Alphonse hugging young, white female volunteers and several others of him drinking at New York Nick's, Intermission and other bars.

The website went viral, drawing reporters from around the state to call the couple for quotes. They handled the inquiries with no miscues, and Jen's husband was very positive, wishing the couple well. Still, this was not a good news day for the campaign.

At the *Insider* staff meeting, Mal wanted to scrap the news stories and devote the space to Gravy and Alphonse. I didn't fight her because our credibility would be questioned if we were the only media outlet not reporting on their problems.

"We have to move quickly," she directed. "I'll call the printer and ask if we can move our print deadline to eight o'clock."

Teddy offered, "I can pull together photos for the cover. Any ideas about the headline?"

Wired on Starbucks' vanilla lattes, Jeremy jumped in, "How about 'Bombshells Rock City'?"

Mal leaned forward slightly in her chair at the head of the table. "I like how you're thinking, but with the jail blast still fresh in everyone's minds we might want to avoid explosions and bombs."

Pantoni spread her hands in front of her face as if unrolling a banner: "How about 'City Stunned' and we make the cover look like a grocery store tabloid."

I cringed inside, but it would be eye-catching. Teddy smiled, "I can work with that. Are you okay with it, Walker?"

"I'll admit it bothers me some because these are my friends being railroaded, but it'll get people to pick up the paper."

"We'll interview them and let them tell their story," Mal assured me. "We still have to include the known facts, but we can provide a balance to the narrative—which is all anyone can expect." She gave out assignments, set new deadlines and then adjourned the meeting. My policy had always been to never interfere with a news story while a reporter was working on it. I refused to talk to people at the center of those pieces to eliminate any impression that they could influence the article. This time Mal would have the final say to preserve our editorial integrity.

Frost's press conference never happened. The word we got was Spencer didn't intend to prosecute Gravy, but the official announcement was still a few days away. Frost didn't want to be embarrassed by Spencer's decision when it came out, but he really didn't care about the presser since he had gotten the arrest above the fold of the daily newspaper.

Mid-afternoon, the *News Herald* added another layer to Gravy's misery when it posted online that Barry Brown, owner of Sheriff Frost's favorite breakfast diner, Mama's Kitchen, had filed a Florida Bar complaint against him, saying that the attorney lied under oath in his notices. Brown asked The Florida Bar to impose "the harshest punishment."

On the evening news, a confident Tyndall was interviewed in front of his campaign office with a smiling McLean by his side. The *Insider* staff took a break to see how the local television station covered the story.

"I know some are wondering who might be behind this anonymous personal attack," Alphonse announced. "The sheriff assured me last night that his campaign was blindsided by this cowardly act, and he pledged his investigators would aggressively pursue the culprits."

Watching the broadcast with me, Mal smiled, "Good move on Tyndall's part, drawing attention to Frost without saying his campaign created the attack website."

We beat the deadline by nearly thirty minutes. Gravy's bogus arrest was the feature story using quotes from the state attorney and other legal experts that debunked the charges, which we predicted would be dropped especially since Frost had cancelled the press conference. The Florida Bar complaint was a sidebar.

We also covered the AlphonseAffair.com website. Mal had Jeremy couple his coverage of the website's sections with quotes from Alphonse, Jen, Thomas McLean and the campaign volunteers in the photos—a creative approach to the news story that our readers would appreciate.

While we worked, Tiny cooked spaghetti, another example of his ever-expanding role in our lives. As the last pages were being finalized, he yelled down the stairwell, "Supper will be ready in ten minutes. It's my momma's recipe."

At eight, we gathered around the kitchen island in the loft as Tiny put plates in front of us. The cat and Big Boy stayed on opposite ends of the room, ignoring each other. After wiping down the counter by the stove and rinsing the pots as he put them in the dishwasher, Tiny headed for the door and announced, "I'm volunteering at the community center. Be back by ten."

In unison we shouted, "Thanks."

Summer opened a bottle of red wine and poured her and Mal a glass. Teddy grabbed a Stella out of the refrigerator, and I continued to drink my bottle of water. Mal raised her glass in toast: "To the land of misfit toys."

The meal was delicious. We filled each other in on our various conversations over the past two days. Mal was concerned that my relationships with Gravy and Alphonse would interfere with our future coverage and took time to reinforce her position with me. "You must stay on the sidelines for this story. The *Insider* can't be about defending your friends from their blunders and miscues. Pantoni handles anything to do with Tyndall or Graves. Agreed?"

"For now," I replied, knowing that she was right. "I've got a few leads on the jail explosion. I'll focus on them."

"Like what?"

I told them about my record requests for documents related to the CBD's basement renovation, but I didn't share anything about the Klan, wanting to withhold that until I had more information because the idea seemed too unbelievable. "I'll post what I discover on the blog. With some luck, people will come forward, and we can pull it together into an in-depth cover story in a couple weeks."

Changing the subject, Summer pointed at my forearm, "When are your stitches coming out?"

"Tomorrow actually. Should've done it last week but things got hectic."

Mal picked up her plate and took it to the sink. "When are you going to tell us about how you were jumped in the alley?"

"I guess now. How'd you know?"

"Lum," she confided. "Also, my sister still works in the emergency room at Sacred Heart."

"I was so drunk I barely remember anything."

Mal smirked, "No surprise there, but who would want to mug you?"

I got up to stretch, no longer feeling like eating. The sun was setting, and I saw through the loft windows people were leaving the bars and heading home. A new crowd would take their place in a couple hours. "It wasn't a robbery. I'm sure it was Lester Judson."

"What makes you say that?" asked Teddy as he followed Mal's lead and took his plate to the sink.

"He texted me afterwards."

Summer beat the others to the obvious question. "Why didn't you go to the police?"

"I filed a report, but the investigation went nowhere. Judson used a burner phone that was untraceable."

Teddy moved next to Big Boy on the couch. "You're not superhuman, tough guy. You bleed."

Waving my left arm in the air, I answered, "I know, but I was too screwed up to face it."

"Hell yeah you were," chided Mal. "But we've moved on. Have you received any more text messages?"

I tossed her my phone so she and the others could read them. Concern showed on their faces as they scrolled down the screen. Upset, Mal scolded me: "I know you don't trust law enforcement, but you need to talk with someone and get this on record."

Teddy agreed with his wife and added, "We need to do something. The lighting in the alley is awful."

Summer offered, "I've got a friend who can install better lighting. He'll do it on trade."

"Maybe you also need to have someone with you when you go out," Mal suggested.

"I'm not having a babysitter." I folded my arms across my chest and glanced around the room to make eye contact with each of them. "I'm not giving in to threats."

Ted warned flatly, "But you're no good to us dead."

19

"**Walker, what the hell's going** on?" Dare asked when I answered my phone Saturday morning.

"At this moment, my shadow, Tiny, and I are walking Big Boy," I replied, passing the Barkley House as we strolled on Bayfront Parkway toward the Pensacola Bay Bridge.

"So it's true, you now have a bodyguard."

"I don't. He's the dog's."

Dare laughed but returned to her serious tone. "I'm going to repeat my question—what the hell is going on? You've been threatened. Jackie's now best buds with Frost, even talking about spending the summer on Pensacola Beach and working on his campaign."

"Do you have any coffee? I'm five minutes away. We can sit on your deck and talk. Tiny and Big Boy can continue their jaunt without me."

Of course Dare had coffee brewed. She always had a pot of coffee available. When I arrived at her home, she was dressed in workout clothes having finished her time with her personal trainer at Anytime Fitness. She had paid for a trainer to work with me too, but that only lasted two sessions because I didn't like to be told what to do and the trainer didn't like being cussed out.

Sinatra played in the house and could faintly be heard as we sat around her patio table out on the deck. We didn't speak much at first and savored the coffee instead. The morning sun gave everything a golden hue while a light breeze came off the bay.

"We talk about Jackie last," I said, wanting to set some boundaries for our conversation. "She takes up too much energy."

Dare nodded, waiting for me to begin. Showing her the long adhesive bandage on my left arm, I started, "I got the stitches removed and will have to wear this for a couple weeks to make sure the skin heals properly."

"That's an improvement over that awful gauze wrap you had before. You never told me what actually happened."

"Lester Judson jumped me in the alley behind the office and has been taunting me ever since."

She shook her head. "And you kept it to yourself. The invincible Walker Holmes."

"I wasn't thinking too clearly back then."

"Damn right you weren't."

I held the coffee under my nose enjoying its aroma. "I did file a police report on the taunts and agreed to call them if Judson came after me again. Until then, Tiny has taken it upon himself to look after me."

"Walker," Dare sighed with concern on her face and reached out to touch my arm. "Please stay safe. I don't want to lose you."

I put my hand over hers. "Yes, ma'am."

Dare looked out over Pensacola Bay, threw her head back, closed her eyes and absorbed the rays as if recharging. I took a couple sips of coffee, admiring the sight. Then sensing I was lingering too long with my admiration I interrupted her solitude, "Judson was the prisoner that Tim was taking to the CBD when it exploded. He somehow escaped in all the confusion."

"What?" she straightened up. "Why hasn't that been reported anywhere?"

"The message that Frost wants out is all prisoners have been accounted for. The police chief doesn't want to cross the sheriff, and the dispatch records have been deleted."

"Is Judson still in the area?"

I shrugged. Just then, we heard Big Boy's dog tags jiggling as he ran towards Dare's house. Tiny shouted his name a few times but stopped when he realized where the dog was going. Big Boy came around the side of the house to the deck dragging his leash and immediately jumped on Dare's lap. She nuzzled him and kissed his snout.

"Come on, boy." She got up and undid his leash. "I've got some treats for you in the kitchen."

Tiny followed, out of breath. "Sorry, Walker. That dog has a mind of his own."

"That he does, Tiny," I said smiling. Dare got Big Boy and his bodyguard settled in the kitchen. Back on the deck, it was Dare's turn to share her latest news. "We're still not getting our share of the repair work. Dammit, we're the largest road contractor in Northwest Florida."

"Sorry, I got sidetracked last week and haven't had time to check on the county contracts."

"Well, my brothers-in-law definitely blame you for the lack of business," Dare shared. "Plus, Commissioner Tatum is telling them over drinks at the Yacht Club that he can smooth things over if we contribute ten thousand dollars to his campaign."

"Slime ball."

"Yeah, but the Evans family has always played that game. Business is business."

I was tired of the game. "Has Frost asked for a contribution too?"

She shook her head. "He's too smart for that."

"I guess Tatum has also offered to help with the building inspectors."

"Of course."

"Can you string him out? Maybe give him a thousand dollars and see if he helps you with the inspectors. We can look into the repair contracts. A little pressure from the media might get the purchasing department to rethink its actions."

Dare was doubtful. "We don't have a lot of time. All the work will be under contract over the next three or four weeks."

She drank her coffee. I hated how Pensacola made people compromise, but I understood her predicament. Tiny's loud laughter at something he was watching on the television drifted from the kitchen. Dare brought up my least favorite subject: "What are we going to do about Jackie?"

I almost flinched at the sound of her name as if I had been pricked by a thorn, or as I liked to say thorned by a prick. "She believes Frost is helping her find out how her brother was killed, and all the sheriff's doing is trying to avoid a lawsuit and get at me. They make a beautiful, malevolent couple joined together by their hatred of me."

"Jackie doesn't hate you. She's just hurting."

I wasn't buying it. "Is she really going to stay here all summer and help Frost's campaign?"

"She's bought a condo and will be around for a while, but I can't imagine her working on anything, much less a political campaign."

"To get back at me, she will."

Dare promised, "I'll work on her."

"The last thing I need is Frost putting out flyers with my ex-wife in the photos."

"He already has. Jackie's hosting a fundraiser for him on Pensacola Beach next week."

"Perfect."

With that painful topic handled, Dare moved to the next item on her mind. "Walker, you've got bigger problems in that race. The affair website is the talk of the town. I can't go anywhere without hearing about Tyndall's love interest. It's hard enough to persuade Escambia County to elect a black man sheriff. A black candidate dating a married white woman may be too heavy of a lift."

I tried to defend my friend's relationship. "Jen McLean has been separated from her husband for nearly a year."

"It's the optics, not details," warned Dare.

"At least the election is over five months away. Plenty of time to change the narrative."

Dare wasn't satisfied, "He better do something quickly. Tyndall is losing votes in both the white and black communities. Add to that, his campaign manager is technically still married and support could become more problematic even among the most open-minded ministers."

I countered, "I told Alphonse and Jen to meet it head-on."

She smiled. "Thought that strategy came from you. It helped, but people aren't as tolerant in the voting booth as they are in public."

I nodded my agreement. We drank our coffee and felt the breeze off the bay. She opened the final round with: "How's Gravy doing since his arrest?"

"The state attorney will drop the bogus charges, but Spencer's waiting for the sheriff's office to finish its investigation, which Frost is dragging out. Meanwhile, Gravy's fighting to keep his clients and having to deal with a complaint filed with The Florida Bar."

"That takes another one of your chess pieces off the board. You need to be careful. Not many pawns separating you from the King."

I nodded and slowly smiled. "Being careful is never fun."

I collected Big Boy and Tiny, my motley crew that no one feared, and headed back to the *Insider* office. Tiny whistled Otis Redding's "The Dock of the Bay" as we walked west on Government Street. My cellphone vibrated. It was Harden: "We need to meet, and it needs to be somewhere discreet."

"A friend has a house on Jackson Street," I replied. "Mr. Reeves and his wife have gone fishing and asked if I would check on it. I'll text you the address." King Reeves and his wife had owned and run King's Bar-B-Q on the corner of Maxwell and North Palafox Streets for nearly forty years until they sold it in January. I loved that couple because they kept me anchored to the real Pensacola.

"My wife has gotten tired of cooking every day," Mr. Reeves had told me before he signed the sales contract. "I want to fish with my great grandchildren, and she wants to sell her pottery at arts and crafts festivals." The big, gray-haired black pitmaster wiped his brow. His grin showed off his dentures. "But we'll always have briskets, ribs and the fixings for barbecue pork sandwiches at the house."

I saw Harden's truck parked inconspicuously a few blocks from the Reeves' small, yellow brick house as I passed by a little before noon. I heated the shredded pork in the microwave and spread it over two large hamburger buns and topped the meat with Mrs. Reeves' homemade barbecue sauce and coleslaw. Jim found Lay's potato chips in the cupboard and poured Coke into two glasses filled with ice. We sat down at the kitchen table and took big bites of the sandwiches before we talked.

"Walker, I miss these sandwiches," Jim said. "The new owner's recipe isn't the same."

I nodded. My mouth was too full to speak. Jim moved quickly to why he wanted to meet. "I want to go after the Klan and expose its leadership because I think they're tied to this mess. I'm hearing they're making sure county contracts are funneled to their companies, not just recently but for years, maybe decades."

"Shit, can you get me proof?"

"That's my intent. While you analyze the paper trails to find any irregularities, I can try to work my way up their chain of command." He took a small bite of his sandwich followed by a sip of Coke.

I wiped sauce off my mouth with a paper towel. "It might explain why Dare's company hasn't gotten any flood repair contracts."

"Maybe."

I said, "If you can get me some names, I can match them to the contracts. However, the county has been slow to fulfill our public record requests."

Harden pulled out a small notepad. He wrote down a name and phone number, tore the sheet of paper from the pad and handed it to me. "Call her. She works in the county's facilities department."

"Won't her boss block her from giving me the records?"

Harden shook his head. "The head of facilities had a nervous breakdown after the explosion and has taken medical leave. Your record request is probably sitting on his desk. She'll take care of it."

Our plans hadn't been going too well lately, and I had a queasy feeling this one wasn't going to end any differently. "How do you plan to infiltrate the Klan?"

He grabbed the last few potato chips off my plate. "First, I'm going to let it be known I blame you for Jimmy's death." He put a big chip in his month and crunched down. "You didn't do enough to expose the gas leak before the blast. Did nothing to help me get the boy out of the jail and instead wanted to help your black friend Tyndall." He ate a couple more chips. "And I'm going to bring them dirt on you."

I pulled away from him and stilled myself. I definitely wasn't liking this plan. "Like what dirt?"

Harden grinned and tried to assure me, "Nothing, but I'll hint that I've got proof you've been stealing money from your partners."

"But I haven't," I protested, not liking the *Insider* or me being used as bait. "We've got an accountant reconciling the books monthly."

"They don't know that, but I can string them along until they agree to meet."

I folded my arms. "I don't like this. If it gets out, then it would hurt the newspaper."

Harden finished off the chips and took a swig of his drink. "They'll want proof before they go public, and I'll tell them that I will only hand it over to the leaders."

A dog started barking. Harden got up and looked out the kitchen window. Then he walked to the front of the house to check if anyone was outside. The dog stopped.

"Okay, I'm a little jumpy," he admitted as he sat back down. "I've heard these guys don't play around. Killing someone isn't beyond them."

"I don't like this," I said rubbing my jaw. "Why don't we just focus on the construction side of this?"

He shot back, "Because my nephew died. We expose them and tie their greed to the explosion, then we can really change this place."

I pushed back from the table and tried to dissuade him. "I've never known you to be a crusader. You're the one that usually talks me off the cliff."

"I know, but the blast and Tyndall's campaign have put these bastards on edge," Harden explained. "They want to shut you and Tyndall down, which makes them susceptible to mistakes."

He got up to rinse off his dish and grabbed my plate too. Getting a fresh paper towel, I wiped the table where I had spilled barbecue sauce. Harden put the plates into the dishwasher and turned to face me leaning his butt against the kitchen sink.

Seeing that I wasn't happy about his scheme, he changed the sub-ject to distract me. "Tatum's challenger is going to drop out of the race. He was shown a video of him and a young high school boy in bed and decided it was time to focus on his real estate business and family. Tatum will go back on the commission unopposed."

"Why's Tatum hitting up Dare and others for campaign con-tributions?"

"To give his campaign funds to Frost."

"Doesn't Tatum need to get the permission of his donors?"

Looking at me as if I were an idiot, he said, "Who's going to block the money going to the sheriff?" He found a spray bottle with disinfec-tant under the sink and wiped down the counters and table. "You really are a slob."

I didn't disagree. Harden sat down at the table. "The election fix is in, my friend."

"Then we need to upset their plans."

He nodded, "Agreed, which is why my plan is necessary. You go after the public records. That'll add a sense of urgency that you may be closing in on them and they'll get more antsy to stop you. Meanwhile, I'll put out some bait for Peck and see if he bites. I'll keep you in the loop, but we need to be careful that no one sees us together."

I stretched out my arms. "We can continue to use this house. The Reeves won't mind."

He asked, a cynical smile touching his lips, "How's it you collect these people who'll do almost anything for you?"

"The Reeves believe, like I do, that Pensacola can be a better place. They want to help me make it happen. After Hurricane Ivan, I had a radio show and mentioned King's Bar-B-Q several times to help them rebuild their business. If a customer or neighbor had an issue, Mr. Reeves would send them to me. We've helped quite a few people with-out fanfare…. And it was Mr. Reeves who recommended that Rachel Townsend and her parents come see me." The house got quiet. I stared at the blank kitchen wall, fighting off the feelings of failure on how I had let Rachel down.

Harden interrupted the moment, "While I try to infiltrate these assholes, you need to be careful."

"I'm always careful."

He laughed, "Sure you are."

20

On Monday, Alphonse dropped by the *Insider* to talk with Mal and Pantoni about his plans to get the county to spend more on the medical needs of inmates.

"The families have told me that their loved ones haven't seen any mental health counselors, and medical care is being discouraged by correctional officers," he said. "The sheriff has made any visit to a doctor so difficult that road camp prisoners are afraid to request medical care."

Mal asked, "How so?"

"Hurting inmates are taken out of their beds at two in the morning and transported to holding cells in the main jail, where they're isolated for hours, only to have a five-minute visit with a doctor who gives them Ibuprofen and sends them back to the road camp."

"Damn," I said. Unhappy that I had sat in on the interview, Mal gave me a harsh look, warning me to stay quiet.

Alphonse continued, "Guards have tormented prisoners. Many of them are suffering from PTSD. The guards walk around hitting things, then laugh when the inmates jump." He said he had been working with Movement for Progress to hold a march on the jail to protest the poor medical care. "It's on Saturday, June 16th and it'll be peaceful, but we need to make Sheriff Frost realize that we won't tolerate business as usual."

Mal added, with a half-smile, "And the march won't hurt your campaign either."

Offended by the remark, Alphonse responded, "Nothing will point out better that the county needs new leadership at the sheriff's office."

After Tyndall left, Mal said, "Pantoni, call the families that he gave you and work up a full story for the May 31st issue. With Memorial Day on Monday, we have a quick turnaround for that issue. If you finish it by this Thursday, Teddy could get a head start on laying it out."

Then she stood up and shouted to the staff, "Let's go ahead and have our staff meeting."

Everyone refilled their coffee cups and sat around the conference table. Tiny relaxed nearby on the couch, absentmindedly petting Big Boy while reading *Harry Potter and the Sorcerer's Stone*. I smiled at him as he silently mouthed the words he read.

Mal looked around the table, "Are we all set for the Memorial Day Weekend issue? Jeremy, we pulled you off the jail explosion coverage to work on the cover story. Do you need any more time?"

Jeremy shook his head. It was a story he had fought to do for the past couple years and was excited that Mal had finally pulled the trigger. "I did my final interview last night and will turn it in before three." He pulled a flash drive out of his shirt pocket and tossed it to Teddy. "Here are the photos I got from Roy and Hank."

For decades, Pensacola Beach had been the destination for gay tourists for the first three-day beach holiday of the year. Most recently lesbian, bisexual and transgender vacationers had joined the festivities. For a long time, the politicians and local media looked the other way and ignored what was happening. A few preachers had threatened to boycott the hotels and nightclubs that catered to the crowd, but their protests went nowhere because the money was too good.

This would be the first time we dedicated an entire issue to LGBTQ events. I privately worried about the impact on our advertising, but the team had been discussing it weeks before the jail explosion and Mal wanted to make a statement. Jeremy had found Roy and Hank Hiller, the couple who had founded the gay weekend. When law enforcement harassed the gay community during the sixties and seventies, the Hillers had established a post office box under the fictitious, nondescript name of Emma Jones to create a gateway for communications for the national gay community to connect with Pensacola.

Along with their friends, the Emma Jones Society held invitation-only parties on the Fourth of July on secluded parts of Pensacola Beach. Those parties eventually became a traditional weekend celebration before Memorial Day with concerts, dance parties, beach cookouts and plays.

Teddy smiled, "I'm going to use one of the early Fourth of July flyers for the cover. It's George Washington hugging Abraham Lincoln with the slogan 'Let's Get Together.'"

The staff looked at me to see if I was cringing, but I just smiled. "I was told when I started the *Insider* that if I didn't publish something that made me a little uneasy every week then I wasn't really an alt-weekly. This's the kind of shift in coverage we need after three weeks of floods, explosions and dirty politics."

We talked through the other articles for the issue and discussed the artwork for each. When the meeting concluded, Mal followed me to my desk. "How are the public records coming?"

"Slowly, but I've gotten some documents." I logged on to my Mac and pulled them up. "The emergency purchase orders resulting from the jail explosion have cost Escambia County almost four million dollars to date."

Mal whistled. "How much for healthcare?"

"Ninety-two thousand."

"That seems awfully low," she said. "Send the info to Pantoni. She can put it in her article."

Summer joined us. She was beaming and couldn't hold back her good news. "Dare's found a carriage house in North Hill that Mal, Ted and I can rent. It has two bedrooms and is furnished. The former tenants were Navy pilots that received orders and shipped out last weekend."

Mal smiled. "It'll be good to have a little more privacy and should hold us over until July or whenever the insurance company gets our townhouse repaired."

"My roommate has moved in with her boyfriend permanently, which leaves me unable to afford my apartment," shared Summer. "The carriage house will give me time to figure something out."

Tiny put down his book. "What about me? Do I have to move out too?"

I assured him, "Big fellow, you can relocate into the conference room, and I'll move back upstairs. Big Boy will love to have the loft back."

Summer, Mal, Ted and the cat whose name had remained still unspoken by me relocated to the North Hill carriage house over the weekend, and Tiny converted the conference room to his one-room apartment. Every time I tried to talk to him about the veterans' halfway house reopening, he would wander off and start cleaning the office or put a leash on Big Boy and go for a walk.

After two weeks, I forgot he was there. Tiny would follow me on my interviews and rounds about town. He wore khakis and button-down white shirts that Summer had bought him. He liked to drive the Jeep Cherokee with me in the passenger seat. I objected initially, but it gave me time to review emails and make phone calls. When I had an interview in a restaurant or bar, Tiny would find a seat in the corner and drink a cup of coffee. Pensacola got used to seeing him with me. I was sure there were jokes being told about my new partner, but never within my earshot.

On Saturday morning, I had breakfast with Gravy and Alphonse. Tiny sat at the counter by himself eating a fried egg sandwich. I had talked him into wearing a Crawfish Festival t-shirt and jeans so I wouldn't have to deal with teasing from my friends. He agreed, but with the condition that I let him take his white shirts and khakis to the cleaners to be washed, pressed and starched.

Gravy had already started eating his biscuit. Alphonse, whom Jen had placed on a diet, was drinking black coffee. I ordered two eggs scrambled with bacon and skipped the cheese grits and toast out of empathy for the candidate. It also messed with the waitress who was accustomed to me ordering an omelet. I filled them in on my investigation into the renovation of the CBD and how State Attorney Spencer had intervened to get the county to release within ten days all invoices, inspection reports and contracts regarding the project.

Spencer had also announced he had no grounds to prosecute Gravy regarding the notices, and Frost had returned the computers and files, but my friend was still struggling to keep his clients.

Gravy wanted to talk about something other than his law practice. "Have you talked to Harden lately?"

"I've gotten a few texts. He's working on some leads. When he wants to meet, he'll let me know."

"I see you still have your shadow," Alphonse teased, nodding toward Tiny. "How long will he be tagging along?"

"Yeah, I can't figure out how to cut him loose. The staff loves him and would commit mutiny if I kicked him out."

Gravy asked, "Are you paying him?"

I shook my head.

"Then maybe I need to talk to him about our state's employment laws."

We all laughed. Tiny turned our way, smiled, nodded and then returned to talking with the waitress while he ate his breakfast. The three of us chatted about the latest town gossip. After my order was delivered to the table, the conversation turned serious.

"The march is set for next Saturday," said Alphonse, as he stroked his mustache. "Tomorrow, the black pastors will ask their congregations to participate. The NAACP and Movement for Progress will join us. Television crews should be there too."

Gravy asked, "Remind me again, what are you protesting?"

"We are marching for medical care for those hurt in the blast and the overcrowded conditions for those still incarcerated."

"Won't people see it as a campaign stunt?" I asked as I motioned for the waitress to refill our cups. She also brought Gravy a Tab.

"This is a human rights issue. People want to see compassion mixed with law and order."

Gravy chimed in, "Besides, there's nothing wrong with holding the march to rally the churches around you."

Alphonse responded, "I'd do this march even if I wasn't running. We can't sit silently and let the sheriff's office return to business as usual."

Sipping his soda, Gravy said, "My firm will be there."

"I'll go to the early service at Antioch Missionary Baptist Church and listen to Pastor Bates," I offered. "Tiny has been begging me to go to his church so I'll write an article on Bates' sermon."

Alphonse liked the idea. "Good, Bates is a big supporter of the march."

"And the early service is guaranteed to last less than ninety minutes. Or at least that's what Tiny has promised."

The next morning, I dressed in my blazer and found a tie that took me three attempts to get the knot and length right. Tiny met me downstairs dressed in a suit that was a little tight but expensive looking. "Thank you for going to church with me, Walker."

Antioch Missionary Baptist Church was founded in 1886 when the First Baptist Church decided that blacks and whites should no longer worship together. John the Baptist Church was designated for black people on the east side of Pensacola. Antioch took care of the black families on the west side. Over the next century, several black Baptist churches spun off from Antioch, but it, and St. John Divine—the successor to John the Baptist—were considered the heart of the local civil rights movement.

Bates and I had shared many meals at H & O Cafe and Five Sisters Blues Cafe. When we had first met at New York Nick's, I knew he was wary of this white boy from Mississippi so I told him to watch me for a year and read our reporting before he passed judgment. When he organized a hundred-man march to support mentors for black male elementary students, I not only covered it but also walked with the group.

At the Sunday service, Pastor Bates stood before his congregation and asked them to get out their Bibles and find Luke 18:1-8. "Jesus wanted to show his followers that it was necessary for them to pray consistently and never quit. Our Lord told them about a judge that never gave God a thought and cared nothing for people and how a widow in that city kept after him shouting her rights had been violated."

He continued, "The judge never gave her the time of day. But after this went on and on, he said to himself, 'I care nothing what God thinks, even less what people think. But because this widow won't quit badgering me, I'd better do something and see that she gets justice—otherwise I'm going to end up beaten black-and-blue by her pounding.'"

The pastor read from the Bible, "And the Lord said, 'Listen to what the unjust judge says. And will not God bring about justice for his chosen ones, who cry out to him day and night? I tell you he will see that they get justice, and quickly.'"

He closed his Bible and held it high. "This is a rather simple parable. We have a judge who's accountable to no one as he dispenses justice. The protagonist of the parable is a widow whose rights were being violated. Why did Jesus use a widow? Because she had no standing, no access, no power and no one who would speak for her."

He walked down from the pulpit and stood in front of the first pew. His deep, baritone voice didn't need a microphone to be heard: "If Jesus told us this parable today, the protagonist might be a poor single mother or an unemployed young man with saggy britches or any number of other people who are seemingly powerless against an oppressive, impersonal system."

He began pacing while maintaining eye contact with his congregation. "The widow in Jesus' parable is a victim, and her avenue for justice is through this judge who doesn't respect God and is accountable to no one. Does the woman give up? No, she shuts down the court system. The widow badgers the corrupt judge until he cannot take it anymore. He finally gives her justice because she made his life miserable."

Pastor Bates compared the parable with how J. H. Jackson, president of the National Baptist Convention, had clashed with Dr. Martin Luther King Jr. over King's nonviolent protests. "Thank God Dr. King and his followers believed that their protests were cries to God and to the leaders of our nation to make justice for all a reality and not an empty promise. However, not all black ministers agreed. Even when they had sheriffs, lawmakers and governors open about their hatred of black people, some black clergy eschewed politics and protests."

When he climbed the steps of the pulpit and returned to his podium, Pastor Bates had the full attention of his congregation. "Today, we have black preachers in Escambia County that have discouraged protests after the explosions at the county jail. They are angrier about saggy pants than police brutality. They treat social justice like it's an elective."

A sprinkle of "Amens" and "Preach, preacher" came forth from the congregation as the pastor paused and wiped his brow. He raised his voice, "Social justice isn't an elective here at Antioch! We have a sheriff that believes he is accountable to no one! We must hold Sheriff Frost and all elected officials accountable and seek justice for those injured in that terrible explosion!"

Pastor Bates announced that next weekend the community would march on the county jail to let Sheriff Frost, the board of county commissioners and the whole world know the status quo was no longer acceptable. "I'll be there. We'll be peaceful. We'll be respectful. But we'll also be persistent and relentless." More "Amens." Louder this time, the pastor closed with "And God will hear our prayers and give us justice. Amen."

21

The following weekend, protesters gathered in a parking lot two blocks away from "The Tower," Sheriff Frost's administrative building. The CBD explosion had occurred about six weeks earlier, but many in the crowd felt like they had been dealing with the aftermath for ages.

Several black pastors had followed Pastor Bates' lead and encouraged their congregations to participate, and they were joined by young white college kids and old hippies, many carrying homemade signs on poster boards: "A change is coming!" "Frost Must Go!" "Lives over Politics!" and my favorites, "What's that smell?" and "Who left the gas on?"

The air was humid and heavy as Tyndall climbed onto the back of a red pickup truck and used a megaphone to address the crowd of about two hundred. "This is a peaceful demonstration. I know you're hurting. You want to lash out, but we can't give the sheriff any excuse to break up this march."

"Screw Frost!" a man yelled from the back of the throng. More than a few cheers followed his outburst.

"Brother, I know how you feel," responded Alphonse. "The explosion and how our friends and families have been treated since are not acceptable. That changes today. The sheriff's office didn't give us a permit so we must stay on the sidewalks. If you walk in the grass or in the street, you might get arrested. Deputies will be all along our route, watching our every step. As hard as it may be, please be respectful of law enforcement."

Pastor Bates climbed on the truck's bed waving away the megaphone, not needing any artificial enhancement. "Heavenly Father—the God of Abraham, Moses, the Apostles Peter and Paul, we stand before you asking for your forgiveness for not only ourselves but also for those who have wronged our friends and families."

Just as at Antioch, a murmur of "Amens" was heard as he continued. "The death and resurrection of your son Jesus showed us that we'd never again be prisoners of hatred and fear. We stand together today as a physical sign of our faith in you."

The "Amens" got louder. Several women jumped up and began waving their arms praising God. Holding up a worn, black Bible, the pastor prayed, "Lord, we walk together as one family to let the world know that we are heirs to your promise and can no longer be silent while our brothers and sisters suffer unjustly. Please, Heavenly Father, help us remember the words of Dr. Martin Luther King Jr.: 'Darkness cannot drive out darkness; only light can do that. Hate cannot drive out hate; only love can do that …. Our lives begin to end the day we become silent about things that matter. Free at last. Free at last. Thank God almighty we are free at last.'"

Led by Pastor Bates, who was followed by Alphonse and Jen holding hands, the crowd walked slowly west on Leonard Street to what was left of Central Booking. Near the front walked the choir from Greater Little Rock Baptist Church singing:

Well I'm on my way to heaven
We shall not be moved
On my way to heaven
We shall not be moved
Just like a tree that's standing by the water side
We shall not be moved

Deputies stood stoically along the route, occasionally telling the marchers to stay on the sidewalk, but otherwise, they were respectful. Big Boy, Tiny and I were in the middle of the somber crowd. When Pastor Bates signaled for the marchers to stop at the site of the deadly explosion, everyone bowed their heads, many kneeled, and a few made the sign of the cross, as I did. Behind me, a mother with a small child began to sob loudly. When we began walking again, the choir continued to sing. As we passed the jail, I noticed Peck standing under a tree along-side a deputy holding a video camera, and I waved as we passed them.

When the march finished, reporters gathered around Pastor Bates and Tyndall. The pastor spoke first, "We need to shine as much light on this problem and call attention to it so that the necessary changes can be made. We know we cannot stop death. That's not in anyone's hands but God's, but we should ask: could this have been different?"

Tyndall focused on the victims. "My heart hurts for these families. When I look at those killed and injured in the explosion, I remind myself that they have a mother, they have a father, they have a sister, they have a daughter or son. They deserve to have a full and open investigation. They deserve to have answers."

Pointing to people still milling around in the parking lot, Tyndall added, "We need to thank God that we can come together in a peaceful way, a professional way, because we're going to get this changed."

The TV crews got powerful images for their evening newscasts, probably picking up a few more votes for Alphonse. Frost exacted his vengeance on me three days later.

Tuesday afternoon, Tiny and I got off the elevator on the fifth floor of the SunTrust Building, one of only three downtown Pensacola's build-ings that had more than nine stories, and entered the reception area of the Chipley Development Group. Sitting on a couch were the chief dep-uty and my ex-wife. Folders stuffed with papers were stacked on the cof-fee table in front of them. Peck's biceps bulged out of the short-sleeved shirt of his dark green uniform, while Jackie sat relaxed in white slacks and a polo with a "Re-elect Frost" button shaped like a badge pinned on it. The pair stared at me and didn't say a word when we got off the elevator. I ignored them. Tiny acknowledged them both with a nod and sat in a big stuffed armchair at the end of the table near Jackie. Then he shut his eyes as if he was going to take a nap.

I had been summoned to a shareholders' meeting that I had been avoiding for six weeks, but my partners insisted I show up. I nodded to the receptionist and walked back to Jackson Chipley's conference room. Jackson "call me JC" Chipley was short and slightly overweight. At fifty-two, his well-trimmed beard had begun to turn gray, which made him look like an affable garden gnome.

JC had inherited the Chipley Development Group from his father. Papa Chipley had owned all the Western Sizzlin Steakhouses from Bay St. Louis to Jacksonville, and the chain thrived because Southerners loved eating steaks at cheap prices. JC worked in the restaurants as a roving manager when he graduated from Wharton Business School with an MBA in 1981. Then in early 1990, his dad died suddenly in his sleep and the popularity of Western Sizzlin began to wane. Seeing his revenues drop, JC began to sell off the locations and invested the proceeds into developing subdivisions and golf courses. Then, he began to liquidate those investments, sensing those markets were set to crash also.

JC had invested in the *Pensacola Insider* because he had a crush on Dare. He knew we were friends and wanted to impress her. It worked for a year or so, but Dare gradually tired of him. However, we stayed friendly, and he rarely gave me trouble because JC never expected to make any money on his investment with the newspaper and was happy as long as I didn't ask for any more cash. He also usually backed me in any disputes with Crutcher.

If there were ever any editorial problems, Reuben Crutcher, my other partner, would be the source of the conflict. A ginger with a weak chin that he tried to cover with whiskers that never grew into a beard, Crutcher was a forty-seven-year-old legacy boy that worked for his mother's bank until the year before when she sold it to a larger bank based in Atlanta. A condition of the sale was that Crutcher stay on as vice president for three years. The new owner gave him an office by the break room and no specific responsibilities, which left Crutcher free to spend his days playing golf at the Pensacola Country Club, bugging me, and trying to be a power broker in local politics.

When I entered the conference room, I found Sheriff Frost sitting smugly between Crutcher and Chipley on one side of the long table. He had on the table a blue folder that he strummed with his fingers while he chatted with my partners. I took the chair opposite Frost and smiled.

"Hello, sheriff. If you're here to ask me to sign your candidate petition, I'll pass."

JC wasn't amused, "This isn't a joke, Walker."

"You've crossed the line this time," injected Crutcher. "You put our newspaper and the money we invested in it in jeopardy."

"How's that, Reuben?"

Crutcher couldn't contain himself. "Your reporting on the Escambia County Sheriff's Office is biased. Your friendship with his opponent has clouded your judgment."

"What in the hell are you talking about? A jail exploded, people died, and we're trying to find out why. Standard reporting."

Crutcher looked at Frost. "Show him the photograph."

The sheriff gave me an evil grin, opened the folder and passed a black-and-white photograph toward me. The photo was of Tiny and I walking at the march with Big Boy in tow. In front of us were two attractive women holding protest signs. Crutcher asked, "What do you have to say about this photo?"

I took my time examining the photograph, then asked, "Could I have a copy? That may be the best one I've seen of my dog."

JC dove in. "You're participating in a protest against Sheriff Frost that was organized by his opponent."

"And the two girls walking with you were witnesses in the trumped-up bribery charges against the sheriff last October," added Crutcher. "The grand jury cleared him, and you're buddy-buddy with them."

"I didn't know who they were." I pulled the photo closer to my face. "I think my dog invited 'em."

Frost sneered, "Always a smart ass. You've got this vendetta against me that already cost me my brother's life." I remained silent. "You're lucky that I don't file a false light lawsuit against you and your newspaper. The only reason I don't is my respect for your partners."

Clever, I thought. For years, parties claimed they had the right to sue a newspaper if the publication published an article that wasn't technically false but was still misleading.

"There hasn't been any such thing as false light in Florida since our state supreme court issued its ruling in the Jews for Jesus case, declaring there was no such thing," I corrected him. Turning to my partners, I added, "If the sheriff has a problem with our reporting, he could try to claim defamation, but he's a public figure and the bar is set pretty high in those lawsuits."

"You can't afford the legal fees," said Crutcher.

"There are plenty of First Amendment foundations that would defend me pro bono," I replied as I picked up the photo again. It really was a good one of Big Boy. "Can I keep this? I'd love to send copies to my friends at *The New York Times*. This could make us famous."

Chipley snapped, "Your flippant attitude isn't helping. We told the sheriff that your reporting will be more objective, and that you wouldn't report on the march."

"You shouldn't promise something that you can't deliver." I folded my arms. "I've already turned in the story, and it's been sent to the printer."

That wasn't true. The pages wouldn't be sent until five, but they didn't know that. Crutcher shoved the phone on the conference table toward me and shot back, "Call right now and tell the printer that you're sending new pages."

Frost grinned. The meeting was unfolding as he wished. I stared at him and said nothing. Crutcher barked, "All it takes is two votes to remove you as editor and publisher."

Frost gestured as if about to stand, "Gentlemen, do you want me to step out of the room?"

I looked at the sheriff and then my partners. I kept my voice steady, but I didn't hide my anger. "No, you need to stay and hear this. You started this shit storm."

"No, this shit storm is your making," retorted Crutcher. His voice was getting shriller as he got more excited. "You think if we take this newspaper away from you that you can start another tomorrow."

"Damn right."

"We'll tie you up in lawsuits and ruin you!"

"I don't have a non-compete clause, and my staff doesn't either."

Trying to lower the temperature of the room, JC asked, "What has gotten into you, Walker? Is this worth you losing everything? Why do this?"

"A newly renovated jail exploded. People died. Hundreds were injured. It's our job to find—"

"Hell, you've already endorsed Alphonse Tyndall," Crutcher cut me off. "You're biased!"

I stared at the banker, and he pulled back as if I was about to jump him. I was tiring of this shit. "Newspapers endorse candidates. However, it doesn't change how we investigate."

"That all sounds nice," remarked Frost. "But you're doing whatever you can to get that black man in office."

I abruptly stood. "Sheriff, I'll make a deal with you. You quit covering up what happened and get the inmates the medical care they need, and I'll write positive things about you."

I walked toward the door and said over my shoulder, "Until then, you're on my shit list."

Tiny met me at the elevator, and we left. I didn't even glance to see Peck and Jackie's reactions.

"How'd your meeting go, Walker?" Tiny asked while we listened to the hum of the elevator as it returned us to the first floor.

"Not well."

As we walked outside in the late afternoon heat, thunderclouds rumbled in the distance. My phone rang with the usual "Help" ringtone: "Help, you know I need someone, help …" I tossed my keys to Tiny and told him to start the Jeep Cherokee and let the A/C run to cool it down. "… please help me." I stepped away to take the call from Gravy.

He began: "They found Harden. Someone has beaten him pretty bad. An ambulance is taking him to Sacred Heart."

"How serious?"

"My source is an EMT. She heard over the radio that he's unconscious. Can you meet me at the hospital?"

"Sure." In that moment I looked over to see Tiny leaning in with the key inserting it into the ignition to start the car. There was a flash, then a boom. I was blown off my feet and showered with broken glass. Merciful unconsciousness stole me away from the horror and pain. My last thought was *Tiny!*

22

Does a person have a quota for funerals he must attend? *If so, I must have met mine,* I thought as I dressed for Tiny's memorial service. For a man with few friends, my life had become a procession of wakes, rosaries, funerals and memorial services, or so it seemed.

The worst was Mari's. I sat on the front pew of St. Anthony of Padua Catholic Church looking at Mari's open casket in front of the altar where we were to be married, squeezed in between Grandma Gaudet and her twin sister Alice while they clutched my biceps and held crumpled tissues in their free hands as their bodies trembled with grief.

No one blamed me for Mari's death because I never shared that it could have been avoided if I had picked her up at the end of her shift. The extended Gaudet family tried to comfort each other and me, and I did my best to cooperate and ease the nearly overwhelming sorrow that enveloped Eunice. Deep down in the darkest corner of my soul, I knew my obsession with journalism caused their anguish and cost me the one person who truly loved me.

Every funeral since had brought back the memory of sitting in that pew. My arms would ache—muscle memory of how those two elderly women had grabbed them so tight that I had lost the circulation in my hands. Oftentimes after a funeral or memorial service, I would put Big Boy in the car and make the five-hour drive to Eunice to visit Mari's grave. The first time we made the trip I called ahead and visited Mari's parents and Grandma Gaudet but seeing how painful it was for them to see me, on our later sojourns I drove by their homes without stopping.

The bomb that had taken Tiny's life had also completely destroyed my Jeep Cherokee. The police had interviewed people in the SunTrust Building that witnessed a pickup truck pull into the parking lot and then saw a petite female in a tank top and low-cut jeans and a wiry older man approach the Jeep. The witnesses assumed it was a father trying to help his daughter get her car on the road. Since we never locked the Jeep, the man was able to pop the hood and spent several minutes pretending to work on the engine. After about fifteen minutes, the couple gave up and drove away in the truck.

"Was the bomb wired to the car's ignition?" I asked the police investigator who visited me the next day at the hospital. She shook her head, "That only happens in movies. The suspects didn't have the time to do that. Besides, those bombs aren't always effective."

She brushed back a soft wave of sandy blonde hair out of her eyes. "We suspect the bomb was magnetically attached to the car, underneath the driver's seat. Your friend triggered the detonator when he applied pressure to the gas pedal. Descriptions of the couple and vehicle have been released to the media."

The loft and office were lonely without Tiny. I missed his humming and the sound of him puttering around the place. Summer and Mal had planned the Sunday afternoon service, and thanks to Dare's influence, they got the city to approve having it in Ferdinand Plaza, a fitting place to honor the man who once called himself the "Mayor of Palafox" and had often counseled homeless veterans who gathered on the benches in the plaza.

Pastor Bates was to lead the service, and the Antioch Missionary Baptist Church choir would accompany him. Congressman Miller had arranged for a military color guard to be in attendance, and I was to give the eulogy.

Pantoni attempted to use her investigative skills to locate Tiny's family. He had grown up in Mississippi, joined the Army Reserve when he was twenty-two and served two tours in Iraq before losing his foot to an IED. Suffering from PTSD and addicted to pain pills after he was discharged, he wandered the Gulf Coast living on the streets until a buddy from his unit got him the counseling he needed. Tiny had been off booze and drugs for three years.

Having learned from the VA that Tiny's name was Titus Smith, Pantoni had traced his family to Moselle, a tiny community about fourteen miles from Hattiesburg. When she called the postmaster of the little post office there, she learned Tiny's parents had died in a trailer fire last year. There were no other Smiths left in Moselle.

I shaved while Big Boy laid outside the door of the bathroom. "I'm sad too, boy. Seems like death and disaster follow us." He lifted his head and put it back down. *Was he nodding in agreement?* I had *Al Green's Greatest Hits* playing, an album that Tiny loved, and tried to organize my thoughts.

Since the jail explosion, every plan I had made had fallen apart. Gravy was fighting for his professional survival while facing a Florida Bar investigation. Alphonse was valiantly campaigning for sheriff, but Frost had three times more money in his war chest. Harden was in a hospital bed in a coma as doctors tried to figure out how to fix him. Titus "Tiny" Smith's ashes were in an urn because the gentle giant who overcame his personal demons had died trying to protect a man who had refused to face his.

I gingerly put on my undershirt and white button-down. The blast had skidded me across the concrete, grinding away a layer skin off my shoulder blades. The doctors said it had scabbed over and was healing well, but it still stung like hell. I skipped wearing a tie and donned my blazer.

In the mirror, I examined the bruise that started as purple stain above my left eyebrow and sunk into the delicate flesh around my eye, then decided to put on a pair of Ray Bans to cover it. My face had a dozen or more little cuts from the flying glass that the nurses had painstakingly removed. There was little I could do to hide those.

Big Boy and I walked two blocks to Ferdinand Plaza listening to the choir singing "Amazing Grace" as we approached.

Mal and Summer had worked out a deal with a rental company to set up chairs under a huge white tent in exchange for advertising in the paper. The first few rows were filled with the *Insider* staff, his fellow veterans, and co-workers and friends from the Bodacious Brew and the Fricker Center. Dare and Taylor were on the fourth row with Alphonse, Jen and Gravy. Next to them was Bree, alone. The homeless gathered in the back, barely fitting under the tent.

I acknowledged my friends as I took off Big Boy's leash, and he ran to sit at Summer's feet while I went to join Pastor Bates who was seated beside a podium that was surrounded by floral arrangements. A nearby wooden table held Tiny's urn, a shadow box with his medals and a framed portrait of him in a slightly too tight gray pinstripe suit, red shirt, and black tie. The photo was the one Teddy had taken years earlier when Tiny visited our office and shared how he was injured in Iraq and struggled to fit back into society since returning stateside.

While the pastor read from the Bible and preached a sermon about Tiny going home to God, I pulled out scraps of paper from my sports coat and tried to make some sense of my notes. What do you say to honor someone who died because of your reporting? I hadn't found the words more than two decades ago when Mari was murdered. What made me think I could do it now?

Everything got quiet, and I realized the pastor had finished and was sitting down. My turn to speak had arrived. I walked up to the podium and put my notes back in my pocket, realizing they weren't any help. I looked over the gathering and saw the tear-filled faces of my friends. In the back, standing in the sun, I spied Jackie in sunglasses and a big hat, clutching a handkerchief. Maybe Dare was right, maybe my ex did have a heart. I looked down at the podium, cleared my throat, took off my sunglasses, lifted my head and began to speak.

"We have lost a hero and a friend. Tiny fought for freedom in a faraway land and left a piece of himself there. The Army awarded him a Bronze Star for his bravery and service, but Tiny didn't stop being a hero when he was discharged. Here he had to fight new enemies—PTSD, depression and drug addiction. He could've become another sad statistic, another military veteran suicide, but Tiny fought back."

I looked over the heads of the crowd, avoiding eye contact. "But his heroism didn't stop there. He gave of himself unselfishly to his fellow veterans trying to help them cope. He worked with children at the Fricker Center. And ... and he died protecting me. He never hurt anyone, he only tried to help people."

I blinked away my tears. "Tiny became my friend before I realized he was. One day he walked in and wanted to tell his life story. Then for the next two years whenever I walked down Palafox, he would greet me with a smile and a kind word. Occasionally, he would stop by the office with a news tip about something that he had heard on the street or offer to take Big Boy for a walk."

I talked about how Tiny had moved into the office after the April flood and stayed on after the staff had found new places to live. He wanted to look after me and called himself my bodyguard.

"For the past two months, Tiny has—had— been with me every day. Gravy joked, calling him my 'shadow.' Tiny didn't intrude, but rather was a calm, reassuring presence who laughed at my jokes and kept my temper in check. And the son of a gun worked himself into my heart so deeply that now there's just a big hole. I'm sure many of you have a similar emptiness. Wise people, like Pastor Bates, give us hope that the emptiness will one day be filled, and I'm grateful for that. But forgive me, pastor, I'm not ready to fill it just yet."

I paused and gathered myself. "Tiny was too kind, too giving and too gentle a soul to be forgotten so quickly. We all have our memories of him, our bits of conversations that we can still hear in our minds. Please share them with your friends. Keep his memory alive."

I looked to the sky, "Tiny, you'll be missed greatly and deeply."

Then I sat down, and Big Boy came and put his head in my lap. I stroked him as the choir sang the closing hymn:

Soon and very soon,
We are going to see the King,
Hallelujah, hallelujah,

We are going to see the King.
No more crying there,
We are going to see the King

I wept.

After the memorial service and thanking the dozens that came, I huddled with the staff under the tent. Though they were mourning the loss of Tiny, I saw the determination and fire in their eyes. They weren't walking away from this fight. I passed on joining them at New York Nick's and chose to have my first bourbon in weeks alone at Intermission.

I wasn't ready for company, or so I thought, until Bree walked into the bar and sat next to me. I didn't see her enter, but her perfume told me she was there before she took the stool next to me. I also noticed the bartender straighten and suck in his gut, a sure giveaway that a beautiful woman was in the room.

"I leave you alone and Pensacola implodes," she said in a husky voice, and with a hint of the playful smile I missed more than I'd ever let myself believe. She was dressed in a black sleeveless blouse with a high collar over white slacks. Her midnight-dark hair had been styled and feathered in layers a little past her shoulders. She was tanned, which made the colorful tattoos on her arms stand out even more. Bree had worn a light cover-up to hide them during the service, but now they were on full display.

"Explode is more like it. It's never good to leave me unattended," I replied as the bartender brought Bree a beer. I noticed that Asher wasn't with her and I had no intention of bringing him up. I raised my glass, "To Titus 'Tiny' Smith, may he rest in peace."

We touched our drinks.

"Good job at the service," she said.

We drank and looked ahead. Baseball was on the television, but the Dodgers weren't playing so I couldn't even pretend to care. Bree said, "I heard you had cut back on your drinking."

I shrugged, "Yeah, the world demanded a sober Walker Holmes."

She pulled my left arm toward her and examined the pink scar that run below the wrist to the elbow. Her touch sent a jolt through my nervous system. "I also heard you had been cut up pretty bad. I remember seeing the bandage when I picked up my stuff, but you were too drunk, and I was too angry to ask you about it. What happened?"

I told her about the attack and the subsequent threatening phone calls. She asked, "Is that why Tiny was with you? He was protecting you?"

I nodded and let down my stoic facade. "Bree, I feel so guilty, and I should've taken the threats more seriously. Tiny was with me to placate Mal and the staff and because it made him feel important. I never thought someone would try to kill me. Beat me up? Maybe. Murder? No."

She almost put her hand on my shoulder. Instead, she drank her beer slowly. She said rather wistfully, "You've never understood the risk you put yourself in. You never stop to think about it, which is one of the things I loved about you. But it reached a point where I couldn't tell if you were courageous or just had a death wish."

I shook my head slowly and sighed, "I don't know either."

We drank. She didn't face me but looked at my reflection in the mirror hanging behind the bar. "I check the *News Herald* and your paper and blog to keep up with what has been going on. Everyone close to you is struggling—Gravy, Alphonse and Dare. Read yesterday that Harden was in critical condition after being found nearly dead on some country road."

I let out a deep breath and looked at her. "It's like my secret identity has been exposed and my friends have suffered. The truth is even worse than what you've read."

This time she touched my hand, squeezed it and didn't pull back. "What are you going to do?"

Putting my left hand on top of hers I stared into her whiskey-brown eyes, "Fight." I let the word sit there for a few minutes, absorbing its power. She kissed my cheek, pulled away and motioned for the bartender to bring us another round. She winked and smiled, "That's the Walker Holmes I know."

"How long are you in Pensacola?"

Bree's smile got broader and a little more mischievous. "As long as it takes me to finish this beer. I've got to be at work first thing in the morning."

I suggested, "You can have dinner, stay the night, and head back before sunrise. Big Boy misses you."

She laughed, "Big Boy? You're going to seduce me using your dog?"

"He was talking about you this morning."

She threw her head back and grinned, "Sure he was."

"I'll sleep on the couch downstairs."

"Right, sure you will," she raised her beer to her lips.

"Bree, I let my work get to me and was an ass." She nodded in agreement. I added softly, "I miss you."

She straightened her back and took a serious tone. "Your work is to find Tiny's killer and turn this place around." She drank her beer. "Yes, you were an ass, and so was I. We don't need to rush back into bed, but we don't need to stay strangers either."

"I'm not sure I can handle us just being friends."

"Give it a try for a few weeks," Bree smiled. "You might like it."

I shook my head and tried to put my hormones in check. I wanted to hold her so badly and kiss her lips and neck. But, dammit, she was right. Bree could easily become collateral damage in this hell. I already had enough people in my life to protect, and I had been doing a pretty crappy job of that.

"Can I call or text you?"

"Of course, but go slow," she said. "I've just gotten out of a relationship."

I thought, *Bye Asher.*

Bree saw my smile. She warned, "Don't get any ideas. We've got a lot of things to work out. Please let's go back to being friends for a while."

"I was thinking about how happy Big Boy will be," I said innocently.

"You really are an ass," she said laughing.

"Thank you for coming today. It was great to see you."

"Walker, I missed your sorry ass too."

We continued to drink, and she filled me in on her career. The conversation was light, exactly what I needed. Bree was happy in New Orleans and had a good life there. She was too talented for Pensacola. One day, she might spend a night or two in my apartment, but her future was elsewhere.

Did I have to live in Pensacola forever? New Orleans was a writer's paradise where I could pen that novel every journalist thinks he has inside himself and become a famous author. Bree and I could be together, but first I had things to settle here, a fight from which I couldn't walk away. We finished our drinks and then she kissed me on the lips. But didn't linger afterwards too long, though her parting words did: "Take care of yourself Walker. The world needs assholes like you."

23

I had two ways of dealing with grief—returning to drink or returning to familiar routines. The next morning, I chose the latter and donned khaki shorts and a Dog House Deli t-shirt. Big Boy began to do his "happy dance" as I laced up my ancient Reeboks. He brought me his leash while I grabbed my Dodgers cap.

We walked in the early morning humidity, and Big Boy tugged me down Jefferson Street toward Pensacola Bay. I begged for a hint of a breeze as I tried to clear the cobwebs from my mind while the dog stretched his leash to the point of choking himself, pulling me south past Seville Quarter's parking lot where the morning crew was picking up beer bottles, plastic cups and cigarette butts. We passed two workers laughing at a red push-up bra they found under a bush.

Big Boy ignored them and jerked me towards the bay, forcing me into a run several times. I hadn't jogged in weeks and the tightness of the waistband on my shorts gave witness to my lack of fitness. The walk became a tug-of-war that evolved into a series of lurches punctuated by the dog stopping at irregular intervals to sniff a weed in the sidewalk or whiz on a tree.

Ferdinand Plaza had no evidence of Tiny's memorial service, except for a small cross made from scraps of wood with a program from the service hanging on it. Big Boy paused and sniffed the makeshift monument before pulling me across Main Street toward the bay. My shirt was soaked by the humidity and I was dripping sweat when my phone vibrated. The caller ID showed it was my ex-wife, and though tempted to let it go to voicemail, I knew it was time for me to confront life again.

"I've been a fool," Jackie blurted, skipping any formalities. "Wouldn't listen to you or Dare when you warned these people are dangerous. I thought it was more of your bullshit, trying to make yourself out as a hero, and Dare was sticking up for you like she always has."

"It's okay." I attempted to calm her down. I couldn't remember the last time anything close to an apology had come out of her mouth. "Pensacola seems simpler and more tranquil than it actually is."

Her temper flared, but not at me. "This fucking place killed my little brother, your bodyguard and almost you!"

I wanted to say Tiny was my friend, not my bodyguard, but I didn't want to fight with her because there were bigger battles ahead. Jackie continued as her cadence sped up with each sentence: "When I tried to talk to Sheriff Frost about it, he mumbled something about you playing with fire and seemed disappointed that you weren't killed in the explosion. I started to tell him how screwed up he was, and he had me escorted out of the building. Now he won't take my calls. Hell, I've given his campaign over twenty-five grand!"

Big Boy relieved himself on a weed in the sidewalk. "Frost and Peck are dangerous people with greedy, powerful friends. You need to be careful."

Her voice softened, "I want to help your friend, Tyndall. I'll donate to his campaign."

"Maybe you should sit this out."

She insisted, "The check is written and will go in the mail today." Again, I didn't argue with her because Alphonse needed the money. The phone went silent, and I didn't rush to fill the void. Jackie whispered, "Are you still there?"

"Yes."

"Is there a connection between my brother's death and the car explosion?"

I pondered her question. "Maybe, but I'm really not sure. I had a private investigator looking into the prisoner that Tim was booking into the CBD at the time of the explosion. The man isn't on any of the jail logs and appears to have escaped—"

"Sheriff Frost said all prisoners were accounted for," Jackie interrupted. *Old habits die hard*, I thought. She couldn't stop from interrupting me.

"Well, our sheriff has been known to stretch the truth." Big Boy and I started to move again. "I've got a lot of pieces to the puzzle but no idea how they fit together. When I do, I promise to tell you."

"What did your PI discover?"

"He's in a coma in ICU at Sacred Heart."

Jackie gasped. "Oh dear."

An idea hit me. "You've been around Frost and Peck. I need to know what you saw and heard, especially anything about the jail explosion."

She jumped on the opportunity. "I'll tell you everything, but I need some time to gather my thoughts."

"Let me send a reporter your way. You can unload to her with a recorder running. Don't hold anything back."

She agreed and hung up. The dog and I headed back to the loft. After I showered and dressed for the day, I turned on my computer for the first time since Tiny's death and read that the qualifying deadline for local candidates had passed, and as Harden had predicted, Monte Tatum's expected opponent dropped out of the race leaving the commissioner unopposed and automatically re-elected.

Frost and Tyndall were the only two to qualify for the sheriff's race and would face off in the general election on November 6th. I emailed Alphonse, "Reviewed the list of candidates that qualified. Your strategy of intimidating Frost to drop out of the race failed." Within two minutes, he replied, "Frost had to stay in the race. Couldn't figure out what to do with the two hundred grand in his campaign account."

The staff rolled in around nine. They had moved the big table back into the conference room and taken Tiny's clothes to his church for its clothing ministry. The room had been returned to its pre-flood condition, except for Tiny's urn, shadow box and portrait on a small table between the two windows. It would always be his room.

The staff seemed uncertain about how to approach me. Mal met the doubts head-on and began the staff meeting in her direct fashion: "Walker, a lot has happened since the incident last week."

She and the staff had agreed not to mention the Jeep explosion. For them, it would be referred to as the "incident." Mal continued, "Videos of the march have gone viral on the web."

She played a couple for me on her cellphone. The mounting public pressure had apparently gotten to Frost. Pantoni said, "The sheriff has hired Life Healthcare to provide more medical services, effective immediately. Mental health assessments will be expanded to cover inmates transferred to the road camp and to the Santa Rosa and Okaloosa jails."

Mal added, a cynical smile twisted her lips, "Mind you, this is after Chief Deputy Peck twice stood before the county commissioners and said that he had hired mental health counselors and an additional doctor. Obviously, that never happened."

Pantoni sat cross-legged in her chair and opened her laptop covered with a big Chicago Cub's decal and stickers from Murphy's Bleachers and Casey Moran's. "I called the county administrator at home. Tired of excuses, he has assigned an assistant county administrator to oversee what's happening in the jail."

She opened a file on the laptop. "Here's the money quote: 'I'm disappointed in how long this has taken on the medical and mental health sides. I want to have so many white coats in those facilities that they are tripping over themselves.'"

Leaning back, at ease and in control, Mal nodded, "That's our feature story this week. The secondary news story will be on the incident and Tiny. I'm writing that one."

I added, "I used my eulogy for a column about Tiny. It's in your inbox."

Jeremy shifted the discussion to coverage for the Fourth of July issue that would be published the following week, and he wasn't happy. Throwing up his hands, he complained, "When did I become the holiday writer? This is freelancer work."

Mal gave him the stare, and Jeremy shrank slightly in his chair and drank his triple espresso. She reminded him, "You wanted to take the next two weeks off. Our freelance budget will cover your sorry ass while you're out. Don't give me any lip."

Summer gave us a sales report, and Mal made photo assignments and set deadlines for the articles. The routine felt good. However, instead of adjourning when she finished, Mal and the rest of the staff looked at me. I sat back in my chair and glanced around, "What?"

Teddy put his elbows on the table. "Man, we know you. Things aren't going to ever be what they were, and you're not going to sit still. You'll find Tiny's killer and blow the investigation into the jail explosion wide open. We know you."

I nodded, absorbing his words. From the moment I had regained consciousness after the Jeep's explosion, I thought of little else than hunting down Judson and destroying Frost, Peck and whoever else was behind the blast.

Summer cleared her throat to get my attention. In a sweet voice, filled with empathy, she said, "We want you to know that you don't have to worry about the day-to-day."

Mal said, "You're free to go after those bastards." She waved her right arm to include Teddy, Summer, Pantoni and Jeremy. "We can handle the newspaper." Pantoni closed her laptop and added, "And we'll help in whatever way you need us."

Mal pulled together all the emotions in the room and tried to set some parameters. "All we ask is that you keep us in the loop. The killers are still out there. They may back off a little because of all the publicity, but you're going to step on some toes, and they'll react."

Their bodies were tense, they stared at me waiting for a reply. I drew forward and folded my arms on the table to match Teddy's pose, "Thank you." I rotated my head and looked in the eyes of all five of them. "I don't have a plan ... yet. Each one that I've made has either fallen apart or backfired horribly. Having the freedom to solely focus on the explosions will help, and I completely trust you with our newspaper."

They nodded with me when I said, "our newspaper."

"Tessie, send me your notes on the flood and jail explosion."

She smiled when I used her first name and asked, "Do you think the car bomb is tied to the jail and Frost?"

"I suspect it has more to do with Judson. The description of the man working on my car fits him, but I need to talk with Harden as soon as he regains consciousness." I got up and stretched my legs that ached from the morning run. "If the paper goes back to normal, our enemies may think that we're backing off while I'm recuperating. I can do my investigation under the radar for a couple weeks."

Mal smiled, "You'll be lucky if you get a week before Frost and Peck figure out what you're doing."

"You're right, but I can dream," I laughed. "Mal, I'll text you what I'm working on and my whereabouts. I may not make the staff meetings, but I'll give you updates as things develop."

"Promise that you'll be careful," begged Summer.

"Cross my heart." I made the sign of the cross like the nuns taught me in elementary school. "I'll stay out in the open and avoid dark alleys."

24

I moved my Mac into the conference room. Using a black marker, I divided the dry erase board into three headings—Pre-Explosion, Explosion and Post-Explosion.

Under pre-explosion, I listed the information I needed to research regarding the renovation of the CBD basement—contractor, subcontractors, contracts, design documents, change orders, invoices and permits. My public records request would supply those documents. I emailed Summer to check and see if the county had the records ready for her to retrieve.

I subdivided the explosion section into four segments to log what had happened in the six-hour block leading up to the blast. It would be a couple of days though before I got to the post-explosion section, however I already knew it would at least contain Gravy's arrest, the website attacking Tyndall, and the assault on Harden.

For the rest of the day, I pored over news articles and reviewed my and Pantoni's notes. I took two breaks to take Big Boy for a walk and check on my emails. Summer brought me a salad from Ever'man Cooperative Grocery when she delivered the county's documents, which I set aside while I created a timeline for the pre-explosion section.

Hearing Big Boy scratching at the door a little before six, I opened it to let him in the conference room. Everyone else had gone home and the setting sun shone through the windows facing Palafox Street, casting an orange glow on the empty office. Big Boy jumped on my lap, and we looked at the board together as I stroked his back. My brain was wasted.

"Big Boy, I know it doesn't look like much for my first day of investigating, but it's a start." I looked at my cellphone. It was 6:11 p.m. I noticed Dare had texted me an hour earlier: "Meet me for sushi."

I replied, "Is your sushi offer still up?"

Almost immediately: "Sure."

"Taylor given you a hall pass?"

"Shut up. Dharma@7."

Dharma Blue was a restaurant with a cool coastal vibe in the historic Smith House off Seville Square, only two blocks east of the *Insider* office. When I arrived, I found Dare wearing a floral dress that exposed her back and long, slender legs, sitting alone at the bar drinking a glass of Chardonnay and talking with the female bartender. As I sat down beside her, she said, "Walker, you've got to hear this ghost story. Their chef walked out today."

According to the bartender, the chef had been preparing food for the day with two assistants in the kitchen when he approached her. Visibly upset, he announced he couldn't take it anymore and quit. The bartender shared, "I went to the kitchen to find out what happened. The workers said they'd seen a pair of little hands on the edge of the prep table. Then they heard a child saying, 'I want my mommy.' The chef threw down his frying pan and walked out."

Dare had more to add to the ghost story. "Rory and his brothers used to talk about how the ghost of a child would appear on Alcaniz Street on hot summer nights. As the story went, in the 1930s a young boy wanted to go swimming one night in the bay, but his mother told him that it was too late and sent him to bed. Later that night, the six-year-old sneaked out after his parents had gone to bed and drowned in the bay while swimming alone."

She swirled the wine in her glass as she paused to build suspense. "According to the Evans, the little boy has been seen by visitors and locals often over the years around dusk. People walk up to the crying child and stop to try to comfort him. The little boy answers every time that he wants his mother. When they look around to see if the mother might be in Seville Square, the little boy is gone when they turn back to him."

The bartender shuddered as she poured me a glass of wine. She asked, "Why is it nearly every place in this historic district seems to have a ghost?"

"Bad parenting," I suggested, which earned a giggle from the bartender.

"Not funny," Dare scolded me, but she also smiled at my one-liner. The bartender left us, and Dare sat back in her chair and assessed the damage to my face. The shiner under my right eye had turned purple. The small cuts on my face were slightly less noticeable. "How are you?"

"Angry, determined, driven."

She shook her head slowly. "I know you. You'll drop everything and become obsessed with finding out what's going on. You'll drink too much, eat horribly and shut yourself off from me and your other friends."

Dare was right. *Could I do this any other way?* She changed the subject, "Jackie says she plans to leave town for a couple weeks. She said she apologized to you for her behavior, but she's worried you'll go off the deep end."

My ex-wife worried about me. Another first. I took a sip of the wine and rolled it around on my tongue before I swallowed. I looked past Dare at a beach painting on the teal-colored wall. A mother in a one-piece bathing suit was collecting seashells with her two young daughters, the wind blowing their hair into their faces and waves covering their feet. Dare tried to shake me out of my fog, a tinge of impatience in her voice, "Walker, are you going to say anything?"

I moved closer to her. "Thank you for caring."

"I worry about you," she whispered, gripping my hand. "I know you think you have this under control, but you don't. Let the state investigate this. There'll be plenty of time for you to report once they finish. No one would think less of you if you sat on the sidelines and healed. No one."

Dare leaned into me and our shoulders touched. With tears in her eyes, she turned to face me. "You aren't Superman. Tyndall can take care of his campaign. Gravy will fight Frost in court and salvage his practice. Spencer will take whatever the investigators find to a grand jury. Let them do their jobs."

I kissed her cheek, put my arm around her shoulder and hugged her. A glass shattered at the bar, ending the moment and pulling us apart. Dare straightened her dress, brushed away a tear, flung back her hair with a toss of her head and lifted her glass motioning for the bartender to refill it. "You aren't going to listen to me, are you?"

I couldn't take my eyes off her, but I also couldn't give in to her demand. I sighed, "I hear and understand what you're saying. For the next few weeks, I want people to believe that—"

"But you'll be investigating. They'll know that."

I ignored her objection. "That I am taking a break from the *Insider* because of my injuries. Meanwhile, I'll pore over all the information I can get my hands on and try to make sense of this mess."

Unconvinced, Dare pressed me. "How long do you think it'll be before Frost, Peck and whoever else that's gunning for you finds out?"

I finished my wine. "I can't worry about that, but I promise I'll be careful. Today, I spent the entire day working on a timeline for the day of the CBD explosion. I'm hoping patterns will emerge. They usually do."

She let out an exasperated huff and asked, " And no one else can do this?"

"Not like I do. This is what I do well. I owe it to Tiny, Tim Sturdevant and all those hurt."

Giving a single nod, Dare studied the wine in her glass while she pondered the situation. Then she lifted her head and made eye contact. "How can I help?"

I grabbed her hand. "Being my friend is a tremendous help. I'm sure I'll have a list of questions after I review the construction documents. I'll bounce them off you."

"Deal, but only if you promise to be careful." She squeezed and released my hand. Dare ordered a couple sushi rolls. As we ate, we talked about the statewide political races and the rumors she had heard. She also filled me in on the flood recovery efforts. With the help of the governor, she had cleared up most of her permit issues. She had decided not to make a contribution to Tatum's campaign, even if the paving company might have to pay the price for not greasing the county's wheels for a few contracts.

"What are you doing for a car?" Dare asked, as she paid the tab, then walked to her BMW.

"Gravy's got a client that owns a used car lot. The dealer has agreed to loan me a used Ford Bronco. It's nothing special, but the A/C works, and no one will know it's my car."

"Having a nondescript vehicle could come in handy," she shot a grin at him.

"I'm not putting any Ole Miss decals on it, that's for sure. It's a bland gray Bronco." I kissed Dare on the cheek when we came to her car and whispered in her ear, "I never said I was Superman. I'm Batman."

25

The next day, I texted Alphonse that I was taking a few days off. When I tried the same with Gravy, he wouldn't cooperate. He knew me too well. "You never take days off. You must've gotten your public records. Let me know what you find out. It might help us in our cases."

"You still have cases?"

He laughed, "Not as many as we had before Frost's stunt. People have short memories. Two months ago, they were thanking me for finding their loved ones and getting them medical care. Now they bitch I haven't done any work for them."

"Did our article help?"

Gravy couldn't hide the worry in his voice. "Some. Thanks."

I changed the subject: "How about my former cellmate, DeSean? Has he stayed with you?"

"My pro bono practice is booming," he chuckled. "He's going to be fine. We located video from the bar. The men jumped him so I think we can get the prosecutors to accept my client acted in self-defense."

"What's the latest on Harden?"

"He's still in a coma. I'll text if there's any change in his condition."

We hung up, and I began to examine the county records which their office had apparently and deliberately put in disheveled stacks. It took a pot of coffee and most of the morning to sort them in a way that made logical sense.

Two years ago, a torrential rain had flooded the CBD basement. Unlike the April storm, the rainfall occurred over several days, not twenty-four hours, and had dumped less water. I found an internal county

202 / **RICK OUTZEN**

facilities report that described how the basement had flooded then. A small amount of water had started seeping into the basement after a night of steady rain, according to the report. By noon the floors of the laundry, kitchen and records storage area were covered with six inches, and the water began rising steadily to three feet, then five feet, causing the basement wall to collapse, knocking out electrical, water and sewer systems, destroying vital records stored in the lower level and disabling the facility's kitchen, boilers and phone system. The report had no mention of any gas leaks.

The rebuild project had two elements—restoration of the laundry and kitchen in the CBD basement and installation of flood prevention measures to prevent flooding from recurring. I found no documents or emails that showed anyone had questioned the wisdom of putting gas dryers back in the basement. The construction documents were on two CDs so I emailed Dare and asked if she would loan me someone to help decipher them. She asked that I drop them by her offices.

Willis Construction had been awarded the rebuild project. My "pal" Tony Willis had signed the contract that included a huge incentive bonus to complete the work before the end of March—a quarter of a million dollars. The certificate of occupancy was dated March 28th, and Willis Construction received its final draw and the bonus check on April 6th. Why didn't the flood prevention measures work?

At four, I heard from Gravy, "We need to pick up your new set of wheels. I'll treat you to Jerry's Drive In after we get it." I gave him no argument since I had been so absorbed with my research that I had nothing but coffee all day.

By five-thirty, Gravy and I were sitting in a booth at the crowded diner in East Pensacola Heights eating bacon cheeseburgers, fries and onion rings. Gravy had a beer, while I drank a chocolate shake. While he chowed down on his burger, Gravy told me that the medical services at the jail had improved, but the care was still lacking. He had clients that had been released from the facility and needed medical care but had no means to pay for it, and the county had shown no interest in providing support for them. He agreed to send Pantoni the names of a few of his clients that were still hurting.

When I asked him about Harden, Gravy didn't have positive news. "Things aren't good. He's hooked up to just about every machine they have, and his brain waves are minimal. His sister told me that they may take him off life support."

"Damn."

Shifting in his seat, Gravy offered, "Maybe the Klan's responsible."

Four softball players in uniforms covered with red clay walked in the restaurant and sat in the booth behind Gravy. Keeping an eye on them, I lowered my voice. "Most likely. He was trying to infiltrate them and identify their leaders. Maybe we could visit his office with his sister's permission and look for any notes he might have."

"You haven't heard?" Gravy drained his beer and slumped his shoulders. "I guess it was while you were in the hospital. Harden's office was broken into and ransacked. His computer was stolen. Only Harden would know if any files were missing."

"Double Damn." I squeezed ketchup on the plate and dipped a couple fries in it. "Someone's worried about what Harden knew."

Gravy continued: "Harden's sister has asked me to check into who attacked Jim, but I have zero access to the sheriff's office since Peck had me arrested. Deputies may be more afraid of talking to me than to you, which is hard to believe."

"It just means I have to work harder to move back to the top of the sheriff's enemy list." I finished off my shake with a loud slurp. "The Klan and Peck are involved somehow."

Reaching for his wallet, he agreed, "But we need hard evidence, and all you have is a couple conversations with Harden."

I gathered my cellphone and car keys. "All I can do is pore over the documents I got from the county and start asking some questions. Maybe something will pop up." I grabbed a fry for the road as I began to slide out of the booth. "Whatever Jim found out upset someone enough to nearly beat him to death."

Gravy grimly looked up at me. "And based on the degree of the beating, Jim didn't give them what they wanted. Be careful, Walker."

As I drove the Bronco back to the office, Benny texted and asked if I would drop by the Backseat. Half a dozen well-worn cars and pickup trucks lined the strip club's parking lot when I pulled in. The bar was half-filled with construction workers, truck drivers and other blue-collar folks as happy hour ended. The second shift of dancers was lining up to take the stage that had a red, white and blue theme in preparation for the upcoming Fourth of July festivities. After all, the strippers were patriots.

The new dancers weren't the top moneymakers but weighed less and had better tattoos than the happy hour shift. A taco bar by the champagne room had only a few broken hard shells left along with nearly empty bowls of shredded cheese, ground beef and salsa. This wasn't a champagne room crowd, but Benny realized spicy tacos sold more beers.

The doorman told me Benny was in his office off the poolroom. Decked out in a powder blue tracksuit with several gold chains around his neck, the bar owner sat in his office that was slightly bigger than my loft's bathroom. He was huddled over a computer screen that had a series of windows opened, each monitoring the inside and outside of the club.

"Holmes, let me get you a beer. Want any tacos? We might have few in back," he said after we bumped fists. I agreed to the beer, passed on the food. Benny pointed to the window that showed my Bronco on the edge of his parking lot. "Why are you driving that piece of crap? I would've loaned you my Hummer."

"A friend of a friend offered it to me." I slumped in a tattered leather chair. "I'm traveling incognito for a few weeks while I look into things. What's up?"

Benny ran a white, monogramed handkerchief over his bald head while the air conditioning clattered and jangled struggling to keep the room cool. The tracksuit probably didn't help, but Benny had an image to maintain and the suit hid his gut, or so he thought.

"Last night, we had this redheaded cracker come in. He drank nothing but top-shelf bourbons and proceeded to get shit-faced. He was nasty to the girls, and the bouncers had to tell him to quiet down several times.

Monday nights are movie nights for my mom and aunt so my manager had to deal with it. When she cut off the peckerwood, the shit-head pulled up his shirt, pointed to a pistol in his waistband and said he'd decide when he'd stop drinking. She told the waitress to serve him a Jack Daniels on the house and then called the cops. Two cruisers were here in less than ten minutes, and the deputies escorted him off the premises without any more trouble."

"Ok, sounds like another fun night at the Backseat," I teased.

"Yeah, except the sheriff's office has no arrest report. I expected to hear from them this morning, asking me to supply witness statements and to press charges. When I didn't hear back, I called and was patched through to Peck."

There was a faint knock at the door, and a waitress brought me a beer. Benny paused until she left the room, then continued: "Peck said not to worry. The drunk was one of their own, not with them but worked for another agency. They'd take care of him. He asked that I forget about it."

"What did you say?"

"No problem," Benny shrugged his shoulders. "The last thing I need is a raid from law enforcement. Strip clubs are easy targets for sheriffs running for re-election." He turned to his computer and begin clicking on a series of video clips. "However, I did pull out last night's video. Does his guy look familiar?"

The black and white video was grainy. The man's face was in shadows for most of the clip until the deputies hauled him off. His face was clear when he was walked past the doorman. It was Lester Judson.

Pointing at the screen, I said with anger in my voice, "That's the man who killed Rachel Townsend and who the sheriff's office is supposed to be searching for. Son of a bitch."

"There's more." Benny sat back and folded his arms and rested them on his belly. "The waitress who served him last night wants to talk with you. She says she knows you." He pushed a button on an intercom and shouted, "Tell Catelyn to come to my office."

Fitting three people in Benny's office was difficult, but somehow we did it. Dressed in a white peasant top over tight blue jeans, Catelyn was nervous, but after encouragement from Benny, she confided: "He was one of the meanest people I've ever met, and I was worried he'd grab me and pull a knife on me. I asked Leo, the bouncer, to please watch me whenever I was at his table."

"How was he mean?"

"His language was nasty. I'm used to cuss words, but Benny has a strict rule about how the women here are spoken to." She pulled at her hair, trying to tame it, as she talked. "Several times, he called the dancers 'cunts' and 'whores' when they asked him to buy 'em drinks. Leo gave him several warnings. Ordinarily, we'd have kicked him out, but he was paying top dollar for his drinks and tipped well."

Benny injected, "It's the waitresses' call most of the time. They know best what they can handle."

Catelyn began rubbing her hands down her pant legs and rocked slightly. "The drunker he got, the more racist his language became, talking to himself mostly. A couple times he tried to engage a group of sailors at the table next to him, but they blew him off. He used the N-word a lot, which I ignored until I heard him mumble your name."

I sat upright. "My name? What did he say?"

"Something about you, Ole Miss and blowing you away." Her voice was shaky, and she trembled slightly. "I started to hang around his table more, but then he began talking about the Klan and cross burning. That's when I went to the manager, and she made the decision to cut him off. Then everything went from bad to worse."

"Catelyn, thank you." I gave her my most sincere smile. "Could you write down everything you remember? You don't have to use full sentences. Jot down impressions and the bits and pieces of what he said." She lowered her voice to a whisper, "I won't have to testify in court, will I? My parents, friends and employer don't know I work here."

I shook my head. "This'll only be used for background. We'll figure out other ways to corroborate what you've told me."

She tugged her blouse in place and half-smiled in relief. In an unsteady voice, she said, "I read about the car bomb and Tiny. He was always pleasant when I stopped by Bodacious Brew."

I agreed, "He'll be missed."

She asked, her eyes wide with fright, "Am I in danger?"

Benny fielded that question because he didn't want her to know that we knew the name of the douchebag or that anything unusual had happened with his arrest. "A guy like him won't remember anything about last night, and he won't be back. You're safe."

Peck didn't know that the strip club owner and I were friends and he would trust Benny to drop it. After Catelyn left to change into her waitress outfit, Benny handed me a DVD of Judson's visit, "Here's your copy. Peck might ask us to erase it so I wanted you to get it now."

"I need to identify the deputies that picked up Judson. Did your people recognize them?"

He shook his head. "They were focusing on getting the asshole away from the girls and our other customers. Maybe you can show their pictures to some of your other sources. I wouldn't recommend confronting Peck. Since he's been on steroids and become a muscle-bound freak, he's too unpredictable."

Back at the loft, I watched the Dodgers get shutout by the San Francisco Giants. My team was on a losing streak and barely holding on to a one-game lead in the NL West Division. Big Boy blamed me for it and slept in the living room.

26

After their morning staff meeting, I sat down with Mal and Pantoni to review the information on the dry erase board. The reporter added a few points to the pre-explosion column and more accurate times on the electricity, water and sewer outages and when inmates began to get sick.

"Why don't you let me work up the timeline for the aftermath, focusing on events that didn't involve you or your friends?" she volunteered. "Some of it might tie back to county documents. Besides, I've got some free time this week with Jeremy working on the Fourth of July stories."

"Sure, that'll free me to focus on Judson and the Klan."

"Klan?" Mal and Pantoni said together, almost spitting out their coffees. Mal didn't hide her disbelief. Her eyes narrowed as she searched my face: "We've got more than our share of racist bastards around here and maybe a few white supremacists in the woods at the north end of the county, but no robe-wearing, cross-burning Klansmen."

"That's what I thought until Harden told me about it, but now I believe him."

"Harden? Did the Klan put him in the ICU?" asked Pantoni, flicking her hair out of her eyes.

"Most likely." I drew a deep, audible breath. "I'm not going to go through all the weird titles they have for themselves. Harden believes Peck heads up an enforcement crew that deals with the Klan's enemies and any prodigal members. I'll send you a link to a *New York Times* article from the seventies describing a Klan meeting held in Warrington that was led by his grandfather."

Still not ready to accept the possibility of the Klan existing in Pensacola, Mal arched her right eyebrow and cocked her head. "And Peck tried to blow you up?"

"I think that was Lester Judson, based on the description of the man who put the bomb under my Jeep. He might have a connection to the Klan too."

I told them what Catelyn had shared about Judson at Benny's and how he mentioned Ole Miss, the Klan and blowing me away. I had downloaded the club's video from the DVD to my Mac and played it for them. Mal requested that I replay it and pause on the man being escorted out of the bar. She agreed it was Judson, "Damn."

"My thought exactly." I turned to face both of them. "The deputies never booked him. Peck told Benny not to worry about it because he was one of them."

Pantoni asked, "Do you think those deputies are some of Peck's enforcers?"

I shrugged. Mal kicked into editor mode, "I can have Teddy see if he can get us cleaner images of these goons that would help us identify them."

"Good idea." I handed her the DVD. She walked out of the conference room and came back a few minutes later with the coffee carafe and filled our mugs.

"Ted has it. Give him an hour or so to work his magic."

We drank our coffee and soaked in the moment. Pantoni asked, "When you going to confront Peck?"

"Not any time soon. I'll call the newspaper in Oxford this afternoon and maybe they'll give me access to their digital archives. They might have something on Judson."

As we broke up the meeting, Pantoni poked me, "I'm meeting with your ex-wife this afternoon to hear what she remembers about her conversations with Frost and Peck."

"I suggest you block out a couple hours. Jax's a talker. Keep her on topic."

She teased, "I can't wait to hear some Walker Holmes gossip."

"None of it's true."

She laughed, "Yeah, right."

At ten, I walked over to Jackson Tower to drop off the CDs with the construction documents. Dare was out, but one of her construction managers promised to review the plans and call me near the end of the day.

I called *The Oxford Eagle* after lunch. As a professional courtesy, the publisher set me up with a password that allowed me to review their archives. Judson's name popped up in three articles.

The oldest was dated August 10, 1987, my sophomore year at Ole Miss. It reported that Lester K. Judson was questioned about arson on the University of Mississippi campus. I remembered the incident but didn't get to cover it for the school newspaper because the seniors pulled rank on me. A fire destroyed the first black fraternity house at Ole Miss two weeks before the Phi Beta Sigma members were to move into their two-story antebellum-style house on Fraternity Row. Fortunately, the house was vacant. According to the article, Judson, who worked at a local hardware store, had mouthed off at several bars about keeping black students off Fraternity Row. He was questioned by police and released. The arson case was never solved.

An October 1997 article had a photo of Judson with shaggy red hair and a scruffy beard dressed in a Confederate uniform being escorted out of Vaught-Hemingway Stadium for bringing a Rebel flag to the football game versus the Alabama Crimson Tide. The flags had been used like pompoms by the fans for decades. Chancellor Robert Khayat had ordered a ban on all sticks at athletic events, starting with that game. He asserted it was for safety reasons, but no one was fooled. Khayat aimed to keep out the Confederate flags attached to those sticks. Judson defied the ban and was arrested.

The last article was about the 1998 trial concerning the murder of "Pizza Bob," the owner of the Pizza Shack. In the wee hours of a Sunday morning after closing the restaurant, Roberto "Pizza Bob" Hosea's car had broken down on Highway 30. As he began walking along the road to seek help, three men robbed and fatally beat him. Hours later, as the sun was rising, a jogger found his body. According to the article, the man considered to be the ringleader was convicted of first-degree murder due to a jailhouse tip from one Lester Judson, who had alleged the black man had bragged about the crime. Judson was released on parole for his cooperation.

I tried to find anything on why Judson was in the county jail. The newspaper's archives had nothing so I went to the Lafayette Circuit Clerk's website and searched the criminal case records. I learned two things: Judson had been convicted of stalking a college coed, which wasn't his first stalking arrest, and his middle name was "Krager."

Damn.

27

Dare texted for me to come by her office at four to discuss the construction documents. She asked that I bring any photos we had of the Central Booking and Detention facility.

We met in the Evans Timber & Land boardroom where Dare and her construction manager were standing over construction drawings. The construction manager, Red, wore scuffed cowboy boots, dirty jeans and a clean white polo shirt. He smelled of cigarettes.

"Walker, these engineering plans had several measures that should've kept the CBD basement from flooding as badly as it did," Dare said as I walked in the room.

"There sure as heck shouldn't have been more than a foot of water in the building, even without the pumps being installed," Red added. "I've circled areas that were designed with measures to protect against water intrusion into the building." He pointed to several spots on the master drawing. "These series of drains were to flow the water into the sewer system. Did you bring the photos?"

I handed him a flash drive on which I had downloaded the files. He plugged it into a laptop that projected the images onto a large screen on the wall, then scrolled through photos. He stopped on one taken near the sally port. "See, only one drain was put in and it's clogged with debris." He clicked past a few more photos. "The parking lot also was supposed to be regraded so it would slope toward the northeast corner, away from the basement. The contractor should've dug a deep pond with a weir on the eastern edge of the property. None of that was done."

Red showed us a photo of the parking taken after the previous flood. Dare saw exactly what I did, "The new parking lot doesn't look any different from the old one."

I asked, "Shouldn't the engineering firm have made sure its design was followed?"

Red shook his head. "The firm is out of Houston. They drew it, got paid and left it to the contractor and the county to make sure it was built correctly."

"Who should've caught it then?"

"The county inspections department," replied the construction manager, fighting off a cough. He shuffled through papers in a manila folder. "This person, RK, signed the CO—certificate of occupancy." He handed me the document. "Based on what I'm seeing, Sheriff Frost never should have been allowed to move into the basement without the flood mitigation work done."

Red left us. Dare and I looked through the photos and collected our thoughts. Dare said, "Corners were definitely cut." I nodded as I scanned the documents, "And people died, including Jackie's little brother."

"What are you going to do with this?"

"Publish it, but not until I have more pieces of the puzzle."

"Mmmm, Walker Holmes thinking strategically," Dare smiled, with a touch of mockery. "Don't think I've seen that before. My role has always been to keep you from running into burning buildings. Let's go to my office and share a drink."

In her office, she poured us Four Roses, no ice. Over her shoulder, Pensacola Bay was filled with sailboats racing. The Pensacola Yacht Club was hosting a regional summer regatta for junior sailors. I needed some information from Dare. "Tell me about Willis Construction."

She sat down in the chair beside me, her perfume lightly drifted in my direction. She watched the sailboats, then spoke without looking directly at me. "The Evans family never got along with Big Anthony Willis, the patriarch who started the company—there was some grudge dating back to when Willis moved to Pensacola from New Orleans after World War II." Dare paused, reflecting on her husband and savoring the bourbon. "Rory wasn't sure what it was, but he was raised to never trust anyone in the Willis family. Willis Construction wasn't allowed to bid on any Evans projects. They approached me after I took control of the family business and tried to get me to partner with them on some projects, claiming they had an inside track on government contracts."

She took a sip, remembering the conversation. She faced me, "Big Anthony Willis, the patriarch, acted so privileged and elitist. He was doing me—a widow—a favor. I should've been grateful."

"What did you do?"

She smiled with satisfaction, "I told him to get up, turn his sorry ass around and get out of my office."

"What about Tony Willis?"

"A sorry piece of dog crap. Little Tony is Anthony's grandson. His dad never had the heart to run the business, literally. He died of a massive coronary a while back, 2008 or 2009. Tony's listed as the CEO. However, the grandfather is still around and pulling the strings."

I got up. Sitting in that chair had brought back my never-ending aches. As I worked them out, I saw out in the bay that one of the small sailboats had capsized and the others were moving to help it. "Is Willis Construction successful?"

"They've done very well on the flood recovery business." Dare played with her pearls. "And they keep getting government contracts like the CBD basement repair. It doesn't seem to matter who's running the company." Dare moved to stand beside me at the window. As we watched the sailors rescue their mates, she put her arm around my waist. She asked, "How's your back?"

I turned to face her and so badly wanted to kiss her, but I didn't and walked back to my chair. "I'm fine. It's the black eye that's hurting my game."

Sitting back down, a sardonic smile flickered on her lips. "Your eye goes well with the other scars. You'll be fine." I laughed, "Chicks do love guys with scars." She joined me in laughing, "That's what I hear." Dare was beautiful when she laughed.

Emptying my glass, I got up again. "Thank you for your help and the drink. I need to find the county inspector, and soon I'll have some questions for Little Tony. That'll be fun."

"Be careful." Dare got up and kissed me lightly on the cheek. "I need you."

I paused to catch my breath. "Yes, ma'am."

When I walked out of Jackson Tower, my cellphone vibrated. Jackie was calling. "Hello," I answered as I went across Government Street and sat down by the fountain in Ferdinand Plaza. A man was sleeping on a bench opposite me. My ex opened with a light jab, "I met with your lesbian, punk reporter."

"Be nice, Pantoni isn't punk."

"I was nice." She emphasized the last word. "She was pleasant and asked good questions. I told her everything I could remember."

"Thank you." Damn it felt strange being civil with this woman.

"How do you get these young people to look up to you so much?" I was uncertain what to say so I ignored her statement. "Pantoni's a good reporter."

The phone went silent for several beats. She asked, "Are you okay?"

"I am. Still investigating, but I'm making progress."

She spoke softly, hesitantly, "Promise to fill me in on the details."

I had broken so many promises during our marriage. Yet, she was asking me to promise one more time. "Jackie, someone will pay for Tim's death. I'll give you all the information I have once I connect the dots. You have my promise."

"Thank you." She hung up.

Inside Intermission, Eva was holding court with a group of Navy aviators that were drooling over her tight, low-cut black tank top, especially when she leaned forward to hand them their beers. I sat down at the bar near the door, where I could watch the Dodgers lose another game. She pulled herself away from the pilots and brought me a beer.

"Long time no see, Mr. Reporter. Sorry to hear about Tiny. Let me look at your eye."

I tilted my head back. Eva looked me over: "I've seen worse."

"Me too." I couldn't help but laugh. "Do you have time to talk? Need your help on a story."

"Is it about Tiny's murder?" she whispered. I got to see what the aviators were so excited about when she bent toward me. I nodded and tried to keep my eyes focused on her forehead. Motioning toward the pilots, she confided, "They're about to settle their tab, and I've got another bartender coming on in fifteen minutes. We can talk at one of the tables in the back."

The Navy boys weren't as easy to get rid of as she had thought. They ordered several more Jäger shots before they finally left in a cab. When the new bartender arrived, Eva waved for me to join her near the pool table. She drank a Diet Coke while I still nursed my beer.

"In early May, the night of the jail explosion, I came in and three drunk rich boys tried to kick my ass. Do you remember that?" I asked.

She flashed a roguish smile and shook out her black curls with both hands as she pulled back her shoulders. "Someone kicking your ass. Hmmm. I need you to be more specific."

When I started to explain, she put her finger on my lips. "Just teasing, baby. Of course I remember. It was Tony Willis and his rat pack. They were hankering for a fight and you were an easy target."

"Is he a regular?"

"He comes in two or three times a week, usually late … after ten, before he leaves downtown. Most nights he hasn't had too much so when he gets here, he's pleasant, flirts some—little bit too 'touchy feely,' but nothing I can't handle. Always tips well."

"How's he been over the past month or so since the jail explosion? I imagined he'd be celebrating, considering the contracts Willis Construction has picked up."

Eva played with her bracelets while she thought about my question. I appreciated that she took time to answer. "The night you ran into them, they were celebrating. We were one of the few bars open. I figured they'd help close the place down until you walked in."

"I apologize if I cost you tips."

She gave a throaty laugh. "There're few things outside of sex and a piece of good Key lime pie that are better than watching how quickly you can get under someone's skin. When I danced, I could coax hundred dollar bills out of the tightest wallets in town, but you can light 'em up with just a phrase."

We touched our drinks and silently toasted our superpowers. Eva continued more seriously: "Tony and his boys came in a week later, and his mood was completely different—worried, almost depressed. I overheard him say several times that he was in deep shit, kept mentioning his grandfather and the jail explosion, but not in a coherent way."

"When was the last time he came in?"

"Last Thursday, he was celebrating something. Had two deputies drinking with him. They weren't in uniform, but I had no doubt they were cops. One of them asked me about my ex-husband."

Eva's ex-husband was a Pensacola Police Department sergeant who had left the force to work for ATF in Tallahassee. She continued, "They were doing shots and toasting Chief Deputy 'Peck' Krager, not Sheriff Frost, which I thought was strange."

I drank my beer and let that information sink in. I ate a handful of pretzels from the bowl in front of us. "Do people from the county inspection department hang around here after work?"

"All sorts of county employees start drifting in after four and are out of here by six," she answered, "which is before I come in."

She waved to the scarecrow-thin bartender, her chalk-white hair that stretched all the way down to her butt. She left her lone customer and came over to us, with another beer in hand for me. Eva asked about the county inspectors, and she said that several of them drink on Thursday afternoons.

I asked, "Do any of them have the initial RK?"

The girl bit her bottom lip and tilted her head down while she thought. She looked up after brief pause, "Robbie Krager."

"Any kin to Chief Deputy Krager?"

She shrugged her shoulders. Her customer waved for another beer, and she drifted back to the bar. Eva said, "I think Robbie is Peck's younger brother. You probably won't have trouble finding out for sure."

I really didn't want another beer so Eva drank it. I pulled out my wallet. "How much do I owe?"

"Three." I gave her a five.

"How's your friend, Gravy?" she asked. "Haven't seen him around since his arrest."

"Gravy's a fighter. The arrest was bogus, a political stunt by Frost. Want me to tell him you asked how he's doin?"

"Please."

"Why is it Gravy gets all the hot women and not me?"

Eva smiled, "Don't get me wrong. You're a handsome fella, but you're too haunted."

28

When she came into office the next morning, Pantoni couldn't wait to tell me about her interview with Jackie. "I've a hard time believing you two were ever married," she said shaking her head. "She's emotional, rambles all over the place. Whatever enters her mind she blurts out without any filter."

"Yeah, well, things happen when you're young and stupid."

She ignored my annoyance. "She still has a thing for you. Don't get me wrong. She hates you, but it's complicated."

"I agree it's complicated," I replied, trying to push her past my past. "What did you learn?"

"Frost and Peck fed her anger, told her stories about you that got her to open her checkbook. Totally manipulative."

"And she realizes it now?"

She nodded, "They pulled her in, promising to find out what happened to her brother and offered to destroy you."

I started a new pot of coffee, since it was my turn anyway. It was also my turn to get bagels, but Big Boy forgot to remind me so that one was his fault. "Did Jackie overhear anything that'll help us?"

She opened her laptop and reviewed her notes. "At one point, Peck and Frost got into a fight over someone. Frost said that Peck and his Mississippi redneck cousin would destroy everything that he had built over forty-plus years. Frost didn't need a race riot or the Feds breathing down his neck."

I went to sit down at my desk but had to go back to the coffeemaker because I forgot to turn it on. "How did Peck respond?"

"Not nearly as repentant as he should've, Jackie thought. Peck told the sheriff to mind his own business."

"Anything else?"

"Your ex thinks Frost has some health issues that he's hiding." She got up. "I'll clean up my notes and email them to you."

Harden's sister sent me a text at little before two. She wanted me to know that they were taking her brother off of life support. Would I come by the hospital? I drove directly to Sacred Heart Hospital and found Mrs. Low huddled with her husband Butch in the ICU waiting room. The Lows looked drained—physically, mentally and spiritually. I shook Butch's hand, hugged his wife and offered my condolences.

"James trusted you, Mr. Holmes." She cut me off when I tried to tell her to call me by first name. "Said you were helping him find out who killed my boy." She paused, losing her train of thought. "You know, Jimmy was named after him."

Butch started to choke up, pulled away from us and left the room. She watched him walk out and then turned to me. "James blames himself for what happened to our son. I tried to convince him otherwise, but no one could stop my brother when he was investigating someone. Kinda like you, I hear."

I didn't know what to say so I listened.

"The doctor told us he didn't know how much longer he'll last without the machines hooked up to him." I noticed she had scratched her left arm raw out of worry. She pulled down the sleeve of her cream-colored sweater to cover the marks when she saw that I had spotted them. "James is a fighter. I thought he might surprise them all." Then she fought back tears and sighed heavily. "But he's not coming back, is he?"

I shook my head. She reached into a huge canvas purse, pulled out a heavy, white envelope, the kind used to ship a book or several magazines, and handed it to me. "The last time I saw James, before he wound up here, he brought this to me. I was to give it to you if something happened to him. I should've given it to you earlier, but there was the explosion that killed your friend." She sobbed. "And I kept hoping my brother would recover."

"It's fine. Jim would understand."

Just then Butch walked back in. He didn't say a word, his face telling us everything, and his wife let go a heart-wrenching wail. Harden had passed. I left them consoling each other.

I should have driven back to the office and immediately dug into the documents Harden had left for me. I should have but didn't. Instead, I drank, not at places that I normally visited. No, I hit dive bars on the west side—places that were dark and smelled of bleach used by the cleaning crews when they mopped the floors in the morning. Each bar had only a handful of patrons, most smoking nearly as heavy as they were drinking, and the bartenders were all female whose ages ranged from forty-six to ninety-six.

At the Cutty Sark, I sat next to a used car salesman and his "date," a large, top-heavy washed-out girl with long frizzy hair. A red halter top barely contained her silicone breasts and cut-off jean shorts failed to cover her butt cheeks. The salesman told me that they had met on the internet, and he was in love. She drooled over his fat wallet and loved the double rums and Coke he was buying her.

I sought less chatty company and drove to The Flight Deck, where I didn't talk to anyone and simply focused on getting drunk until I noticed I was sitting next to an old man with an oxygen tank who was smoking cigarettes while he drank straight shots of Evan Williams. No one else seemed to care, but I left before he blew up the place.

I ended up at Tippy's Tavern, a house on Barrancas Avenue that had been converted into a Tiki bar, and drank bourbon and water, watched some talk show on ESPN and tried to escape everything. But the guilt and pain wouldn't dissolve like it had so many other times when I got wasted. Instead, I was getting angrier. *The hell with playing it safe, screw being strategic. I had to do something.*

Too drunk to drive, I asked the bartender to call a cab to take me to the office. When I was dropped off, I looked at my watch—5:24 p.m.—*a sign from God,* I thought. *I should walk down to Intermission to see if County Inspector Robbie Krager is having a beer with his buddies.*

The skinny bartender with the long, white hair saw me walk in. She picked a Bud Light out of the cooler and waved it at me. When I nodded, she brought it over with a smile. "Eva told me to expect you. She didn't know when, but bet it'd be before happy hour was over."

Returning the smile, I asked, "Is Robbie Krager here?"

"Over there," she pointed to a table by the Golden Tee game. "He's the fat slob with the dirty, blue work shirt and Auburn baseball cap. The other guy's also an inspector. You aren't going to cause any trouble, are you?"

"I'll buy them a round and maybe ask a few questions about county inspections." I took a long drink of the cold beer. "No big deal."

The bartender brought them a round of beers. When she told them that I had paid the tab, they looked in my direction, and I saluted them with my beer bottle and walked to their table. Robbie Krager looked a lot like his brother before Peck had started hitting the weight room, soft and doughy. He was still a lot like him though as both were not too bright.

"Thanks for the beers, mister." He was leery, and when I approached his unease went up another notch. Then another when I pulled up a chair and joined them.

I gave him my most sincere fake smile, "I want to thank you for all the hard work you've done since the flooding. You must've been swamped handling all the inspections, determining whether buildings and homes are okay, and permitting replacements."

The big man to Krager's right nodded, "We really could use four more inspectors, but the sorry commissioners won't approve 'em. They're worried about having money to house the prisoners until they build a new CBD."

I agreed, still smiling, "Yeah, the jail explosion really complicated everything."

The big man nodded. Krager's eyes hardened, "I didn't catch your name."

"Walker Holmes, publisher of the *Insider*."

Krager put down his beer. "Again thank you for the beers, but we're not supposed to talk with reporters. We'll have to ask you to leave."

I replied calmly, "I haven't asked any questions. We're just drinking beers."

"Robbie's asking you nice," barked the big man who clinched his fists and set them on the table, ready to jump out of his chair. I ignored him and stayed focused on Krager: "Why did you sign the CO for the CBD basement without the flood mitigation features completed?"

His cheeks reddened. "Leave."

"The plans called for the gas dryers to be bolted to the floor. Did you inspect them to be sure they were?"

He said louder, "Leave!"

His companion rose, grabbed me by my button-down white shirt and began to pull me out of my chair. Still looking at Krager, I asked, "How many died because of you?"

Krager leaped up and surprised me with a left uppercut. *Hell, I should've noticed he was left-handed.* The blow also shocked his partner, who let me go as my head popped back. I slumped to the floor and that all too familiar darkness embraced me again. When I regained consciousness, I was on a leather couch in the manager's office, alone. I had been out for about thirty minutes, which may have been due more to my alcohol consumption than the blow. *I used to be so much better at this.*

Eva walked into the office. "Well, I see you're alive. I was about to start my shift and they told me what happened. How do you feel?"

"My jaw feels swollen." I touched it lightly as I sat up. The minutest movement sent my nerves ablaze. The accumulation of my recent injuries had my body screaming from being such a dumbass. "I had several drinks before I came here so I've still got a buzz. But I have to admit I feel like shit."

Eva sat down in the manager's chair and pulled it up to the couch. She gave me worried smile, "Thought you'd given up heavy drinking."

"Jim Harden died this afternoon."

Eva sighed and shook her head. "What a shame. He helped me a couple of times."

"I didn't take it well to say the least." I tried to stand but my legs refused to cooperate. Eva eased me into a sitting position on the couch.

"I've got to tend bar," she apologized. "Thursday nights are busy, and the place's starting to fill up. I'll have the barback get you to your place. We can catch up later."

When I got to the loft, Big Boy greeted me, helped me get upstairs and watched over me until I fell asleep.

29

I woke with a hangover and shame, neither of which were unfamiliar bed partners. The booze I thought I had gotten under control, but I had to admit that I was only deceiving myself. A part of me hungered for smoke-filled, crappy bars, cheap liquor and faceless enablers. Harden's death gave me an excuse to embark on an inebriated reunion tour of west Pensacola, but if he hadn't died, I would have found another reason sooner or later.

Could I avoid sliding into another drunken, downward, weeks-long spiral? The stakes were high enough, but the path to oblivion was damn tempting. My sins begged not for absolution but pressed for my obliteration. As I began to sink into self-pity, I thought of Mari, my staff and my friends and recalled Rachel coming to my office begging for help, Harden in his hospital bed and Tiny's smile right before he turned the key in ignition.

I stood slowly, stretched my sore muscles and decided to deal with the guilt over my lack of self-control the same way I did with my grief. Big Boy and I took off on foot toward Tippy's Tavern, a four-mile trek from the *Insider* office, to get my car. I would tell the staff about Harden and the confrontation with Robbie Krager, but I didn't want the additional humiliation of explaining how drunk I got yesterday.

Unfortunately, I was busted by the downtown bar rumor mill. When I later came downstairs after my shower, I was marched into the conference room for an emergency staff meeting. Teddy worked a deejay gig at Seville Quarter and had heard about my scuffle with Robbie

Krager from one of the waitresses and Mal was ready to light into me for getting drunk until I told them that Harden was dead.

"I admit that really isn't an excuse, and I'll be more careful." I pointed to the package from Harden that was in the middle of the conference table. "I'm spending my morning going through whatever's in there."

Mal fumed, cutting me zero slack, "I can't believe you haven't already opened it. Getting drunk and having your ass kicked must've gotten in the way."

I deserved that comment. Teddy tried to take some of the pressure off the situation, "Tell us about the Intermission fight. We heard only one punch was thrown and it wasn't by you."

Also trying to release the tension in the room, Jeremy teased, "It must be hell to get old."

I didn't immediately tell them about the punch. I first walked them through my meeting with Dare and her construction manager, and how Willis Construction hadn't constructed the flood mitigation measures that were in the contract but had still gotten a certificate of occupancy. I then told them about two links to Chief Deputy "Peck" Krager: his cousin Lester Krager Judson, who had a history of violence against women, and his little brother, Robbie, who was the county inspector that signed the CO. Then I shared that Robbie Krager was also the one who knocked me out.

"I thought the plan was for you to work without drawing any attention from Frost or Peck," Teddy said.

Mal huffed, "That plan lasted all of four days."

"But they were four productive days," I said. "This isn't ideal, but we can't go backwards."

Summer asked, "How do we keep you alive? Boss, these people don't care who they hurt."

"The best protection is to be as visible as possible." I stood, walked over to the window and watched the heat rise off the asphalt. "We need to open the blog next Monday with something strong and follow it up with an article in the newspaper. Hopefully, the other media will pick up the story."

Mal protested, "Next week's a horrible time for something like that. The Fourth of July is Wednesday. We've got to get the issue to the printer on Monday."

Jeremy added, "And most of Pensacola is going to be focused on the holiday. You already said I could take two weeks off."

"Face it. No one's going to read a blockbuster news story next week," said Mal. "It's all patriotism, fireworks, hot dogs, hamburgers and watermelons."

I relented, "Okay, we'll keep this issue focused on the Fourth of July and shoot to break something big for the July 12th issue. No more screw ups on my part."

They left me to read through the material Harden had uncovered. Stapled together were 28 pages of "The Kloran of the White Knights of the Ku Klux Klan Realm of Mississippi," a manual that contained the Klan's creed, titles and rituals. The manual was dated April 20, 1998, a little more than fourteen years old, and numbered and assigned to the Pensacola chapter.

The packet had several grainy photos of a cross burning with people in white robes and hoods encircling the cross and holding torches and Rebel flags. Harden had written on the back of one photograph: "Farm outside of Jay. Photos of license plates on flash drive."

Jim had drawn an organizational chart. At the top was a bubble with "Exalted Cyclops & 4 Kaliffs" written in it. I looked up "Kaliff" in the Klan manual. That was the title given the officers under the Cyclops. He had the name "Anthony Willis" and four question marks outside of the bubble.

A solid line connected that bubble with another one beneath it with "Fury—Peck Krager" inside it. To the left was a bubble labeled "Wrecking Crew" and listed underneath were the names of three deputies. To the right was a dotted line to Sheriff Frost's bubble, which was surrounded by question marks.

Three solid lines descended from Peck's bubble to three squares. The first connected to the words "Prostitution" and "Lester Judson (cousin)," the second to "Land Deals" and "R. Krager (brother)" and the third went to "Investments" and "Reuben Crutcher." *Damn.*

Several names were written on the bottom of the chart. Only a few looked familiar. The rest of the contents included a flash drive, a datebook and a small notepad. Most of the notebook was in Jim's shorthand that only he understood. So I moved to the datebook and I looked up his entry from two weeks prior. The last item was "8p AW/KKK."

Anthony Willis may have been Harden's fatal appointment.

30

At the end of the workday, I met with Alphonse and Gravy at The Elbow Room. The jukebox blared The Clash's "London Calling." The crowd ignored the three of us as we sat at the Godfather table. Jimmy and Del kept an eye on the room for us. The people at the tables closest to us were regular customers that they trusted. If one of them left, Del placed a reserved sign on the table until more friends came in to occupy the space.

Del also loaded the jukebox with quarters to make sure it played continuously. The next song was Johnny Cash's "Hurt." The aroma of pizza in the oven wafted from the kitchen. Over the bar, "Star Trek: The Animated Series" was projected on a screen with no sound.

We had driven to the bar in the Bronco because it wasn't in my name yet so if a deputy trolled the parking lot and checked tags, he wouldn't know any of us were inside. Summer had taken Big Boy for the weekend, and I planned to sleep in the Reeves' home that was only four blocks away on Jackson Street. Jen would pick up the guys when we finished and take care of them. We weren't taking any chances.

I told Alphonse and Gravy what I had learned from the county documents and Harden's packet.

"Nothing to tie Frost to any of this?" Alphonse asked when I finished. "Surely Peck isn't operating without his approval. Maybe the sheriff is the Cyclops."

"Jim would've put his name by Willis's," I said.

Gravy sipped his beer. "Walker, you need to take this to the state attorney's office, FDLE or FBI. This is too big for you to handle on your own. Harden and Tiny are dead. You are at risk, especially since Peck's aware by now that you know about his brother."

Alphonse shook his head. He held the organizational chart under the light to better read it. "He can't. This guy's an assistant state attorney. That one's a prick and works for FDLE, and, dammit, this guy Smith is with the FBI. We don't know who to trust."

"Clark Spencer's honest," said Gravy. "He would—"

I interrupted: "Clark left town yesterday. He's fishing all next week somewhere in South Louisiana that doesn't have cell service."

Gravy pleaded, "Why not wait until ATF issues its report?"

"Because of what you said earlier. Peck knows I know something, but he's not sure what, which gives me a little time to pull this together and nail all of 'em before they harm anyone else."

Alphonse wasn't convinced I had a handle on it all. "You expect Peck to show restraint?"

"No, but these guys have a racket and are making tons of money. He doesn't want to shut it down unless he has to. With moles in all the local law enforcement agencies, Peck will bet he'll learn about what I'm doing."

Gravy rubbed his forehead as if he had a headache. "This is a dangerous game."

"I'm not asking you to be involved."

Gravy laughed softly. "Hell, I am involved." Alphonse agreed, "Ditto. What's your timetable for publishing your exposé?"

"Two weeks."

The pair shook their heads thinking I had lost my mind. While they drank their beers, I sipped on a Diet Coke—holding off the demons that had led to my impromptu pub crawl. Jackson Browne's "The Pretender" played on the jukebox, and a young couple took turns on the Dolly Parton pinball machine.

"Frost has got to be a part of this scheme." Alphonse put slices of pizza on Gravy's and my plates. "Our opposition research has found he has overseas bank accounts and several condos along the coast. Either he and his wife are two of the most successful real estate investors in North-west Florida or he has other sources of income."

Gravy wiped cheese off his chin and offered, "Maybe he got a kick-back on the CBD basement contract."

"Maybe," I said as I sprinkled red peppers on my pizza slice. "That'll be what I'll work on this weekend."

"What can we do to help?" asked Alphonse. "Other than find some-one in law enforcement we can trust."

"Keep your eyes and ears open," I said. "Both of you are in contact with hundreds of people every week. Call me if anything comes up."

"And you?" asked Gravy.

"I want it to look like business as usual, and that it was old, drunk Walker Holmes that confronted Peck's brother at Intermission."

Gravy got serious. "You can't go on another bender."

"I made a stupid mistake. No excuses, but Tiny's memorial service and Harden passing got to me."

We finished our meal, but before we left, we toasted Tiny and Harden. After Jen picked them up, I headed to the Reeves' home where I sat on the couch in the living room with the lights off and the blinds open so I could watch the traffic on Jackson Street. The noisy Tom Ann Buddy's Lounge crowd could be heard from a block away, and the street-light flickered and finally gave up, leaving the full moon as the sole light source. I felt there was something I was overlooking. A clue was staring me in the face, but I couldn't pull it out of my subconscious. Something little, but significant gnawed at my mind until I fell asleep on the couch.

Images of Mari flooded my dreams. Little vignettes—when I first interviewed her for an article; finding her crying at Rowan Oak after one of her clients committed suicide; hugging her after I met and won over her family; proposing to her at Lake Sardis; and seeing her body in the morgue. Most times when I had dreams of Mari, I could hear her voice, smell her hair and feel her skin. Not that night. I was watching a silent movie—

Pizza Shack matchbook.

I bolted awake. When Mari's body was found, the Oxford police first suspected I may have killed her, but they found red hairs under her nails. *The Oxford Eagle* articles proved that the red-headed Judson was in Oxford when we were enrolled at Ole Miss, and court records showed he had a history of stalking college coeds. Judson was a jailhouse witness in the trial that convicted the murderer of the Pizza Shack owner. Also, Rachel Townsend's mother had found a Pizza Shack matchbook in her bedroom. Since Rachel's murder, Judson had taken a sick interest in taunting me, attacking me in the alley behind my office and then trying to kill me with a car bomb. This was personal for him.

Lester Judson murdered Mari.

31

started running. I ran for miles toward downtown Pensacola, chasing the rising sun. I ran past the point when my lungs felt like they would burst. I ran with my legs screaming at me to stop. I ran to burn the rage inside myself. I ran because I didn't know what else to do. I ran to Dare's.

Dressed for her morning workout at the gym, she opened the door before I knocked. I was drenched in sweat and must have looked deranged.

"Damn, you scared the crap out of me. What's wrong?"

I took a step back, bent over and put my hands on my knees, trying to catch my breath so I could speak. Dare dropped her gym bag and put her hand on my back, hoping to comfort me. "Lester ... Lester Judson killed Mari," I said as I struggled to breathe. I backed away from her front porch and threw up into the nearby bushes.

"Come in. Let's clean you up and talk, baby."

I peeled off my shirt, washed my face and toweled off in the downstairs bathroom. Finding some mouthwash in the cabinet under the sink, I rinsed out my mouth. Dare tossed me a New Orleans Jazz Fest t-shirt. I didn't ask whose shirt it was. We sat at the island in the kitchen, and Dare poured me a cup of coffee.

Wanting to settle me down, she took a measured approach. "How's Lester Judson linked in any way to Mari?" Her voice was laced with concern. She wore no makeup, except a little lipstick. There were a few slight wrinkles around her eyes, but I still saw the Memphis girl I first met at the fraternity swap. Slowly, over several cups of coffee, I walked Dare through my deductions. Several times she stopped me to ask a question for clarification. Tears were running down my cheeks by the time I finished. Dare was crying too.

We held each other tightly. She and I had so many shared experiences so many happy times, but death had bound us—the deaths of Mari and Rory. They had also kept us apart, but not that morning. I needed her love and warmth. At last, she said, "Let's go into the living room."

We held each other on her couch and watched the sun complete its ascent above Pensacola Bay. She put her head on my chest, and neither of us said anything as the minutes passed. When she finally spoke, her voice was hesitant, "What are you going to do? I believe you, but the facts are circumstantial."

I filled her in on Peck and the Klan connections with law enforcement agencies. "Peck's the nexus for the jail explosion, car bomb and Harden's death. Arrest him, and Judson will soon be in the cell next to him. Judson has such an ego that he may even confess to Mari's murder."

Dare squeezed my hand tightly. "You're dealing with murderers. You can't do this alone."

"We don't know who to trust. Publishing the story is the best protection. I just need to stay safe while I finish the reporting."

In a voice that was slightly unsteady and uncertain about how I would reply, Dare offered, "You can stay here." I thought how many times I wanted to hear those four words, but I shook my head, "No need to pull you into this. I have a safe house. I'll be fine."

She began to tear up again. "I can't lose you." I pulled her toward me and kissed her cheek. "You won't."

"Promise me." Dare got up to find a tissue and regain her composure. She came back and sat down in a chair opposite the couch, putting her legs under her. Her wall was back up. "You didn't mention Frost in your narrative. What's his role?"

"Not sure, but little happens in this county without his knowledge. I've got a week to find out."

"A cornered Peck could be more dangerous than Judson," Dare warned.

"Agreed. But he doesn't really know how much I know and doesn't want to hurt his boss's reelection. I'm counting on Frost to keep Peck in check."

Dare shook her head slowly, absorbing my words. "Remember your promise. I'll kick your ass if you get yourself killed." My reply was two words that I had been saying to her for over two decades, "Yes, ma'am."

As I began the long walk back to the Jackson Street house, my phone vibrated. It was Eva from Intermission. With an excited catch in her throat, she said, "I've somebody at the county who wants to meet with you. He wants to stay anonymous because he could lose his job."

"Do you trust him?"

"Trust is a pretty heavy word. Let's say I believe he wants to help. He saw you and Krager get into it at the bar and wants to talk."

"It'll need to be somewhere in the open. How about Nick's at two? Hardly anybody will be in there." Eva agreed to pass the information along. She texted me after I took my shower to say the meeting was set, and that he would bring his county badge for identification.

A nervous, mousy guy in a green J. C. Penney crewneck shirt, shapeless no-name brand jeans, and a comb-over that didn't come close to covering his pale scalp walked into Nick's five minutes after two. I had seen him stroll past the bar twice before he mounted the courage to enter the place.

The name badge he handed me identified him as Milton Blatt. He ordered a sweet tea while I had my Bud Light and a glass of water. After I promised him that I wouldn't print his name, Blatt opened up: "I handle the paperwork for the inspections office, making sure reports are properly loaded into the computer system. The CO for the CBD basement should never have been signed." He kept his head down, rotating his plastic glass in his small hands while avoiding eye contact. "They shouldn't have been allowed to move back into the basement without the flood mitigation work being done. Robbie knew it but said he was being pressured to sign."

"Who pressured him?"

"The chief deputy and the contractor. Both of them came to Robbie's office and got into a big row behind a closed door. A lot of yelling, cussing and screaming. When it was over, they had a signed CO."

"And it was Chief Deputy Krager and Tony Willis?" I asked.

He shook his head quickly three times. "No, not Little Tony, it was the grandfather, Anthony Willis, and Peck."

"Did you talk with Robbie about the CO?"

Blatt lowered his voice, "He said that the CBD and jail were overcrowded, and the project was behind schedule. Willis would lose a quarter of a million dollars if the basement wasn't ready before the end of March. According to Robbie, the sheriff was okay with the flooding prevention stuff being put off because he didn't want to put in a change order during an election year. Sheriff Frost would ask for that extra money in next year's budget."

I said, "And Willis got his bonus for hitting the deadline and would get the new contract for the flood mitigation work after the start of the new fiscal year. Not bad."

"It's worse," he said, after looking around the room to be sure no one was listening. Yes's "Roundabout" was playing at the standard New York Nick's high volume. "Robbie didn't do a final inspection. He never went to check to see if the dryers in the laundry were properly installed. It's pretty obvious that they weren't. I hear there's video of the laundry that shows the dryers floating before the explosion."

"Who has the video?"

"ATF does. The sheriff's office tried to keep it from them, but ATF confiscated all the video equipment immediately."

"How can I get a copy?"

"Don't know. Above my pay grade. Robbie is scared to death of the ATF report. I caught him going behind my back and changing entries in the inspection log to show he made all the necessary inspections, even though he hardly ever went to the site."

I sipped my beer. "Is there any way I can prove that?"

Blatt pulled out of his back pocket two folded pieces of paper. "Here's the inspection log that I printed out the morning after the explosion. You can see the log has date stamps. There is only one inspection entry. The second log is one I printed out yesterday."

I compared the two. Robbie Krager had been a busy boy. Before I could say anything, Blatt said, "I've got twenty years vested in the state retirement system. None of this can come back on me."

I grabbed his forearm, "You've done the right thing, Mr. Blatt. These logs are damning. You know, if you were to come forward as a whistleblower, you might be rewarded for reporting this."

Blatt lost all of his coloring and for the first time he made eye contact. He shook off my grip on his arm, and his hands began to shake. "No, definitely not. These people would make sure I never collected a penny. I have to stay anonymous. Eva promised that you'd understand. I've risked my life even talking to you."

I sat upright, holding out my palms, and calmly said, "Just a suggestion. Your identity's safe with me. These two logs are enough to show foul play." I knew that the Kragers would probably figure out how I got the documents, but I would deal with that later.

After he left, Nick brought over Orange Crush shots, a sweet mix of "shit on the shelf" shaken up to be the exact color of Syracuse Orange. As he pulled up a chair, he asked, "Did it go well?"

"Very."

He smacked his lips and raised his chin. We tapped our glasses, "To whistleblowers," and downed our shots.

32

My intention for the rest of the weekend was to sleep and in-between naps to outline my story for the July 12th issue, listing the outstanding questions and the interviews needed to answer them—while avoiding getting killed.

Did I have a death wish? Maybe. After Mari was killed, I didn't care if I lived or not, but I did want my days to mean something and to prove that I made a difference. I didn't seek death, but oddly I wasn't afraid of it.

My weekend retreat lasted until early Sunday morning when I was awakened by my phone. Jen McLean shouted, "Are you out of your freaking mind? You're taking these monsters on your own! Walker Holmes versus the goddamn world!"

I had been sleeping on the couch at the Reeves' home. "Law & Order" was playing on the television, and Big Boy was sleeping in the crook of my legs. I fumbled around for the remote, put the television on mute and answered, "Good morning, Jen."

"Yesterday I called a friend in Tallahassee," she said, dropping her voice an octave but not her anger. "He'll be at your office Monday morning at eight. He's your new summer intern and also one of the best on the governor's security detail. He's part of the governor's advance team, works the room without anyone realizing he's security. Looks twenty but is thirty."

"Thanks, Jen, but I—"

"No buts. You aren't the only one in danger. Vince will watch over your staff and keep them from harm too. He can room with them in the carriage house."

"I thought you were worried about me."

"Hell, if you don't worry about yourself, why should I? Besides, your last bodyguard didn't fare too well."

"Stop, Jen. I get your point."

She slapped me down. "I'm not worried about your feelings. Vince Thompson has a social presence that'll support his backstory—Facebook, Twitter, Instagram and LinkedIn. The staff'll love him."

"Why do this?"

Jen sighed heavily, "We need your story on the jail explosion to be published. Anything you write will create problems for Frost and help us." She cleared her throat. "And Alphonse's worried about you."

Noting that it was Alphonse, not her, who was concerned, but she helped anyway, I said, "Thanks, Jen."

"Vince will be at your office on Monday," she repeated and hung up.

A few minutes later, she texted, "BTW you're welcome."

Abandoning my outlining plans, I took the television off mute and went back to sleep, staying on the couch most of day until around four when Benny texted that he needed to see me. He added, "Be sure you aren't followed."

I drove in the rain to Benny's Backseat and circled the place several times. No one was watching the club. To play it safe, I wore a yellow raincoat that I had found in Mr. Reeves' closet and used its hood to cover my face when I got out of the car.

Inside, Benny wasn't his normally jovial self. I closed the office door behind me as he motioned for me to sit. Fortunately, the air-conditioning was working. He said, "We need to have a talk, but before I say anything, I need your word that what we talk about stays in this room."

It bothered me that he thought he needed to say that. "You know you can trust me."

He moved his chair so close that our knees almost touched, and I could smell his Aramis cologne. "What I need to tell you opens a can of worms that you can't ever investigate. You're in danger, and I need you to understand what you're up against. You need to know the magnitude of what you're fighting."

"Are you trying to scare me, Benny?"

"Hell, nobody can scare Walker Holmes, but everyone you love or care about could be in danger." He pulled back and locked eyes with me. "I need your word."

Without hesitation, I replied, "You have it."

Benny started, "Peck came in and took the video from the other night. The asshole actually threatened me and my girls if anyone else learned about it." He shifted back toward me. "Imagine that. I reminded him that I have protection, which got him to back off a little. He stormed out of here, but only after he punched a hole in the wall."

He nodded to a hole in the drywall by the door that I hadn't noticed when I walked into the office. I knew Benny had some criminal connections in his past but never asked about them, but I would now. "What kind of protection?"

Benny shrugged. His anger dissipated as he slumped back in his chair. "You know I worked several years in New Orleans and Biloxi before I moved back to Pensacola. I ran several clubs—some legal, some not so much. Finally, I was offered this place, but I had to give a percentage to the bosses."

"Bosses?"

"Don't ask," he warned me sternly. "You don't need to know. I pay, and we don't have any problems with the sheriff's office or police. It's no big deal. Most of the strip clubs along the coast do it. The ones that don't have problems."

"Peck knew about this arrangement?" I asked, hoping to get another question in.

"That's what pissed me off. He knew and still threatened me. He's definitely worried about something."

"What?"

Benny smiled and shook his head. "You can't help yourself. I tell you no more questions, and you keep asking them. Will you just let me tell the goddamn story?"

I folded my arms, leaned back in the chair and waited for him to talk. He explained, "Peck knew better because his boss gets a cut of the protection money. The sheriff always has. Frost has been the bagman for decades, ever since he joined the sheriff's office." Benny saw the shock on my face. "You really do live in a fairy-tale world sometimes."

He rubbed his hands together slowly. When his fingers intertwined, he continued, "That isn't a rabbit hole you need to go down. You won't ever come back, and all of us will be dragged down it with you. You can't use this to get Frost."

"Do you think Peck is running his own operation, right under Frost's nose?"

"They won't be happy if he screws up their cash cow. The Biloxi Boys have mostly retired now that casinos are legal on the Mississippi Gulf Coast. They own condos in Gulf Shores, Perdido Key and Destin. Sometimes they come in here, and I make sure they have a good time."

"Why tell me this?"

"Peck is a vicious sonnabitch. If you expose whatever racket he's running, you might not have to do much more. The guys will deal with him and Frost."

"That's not how I operate. I want him and Lester Judson behind bars."

"Who?" asked Bennie.

"Judson's the guy with the gun in your club last week. Peck's cousin. He killed Rachel Townsend, and I think he killed my fiancée twenty-something years ago. He and Peck are working together."

"Shit," said Bennie.

"Damn right, shit. I'll keep your secret if it helps me nail both of those bastards."

"There's more." Benny wiped his forehead. "Catelyn, your waitress friend who waited on Judson, hasn't shown up for work the past two days. My manager called her cellphone, no answer. Had one of my bouncers visit her apartment this morning. Her roommate hasn't seen her since Thursday."

"Give me her address and cell number."

He scribbled the information on a coaster and handed it to me. "Be careful, my friend. Keep your eyes open. If I get any more info, I'll text. Probably best you stay away from the club."

"Thanks, Benny." We bumped fists and I drove to Catelyn's place. She lived in the Villa Barcelona Apartments on Chase Street behind the SunTrust building. Her stoned roommate wasn't too worried about anything, except whether Catelyn would pay her share of the rent that was due. Their landlord wouldn't give him an extension unless he filed a missing person's report with the police.

"It's not unusual for Cate to sleepover, but she never misses work, never," the long-haired, shirtless musician said. "Man, she could have a fever and be puking her guts out and she'd still get her ass to work. Not me, I was supposed to deliver pizzas today and blew it off."

I pushed past him. "I'm a friend and really worried about her. Can I check her room?"

"Well, I don't know." He scratched his scruffy beard. "What's your name again?"

"Walker Holmes." I handed him a twenty-dollar bill. "You can watch me when I'm in her room."

He took the money.

"Knock yourself out," he said as he pointed me to her bedroom and fell back on the couch. Before he nodded off, he added, "Lock the front door when you leave, man."

In contrast to the living room that had clothes, empty beer cans and dirty dishes everywhere, Catelyn's room was neat and organized. The bed was made. Textbooks and notebooks were arranged on her desk, but there was no computer or laptop. The closet had several empty hangers, the drawers in her chest were nearly empty, and I couldn't find a suitcase. I tried to call her cellphone and it went immediately to voicemail, which was full.

I woke the roommate when I returned to the living room. "When did you last see Catelyn?"

He took his time opening his eyes. "Don't know." He didn't even sit up to talk to me. "Maybe Thursday morning when she was going to work at the law firm."

"What law firm?"

"McGlinchy something," he mumbled.

"Did Catelyn have a computer?"

"A MacBook. Leave me alone. I need to rest."

I locked the front door as I left. Maybe Catelyn had skipped town and was safe. *And maybe leprechauns and unicorns are real.*

33

As Jen had said, when I came downstairs Monday morning, the expected visitor was on the office couch talking with the staff. I had called Mal and filled her in on our new "intern," and though she was a little skeptical at first, I could tell she liked the idea of having some protection around.

Thompson was tall, around six feet two and wore a maroon t-shirt with the faded logo of some Gainesville bar, baggy khakis and Chuck Taylors that were more gray than white. He had shaggy brown hair, an unshaven face and flashed a movie star's smile as he stood when I walked into the room. "Vince Thompson," he introduced himself as he shook my hand. "Mr. Holmes, I heard a lot about you from Jen."

I walked over to the coffee maker. "It's Walker or Holmes, no mister." I poured a cup and went over to me desk. "See you've met the staff. How's this going to work?"

Mal took charge, "He'll hang around the office and help with the phones. Summer will introduce him to a few of her clients. He'll go on a photo assignment with Teddy, and I'll let him cover a few things."

Thompson smiled with perfect teeth, "I'll blend in."

"Can you write?" I asked.

"Double-majored in journalism and criminal justice." He leaned back on the couch, still smiling and making me wonder if I had brushed my teeth that morning.

Clearly liking the look of our protector, Summer added, "He'll stay with us. We've got room."

Thompson added, "People will get accustomed to seeing us together and not think anything of it."

I asked, "How long will we have this arrangement?"

"The governor has approved four weeks. But you tell me. Can you bust this open in that time?"

Teddy laughed. "You don't know our boss."

"What are we doing about Jeremy and Pantoni?" I asked.

Mal replied, "Both are out for the next two weeks. Pantoni is traveling in Europe with her parents, something she had committed to do months ago. After you called last night, I phoned Jeremy and convinced him to leave early for his New York trip." She rolled her chair back to her desk. "We'll send the Fourth of July issue off to the printer today. Next week's issue is planned out. Pantoni has a piece on the county commission's upcoming debate over mass transit that she already turned in, and Jeremy interviewed a band. Vince can write an article using his notes. And your story is going to be on the cover."

I turned to Thompson. "What do you know about what I'm investigating?"

"Quite a lot." He sat up. "I've read your coverage of the April flooding, jail explosion and this area's recovery. I've seen the police report on the car bombing and this." He pulled out a DVD and a thick, blue binder from his backpack that was on the floor by his feet.

Thompson handed me the disk and the binder. "The DVD has the video from the laundry room before the blast. The binder is the preliminary ATF report. You can't quote any of it directly, but you won't have to worry about any libel suits if you stretch your analysis to include some of the details in your article."

I smiled and lifted my mug as a toast, "Thompson, you may be my new best friend."

"The governor wants to help."

"Please pass on my gratitude." I headed toward the conference room. "Summer will help you get settled."

We agreed that Thompson would use my desk while I continued to hole up in the conference room. Teddy and Mal worked on laying out the issue and getting it ready for the printer. Summer took Thompson on a walking tour of downtown Pensacola and introduced him to her clients. Big Boy slept on the floor in the conference room while I worked.

I called the law offices of McGlinchy, Magee & Moore and asked to speak with Catelyn. The receptionist was a fan of the newspaper so when I told her my name, she shared that Catelyn was on vacation—a nugget I passed on to Benny.

The ATF report showed that its investigators had inspected the exterior and interior of the CBD as best they could. The investigators had interviewed several correctional officers, and those transcripts were included. ATF had determined that the area of origin was in the basement near the center of the structure. According to the report, surveillance cameras in the basement quit operating around noon the day of the explosion because of the flooding. The video showed the gas dryers floating in the water and the presence of gas bubbles, which showed the equipment had not been bolted to the floor and the gas connection had been severed.

"The blast damage indicated that a large quantity of natural gas migrated throughout the structure," the report stated. "Due to the flooding, water is known to have infiltrated the electrical system, resulting in a large number of possible ignition sources that became vulnerable as the floodwaters receded."

In other words, the laundry filled with natural gas as the water receded creating a bomb that needed only a spark to ignite. *Damn.* The ATF investigators expected to complete their investigation by August 1st. I jotted down the names of the correctional officers interviewed, hoping one or two might be willing to talk.

Dare called, "Join me for lunch at Jackson's."

"What about Taylor?" I teased. "Won't he get jealous?"

"Taylor and I have moved on. Good man, but we ran out of things to talk about."

"And you've always appreciated a good conversation."

"Damn right. See you at 11:30. Wear your blazer."

When I arrived at Jackson's, Dare was holding court at a corner table that overlooked Palafox Street and Ferdinand Plaza. Bankers, as well as developers and politicians, checked on how she and Evans Timber & Land were doing.

Looking at her watch, she frowned, "Didn't your momma teach you to never keep a lady waiting?"

"I couldn't find my blazer," I replied while brushing dog fur off the lapel. "I apologize."

Dare handed me a Lighting Security card with a five-digit code on the back. "This is the code to activate the security system at the town-home your staff is renting. The pilots kept setting it off so we had discontinued the service, but I think it's wise we reactivate it considering what you're investigating. It'll go live at five this afternoon."

I thanked her. The waiter handed Dare a martini. "I'm taking the rest of the week off," she shared with a sly grin. "There're no rule that says I can't celebrate the Fourth early." I stuck with water.

Since Jackson's was a fishbowl, we kept the conversation light. Dare talked about Ole Miss and the two of us going to a home football game, narrowing the choices to either the Texas Longhorn game in September or Auburn in mid-October. I agreed to the plan, knowing Dare would have a new beau by then, and he would be joining her, not me.

Dare ordered the fried green tomato and lump crab salad. I got the steakhouse black & blue spinach salad. She caught me up on some of her sorority sisters, and then we pulled out our phones and looked up a few of my fraternity brothers on Facebook and laughed at how much weight they had put on and how little hair they had left. Whenever I almost slipped into talking about the newspaper, Dare would change the conversation. When we finished our salads, she talked me into splitting a crème brûlée for dessert.

While the waiter was getting our check, I noticed Dare's expression change as she looked over my shoulder. Before she could warn me, I heard the familiar voice of Sheriff Frost.

"Ms. Evans, Holmes, how was your lunch?" The sheriff stood behind my left shoulder, forcing me to turn awkwardly to see him. Monte Tatum was beside him.

"Sheriff, it was wonderful," replied Dare. She lightly put her foot on top of mine, warning me not to pick a fight. "We're catching up on some old college classmates."

"Holmes, I can see you're healing well since that terrible car explosion. We've offered the Pensacola Police any help they may need to find the killer."

Dare applied pressure to my foot. I smiled, "Thank you, Ron. I know you've had your hands full finding out why your jail exploded and taking care of the medical needs of those hurt in the blast."

Tatum popped up like a ferret and moved closer to the table, but not close enough for me to strangle him. "Despite what your friend Graves is telling the media, the inmates are getting the very best medical care."

Frost patted Tatum on the shoulder. "Commissioner, don't let Holmes get under your skin. I'm sure he didn't mean anything by the remark." The sheriff took a step toward Dare. "Ms. Evans, have your properties recovered from the flooding? Is there anything I or Commissioner Tatum can do for you?"

"That's kind of you, sheriff," she said with her sweetest smile. She then turned a fierce gaze at Tatum but never let the smile leave her face. "We've had a few lingering permit issues, but I'm sure the commissioner has been working on speeding up the approval process."

Frost looked at Tatum. "Monte, you'll help Ms. Evans."

It was a command, not a request. Tatum replied, "Of course."

Dare picked up her purse and pulled out a small notebook. She tore off a sheet of paper and handed it to Tatum. "Here's the list of properties tied up in your planning department. I keep it with me so I can follow up with my construction managers at the end of each day."

Both Frost and I smiled while Tatum squirmed as he took the list from her. "I'll hand this to the county administrator when I get back to the office."

Frost insisted, "See that you do. Ms. Evans, call me later this afternoon if your problems aren't resolved." He handed her his business card, and Tatum turned red. They started to leave, but I called them back. Dare took the pressure on my foot to another level—I thought she was going to crush my toes. "Sheriff, anything to report on who was behind alphonseaffairs.com?"

"Such investigations take time," he replied. "We're not sure if we've enough evidence to get a judge to approve a warrant to force the company hosting the site to tell us the owner of that disreputable website. Even then, you liberals might attack me for denying the owner's First Amendment rights to free speech. My hands are tied."

Dare gave up and took her foot off mine. I poked Frost, "That's a shame. And the state attorney refused to prosecute William Graves Jr."

That drew blood. Frost's neck muscles tightened. He clenched his jaw. "My attorney still believes we have a case and is negotiating with the State Attorney's Office to bring your friend to trial."

"Sheriff, I can see that I've upset you. I apologize. I can only imagine the pressure you're under with the ATF investigation going on while running for re-election."

Frost barely contained his contempt. "Don't worry about me. Good day, Ms. Evans."

As he and Tatum started to turn and walk away, I added, "Can you give me an update on Lester Judson? Have you arrested him yet?" Sheriff Frost didn't reply. He kept walking.

Dare threw her napkin at me. "You're sick."

I smiled and shrugged, "Dare, if I didn't gig him, he would've been suspicious."

"No, you had to wave your weenie in his face."

That I did.

34

We made it through the Fourth of July holiday without any problems. The Seville Sertoma Club had hosted a downtown street festival that ended with a firework show over Pensacola Bay, and the *Insider* office became party central for our staff and friends.

Mal and Summer set up two tables with plenty of food, and Teddy and Thompson brought in coolers filled with beer. I hardly noticed Thompson, he had blended in with the scene. Dare joined us, and Gravy brought Eva as his date. Most of our freelance writers stopped by, if only to grab a free beer and use the bathroom. Alphonse and Jen passed out campaign flyers downtown and periodically came by the office to cool off.

On July 5th, I drove to Willis Construction to interview Tony, but he wasn't expected to return to work until Monday. I left my business card and asked that he call me. When I returned to the *Insider* office and opened the ground level door, Big Boy bolted down the stairs, jumped up on my legs and then ran back to the stairs. Something was wrong, and he wanted me to follow him. Upstairs, Mal was comforting a sobbing Summer on the office couch.

"What happened?" I asked.

Mal answered, "It was Peck—"

"Did he hurt Summer?"

She and Summer shook their heads. Trembling while taking quick, shallow breaths, Summer tried to regain her composure as she squeezed her eyes shut and kept clenching and unclenching her fists. I sat beside her putting my arm around her shoulders. Summer folded into me and cried, sobbing loudly. Slowly the tremors subsided, her gasps for air lessened as she regained control. Mal got up and brought back a box of tissues from Jeremy's desk.

Summer wiped her running nose and took a big breath, "Teddy and Vince were out of the office on a photo shoot." Tears continued to roll down her flushed cheeks, but she pushed Mal and me away, refusing to be held, trying to recover her composure. She spoke quickly, using choppy sentences. "Mal took Big Boy for a walk. Peck came in, demanding to see you. He walked all around the office shouting your name. When he tried to go into the conference room, I blocked him and locked the door. Thought he was going to hit me. He made a move to go up the stairs and I cut him off again. All the time he was yelling. I screamed for him to back up, hoping someone would hear." She took another deep, long breath to calm her nerves and slowed her speech, "I … I … I threatened to call the police, and he just laughed in that creepy high-pitched voice. He dared me to do it, swept everything off my desk and stormed out."

Mal squeezed Summer's hand, "Big Boy and I must've just missed the bastard. I found her curled in a ball on your couch."

I hugged Summer again. "I'm so sorry."

"It's not your fault, boss. Just … just didn't know what to do. Reminded me of when my father came home drunk. There was no reasoning with him. So soon as Peck left, I shut down."

At that moment, Teddy and Thompson walked in, and we filled them in on what had happened. Thompson took control, "The back door must stay locked at all times. I'll make a run to Lowe's, get a surveillance camera and a wireless intercom that I can install for now. At some point you'll need a more sophisticated door that you can buzz open."

Noticing that Mal was about to ask him the obvious question, Thompson grinned. "My dad is an electrician. I've been his helper since sixth grade. It's no big deal."

I said, "Summer, why don't you take the rest of the day off?"

She shook her head, "I don't want to be alone."

Thompson volunteered, "Why don't you come with me to Lowe's and help me install everything? It'll do you good to stay busy." Summer liked that plan, and Big Boy volunteered to go with them. He wouldn't let anything happen to her.

After they left, Mal and Teddy came over to my desk to talk. I was on the phone with Sheriff Frost. Well, not exactly. I was talking to his voicemail.

"Frost, your piece of shit enforcer Peck came to my office this morning and threatened a female staffer. The whole incident was taped by our office surveillance camera. Threats against my staff won't be tolerated. If he shows up again, I'll put the video on YouTube. Not exactly the best promotion for your re-election campaign."

After I hung up the phone, Mal said, "We don't have a surveillance camera in our office."

"He doesn't know that."

Teddy settled on the couch, then looked at Mal who nodded for him to go ahead. "Walker, Mal and I were thinking about taking off Friday to enjoy a long weekend in New Orleans. The stories are mostly done, and we won't get your cover story until Monday—"

"It seems like the perfect time to get away," injected Mal as she plopped on the couch and reached out to hold Teddy's hand. "But with Summer being attacked," she bit her lower lip, "we aren't so sure."

Teddy put his arm around his wife. "It may be better if we stay and take care of Summer."

I shook my head. "Thompson is here. I'll be poring over documents, asking a lot of questions and shaking the trees to get information. It might be good for you two to get out of town for a few days, maybe even take Summer with you. "

Mal leaned forward brushing her hair off her face, "We don't want it to seem like we're running away."

"That's bullshit!" I said.

Teddy liked the idea of letting Thompson concentrate on me without having to worry about the rest of the staff. He said, "It gives Peck and Frost fewer targets. We know once you start making phone calls, they'll react."

Mal smiled, "We've faith in you that your cover story is going to rock their world."

I sighed, "Nothing like adding a little more pressure on me."

The couple began to make plans to leave Friday morning and stay with friends in the Garden District. When Mal asked Summer about going to New Orleans with them, she seemed relieved to be getting out of town. We debated what to do with Big Boy. In the end, I consented to letting him go with them since Mal's friends had no problems with dogs in their house. The rest of the day Mal and Teddy worked on the next issue, Summer and Thompson completed their security installations and I began to call the list of correctional officers interviewed by ATF.

The sixth name on the list, Corrections Officer Bliss Houser, picked up the phone. It didn't take much convincing to get her to share what she remembered about the explosion. "Throughout my shift, I smelled what I thought was natural gas but was told the odor was diesel exhaust fumes from the generator. I argued with my supervisors to report a possible gas leak to Pensacola Energy but was overruled." She had been on the second floor when the explosion occurred. The ground collapsed underneath her, and she fell through. Inmates carried her out of the building.

I said, "I need you to go on the record. My article needs names and faces."

Upset with the press releases issued by the county and sheriff's office, Houser wanted to expose what really happened, but her attorney had told her not to talk to the media. She said, "If you can get his approval, I'll tell you everything I know, and you can quote me in your article."

It took fifteen minutes of arguing with her attorney, but he finally agreed under the condition that I would run the article by him before publication. Though I was tempted to celebrate finally getting a source on the corrections side, I passed on having dinner with the staff, settling on ordering from Lum's and watching the Dodgers play the Arizona Diamondbacks.

My team had snapped its June losing streak and had a game-and-a-half lead in the Western Division. We scored two runs in the first inning and never looked back. A little before midnight when I got up to turn off the television, my phone vibrated.

"Miss me, newspaper man?" asked Lester Judson.

"No, it's you who missed me. The bodies are piling up, and I'll make sure you'll pay."

"The colored's death was your fault."

"Cowards blow up cars. Cowards stalk young girls and rat out on their cellmates. You're going to have a difficult time in prison."

"Ain't going to prison, newspaper man," he laughed. "No witnesses to testify against me. You're pissing up a rope."

"Police have a witness that saw you and a woman attach the bomb to the car."

"Yeah, well I made sure they never saw my face. The pickup truck is in the Arizona desert and the girl ... let's say she's working off her debts south of the border." He laughed again.

"Why'd you kill Mari Gaudet? What did she ever do to you?"

I sensed he knew exactly who Mari was, but he toyed with me. "Who?"

"The Ole Miss coed you kidnapped and killed in 1991. My fiancée."

He chuckled, "She was available, that's all. Standing outside waiting to be picked up by you, I guess. My, my, the guilt you must feel. Had she not been alone, I would've found someone else."

"Bastard!"

"She was my first, you know. I dreamed about killing one of those stuck-up college bitches for years. They laughed at my clothes, treated me like dirt."

"They didn't know you were a Klansman."

Judson hesitated. "Yeah, yeah, they should've respected me."

"Why'd you kill Rachel Townsend?"

He didn't take the bait. "This ain't no interview, newspaper man. I called to tell you two things. Your chubby girlfriend won't be working at that titty bar no more."

"Who the hell are you talking about?" I asked, realizing that it was Catelyn. I hoped he was bluffing.

"The fat ass waitress at Benny's Backseat. I caught her as she was trying to leave town. She told me that you and her were friends," he snickered. "Not at first, but eventually she told me everything."

"Leave her alone, Judson! She doesn't know anything."

"She disrespected me. I can't do nothing about that smart-ass Benny, but she had no right to mistreat me."

"She didn't mistreat you. She isn't worth getting upset over. Leave her alone."

"Too late. Like I said, Benny needs to find another waitress."

"You killed her?"

"Can't kill an employee at a protected club without permission," Judson said. "Let's say I motivated her to relocate. The broken arm will mend, and makeup will cover the bruises."

Red hot, molten hatred began to build in me, giving an edge to my voice. "What's the second thing you wanted to tell me, asshole?"

"Your pretty salesgirl isn't protected. She shouldn't have disrespected my cousin today. I could have some fun with that—"

"Stay the hell away from Summer and my staff!"

"Continue your bullshit and everyone you care about will die."

"You racist ass—"

The phone went dead.

I immediately called Thompson. They had stopped off at New York Nick's for beers after dinner. "Judson called and threatened Summer. They need to leave tonight."

Mal, Teddy, Summer and Big Boy were on the road by one Friday morning. Thompson slept that night in the lounge chair at the Reeves' residence while I stayed up going over documents and waited for a text message from Teddy that they had arrived in New Orleans. When it came at four, I finally allowed myself to nod off.

35

I started calling Benny's cell at eight in morning and finally he picked up around nine. I got his attention when I told him about Judson and Catelyn.

"That sonnabitch! No one messes with my girls! Where is she?"

"I don't know. Judson said she had moved out of Pensacola and mentioned breaking her arm."

"Sonnabitch!" Benny repeated. "I need to make a phone call. Call you back."

Thompson had begun work on the to-do list that Summer and Mal had left, reviewing their email accounts for ads and sending the freelance writers' articles to the copy editor. After he checked the phone for voice messages, he shouted for me to come over to his desk. "Listen to this message."

Thompson put the phone on speaker. An old voice said, "This is Anthony Willis. Mr. Holmes left a business card at my grandson's office yesterday. Tell him that I can meet with him at the IPC this afternoon at 12:30. No need to confirm. Mr. Holmes will want to talk with me."

Thompson asked, "What's the IPC?"

"The Irish Politician's Club, a private dining room in the back of McGuire's Irish Pub. It's where Pensacola's power brokers dine and cut their deals."

"Are you a member?"

I laughed, "Been blackballed three times. I think now if someone even suggests my name they're immediately excommunicated."

"Are you going?"

I could tell he was thinking about how he could safeguard me. "You can sit at the bar in the restaurant area and watch everyone come and go," I told him. "Nothing's going to happen to me at the IPC."

While Thompson had gone to the post office to get our mail, Benny called. "The boys aren't happy. Judson was already on their shit list. They've been upset about a little operation he was running for them in Gulf Shores."

"You aren't going to tell me about the business?"

"Nope, the less you know the better. I've vouched for you when it comes to my club. Once you start looking into anything else involving the Biloxi Boys, you're on your own."

"Point made. What kind of trouble is Judson in?"

"They don't like the attention he's bringing to their business, too rough with the girls. They got people looking for him."

"Did they know about his Klan connections?"

"They do now," he snorted. "These are Catholics and have little tolerance for the Klan, especially when they interfere with business."

I wondered if they knew Peck and Judson were cousins, but I kept that information to myself. I might need it for leverage later.

A little after noon, I drove over to McGuire's. Molly and McGuire Martin first opened their pub in a shopping center in the mid-seventies. Molly sang Irish ballads and ran the front of the house while her husband, McGuire, managed the bar and kitchen. In 1982, they bought the Firehouse Drive Inn on Gregory Street near downtown and converted the place into an award-winning restaurant that became world famous for its succulent steaks and generous portions. Tourists waited outside for hours to get a table and to staple an autographed dollar bill to the walls. At last count, over a half million dollars had been papered on the walls.

When I walked in, Thompson was chatting up a female bartender and pretending to watch a replay of last night's Atlanta Braves game. I headed down the steps at the end of the bar to a dark hallway that led to a mahogany door with a brass plate: "Irish Politician's Club—Private."

The club had a half dozen semi-private dining areas that seated four people each, and most of the tables were filled. The president of Gulf

Power entertained the Greater Pensacola Chamber CEO at one table while the mayor of Pensacola visited with a group of Japanese businessmen at another. The University of West Florida President shared nachos with the Florida House Speaker in yet another dining area. Most nodded to me as I was escorted by the hostess to the club's only exclusively private dining room.

The massive Anthony Willis sat at the end of a long table intended for eight people feasting on a porterhouse steak, rare, smothered in grilled onions and mushrooms. When I sat down at the other end, he put down his fork and knife, finished chewing his bite, wiped his thin, pink lips with a hand speckled with light brown liver spots, and took a swallow of dark red wine.

He looked at his watch and made a face because I was late, and no one kept Big Anthony Willis waiting. I didn't smile, not having any need to give him insights into what I was thinking. When I had coached AAU basketball, one of the mind games I played was to force the other coach into calling a timeout first. Willis invited me so I would make him speak first.

During the silent stalemate, a nervous waitress came in and whispered if I wanted water. I shook my head while keeping my eyes on Willis. He finally broke the quiet, "Mr. Holmes, I hear you are investigating my construction company, particularly our work on the Central Booking and Detention facility." In a genteel, measured tone, he continued, "I want to answer any questions to avoid embarrassment or legal complications if you print something false."

"The contract with the county had several flood mitigation measures. Why didn't you construct them?"

He smiled, showing small, yellow teeth and a silver cap on his incisor. "Now, we know the April storm was a two-hundred-year event. Nothing would have prevented the basement from flooding."

I replied quickly, wanting to pick up the pace of the conversation, "You cut corners, and people died."

"The project cost more than the county budgeted." He picked up his glass and finished off his wine. A little red began to show on his cheeks.

"The sheriff made the decision to hold off and get additional funds in the next budget year. We did what the client wanted."

Again, I ignored his argument not giving him a second to let his point sink in. "There're no written records showing that. I doubt Sheriff Frost will take the hit for you. Your greed will cost the taxpayers over a hundred million dollars before this is over. And the ATF report will put you and your grandson in jail."

Willis slammed his fist on the table, shaking the table and tipping over his wine glass. "The ATF report is not going to focus on the construction. Willis Construction is not under investigation by anyone but you."

"My reporting will be enough."

"Not hardly, Mr. Holmes. You don't know what you're up against. There are forces at play that can crush you and your little newspaper."

"I grew up with the Klan in Mississippi. A bunch of dumbasses pretending they can win a second Civil War doesn't scare me."

He showed a malevolent grin. I shuddered inside but kept my stony exterior. Willis pulled out a phone from his shirt pocket and texted someone. Afterwards, he gave me a cold stare and barely contained his irritation. "The Klan runs this county, has since the 1890s. We've kept the peace making sure everyone knew their place. Your newspaper has been allowed to exist because we didn't see it as a threat, but now you're threatening the society that made this place prosper."

"Prosperity for a chosen, white few." I matched his stare and tone. "You're destined to fail. Shit, this jail explosion shows your grandson isn't smart enough to keep the Klan in power. His greed and ego have exposed you to criminal and civil prosecution. When you die, the Klan will disappear."

"Maybe so, but you won't be here to see any such demise."

There was a knock at the door. Reuben Crutcher, dressed immaculately in a seersucker suit and baby blue tie, walked into the room looking down on me with eyes filled with hate. He sat next to the old man and handed him a folded document. With a grunt Willis strained to pull an envelope out of a black sports coat that was on the back of the chair next to him and gave it to Crutcher. The banker got up and left the room, sneering as he passed me. I willed myself to show no emotion and resisted speaking. I needed Willis to play out this drama.

He didn't disappoint. Willis made a show of opening and reading the document. "Well, Mr. Holmes, it looks like I'm your new shareholder," he smiled, once again flashing his silver cap. "I've purchased Mr. Crutcher's interest in the *Pensacola Insider*."

"Crutcher can't sell his interest to anyone without the approval of Chipley or me," I said, hoping I sounded confident. "Even then, I've the right of first refusal and can match the offer."

"Fine. Do you have a hundred thousand dollars?"

I ignored the question. "It takes two votes to sell. Chipley will never agree to let you be part of the ownership group."

He snorted a laugh. "You sound a little worried. Everyone has a price, and your partners are tired of your antics."

"I'll start another newspaper."

"Reuben said you'd make that threat," Willis countered. "We both know that's easier said than done, especially if we tie you up in court."

"Chipley will hold fast," I said and got up.

Willis raised his arm beckoning me to stop. "I have a one-time offer for you, Mr. Holmes, good until midnight Sunday. In my jacket, I've another check for a hundred thousand dollars for you. Sign over your shares and leave town."

"And if I refuse?"

"You may lose more than your newspaper."

36

I passed Thompson on my way out of McGuire's without looking in his direction. As I got in the Bronco, he texted me to wait for him as he settled his tab.

"Go to office," I replied. "See you in two hours."

"Is that wise?"

"Screw wise."

I tried to call Chipley's cell, but the call immediately went to his voicemail. The message said he was hiking the Appalachian Trail, had turned off his cellphone and wouldn't be back until the first of August. *Damn, another baby boomer seeking me-time with nature.*

I parked at the Palafox Pier, found an open bench and phoned Dare. She stepped out of a meeting to take my call: "Anthony Willis has bought Crutcher's stock in the *Insider* and says he can convince Chipley to sell his share, too."

"Don't you have a right of first refusal?"

"My best protection has been no shareholder could sell their stock without the approval of one of the other shareholders." Nearby, two seagulls were fighting over a scrap of a hamburger bun so I moved to the railing away from the scuffle. "But if Willis buys Chipley's stock too, then I don't think that clause will hold up."

"Did you call Chipley?" Searching for solutions, she offered, "We're still friends. I could talk to him."

"Thanks, but he's out of town until the end of the month." A hot breeze drifted off Pensacola Bay, and I paused for a few seconds to let it wash over me, smelling the saltwater. "I don't know how much Willis has already said to him. The prick sounded so confident."

"Then you're back to the right of first refusal. How much did Willis pay for Crutcher's shares?"

"A hundred grand," I replied.

Dare whistled. "Damn. Can you borrow that much using the newspaper as collateral?"

"We just moved into the black the first of the year. I've still got two credit cards that I have to pay off. My credit is shot."

The phone went silent. A plump, brown pelican plopped into Pensacola Bay, dove under the water and came up with a fish that it promptly swallowed.

Dare asked, "What if I loan you the money?"

It was my turn to be quiet. I let the question linger for a few heartbeats before I responded. "No but thank you. We're too good of friends to be business partners."

"What other options do you have?"

"Willis offered to buy my shares for a hundred grand if I leave town."

"You told him to go to hell, didn't you?"

I laughed softly, "Of course, but he gave me until Sunday to tell him my final answer."

"You can't sell to Willis, and you can't leave Pensacola. Go see Gravy and review your shareholders' agreement. And promise you'll talk to me before you do anything with Willis."

"Yes, ma'am."

Gravy had represented me when the agreement was drawn up. He would help figure out my legal remedies but finding him on a Friday was a feat. His last deposition of the day was before noon, and his office didn't expect to see him until Monday morning. He didn't answer his cellphone either.

Instead of going to back to the office, I checked all along Palafox and found Gravy at Blend Lounge, the full-service bar attached to the back of World of Beer, where he was drinking with a group of attorneys and cheering UWF coeds in tank tops and tight shorts as the young women played cornhole in the courtyard. Seeing the look on my face, he disengaged from the lawyers and joined me on the far end of the bar.

When I told him about Willis and his move to buy the newspaper, he said, "I put in the two-vote approval of any sale of stock as your safeguard, figuring you could keep at least one of them happy." Cheers came from the courtyard, and I lost Gravy's attention while he turned away to check who had won the match. He had a sheepish look on his face when he turned back and shrugged his shoulders, "I had ten on the stacked brunette."

Seeing I wasn't amused, he returned to lawyer mode. "The agreement is straightforward and unambiguous, but if Willis has both Crutcher and Chipley's shares, the clause is worthless. Can you keep Chipley from selling?"

"Not sure," I replied, rubbing the back of my neck. "Chipley and Crutcher both wanted me removed as publisher after the protest march. The car bomb stopped them from carrying out their threat. I don't know where Chipley stands."

"And I guess you don't have the money to exercise your right of first refusal?"

"Dare has offered to loan me the money, but the paper can't handle any more debt." The bartender refilled Gravy's drink. I ordered a club soda with a lime and noticed Thompson sitting on the patio coaching the UWF coeds on the finer points of cornhole while he kept his eyes on those inside the bar. He must have followed me after all.

Once the bartender moved away, Gravy's legal mind continued to work, "There's another option. Willis threatened to tie you up in court if you tried to launch a new paper. Well, you could go on the attack and file a lawsuit blocking Crutcher from selling his stock."

"Won't he just have a judge dismiss it?" I asked. "Anyway, I don't have the funds for a protracted legal battle."

Gravy smiled, "All you need to do is delay the sale and buy a little time."

"For what?"

"Until you can talk to Chipley and convince him not to sell," he said smiling even broader, "or get Willis arrested. The shareholders' agreement has a clause that if any shareholder is arrested for a felony, he forfeits his voting rights until his case is adjudicated. If he's convicted, the two remaining shareholders split the holdings."

"So all I need to do is get him arrested."

Giving me a half-smile, Gravy tipped my glass with his. "That's one of your specialties."

"Nothing like a little pressure."

"Well, there's one more condition under which stock is surrendered." His smile vanished. "If you die, your stock goes to the partners. You need to publish your story and stay alive."

I looked across the bar and nodded to Thompson. The poor guy was going to have his hands full protecting me.

37

Saturday night, the Zion Hope Primitive Baptist Church auditorium was set for the first debate between Sheriff Ron Frost and challenger Alphonse Tyndall, and the excited buzz in the room grew louder as the minutes ticked off on the clock above the stage. The crowd of over three hundred people expected fireworks.

On the left side of the stage, reporters from the *News Herald* and WUWF, the public radio station affiliated with the University of West Florida, sat at a table preparing to ask the candidates questions. Frost had refused to participate if the *Insider* had someone on the media panel.

Thompson had driven me to the hall and sat with the rest of the media in the first row of chairs in front of the stage while I hung out in the back to capture the entire spectacle. Uniformed deputies and Frost's other supporters filled the three rows behind the media, but they were in the minority. Behind them, rows and rows were packed with the families of the jail explosion victims; they wore orange shirts and "Vote Tyndall" buttons.

The room was probably more hostile than Frost had expected. Across the aisle from me sat Peck. The chief deputy looked ready to explode with his right leg bouncing up and down while he swayed back and forth with his arms folded. When he saw me, I smiled and waved. He popped up. I thought he was going to charge me, but instead he hurried away in the other direction.

I turned back to the stage where the candidates stood behind two podiums. Dark, handsome and nearly radiating good health and vibrancy, Alphonse was almost as tall as Frost, who appeared more pasty and gaunt than usual.

While a member of the Zion Hope choir sang the national anthem, a young child, probably eight years old, tapped my arm. He whispered that a minister wanted to talk and led me to a door that opened into a long hallway that bent to the right. When I turned the corner, Peck and his pistol were waiting for me. Though his gun was pointed at the floor, it got my attention, nonetheless.

"When did you become a preacher, Peck?"

He looked confused at first, but then he caught my reference. He sneered, "Always a comedian. We're going for a ride."

"Is this a good idea? There are hundreds of people a few seconds away." I backed up but kept my eyes on him. "You aren't going to pull the trigger."

Steps echoed behind me, and two deputies appeared, blocking my retreat and placing their meaty hands on my shoulders. Either one of them could have broken my collarbone with a tight squeeze.

"I don't have to use this." Peck waved the pistol. "The walls are reinforced cinder blocks filled with concrete. No one'll hear your screams if we rough you up and carry you out of here unconscious."

"But I'll be missed. I came with my intern. He'll look for me."

Putting his gun away, Peck shook his head and gave me what he thought was a reassuring smile. "I'll have you back before the debate is over. There's someone who wants to talk with you, and it won't take long."

He was lying. He was talking a little too fast, a little too excited. The deputies shoved me down the hall, forcing me to follow Peck to his Tahoe, where Lester Judson was behind the wheel and laughing as I approached. I tried to run, but the deputies grabbed me and threatened to beat the crap out of me. As Peck climbed into the passenger's side of the front seat, the deputies handcuffed me, put a thick, canvass bag over my head, threw me in the back and told me to be quiet.

For the first ten minutes or so, Judson changed directions several times to confuse me, while the radio blasted so I couldn't hear any sounds outside of the vehicle. When we stopped, I sensed we were in a warehouse. Keeping the hood over my head, the deputies led me up a flight of narrow stairs, then down a hallway and sat me in a hard, metal chair in a dark room.

I waited and listened to ceiling fans rotating above me and the rattling of a window air conditioner unit as both technologies struggled to keep the room cool. I settled my nerves by picturing the cool being drawn from the window unit by the fans and circulating around the room. Then two people entered the room and flipped on fluorescent ceiling lights that crackled as they brightened. The sound of metal chairs scraping across the floor was unnerving, especially since my visitors made no other sound when they sat in them. Instead, a third man spoke, a man who had been in the room all along.

Anthony Willis asked, "Mr. Holmes, have you made a decision about my offer?"

"Shouldn't you, Peck and Judson be wearing hoods instead of me? Take this damn thing off."

Someone got up and walked toward me. His godawful cologne gave away the man was Peck. He struck me before he removed the canvas bag. The other visitor was Judson who sat wild-eyed with an aluminum baseball bat balanced on his lap.

"Well, Mr. Holmes?" Willis repeated. He sat behind a cheap, green metal desk, which probably had been purchased at some government auction.

"You told me I had until tomorrow. You know I tend to procrastinate."

Judson popped up and swung the bat at my kneecap but missed and hit my calf instead. The blow glanced off, but the pain sizzled along every nerve ending. They definitely had my attention.

Willis tried to persuade me in his honey-laden Southern accent, "I am not a violent man, but my companions don't like you. I've tried to tell them that you're a Southerner, your great-great-uncle served under General Nathan Bedford Forrest at the Battle of Vicksburg, and you went to Ole Miss. Your heritage is why we haven't bothered with you before now."

The feeling was starting to come back in my foot while I shook it to get the circulation going. "This isn't about anyone's Southern heritage. It's about money and power."

Judson stood up again and cocked back his bat.

"Judson," Willis shouted, "it's time for you to leave!"

Peck added, "Lester, you have some place you need to be."

Judson glared at me on his way out. He tossed the bat across the room, nearly hitting me. It bounced on the floor, pinging several times until it hit the wall and rolled to a stop. I wondered where Judson was going and who else was in danger.

Willis offered me a smile and adopted a soft, fatherly tone, rich with phoniness. "As I said, these men don't like you. Sign over your shares, and they won't ever bother you again."

I said, "Judson's a rabid pit bull. He killed my fiancée, the Townsend girl, and my friend Tiny. He'll keep on killing until someone kills him."

Peck snickered, "Like you'd ever have the guts to do anything."

I looked at Willis, "Peck heads your Wrecking Crew. He's amped up on steroids and bringing too much attention to you and the sheriff."

It was Peck's turn to get up. Willis let him backhand me. The world around me spun. He had busted my lip, and I spit blood as he pulled me back onto the chair. He hissed, "You better take Willis' offer or I'll pick up that goddamn bat and crush your skull."

I needed to stall. I wanted to ask Willis about who killed Harden, but didn't want to rile Peck anymore, so I tried: "How about upping your offer to a hundred twenty-five thousand? I can have my attorney draw up the agreement on Monday."

Willis laughed so hard that he had a coughing jag. He spit mucus into a wastebasket by his desk. "The offer's currently one dollar, Mr. Holmes." He waved a document. "You'll sign this sales agreement, and then you'll leave town tonight."

Peck's cellphone on his belt vibrated. He read a text and looked at Willis, "Frost cut off the debate early. Crowd got hostile. He's on his way here."

Willis rubbed his hands together. "Then we need to settle this matter before he arrives."

Peck picked up the bat and rammed it into my stomach. When I collapsed forward, he pushed me to floor and kicked me several times. Willis ordered the chief deputy to put me back in the chair.

"This death by slow beatings is getting tiresome. Call off your pet monkey," I said between shallow breaths. "Your offer is generous, but let's not kid ourselves. You're going to kill me no matter what I do—just like you killed Jim Harden."

Willis shook as he suppressed a laugh and fought off another coughing jag. "You've a very active imagination. We're fellow Southerners. You have my word."

Peck barked, "Just sign the damn papers, and I'll take you back to your car." He unlocked the handcuffs and directed me to sit in a chair by Willis' desk.

The phone on the desk rang. Willis answered. "Mr. Judson, are you in place? Good. Let me put you on speakerphone so you can tell Mr. Holmes your location."

Willis switched the phone to speaker. "Go ahead, Mr. Judson."

"I'm sitting on a bench in Ferdinand Plaza. It's dark, but I can see into Jackson's Steakhouse. Holmes, your girlfriend Evans is sitting by the window talking to some fag. I can see why you've got the hots for her, her tits are impressive and—"

"Don't you touch her! I'll kill—"

Peck slapped me on the back of the head to shut me up, then said to Lester, "How much longer before she leaves?"

"Not long. Looks like they're ordering dessert. Holmes, she'll slice up real nice—"

Willis cut him off, "That's enough. No need to be vulgar. We'll call you in a few minutes after he signs the agreement." He hung up and turned to me, "You don't have any options left."

Peck pulled his pistol and pressed the barrel against the base of my skull. "Sign the damn papers."

"What the hell are you doing?" shouted Frost as he walked into the room. "Put that gun away, you idiot!"

Peck eased the pressure off of my head and took a step back. "We need those papers signed. They were going to be our gift to you."

Willis spoke up, trying to maintain control of the situation. "That's right, sheriff. Once he signs those papers, the *Insider* and Walker Holmes go away."

"You're a bigger dumbass than Peck if you believe that," said Frost, walking across the room to face Willis. "The whole state is watching Escambia County and the sheriff's race. This 'Mickey Mouse' thuggery might've worked fifty years ago but not today. Willis, you're a senile old dinosaur with more money than brains."

If he hadn't been so heavy, Willis might have leapt from his chair and confronted Frost. "How dare you insult the Grand Dragon of the Ku Klux Klan! We run this county! You work for us!"

Frost slapped Willis twice. The sound of the openhanded blows echoed in the room. He said with contempt, "You crazy fool! You exist because I allow it! As long as the funds kept flowing into my campaign account and your Klan held your stupid ceremonies in the woods and stayed out of sight, I looked the other way."

He grabbed Willis by his shirt. He was too heavy to lift, but Frost pulled him close to his face. "You got too greedy. You cut corners on the CBD project, guaranteed nothing would go wrong. You said you'd install the pumps and do the other work later. No big deal. Hell, you didn't even bolt the goddamn dryers to the floor, you cheap sonnabitch."

Frost pushed Willis away. The old man wilted in his chair. He had never faced the full fury of Sheriff Ron Frost.

"And as far as my re-election, who else are you going to support? The colored Democrat? Shit, I should arrest you all! That would help my campaign more than any contributions you can give me."

I glanced at Peck. He stood with his feet planted wide, nostrils flaring and beads of sweat collecting on his forehead. He had lowered the revolver until it was pointed at the floor, but he hadn't put it back in its holster. His eyes darted back and forth as if he couldn't decide whether to aim it at Willis, Frost or me.

Frost noticed Peck's confusion. "Chief Deputy Krager, I said put the gun away. This KKK bullshit has nearly ruined everything. You're supposed to be my successor, but then your piece of shit cousin came to town. Killing girls, blowing up cars. He's a danger to you, me and this community. I'm locking him up."

Peck raised his gun but still seemed uncertain what to do. "Leave Lester alone."

Willis pointed at me. "What do we do about him?"

"You apologize and let him go," said Frost.

"But ... but he'll expose us," sputtered the old man. "He'll ruin us."

"There is no 'us.' The jail explosion is all on you. The car bomb and the Townsend girl are Judson's. Holmes knows I had no part in those crimes. Right, Holmes?"

I nodded. "But now they've got Judson stalking Dare Evans."

Frost cursed, "Dammit, dammit, dammit! Willis, call him."

Peck waved his gun at Frost and me. "What about me? I'm your chief deputy, the next Escambia County Sheriff. What about me?"

"It's over," growled Frost. "You'll resign. The state attorney will take it from there."

"No!" yelled Peck as he fired his gun. Frost was hit and thrown back against the wall. He slid down it slowly and slumped over on the floor. Across his chest a huge stain of blood began to spread like a grotesque ink blot. Before he could turn the pistol on me, I let out a roar and rushed Peck, trying to wrestle the gun away from him. Willis had screamed when Peck shot Frost and was frozen with the phone receiver in his hand. He kept repeating, "No, no, no...."

Peck was strong, but I refused to let him shake me off, throwing the last of my energy at getting his pistol. He slammed me against the desk, but I kept both my hands on the gun, pointing it upward. He pushed me against the brick wall and head-butted me. Dazed and off-balance, I slipped on the baseball bat Judson had thrown across the room and fell. Pain tore through me like shattered glass when I hit the cold, hard concrete floor.

Grinning, Peck stepped back and sighted his pistol at the center of my forehead. I held my breath and tensed every muscle in my body, waiting for the bullet. A shot fired. Blood spurted in my face. Half of Peck's head was gone. His brain matter splattered on the wall behind me. The sheriff had taken out his pearl-handled revolver while still lying on the floor and shot Peck. Then Frost dropped his gun.

I ran to Willis and shook him. "Call Judson now! Call him and tell him to come here!"

"I'm ruined, I'm ruined." He held the receiver but still hadn't started dialing.

"Willis, call the damn number and tell him I've signed the agreements. Tell him he can come back now."

When Judson answered, Willis spoke into the phone: "Holmes signed the agreement. You can …" Willis looked at me. "Run, get away now. Your cousin and the sheriff are dead. Run."

I snatched the phone from him, but the line had already gone cold. I quickly dialed again: "C'mon, c'mon … pick up … Dare, don't leave the restaurant!"

"How do you know where I am?"

"No time. Wait for the police."

"Walker, you're scaring me."

"Please, just stay there."

Then I called 9-1-1 and told them Dare was in danger and reported that Sheriff Frost was down and Chief Deputy Krager was dead. Willis gave me our location, which I passed on to the dispatcher. Frost was coughing up blood and I could hear a faint whistling sound from the bullet hole in his chest. I stripped off my shirt and used it to keep pressure on his wound. The room's air was thick with the sweet, metallic smell of fresh blood puddling on the floor.

38

I was suspected of murder for about thirty minutes when Willis tried to convince the police of my guilt as he stuttered and sputtered nonsense that I had burst into the warehouse office attacking the sheriff and his chief deputy. The officers looked at my busted lip and bruises and believed me for a change. Plus, since I hadn't touched either gun, the crime scene tech quickly proved my innocence when she found no gunpowder residue on my hands. They took the old man into custody and charged him with kidnapping with the likelihood of more charges to be added later.

Peck's henchmen deputies had run as soon as they heard the first gunshot but later turned themselves in when reports of the shootings got out. They claimed that they were simply following Peck's orders and knew nothing about why I had been taken from the church. But they ended up in jail cells without bail.

Frost was alive, and Peck was dead. The investigators had no second thoughts about declaring that Peck's death was in self-defense. The sheriff would have explained what happened, but he was unconscious when the police and ambulance arrived. The bullet had lodged in his chest, breaking several ribs and collapsing his lung. He was transported to Sacred Heart Hospital, where cardiothoracic surgeons saved his life. His wife told the police that he was in the early stages of thyroid cancer and had delayed further treatment until after the election.

The Sunday edition of the *News Herald* proclaimed Frost a hero for saving my life. They must have literally stopped the presses and rearranged the front page to tell of the gun battle between the sheriff and his chief deputy. They had only the barest of details, but the daily needed to get something in print before we did. The editors knew my own story would be out soon.

I told my version in three separate blog posts over two days with a promise to publish the exclusive story in the *Insider* on Thursday. My Monday morning post covered the specifics of my kidnapping, beating and the gunfight in the warehouse. I wrote how Willis and Peck tried to get me to sign over my share of the newspaper. I didn't mention Lester Judson or his stalking of Dare at the request of the police who were searching for him, but his presence would be in the newspaper article. I teased readers that future posts would cover the reasons for the jail explosion and expose connections to the Ku Klux Klan. By the end of the day, the State Attorney's Office added extortion to the charges against Willis.

The second blog was posted after lunch and covered how Willis Construction's greed led to the jail explosion. I laid out how the contractor had cut corners and not installed the pumps or built the other flood mitigation measures. I included how the county inspection department, with the help of the brother of the dead chief deputy, had looked the other way and issued a certificate of occupancy that allowed Willis Construction to receive a big bonus weeks before the explosion.

Little Tony was arrested on the Pensacola County Club golf course on charges related to the explosion. State Attorney Clark Spencer announced he might go after both Willis men under Florida's RICO laws for a "pattern of racketeering activities." County commissioners, including Tatum, called for a special meeting to discuss an independent investigation into the county inspection department.

The final blog post on Tuesday morning gave the commissioners more to investigate. I laid out the political influence of the Ku Klux Klan, how the organization had controlled local government contracts, infiltrated law enforcement, and likely played a role in the death of private investigator James Harden. I shared Harden's Klan organizational chart and some of the names of the Klansmen inside the Escambia County Sheriff's Office, State Attorney's Office and other law enforcement agencies.

I promised to publish the entire list in the *Insider*. Because of my pledge to Benny, I didn't mention the Biloxi Boys.

Within an hour of the Tuesday post, I had to field angry phone calls from State Attorney Spencer and the offices of the US Attorney for the Northern District of Florida and the Florida Attorney General. They were upset about the names I had released and demanded that I turn over all of Harden's materials. I told them to contact Gravy.

Crutcher called me Tuesday afternoon. "Willis coerced me into signing over my shares. My attorney says the courts will void the agreement."

"Reuben, thank you for calling," I said. "Now can you give me quote about your role in the Ku Klux Klan and the rigging of county bids?"

"What? You print a damn word of those lies and I'll file a libel suit!"

"Not if we use the documents filed with the court when the state attorney hits you with money laundering and bribery charges. You've got more than the *Insider* to worry about."

Newspapers across the state picked up the stories. The traffic on the blog was so heavy it almost shut down our host's server. Advertisers called and desperately tried to get last-minute ads in the print edition seeing that the issue would fly off the racks.

Tuesday evening, I received a message that Sheriff Frost wanted to see me. He was still under observation in the ICU. Looking frail, weak, a ghost of the formidable opponent that I had battled for eight years, the man was hooked up to a machine that tracked his vital signs. A drip kept him medicated.

"You look like shit," I said as stood at the foot of his bed.

He wheezed and spoke in a raspy voice, barely above a whisper: "Shouldn't you thank me for saving your life?" I stared at him and didn't reply as the heart monitor beeped softly, and the oxygen hissed as a clear plastic tube pushed air into his nostrils to feed his lungs.

"State Attorney's Office and I have an agreement." He winced as he tried to take a deep breath but couldn't. "I've submitted my resignation and withdrawn from the race." His breathing was limited to a series of short huffs as he fought off a cough and its accompanying pain. "Cited health reasons."

I closed the curtain that separated his room from the nurses' station and sat in a chair near the bed. "So, you cut a deal."

Frost started to chuckle, but it turned into a hacking cough. "Pensacola likes neat, Holmes. I agreed to cooperate in Spencer's investigation of that fat dumbass Willis and the Klan."

I nodded and remained quiet. My silence got under his skin, and two rosy splotches appeared on his cheeks. I noticed his heart rate pick up on the monitor, and the volume of his voice went up too. "You know this is bullshit! I'm innocent!" He struggled to calm himself. "I had nothing to do with the jail explosion, Willis Construction or the goddamn Klan." He let out a sigh. "Dammit, I didn't murder your friends or kidnap you."

I said coldly, "You weren't ever innocent. Maybe you aren't directly guilty of those crimes, but there're plenty of others. You've taken kickbacks and gotten rich while you've worked in the sheriff's office. You're lucky that you got a deal. You should be in the cell next to Willis." Frost coughed again. When he wiped his mouth, I noticed blood on the tissue. Still I felt no sympathy for him.

"You've always been a hard ass, Holmes." He tried to sit up but failed. He had no strength in his arms to lift himself off the mattress, and the remote that would have adjusted the bed dangled out of his reach. "Don't think your black friend will be elected. The Republicans will get another candidate on the ballot. You haven't won."

"I heard they tapped one of your commanders to replace you on the ballot." I sat back in the chair and crossed my legs. "They don't know yet that he's also in the Klan, but they will Thursday when my paper hits the stands." The commander wasn't on the list compiled by Harden, but I wanted to screw with Frost. Anyone the Republicans selected out of the sheriff's office would be under a cloud of suspicion. Tyndall would still have to fight to win the election in November, but the odds of his victory had improved considerably.

"My friends will find someone," Frost replied with a little less confidence.

"Your Biloxi friends have moved on." The sheriff's jaw dropped, and his eyes opened wide. He couldn't hide the shock on his face, and grew speechless, not knowing how much I knew and was clearly afraid anything he said would get back to the State Attorney's Office. He had no idea that I only knew the few cryptic clues Benny had shared.

"You and I both know they're the reason you're resigning. They don't like the attention you've brought to their operation. They blame you for Peck and Judson and gave you no choice but to walk away."

Frost fumed. I smiled and relished the moment until finally he couldn't take my smugness any longer. "You've got it all figured out, you little pissant …," he tried to shout, as a vein on his forehead started to throb, his eyes began to bulge, and his breath slowed to a wheeze. "You haven't won."

I stood up and laughed. A loud boisterous laugh. His pulse quickened causing the monitor's alert to sound. Frost croaked, "I'll be back. I'll …" Then the alarm hit another octave and become more frantic and shriller. He struggled for air, his face flushed beet red.

"Sure you will," I replied. Then I pulled back the curtain as I heard nurses running down the hall toward the room and left the hospital.

ABOUT THE AUTHOR

Photo by Barrett McClean, Barrett McClean Photography

RICK OUTZEN is the publisher and owner of *Pensacola Inweekly* and creator of "Rick's Blog," one of the most influential blogs in Florida. His investigative reporting on crime, corruption and the BP oil spill for his newspaper and the Daily Beast earned him international attention and awards.

His 2018 debut novel, *City of Grudges*, was honored by the Florida Writers Association and Killer Nashville. In 2014 he self-published a digital book on his "Outtakes" columns: *I'm That Guy: Collected Columns of a Southern Journalist.*

Rick grew up in the Mississippi Delta and graduated from the University of Mississippi.

He has lived in the Pensacola for nearly forty years.

www.ingramcontent.com/pod-product-compliance
Lightning Source LLC
Chambersburg PA
CBHW050355260626
47156CB00003B/740